"Jory paints word pictures with remarkable skill. His characters come to life against a rich historical background."

—Janet Dailey

"An outstanding storyteller. Sherman portrayed the characters, their problems, and scenes so well it brought back memories of people I've known and ranches I've visited."

—*Tulsa World*

"Blazing out of the Texas ranch country with absolute authenticity, Jory Sherman in *Grass Kingdom* tells a pulsating story of love, hate, revenge, and redemption, a story of sons avenging fathers and making peace in an unforgiving land."

—David Nevin, author of *1812*

"*Grass Kingdom* is on the mark, Sherman's big one—with great characters, great dialogue, and a wonderful story."
—Dee Brown, author of *Bury My Heart at Wounded Knee*

THE BARONS OF TEXAS

JORY SHERMAN

FORGE®

A TOM DOHERTY ASSOCIATES BOOK
NEW YORK

THE BARONS OF TEXAS

A Forge Book
Published by Tom Doherty Associates, Inc.
175 Fifth Avenue
New York, NY 10010

Forge® is a registered trademark of Tom Doherty Associates, Inc.

ISBN: 0-812-52075-0
Library of Congress Card Catalog Number: 97-18697

First edition: October 1997
First mass market edition: April 1999

Printed in the United States of America

0 9 8 7 6 5 4 3 2 1

For my wife, Charlotte, *mis ojos y mi corazon*

It is manifest that nobody is going to write all about Texas in any one book, or in any one reasonably long shelf of books. The subject is myriad, multifarious, and endless.

George Sessions Perry,
Texas: A World in Itself

Cast of Characters

Martin Baron—sailor who settles Southwest Texas
Juanito Salazar—the Argentine from the Pampas
Jack McTavish—Baron's crew
Ken Richman—drummer, ranch hand
O. B. Clarke—ranch hand
*Gene Andereck—lawyer
Jaime Lafcadio Aguilar—rancho owner
Benito Aguilar—brother of Jaime
Pilar Aguilar—Benito's wife
Victoria Aguilar—Jaime's wife
Antonio Aguilar—son of Benito
Matteo Miguelito Aguilar—Jaime's son by Pilar
Captain Richard Grimes—landowner
Polly Darnell—pioneer woman
Lawrence Darnell—pioneer rancher
Kenneth Darnell—son, sixteen
Caroline Darnell—daughter, eighteen
Samuel Robbins—friend of Captain Grimes
*Jerome Winfield—Martin sells his boat to him
Anson Baron—Martin's son
*Matt Baron—Anson's son
Edith Baron—Anson's daughter, Matt's sister
John Fitzroy Killian—Ben's grandfather
*Pedro "Horky" Horcasitas—Jack Killian's sidekick
and foreman
*Jethro, "Jeth"—Jack Killian's bluetick hound

*Characters not appearing in this book are identified here with an asterisk.

*George Killian—Ben Killian's father
*Jane Houston Killian—Ben's mother
*Ralph Houston—Jane Houston's father
*Doris Houston—Jane Houston's mother
*Roy Killian—Jack Killian's son, George Killian's father
Lázaro Aguilar—Pilar Aguilar's blind son
*Esperanza Cuevas—Lázaro's nanny
*Alonzo "Lonnie" Guzman—trail cook
*Joselito Delgado—Lonnie's helper
*Charles Goodnight—cattle rancher and trailbreaker
*Oliver Loving—cattle rancher and trailbreaker
*Jéfe—lead steer in Anson's first cattle drive
*Samuel Maverick—legendary cowman

1

YEARS AFTERWARD, HE would swear that the land had called out to him, that he had heard it call to him, not with words that he could hear with his ears, but through some vibrant, almost celestial tone in his brain, some preternatural tug at his senses that drew him to the land and made him want to step ashore. Others coming into Texas for the first time in those olden days—as measured in blood and sinew, in extreme weariness to the point of despair and soul sickness, and sometimes in high unearthly salt-laden winds blowing off the Gulf—had similar experiences.

The earth was blood-red when he first saw it, flaring with the crimson dawn, seemingly running with consanguineous shadows until he thought it must be some madman's abattoir, an island risen from hell and caught there off the Gulf shore for a brief moment in time—desolate, haunting, frightening to witness. But that feeling lasted only a split textillionth of a second, because the land changed even as he watched it and the holocaustal dawn faded quickly when the sun was finished unfurling its banderas on a faraway battlefield in the heavens.

Martin Baron stood on the deck of his boat, staring at the flaming shore, the sailor's wine-red warning sky, as if he was in a trance, mesmerized by the strange glow on the eastern horizon, the earth reflecting the carmine hue of each cloud forged from shimmering metal strips yanked steaming from a blacksmith's fiery forge. He had never seen a sky so beautiful and blazing, as if it was the first sky ever created, had never seen it bleed onto the earth with such intensity. Had never seen a sun rise so militantly and proudly as if engorged with other flaming worlds from some unknown sea of the universe.

"Cackle Jack, get your ass up here!" Martin hollered to his companion below. A rattle of pans in the tiny galley, a muffled curse, and a grizzled old man, his beard a scraggle of black and white hairs soaked to a hideous prurient yellow from the drip of half-raw eggs, poked his head up as far as the third step in the ladder, his torso strangely compressed from the angle of Martin's vision so that he appeared to be a stub-legged dwarf.

"What ye got, Martin? Pirates? Brigands?"

"Just look at it, Cackle Jack. Just looky there."

Jack McTavish, called Cackleberry Jack because of his fondness for hen's fruit, ascended the steps, regaining the full length of his legs until he stood on the deck, bathed in that same roseate glow as Martin.

Baron grabbed Cackle Jack and turned him toward the land as if he was a dressmaker's dummy on a swivel. Martin stuck out his arm, pointed toward the shore. Killdeer raced on the sand, their spindly pencil legs moving like knitting needles stitching crazily on a cockeyed loom. Their high-pitched *screet, screet* carried on the wind like tiny monotonal flutes. Gulls wheeled in the staggered sky over landfall, little etch-

ings come to life, antic white pinwheels fluttering out
of control, aimlessly flapping toward nowhere and
everywhere, gawking wanderers adrift on invisible air
currents.

"That?"

"Did you ever see such a sight?"

"Aye, the Matagorda. Hideous, ain't it?" Cackle
Jack eyed Martin with a suspicious glare from rheumy
blue eyes.

"It's plumb beautiful, Cackle Jack."

"Teemin' with Apache niggers and ravenous
wolves, sand fleas, poisonous lizards and crazed
jackrabbits."

Martin stepped around Cackle Jack and seemed
about to walk through the gunwale and into the grena-
dine dawn. His face was struck with a blissful expression, his dark hazel eyes pulsating with that carnal
light, his face bathed with the sun's fire like a slab of
raw meat plucked from a bed of raging embers.

"You been at that Messican aguardiente, lad?"

"Just look at it, Cackle Jack. It's like looking at the
face of God."

Cackle Jack spat out a gobbet of egg-white phlegm
through carious teeth gapped like missing slats in a
picket fence. The goo hit the gunwale and slid down it
like an aqueous fragment of oyster.

"Blasphemous."

Martin stood there, unmindful of Cackle Jack's
blindness. He shook his head with the wonder of it all,
stood gape-mouthed in awe as the bloody land softened and turned pink as salmon meat, the creosote and
the mesquite trees stark against the sky, the deep curly
mesquite grass thickened with Siberian clover, live
oaks twisted to arabesque forms, dripping with Spanish moss all spangled in the light, shining with an eye-
searing brilliance. And as the sun rose still higher, the
land turned green as an emerald buffed to a high virid-
ian sheen. And the sky all daubed in gray on the west-

ern horizon like a painter's canvas, the clouds thick
and rolled, stacked against the northwestern horizon
like fluffy rugs fresh from the weaver's loom.

It seemed as if he was watching two separate skies,
each moving toward each other slowly, the one in the
east open and big with tatters of clouds hanging like
streamers over the rising sun, the one in the west closing up and graying with winter shadows, as if morning
and afternoon were watching each other from a distance and moving to meet in some center of heaven
and do battle on a solemn silent field.

"That's the place," murmured Martin.

"Eh?"

"The place I've always dreamed of."

"Nightmares, ye mean."

"Cattle. And goats and horses."

"Aye, and ye're daft as a spoon. You been talkin' to
that Argentine too damn much. Juanito ain't got the
brains of a Port Aransas clam."

Martin drew a deep, satisfying breath, and in the salt
tang he smelled the sweet clover, the ripening beans of
the mesquite trees, the loamy musk of Spanish moss,
the heady sweat of prickly pear and the delicate aroma
of cholla blossoms.

"Just look at it, Cackle Jack," said Martin. "Just shut
your mouth for ten seconds and look at it. That's graze
yonder, feed aplenty for cattle, for hundreds, thousands."

McTavish blinked in the sun, waddled to the gunwale to stand beside his young captain. Line snaked
against the single mast of the sloop, its sail furled and
bound, the jib lashed to its spar. They had anchored in
the bay, in a harbor of stars the night before, after
scrubbing the decks of the reek from their last catch,
which they had sold wet in Corpus Christi.

"I seen it before, lad."

The sloop swung slowly on its anchor hauser, turning them broadside to the land. Martin had bought an

old dilapidated shrimp boat, stripped it of its outrigging, patched it up, rebuilt the cabin with new pine bunks and a galley, put in a doghouse to stay dry in rough weather, attached a bigger keel, filled its ballast with pig iron, set the mast, all before his fifteenth birthday. For the past year, he had earned his living from the sea.

"When?"

"Two year ago, we come here, blown like a cork before the storm, sea anchor shredded to lint, jib wearin' ten pound o' salt water to the inch, mains'l tangled like a whore's bedsheets."

And Cackle Jack looked at the land and it was not the same, not bleak and hostile as it had been, but green and growing, gentle under a slowly rising sun, gentle as the calm glass sea beneath them. But Cackle Jack didn't tell any of this to young Martin Baron. Instead, he fished for his clay pipe and leather pouch of fresh Carolina tobacco while checking the angle of the sun for his burning glass.

"And look at it now," said Martin as if he had been there on that bleak wintry day, as if he was inside Cackle Jack's thoughts, inside his skeptical Scot's heart.

"Aye, look at it now," breathed Cackle Jack as he dipped his bowl in the pouch, released aromatic gusts of tobacco musk that floated to his nostrils. He tamped the bowl with his horny thumb and folded the pouch tight, put it back in his pocket like treasure. He fished out the burning glass, stuck the stem of the pipe in his mouth, between pudgy lips, worried it into position with his tongue. He held the glass up to the sun, centimeters away from the tobacco, caught the light prisoner and sent a beam into the bowl. A lick of smoke curled upward and he began to draw air through the pipe. The tobacco flamed and caught; smoke fumed through the pipe, caressed the inside of his mouth. Cackle Jack fanned the glass to cool it, then put it away, back in the soft cloth that kept it smooth and safe.

"I want to go there," said Martin. "All over. Walk it, see every inch of it."

"And where will ye catch your fish, Martin? Or is it sand crabs and turtle eggs you're after?"

"We could anchor the *Mary E,* go ashore in the dinghy. Take pistols, rifles and bedding." He looked toward the stern where the dinghy was lashed to davits. It was a rugged boat, built for rough weather. He had put in storage lockers, rigged up removable reels that fit into iron L-shaped rods that slipped into fittings inboard of the gunwales. He could fish seventy or eighty fathoms, using double rigs and treble hooks. The dinghy had its own oars, was stocked with provisions. The *Mary E,* named after his favorite aunt, could be battened down, secured in the harbor with anchors fore and aft, heavy Danforths attached to sturdy hausers.

"And leave the *Mary E* for thieves?"

"You can stay aboard if you like. I'm going," said Martin. He was a tall, strapping youth, barely sixteen, but already possessed of sea legs and a fishing savvy that belied his years. He had left home at thirteen, traveled down the Mississippi to New Orleans, apprenticed with a fisherman for a year and then bought the tug. His parents had been murdered by Indians when his father had refused to give them corn. Martin was spared, but made prisoner by the Shawnee band. He killed his guard after a month of captivity and escaped with a rifle, powder, ball and a knife. He went west from Illinois to St. Louis and worked his way to New Orleans. In his hazel eyes there was already wisdom and flickers of painful memories whenever he thought about his parents, but he had grown into a man early, was already over six feet and still growing.

"Well, I see a red sky of morning what says sailor

take warning. I think you ought to take the _Mary E_ well out from shore."

"Might be best, at that. Set anchors fore and aft, batten her down."

"Even so, we could have to hunt her when we come back. A good blow could move her out to sea, anchors dragging seawater."

"Or we could just leave her where she is, come back in the morning."

"Be takin' a chance, lad."

Martin knew it was a risk to leave the boat at anchor so close to shore with the sky arage and blazing like an open furnace that morning, but the pull of the land was so strong he felt reckless almost to the point of despair. He had been looking at it too long, dreaming about it for too many nights, talking about it in New Orleans and Corpus and Galveston.

The Argentinian he had met in New Orleans had put the idea in Martin's head about cattle. Juanito Salazar. Odd little fellow. Talk, talk, talk. Drink, drink, drink. For a small man, Juanito could hold a lot of whiskey and rum. He had a smile bigger than he was and he was homesick for something he called the pampas. Worked on a shrimp boat, smelled of brine and the sea. But Juanito talked of cattle as if they were living gods, talked of eating the cooked meat over a campfire as if he had dined on a king's feast.

"Didn't you ever dream of sitting in a cabin on a sea that doesn't move? Of sleeping in a bed that doesn't rock in the swells and throw you against the bulkhead when the wind rises?"

"I been on dry land. That there is a-crawlin' with rattlesnakes and scorpions, pizenous lizards and red niggers that'd cut you into a girl. It ain't safe to be anyplace where a man can walk up on you 'thought you seein' him. And the sea don't have no ticks or fleas or sand crabs."

"Nor grass nor cattle nor horses, neither."

The argument between the two men was not new, but it had grown gamier over the months since Martin had met the Argentine in Barque d'Or, a French tavern on the waterfront that the Americans all called "the barking door."

"Not a good day to go ashore, Martin. Specially on such a day as this. I'll wager the glass is falling like a round stone rolling down a hill. When was Juanito supposed to come down here and meet us, anyways?"

"Tomorrow or the next day."

"Well, he won't make it out of port tomorrow, 'less I miss my guess. If we get a storm real quick, it ain't gonna be no one-day blow."

Then he heard a sound and saw dust rise in the air offshore. Hoofbeats.

A moment later, he saw men on horses ride into view, half-naked men with bronzed skin, their lances trailing eagle feathers, shiny points glistening in the brightness of morning. The riders saw the boat and reined in their stocky horses. One man rode away from the group of five, heading toward the bank nearest to the boat.

"Well, looky there, will you?" said Cackle Jack. "If'n we ain't got us a boarding party of red Apaches all primed to lift our hair and cut our throats."

"Apaches?"

"Looks to be. Bloodthirsty savages."

The Apache stopped at the bank, stared straight into Martin's eyes. Martin lifted a hand in greeting, turned his empty palm toward the brave on horseback. The Apache glared at him, shook his lance. Then he pointed to the dark western sky, raised his spear and moved it in a circle. Then he dropped the tip and wiped it across the face of the sea like some sandaled prophet from an ancient desert land.

"What's he doing?" asked Martin.

"He's likely saying there's a storm a-comin' from the west and it's going to wash us away."

The Apache dropped the tip of his lance as if underlining his prophecy. Then he yipped and the others took up the chorus. The warrior wheeled his mount expertly and rode back to join his companions. They all lifted their lances and shook them against the heavens as if defying nature to vent its rage upon the land and the sea. And then they rode off as one being, galloping out of sight in a twinkling shift of the universe. And they left no sign on the land, disappeared until the emptiness blinded Martin and he wondered if they had ever been there at all.

"What do you make of it, Cackle Jack?"

"I think it would be one big mistake to go ashore. Now or any other day."

Martin wrestled with the decision to go ashore, walk the land, dig into it, taste it, roll in its grasses and measure its width and breadth on solid footing. He felt the gentle roll of the boat beneath him and listened to the tapping of the line against the mast, the creak of the hauser. He felt trapped, caught in some seaborne prison when his heart had already flown to dry land, soared with the hawk that grazed the mesquite as clouds of blackbirds rose behind it, startled from their night perches. Several gave chase to the hawk and it zigzagged out of sight over land that Martin could not see.

"The glass is falling, all right, but we have this chance. The boat is empty, clean, and we've grub to last a fortnight or more. And all that land out there just waiting to be walked."

McTavish snorted.

He did not have this yearning that Martin had borne ever since leaving New Orleans after still another drunken night with the Argentine. That damned Juanito had even learned Baron the Spanish and two

chattered like magpies over cheap brandy, waving their
arms in the air like fishwives and cutting their talk
with English so hardly a man jack in the Barking Door
could understand what they were talking about.
And always afterward, Martin would set to sea all
bleary-eyed and bleary-brained, talking of this damned
Matagorda and all the land unfit for habitation as if
it was a treasure to be sought.

But this time was the worst, Cackle Jack admitted.
Martin seemed possessed, tugged so strongly by the
land that he paid no mind to the weather or his boat or
his fisherman's trade. They made a good living plying
the sea for its plunder, drying the catch in the sun,
drinking good Portagee rum and selling their catch in
the coastal towns where scarce a soul had ever tasted
beef, let alone seen a cow that didn't squirt milk.

"You ain't a man to bend to a plow," said Cackle
Jack, his tone laced with a seaman's bitterness. "You
busted sod once't and what did it get you? Made you
an orphan, that's what."

"I aim to ride a horse and let others break their
backs on such," said Martin stubbornly.

Cackle Jack leaned against the doghouse and
squinted at the sky, traversed it with his gaze from
horizon to horizon. Martin was not looking at him, but
seemed rooted to the deck, mesmerized by the coast,
the land beyond.

"Be a hell of a blow," said Cackle Jack. "Them
mare's tails are near gone in the east. Be a nor'wester,
cold as a bitch's heart, and when it meets up with this
sweat off the Gulf, it'll howl and dump water by the
long ton all over us and that damnable land you're
gawking at like a ripe schoolgal. I wouldn't be surprised to see a waterspout or two come rippin' across
the water like a bucksaw."

"Cackle Jack, you worry too damned much."

"I been readin' weather for thirty years and ain't

been wrong yet. This one'll be a bitch willy, you watch."

Martin sniffed the breeze. A vagrant gust of wind rattled the rigging, made the canvas crackle against its lashes on the boom. The spinnaker rippled as if it had a snake in it. A cloud of blackbirds rose from the marshes and wheeled in the sky as if activated by a single mind, not a wing out of place. Shorebirds lifted off the beach and fluttered like flung kerchiefs as the wind caught them.

"Damn," muttered Martin as the breeze stiffened again. It had been so calm last night and he had his heart set on walking the land for the first time, walking through the dream he had been carrying in his heart ever since he first laid eyes on it and all the times Juanito spoke of the pampas and the cordilleras in the Argentine. He had made his country seem like a magic land, and Martin had transposed Juanito's descriptions to this place lying off the Matagorda coast.

"We better look for a quay or run to sea," said Cackle Jack ominously. "This one ain't goin' to wait. They's ice in that wind, barracuda teeth."

Martin looked to the east again, where the sun was struggling to rise and clear the scattered clouds, and already the blue was fogging over as the western clouds moved across the sky, pushed by a chill wind from the north.

If they got caught there offshore with the sails reefed, they could be blown to kindling wood should the wind stiffen beyond forty or fifty knots, which seemed likely. He wet a finger and held it up, as if needing further proof that Cackle Jack was right. They had to find shelter or sail far out to sea and ride it out with the drogue.

"We'll find a quay," said Martin. "Set the jib. I'll hoist anchor." He looked out into the Gulf and saw that the sea was beginning to roll. Small waves curled

in green combers and an occasional spray lifted off the
ocean in a spurt of mist. Cat's-paws dotted the waters
with every swirl of wind.

Cackle Jack beamed. "Now you're talkin'," he said.
He raced to the bow and unlashed the jib, ran it up the
spar while Martin weighed anchor in the stern. The
wind caught the small jib and the boat eased up the
coast, graceful as a swan.

The wind began to lash the sea, crowning the small
waves with foamy whitecaps. The boat rolled beneath
their feet as the swells increased. The water grew
choppy, the number of whitecaps increasing alarm-
ingly.

Martin flaked the anchor hauser, set the Danforth in
the locker. He took the wheel, guided the boat as they
beat against the wind off the starboard bow on a close
reach. But the wind was circling, ever circling, so that
the jib was spanking and crackling while Cackle Jack
wrestled with the boomline, trying to tie it to a davit.

"Twenty-five-knot wind at least," yelled Cackle
Jack as he lashed the boomline fast. The *Mary E* began
to pitch and toss atop the growing swells. An occasional comber rose up before them, and when they
broke through, doused them with spray.

"Gusting to thirty-five," said Martin, fighting the
tiller to keep from dousing the sail as the *Mary E*
heeled over at the bow. Spray whipped their faces as it
sprung from the bow, and the sky darkened suddenly,
wiping the sunlight from the sky so fast that the two
men looked at one another empty-eyed in wonder-
ment.

A ferocious squall sprang up as the wind dove off
the escarpment and swept across the Gulf, dashing icy
gusts into the warm waters. Blinded by windblown
spray, Martin closed his stinging eyes. In seconds he
and Cackle Jack were drenched as the sea rose up
around them, propelled by thirty-five- and forty-knot
winds. The boat began to tumble between the brute

waves that swelled up, dropped them into troughs where they wallowed until the next swell lifted them up, only to be buffeted by winds and waves.

When Martin opened his eyes again, the shoreline was blotted out, and sheets of rain scourged the decks, lashed their flesh. All of Martin's bearings disappeared in an instant as the darkness enfolded the small fishing boat. Sea and vessel became a single creation. With a sickening dread, Martin knew that Cackle Jack would not be able to hoist the mainsail. The storm jib was not enough sail to take them out to sea, away from the dangerous shoreline, where rocks and sandbars lurked in a thrashing tumult of water and wind.

He heard Cackle Jack shouting, but could not see him in the driving rain. Martin spun the wheel, hoping to turn away from the shore, pick up a following wind. He needed distance, any distance, away from the treacherous shore. As the boat spun to port, he heard a terrible ripping sound and the wheel whirled crazily.

The boat shuddered to a halt, standing helpless at the brunt of the needling rain and ferocious wind, and he knew the *Mary E* was dead in the water, at the mercy of the angry, howling seas that enveloped them with a furious savagery as it rose hot and steaming to close with the gelid rain from the maw of the north like some angry ancient god landed on earth to smash and devour everything in its barbaric path.

They fought the storm all that day. Late in the afternoon the wind suddenly lost its strength and the rain turned to drizzle. But just before dusk, when the wind gained new energy and the rain slapped against Martin's face, he knew they were in for a rough night.

2

A ROGUE WAVE crashed over the port side of the sloop, striking Cackle Jack broadside. The force of the water rammed the Scot against the starboard rail, staggering him. The spinnaker boom swung toward him with blinding speed as the gusting wind struck its sail and released its lashing. Jack threw up his arms to avoid the blow. Blinded by the water, he saw only a blur, felt the rush of wind and spray across his face. The boom struck his left forearm. Pain shot through the bone and paralyzed him to the shoulder. A numbness set in an instant later.

"Reef the spinnaker," Baron yelled and his words were snatched away by the wind, doused by the stinging spray. He did not know if Jack heard him, but the wind took the small sail again and the boat lurched like a skidding sledge to starboard.

Water streamed through the scuppers, washing the deck, making the footing slick and treacherous. Martin fought the helm, trying to hold the *Mary E* steady until Jack could furl the spinnaker. He yelled at the first mate again. Through a gap in the rain he saw that Jack was in trouble, holding his arms up defensively like a blind man fighting off a pack of wild dogs.

Martin released his hold on the wheel and, bent to the wind, struggled forward. When he was halfway to the bow, a wave washed across the stern and sent the boat skidding again. He fell to port, his bare feet sliding across the deck as if it was oiled. The wind howled in his ears and he gasped for a clean breath in the thick spray. He caught himself before he went down, crawled along the gunwale toward the spinnaker boom, the boat at the mercy of the seas and wind.

Shimmering light scalded the clouds in the distance, like coals in a fire. Thunder boomed across long, rolling lands, sounding like cannon rumbling as lead streaked across a battlefield.

Jack grabbed the boom and held it steady just as Martin came up alongside.

"Get back to the helm," yelled Jack. "I'll reef the sail."

"Cut the lashings if you have to."

The wind howled through the rigging, whistled through the stays as Martin made his way back to the stern of the *Mary E.* The boat crashed through waves and wallowed in heavy troughs as the seas rose about it in a frenzied rampage of spray and foam, with the watery muscles underneath giving force to the crashing waves. Streaks of lightning cut through the fat of black clouds, opening silver veins. The hollow bass boom of thunder followed each flash of jagged light that cracked the pane of darkness.

Martin grabbed the wheel and held the prow into the teeth of the wind as Jack reefed the spinnaker. Still, the *Mary E* tossed like a chunk of driftwood and the craft strained to stay nose to the wind. The sky darkened until it was like night, the whitecaps like boiling sea beacons in the tumult. Then the whitecaps disappeared under the hammer of rain as the sea turned to a leaden dark, with great swells rolling under and over them.

Jack lashed the boom with slippery fingers, made his way aft on rubbery legs, drenched from head to foot, shivering until his teeth clattered like castanets. Thunder and lightning sketched a dark horizon ashore and balls of orange light bounded from cloud to massive thunderhead like an explosion in an armory.

"One whale of a blow!"

Martin stared at Jack with slitted eyes stung red by the rain. He smiled through gritted teeth as he fought the wheel, careful not to oversteer, for the rudder stood in air much of the time as the boat tumbled in the waves like some blind lumbering beast.

"God, where did it come from, Jack?"

"There's two of 'em—one from the south, one from the north."

Martin shook his head.

"Should we break out the slickers?"

"Too late, Martin." Jack leaned into the wind, his fingers gripping a davit, his right foot rammed against a bulkhead rib. "We may have to jump ship."

"Abandon the *Mary E*?"

"Lest it abandon us. This ain't no squall, Martin. It's a hard blow."

The wheel wrenched in Martin's hands as the rudder struck a wave sideways. Pain skewered his wrists and the wheel tried to spin out of his slick hands. He felt as if his bones had been splintered into a dozen pieces.

"Better batten down," yelled Martin as the boat leaped on the crest of a huge wave. "See if we're taking on water below."

"Hell yes, we're takin' on water."

"Get to the bilge pump then."

"Martin, it's no damned use."

Baron glared at Cackle Jack.

"What in hell do you mean?"

"You don't want to hear it. You're goin' to lose the boat. Don't you hear them timbers a-groanin'? She'll break up in water iffen we don't run aground."

"Damned if she will, Jack." Lightning lit his face for a flash of a second and then his image plunged back into darkness, its afterglow burning into Martin's eyes like a photo negative floating in a pan.

Jack shook his head, staggered to the doghouse, down the ladder. The boat was leaden with sloshing water below. The pump was in the fo'c'sle, invisible in the darkness, the hose wriggling like a snake just below the surface. Wooden bowls and cloths, pages from a book, a belaying pin, a piece of line, a spool of thread, dozens of other things all spun around in the black muck, knee-high to a man below.

The boat twisted and groaned as Jack hung on to the teak railing. The bilge smells swirled up to his nostrils, making him gag. He turned and headed up the ladder as the boat landed in a trough with a tremendous shudder. He heard the timbers screeching, the decks moaning, the wind howling and keening in the rigging.

He gulped in fresh air, clambered on deck, where the force of the wind nearly knocked him down. Rain pelted his face like flung shot, stinging his eyes and cheeks and mouth. The wind was a bellowing roar, and he saw that all the lines were being jerked by the powerful gusts. He staggered over to the helm, where he grabbed the wheel with one hand to steady himself, grabbed Martin's arm with the other hand.

"We took on too much water. She's founderin'."

"I know. I can feel it in the wheel."

"She's goin' down, Marty."

"I'm going to try and run her up on the beach."

"She'll be scrap."

"She can be rebuilt."

The wind tore at them; the rain lashed them with savage force. It seemed to be coming down in sheets like guillotine blades, one after the other, relentless as a mighty waterfall tumbling from a great height. Both men fought the wheel. They heard the lines strain and snap, the rudder groan.

Martin wished he still had the spinnaker up. He might be able to catch the wind and run the craft up on shore. But that was dangerous business, he knew. They could just as well be blown out to sea, where the boat would sink, taking them down with it.

"Cut the drogue," he told Jack.

Jack cursed and turned to the stern, drawing his knife. The wind hurled him against the bulkhead of the doghouse as the bow rose like a sounding whale, straight into the wind. He gripped the knife with slippery fingers, found the rope that held the sea anchor. He slashed at the hemp until the strands parted. The drogue pulled the line away from the boat and the *Mary E* lurched with the sudden freedom. The bow swung toward the shoreline, but the boat was sluggish in the water, low from its heavy load of seawater.

Jack slid his knife back in its scabbard and braced himself on the rolling deck. Then he leaned forward and stepped toward the helm to help Marty steer the boat.

A gigantic wave rose up before them, knifed downward in a green-black curl. The two men ducked, but the wave struck them, slammed them against the starboard gunwale. The wheel spun crazily, and as the water drained from the scuppers with a terrible sucking sound, both men heard the steering lines snap like matchsticks. Then the waves tore away the rudder, and the boat swirled in a sickening circle before it was caught by a swell and rose high in the air on a tremendous crest. The boat came down on its starboard hull and the spinnaker spar cracked like a rifle shot. Sheets flew in the wind like ghostly apparitions, sailed into the darkness and the rain with a dull flapping sound and then were gone.

Half drowned, Marty and Jack grabbed davits and

hauled themselves to their feet as the boat righted. A deeper darkness loomed over the port bow, and a moment later, the boat jolted to a halt with the sound of wood screaming and cracking as the hull broke up on rocks.

Martin heard Jack scream and felt a hard object ram into his back. Then he heard the mast snap and there was the sound of wood splintering as it crashed into the doghouse. The boat shuddered and he heard it moan like a living thing. Splinters flew in the air and the wind hurled them into his face like wooden needles. Blood streamed from a half-dozen wounds and the waves pounded against the exposed hull with tremendous force. The boat bleated each time it was struck and heeled over until Martin lay crumpled on his back against the bulkhead.

The boat began to disgorge its flotsam. Water washed over Martin's legs, water laden with airtights, wooden utensils and bowls, dark hard objects that he could not see, but which battered him again and again as the water sloshed up and down the deck.

"Jack, you there?"

There was no answer. Only the howling of the wind, the flap of the sheets tattering against the booms. Martin tried to get up, but each time he got ready, another wave crashed against the hull. He knew he couldn't lie there at the mercy of the sea and the rocks. He had to get out of the boat.

Where was Jack?

"Jack?" he called again.

In the keening of the wind he heard the cry of wolves on the plain, the bugling of an elk in the forest and the wails of children weeping. But he could not hear Jack answer him. He tried to peer through the darkness and the slashing rain, but the water blinded him and the boat was cockeyed on the rocks, shuddering with every smashing wave, rocking back and forth and up and down like a cradle on an uneven floor.

Martin turned over on his stomach and reached out for anything solid his hand might touch. The boat lurched again, this time in a different direction and he felt the stern give way, twist to port. He heard the sound of the hull sliding over sand and rock.

"Martin, Martin," came a cry from forward.

"Jack, you okay?"

"Hurt bad, Marty."

"Hang on."

Martin heard no more as he pulled himself along the gunwale toward the bow.

The wind circled, came from a different direction. The stern swung wider and then the boat was floating, off the shore. Martin felt his stomach roil with a green queasiness. But the deck was no longer tilted and he struggled to his feet, still holding on to the gunwale. He inched along, battered by wind and rain, thrown almost off his feet as the waves lifted the boat and brought it down again, a five- or six-foot difference in height, it seemed to him.

Martin tried to get his bearings, but it was impossible to see more than twenty or thirty yards, the sky so dark it was like being inside a charred oaken barrel. He fought with a nagging fear that the *Mary E* was being swept out to sea and he was powerless to do anything about it. The rudderless vessel wallowed like a sick cow in eight- or ten-foot troughs and rode crests that were at least that high.

But the boat was moving and some of the water in the hold seemed to have drained out when the boat was tipped. It felt lighter in the water, but that could have been because of losing cargo and deck fixtures. There was no way to tell. The wind had picked up and the sound of the rain on the deck deafened his ears.

"Jack," he called, but he could hear no answer above the roar of the wind, the racket of rain on every square inch of boat above water.

The stern slid away still more and then the wind

shifted and the boat headed on a course to starboard. Martin tried to remember his bearings, whether or not they were heading out to sea or back to shore, but his head hurt and his thoughts turned to mush as he struggled to move forward on a slippery deck against a brute wind that stabbed him with lancing rain.

With the wind now at his back, Martin made better progress. And the boat surged ahead, borne by a raging tide and wrathful swells. The wind seemed to catch its breath for a moment, but he knew that was only an illusion. He felt it blow against his back and no longer batter him from either side.

"Jack, we must be heading into a cove," he yelled.

The wars of sky gods raged across the heavens, orange light exploding like spotlights on a stage backdrop to the wind and rain. Huge fireballs appeared magically behind monstrous black thunderheads and silver streaked from cloud to ground in savage bolts hurled by shadow-faced Norse deities.

Martin heard no sound from Jack and it was too dark to see. He hung on to the gunwale with one arm while he shielded his eyes with his left hand in a vain attempt to locate Jack while the sky overhead gave him brief flashes of light as the thunder pealed in the aftermath of hieroglyphic lines of mercury that left images in the clouds like the staggered stair steps of prehistoric ziggurats.

In those lucid intervals Martin saw the dim outlines of a shore off his starboard beam, and when he looked to port, he saw a similar sight, although he could not be sure. The boat seemed to be weaving out of the brunt of the weather, though. He knew that much, but it gave him little comfort. Jack was hurt, probably unconscious, and he was powerless to come to his aid.

He wondered how Juanito would act in such a situation. For a young man, the Argentinian was very wise, and he was a good seaman from all that he'd heard. Smart and tough, that was Juanito. And he had weathered many storms around the world. But this was a storm to test the mettle of any man on any sea.

Martin heard the sound of the hull scraping against a sandy shoreline. Yet the craft was under way, slowly heading into some unknown landing as if it had sought shelter on its own. Like many men who had gone to sea, Baron was superstitious, and he had heard many a tale from men who had spent long days and nights on the ocean. He believed them all. And now, he thought, he would have a story of his own to tell—if the *Mary E* was indeed heading to safe harbor without anyone manning the helm.

"Martin, I'm hurt bad."

Jack's voice. A harsh croak, but he was still alive. Martin's heart jumped. "Hold on, Jack. I'll find you."

Even though the boat rocked with waves and wind, Martin crawled along the gunwale toward the bow. The mainmast boom was swinging to and fro, so he lowered his head, walked in a stoop to avoid being brained.

Groping blindly through the darkness, Martin reached the foredeck. "Jack, where are you?"

"Over here." Jack's voice was very weak. It was hard to determine just where he was. Martin dropped to his knees just as the spinnaker boom swung over his head with a loud swish.

"I'm coming," said Martin. A loud groan told him that Jack was just ahead, somewhere on the bow.

Martin touched a shoe. He felt it and moved his hand forward. "That you, Jack?"

"Unnnh."

"Where you hurt?"

Another groan.

Martin scooted up. A burst of lightning lit the foredeck for a fraction of a second. Jack lay against the bulkhead, pinned there by the Danforth anchor. The hackles rose on the back of Martin's neck when he realized that one of the shivs seemed to be buried in Jack's leg.

"What happened, Jack?"

"Anchor busted loose from its housing," McTavish said breathlessly. "Caught me in the leg."

"You bleeding?"

"Pretty bad," Jack breathed.

"I can't see a damned thing."

"I know."

"I'll try and get it off you."

"Better tie me up right quick if you do."

Ominous words to Martin's ears. Jack knew how bad it was, even without looking. The pain in Jack's voice came from a deep place.

"I might hurt you more."

"Can't be helped. Damn thing's buried in my leg. Must have cut loose from the windlass."

Martin felt for the anchor, found one edge of the Danforth jutting upward at an angle. When he touched it, Jack groaned, then let out a quick sigh.

"That the one?" asked Martin.

"No. Other side."

Martin felt around the anchor, tracing its shape in the darkness as the sea kept running before the wind that rattled the rigging, swung the main boom back and forth like a scything club.

He touched the metal gingerly, but still Jack groaned and stiffened with pain at every contact. Finally his fingers touched the point where the anchor made contact with Jack's leg.

Martin sighed and gritted his teeth. He grasped the anchor firmly, lifted it away from Jack. Jack cried out. Martin set the anchor behind him, against the windlass, made sure it was secure. The chain rattled as he pushed it away. The hauser whispered where it was attached to the chain as Martin slid it out of his way.

"God, it hurts," said Jack.

"I'm going to rip off a sleeve and tie off the wound. You'll have to guide me, Jack."

"You do it, Martin. Do it quick."

Martin felt the gash in Jack's leg. He felt the slime of blood lining the wound. Fresh blood pulsed against the tips of his fingers. He drew his hand away, then grasped his shirt at the shoulder seam, ripped it apart with both hands. He could barely hear the sound in the roar of the wind.

"I'm going to tie it off just above the cut, Jack."

Jack said nothing. Martin wondered if he had passed out.

Quickly Martin found the wound again, in the fleshy part of Jack's thigh. Very near an artery, he thought, although he was not an expert. He knew there was a large artery in the leg somewhere. He wrapped the sleeve around Jack's torn trousers and felt to see if it was above the wound. It was. He tied it tightly.

"I'll have to find something to use as a tourniquet. Otherwise . . ."

"Martin . . ."

"Yeah?"

"I've lost a dram or two of blood."

"Probably."

"Did it stop?"

"Yes, I think so."

"Good."

Martin felt the bandage again. It was very tight. Too tight. He would have to loosen it soon or Jack might lose his leg. He knew it was a dangerous wound. How severe he could not tell until it was light enough to see, and dawn was hours away. An eternity from that moment.

"Hell of a blow," said Jack, and Martin heard the trembling in his voice, the hard sharp edge of it breaking up.

"I'll see if I can find the whiskey." Martin knew it would be a miracle if he could find anything in the hold. But anything to get away from Jack for a few minutes, to collect his thoughts. The storm had come up on them so sudden and the boat had gotten away from him and that was a loss, a heartbreak, a failure.

"I could use a drop," said Jack. A bone of a whisper, a scrape of sound struggling through the vocal chords. He tore at Martin's heart. Tore at it like a jagged knife.

"Loosen that bandage if it . . ."

"I know. See can you find old Cackle Jack some whiskey, Marty. There's a good lad."

Raspy whisper in the roar of the wind, eerie and clear despite the tumult of the storm. Death's whisper, cold in the cockleshell of Martin's ear. Sand pouring through an hourglass. A broken watch ticking down.

Martin made his way to the doghouse, stepped down into the pitch cabin, made his way into the hold. Water up to his knees. He heard the boat run aground and it stopped with a jarring shudder, plunging Martin into the cold water. He rose out of it, shook his head and felt the overhead lockers to see if they were still closed. They were, at least on that side of the boat.

He found the one where the whiskey was stored, opened it and felt for a bottle. Rum, brandy, anything would do. He knew that Jack had to be in terrible pain, had to be shivering in the nightchill.

He grabbed a bottle, unable to read the label. The bottle was wet, slippery. He clutched it to him as he waded for the ladder. He climbed back up and went out on deck. At least the boat wasn't rocking anymore. He could hear the scrape of the hull as it settled, the hiss of sand, the thunk of rock against the timbers.

"Jack?" Martin knelt down beside the injured man. Jack didn't answer.

Martin felt Jack's face. His eyes were closed.

"Jack, wake up. I've got a bottle for you." He gently slapped Jack's face.

"Huh? Oh, Marty, that you?"

"You passed out."

"Sleeping. Dreaming. Calm seas, a sunny shore."

"Do you want a drink for the pain?"

"The pain. Jesus, Marty. It was in the dream. It's all over me. All through me."

"I know."

Martin pulled the cork. The fumes of strong whiskey wafted to his nostrils. He put the bottle to Jack's mouth. Jack drank. Martin could hear the whiskey gurgle in his throat. Then Jack coughed.

"Can you hold it down?"

"It's down and hot in me. Helps."

"Jack, we're going to make it. Just hold on until morning. I'm going to loosen that bandage for a minute."

"I can feel the blood pounding in my ears. Like the sea."

Martin loosened the bandage with cold, wet fingers. Jack let out a sigh.

"Marty," he rasped. "Listen."

"I'm listening."

"I'm dying, Marty. Dying slow and hard. Can you hear it? It's like someone singing far off. And I can't make out the words."

Martin closed his eyes to shut back the tears.

3

MARTIN TIGHTENED UP the bandage on Jack's leg for what seemed like the hundredth time. He had long since lost count. But he was pretty sure he had stopped the bleeding. At least there was no blood pouring from the wound. Inside Jack's leg it might be different. Jack had put away enough whiskey to keep him quiet and, if not asleep, in a stupor. Martin had been drinking the whiskey, too. There wasn't a dry blanket on board and the two men huddled together in the rain-lashed darkness like mendicants on a deserted street.

The rain swept over them like a watery hail. Sped by the wind, the droplets shattered against every surface of the beached boat, kept them drenched to the skin. The wind was gusting now, pausing intermittently as if gathering force before lashing out again. Martin shivered, despite the whiskey warming his innards, shivered and wondered about Jack, how badly he was hurt, whether or not he could sew him up when he could see well enough to find the awl.

For hours the two men shivered in the darkness while the wind raked the *Mary E* with a howling savagery, as if trying to tear it to pieces. But the boat held to its precarious perch on the shore and finally the wind abated and the rain no longer lacerated their faces, but shook down on them in brisk contemptuous gusts whenever they began to feel the storm was over.

"Martin," husked Jack, during a long lull just before dawn broke.

"Yeah, Jack?"

"I'm still alive."

"Sure, Jack. We'll fix you up."

"I heard them calling me."

"Who?"

"Angels, maybe. Ghosts."

"Sure, Jack."

"No, really, Martin. In the wind. Underneath it, maybe. Pretty voices, soft. Soothing like a mother's lullaby."

"Jack, you're delirious. Whiskeyed up, maybe."

Martin felt Jack's hand on his arm, pulling at his sodden sleeve.

"No, no, Martin. I could hear 'em. Like a chorus. Calling my name, calling to me from the sea, from the sky. It was beautiful, Martin. Beautiful as anything."

"Okay, Jack. Whatever you say." Jack's grip tightened on Martin's arm and he wondered if the old sailor was slipping away, slipping into the final deep.

"I know it was true, because they called my true name."

"Jack?"

"No, Jonathan. Like that. Like a song. Real drawn out. Joooooonaaaaathaaaaaannnnnnnn."

Martin felt chills run up his arms, his back, like the cold hairs of spiders.

The wind softened and purred in the rigging and Martin felt Jack stiffen.

"There it is again. Hear it, Martin? Do you hear it, lad? Listen. Angels calling me."

Martin listened, but all he heard was the soft keening of the wind. It did not sound at all like voices to him.

"I hear a noise in the rigging, Jack."

"No, underneath. In the wind, carrying on the wind. Way down low. Listen."

It was eerie, Martin thought. For a moment he almost thought he could hear something in the wind, beneath it. But, it sounded like nothing human. Only a sighing, a long whisper—hollow, empty.

"I hear it, Jack," Martin said.

"You do? Really?"

"I—I think so. Like singing. Kinda."

"Yes, that's it. Singing my name. Calling me. It won't be long now. I feel real light-headed."

"You've lost a lot of blood, Jack."

Jack didn't say anything for several moments, as if he were listening to the dying breath of the wind, the faint rattles in the rigging, the creak of the boat rocking against the shore.

"The song makes me feel real peaceful, Marty."

"Good. It'll be light soon and I can take care of that wound, sew you up."

Jack sighed and didn't speak for a long time. Together they waited for the dawn as the rain spattered them and tapped a hushed tattoo on the deck that they could hear when the wind retired to some dark cave beyond the sea where the winds slumber between storms.

The first peep of light startled Martin, jarring him out of his shivering stupor. He began to make out the boundaries of his prison, the deck, the rails, the mast, the white shroud of mainsail, the tattered jib in rags on its battered spar. Jack came awake, too, but did not move. Martin felt for the bandage and it was soaked with rain and blood, had tightened down so that he had to tug at it with gelid fingers until it loosened.

Blood broke over his fingers, so hot he jerked his hand away. He quickly retightened the bandage. He might have to cut off Jack's leg, but he was damned if he was going to let him bleed to death.

Martin rose to his feet, stood leaning against the starboard rail, staring at the eastern horizon as the dawn spread a pale gray light across the sky. Clouds floated thickly overhead, blowing to the northeast, and he felt the breeze against his face begin to turn warm. The land appeared to rise out of the darkness like some sleeping beast. He could make out trees and grass. He looked over the bow and saw land's end. The *Mary E* rested in a narrow inlet, gently beached on sand. She would rock off and slide back into deep water when the tide came in.

He felt the wind tugging at him, tugging at the tattered sheets, probing fingers into every crevice and cranny of the boat, and it was a warm south wind, holding the boat to its precarious mooring, not yet strong enough to raise the tide, but gentle and soothing. The rain dropped in sporadic bristlings that rattled the water and tacked harmless silver needles into the deck.

Martin turned to look at Cackle Jack, crumpled up in the bow, his bad leg stuck out straight, the other bent up against him. The injured man was sleeping, but not deeply. His head jerked and twitched every so often and he made low sounds in his throat.

"Jack, I'm going ashore. Need to get some driftwood, start a fire."

"Huh, that you, Martin?" Jack's eyes blinked open and he stared toward the stern.

"Over here," said Martin. "Did you hear me?"

"What'd you say?"

"I said I'm going ashore, get some firewood."

"Oh, good, good. Have you seen my mother?"

"No. You've got to fight it, Jack."

"Fight?"

"Don't give up."

"I'll na' give up yet, laddie," said Jack, his voice slipping into a Scot's brogue as Martin picked up the anchor, threw it over the side of the boat. It hit the gravel with a crunch. Baron hauled in on the hauser until the blade of the Danforth dug in hard. Then he secured the hauser around the large deck davit.

"I'll be back in a while, Jack."

No answer. Jack had slipped back into his dark world of dreams once again, where he encountered people gone to ghost and heard the voices of angels, sirens of the sea.

Martin threw a rope ladder over the side so he could climb back aboard after he had built a fire with wet wood.

The sound awakened Jack. Martin stared at him to see if he was going to stay awake. It would be better if he slept for a while.

Jack turned to look at him then, and his eyes were rheumy, filled with rain or tears. He looked pitiful in his sodden clothes, his bandaged leg reeking of death, the blood so dark on it Martin wondered if he would ever be able to stop the bleeding. If he could get Jack ashore and by a fire, that would help. He could boil some water, find an awl and patch him up. They could build a shelter out of blankets up in the mesquite, dry the boat out and patch it up.

"She was here," said Jack, and Martin left him that way. He climbed over the bow, dropped to the shore. Stepped onto an alien land of sand and rocks and stubborn plants growing out of the soil. A spat of rain dusted him as he walked away from the boat, an insulting spit that dripped water down the back of his neck.

He walked around the bow, saw no hole in the side. He wouldn't know the extent of the storm damage until he had gone into the hold to inspect it. He looked at the morning sky, much lighter now, and wondered if he'd be able to find wood that he could burn. He would have to start it with whale oil, probably. The bank rose steeply above the narrow inlet, but there was a place of erosion where he could climb to the top.

He remembered the Apache warriors and shivered. Where had they gone when the storm hit? He thought of their horses, so sleek and fleet, so unlike the draft horses he was used to back home and in New Orleans. These horses were agile as deer and the redmen rode them expertly. He had never seen such horsemanship before, as if animal and man were just one being, like mythical centaurs galloping across a dreamscape.

Martin shook the thoughts out of his mind and climbed a narrow fissure in the bank until he was looking down on the crippled *Mary E.* He wondered if he should have brought an axe and a weapon of some kind. He had a knife on his belt, but it would be of little use in a fight with men on horseback. And of no use whatsoever in cutting firewood.

But he found plenty of deadwood beyond the bank. He gathered it in his arms, carried it back down to the shore. He made several trips, working well into the morning. He didn't want to have to leave once he got a fire started. And he wanted to tend to Jack's wound without interruption.

He studied the land as he would a map on each trip into the mesquite. It seemed desolate, ravaged after the storm. The rain had washed out all tracks, but there were puddles where deer had left depressions and birds flew overhead under a bleak slate sky. It was a wild land and a stark land, but he longed to roam its broad reaches and explore the depths of the country, not as a man walking but as a rider on a horse like those ridden by the Apaches.

He felt small and alien in such a land, and he gathered the wood like a thief, like a plundering intruder. Yet he knew that the land was probably not deeded to any person, for it was uncultivated and untended. The earth where he walked had never seen a plow; the trees had never known the axe or the saw, for he saw no stumps.

Martin felt a thrill as he ventured into the mesquite thicket and when he walked across open spaces unmuddied by the rains, for the grass was thick and seemed woven through the soil. There were places where the water had made furrows, of course, and washes where floods had raged in the night.

He lingered long in the open patches, dreaming of fences and stock, barns and a house. He could almost hear cattle lowing beyond his sight and his veins tingled with an electric singing. The wind burned his face, dried his hair and clothes—the warm Gulf wind that he knew so well, the wind that had filled his sails and brought him to this place as if by mysterious design.

When he was finished bringing firewood to the beach, the stack was high and not all of the wood was soaked.

He climbed up the ladder and took a deep breath. Jack was still asleep. Martin tiptoed across the deck and entered the doghouse, went down to the hold. It was dark and wet, but most of the water had drained out or stood dank and oily in the stern.

He groped through the cabinets and storage lockers, and found the whale oil, dry punk, flint and steel, a small hatchet, a knife. His pistols were wrapped in oilcloth, safe and dry, and he set them on the galley plank to retrieve later. The powder was in tins, both the fine and the coarse. He would break out one of the rifles later to load and prime, for he was sure they would be landlocked for many days while Jack healed and he worked on the boat to make it shipshape.

There was plenty of beach for a camp, and Martin set about building a shelter. He used rocks and mesquite that he felled with the hatchet to make a hut for Jack and him. He dug a pit for a fire, set stones around it. He set the hut against the bank, giving them protection from the rear and a wide, long field of view in case anyone attacked them by sea or from the other end of the cove.

When he was satisfied with the temporary quarters, he brought down his pistols and two rifles, loaded and primed them. He carried one pistol in his sash, in the hollow of his back, within easy reach, but out of his way.

Then he put Jack on his shoulders and climbed down the ladder. Jack was delirious, only partially conscious when he laid him in the shelter on blankets that had dried in the morning breeze.

"Jack, we're shorebound for a while."

"I thought you was a-carryin' me down to bury me."

Martin laughed. "Not yet, old friend. We're going to work on that leg, get you well."

"Likely you'll have to cut it off. I heard you whackin' with that little hatchet. Practicin' up, I figger."

Martin winced. He had thought the day when the Indians came to their farm had been long ago, caught somewhere in a tangled dream, not real anymore, but just a jumble of disconnected images that could no longer assemble and become part of his mind and memory. But he had watched his father die slowly as the flint arrow tip worked its way through a part of his body that he could not reach with his knife.

But Martin had cut off his father's leg in an attempt to save him. And lied to him about his mother, saying she was still alive, when she was lying in a grave in pieces, the way he'd found her in the corncrib after the Shawnees swept through their farm like a savage horde of locusts, stealing, killing, burning what they could not take. And scalped his mother in two places and took his father's hair, thinking him dead with blood all over him and so many arrows in him, it was a wonder he had any blood left.

"Cut the leg off, Marty," his father had said, and Martin, only twelve years old, had cut off most of his leg with a rendering knife, and he could still hear his father's screams until Conrad Baron had passed out. And now he could smell again the stench of the cauterized wound that still turned gangrenous and see his father writhe as an arrow in his groin worked its way to an artery, slicing through him every time he moved until finally his father was too hoarse to scream anymore and had just prayed and talked about death until Martin could stand it no longer and stuffed cotton wads in his ears until his father stopped breathing. And Martin burned down what was left of the house and rode a mule along the Ohio River until he came to the Mississippi and hired on a steamboat in the black gang and made his way to New Orleans.

"Jack, I think you'll keep your leg. I'm going after an awl now and some more whiskey."

"Yes, Martin, more whiskey to keep the pain at bay, though it snarls and snaps at me like a mad dog. And bring your needle and thread and sew me up like a rag doll."

"Try not to think about it so much, Jack."

Martin felt badly about that bit of advice, but he didn't know what else to say. He knew Jack was in pain, knew he was probably dying. But if he got into that world with him, it would be like watching his father die all over again. He was glad he had not seen his mother linger on, although he wished he had not seen what the Shawnees had done to her.

Martin found the awl in a locker and a roll of oiled sinew, a rattail file. He grabbed a bottle of whiskey from another locker, took along a pot, a deep pan and some cloth towels, and went back up on deck. The clouds were moving fast, to the northeast, but he knew they could still get more heavy rain. He hoped it would stop drizzling, that the sun would come out.

Back at the camp, Martin sharpened the awl, threaded it with sinew. He filled a pot with water from the Gulf and started the fire in the ring of stones.

"I'm going to clean that wound, get a good look at it, Jack."

"How about a pull on that whiskey?"

"Take as much as you want." Martin handed the bottle of whiskey to Jack.

When the water boiled, Martin dipped a towel until it was soaked. He slit Jack's trouser leg, cut it off well above the wound. He bathed it clean while Jack poured whiskey down his throat. The wound was deep, bleeding profusely. He wondered how much blood Jack had lost. It looked as if he had been hacked with an axe. The bone was splintered inside and he knew there was no way to put it together so it could knit. Every time he touched the splinters and tried to mash them into place, Jack screamed.

"It'll hurt worse when I use the awl on you."

"Damn, I know it. Martin, you just do the best you can. That's all any man can do."

Martin dipped the awl in the boiling water. There was no other way to sterilize the sinew. He pinched the flesh together and stuck the curved hollow needle through both sides of the parted skin. Jack clenched his teeth and his face went bone white. But he did not scream. When he had a loop, Martin took the bitter end and wove it through, then tightened it down. Jack's eyes snapped wide for a moment, then closed tight as the shock knocked him cold.

Quickly Martin stitched up the wound, pulling each loop tight so that the flesh was sealed. A few droplets of blood seeped through the stitching, and then it stopped. Baron heaved a sigh of relief and cleaned up the bloody awl, put it away.

He began to bring provisions ashore while Jack slept. He built the fire higher, changed his and Jack's clothes, put the wet ones out to dry in the wind.

When Jack awoke, he was hungry. Martin had a stew ready for him, poured it down his gullet with a tin cup. It was late afternoon and Jack slept again, but he didn't ask for whiskey before he fell asleep. Martin felt his forehead. It was hot and clammy, but he had not yet started to sweat out the poison that was probably building up in his body.

"Maybe you'll make it, Jack," Martin whispered so that Jack could not hear even if he was awake. "I hope to God you do."

There was no more rain, but the clouds held the sky hostage in gray bunting from horizon to horizon. Martin gathered more firewood, neatened up the camp. He carried a rifle, besides the pistol he wore in his belt, when he went up on the plain. The images of the Apaches were still vivid in his mind, but he saw no sign of any other human.

As the sky darkened for evening, the coyotes began to yip and call. Martin listened intently, thrilling to the wild chorus that floated over the Gulf. In a strange way, their cries reminded him of the Apaches they had seen the day before. Both men and coyotes wild and free. The clouds began to break up and the western sky blazed softly. Jack woke up, groggy, unfamiliar with his surroundings.

"Huh, where in hell are we?"

"Shore camp, Jack."

"I thought I had died and gone someplace where there was fire." He stared into the blaze of mesquite, sniffed the aroma.

Martin laughed.

"I'm glad to see you're feeling better."

"Dry clothes and all. But I've been to the brink, Martin."

"What's that?"

"I've looked over the edge. It's mighty dark in there."

"Dreaming again?"

"Didn't seem like a dream. Seemed like Death himself was waiting just beyond."

"Imagination, Jack."

Jack looked down at his leg, orange in the firelight. Martin had cut the pants off above the wound, so he could keep an eye on it. He wanted to see if it changed color or any blue streaks ran up Jack's leg.

"No, I can feel the poison in me. It hurts like hell, too."

"I'm sorry."

"Not your fault."

"How'd it happen?"

"I thought we might hit bottom, so I picked up the anchor. Wind blew me down and it came crunching into my leg. I heard the sound in my brain. Bones breaking. Blood running like a river."

"Bad."

"I should have let it alone, but I thought we were going to hit some rocks. I thought I heard surf breaking. It was just a quick thing. I thought it was pretty smart of me at the time."

"We got out of it," Martin said.

"I reckon."

"Hungry?"

"No. I'm hot. I don't know if it's from the fire or the fever. Hear them coyotes?"

"Yes. Beautiful."

"They probably smell me. I'd hate to be eaten alive."

"I doubt if they'll bother us. But I've got some rifles and pistols loaded if they get curious."

"It's not the wild dogs I'm worried about," said Jack. "It's them scalp-huntin' Apaches. They seen us plain and they'll be back."

"We've got a good defensive position here."

"You can't stay here forever. They'll see the *Mary E* there and wait for us to make a run for it, then shoot arrows into us. They'll be like a fox at a rabbit hole. They can wait us out."

"We'll cross that bridge when we come to it."

Jack sighed and leaned back against the bank. The sun was well down over the horizon and it was dark except for the light from the fire. Martin didn't look into it, but kept his eyes on the upper bank, a rifle across his lap. He was hungry, but he wanted to wait and see if Jack wanted to eat with him.

"You'd best take some supper," Jack said as if reading his mind.

"I'll eat with you."

"Ever think about dying, Martin?"

"Yes, some."

"I've thought about it a lot. Wondered how I'd be when the time came."

"You're doing just fine. You're alive."

"I did a lot of wondering."

"Might be best to let it lie for now. We can talk about it when you get well."

"I'm not going to get well, Martin."

"Sure you are."

"It's too close. A man knows. I didn't know for sure before, but I do now."

"Jack, you're just full of fever and your mind is hot as a skillet."

"No, Martin. Listen to me. I'm dying. I can feel it all through me. Death. I'm not afraid, I just want to remember all I can before I go."

"It won't be that way, Jack."

"How do you know?"

"I watched my father die. It took him five long days. He didn't feel good about it. He didn't think about the good life he had. He only thought about death."

"Well, it's a big moment in a man's life."

"Yes. It's not very pleasant."

"Well, I'm dying, Martin. It might take a few days, but I'll never leave this shore."

Martin got up, leaned the rifle against the bank where he could reach it in a hurry if he had to. Maybe Jack was going to die right where he lay, but he didn't want to listen to him talk about it night and day. His father had been terrified of death and death had terrified Martin.

"I'm going to eat and get some sleep," said Martin.

"Don't worry. I won't dwell on my death, but I've learned a thing or two in my life and before I go I want to tell you a thing or two."

"Not now, Jack."

"No, not now." Jack sighed. "Later, when I've got it all sorted out. Tomorrow, maybe. Before Juanito finds us."

"Juanito?"

"He'll be here in a few days. He knows we had a storm and he'll be curious. I'd like to see him one more time before I go."

"You'll see him, Jack."

"Yes. One way or the other." As Martin looked at him, Jack's eyes frosted strangely in the light. For a moment it seemed he had no eyes at all. They seemed to be looking at some region far beyond the sea, some place of clouds and craggy, snowcapped peaks in another world.

Martin knew, just in that instant, that Jack was going to die.

4

JACK STUMBLED THROUGH the thicket of brambles. There was a path, but it was narrow and striped with dark shadows. There were many converging pathways and they kept leading into ever more complex labyrinths. He felt in his pocket for the crimson string that a man looking like Martin had given him. He pulled out a bundle of thread that looked like sinew, only it had a silvery cast and the thread slithered in his hands like snakes. He began to walk down one of the tributaries and let the string unwind to mark his path.

It grew ever darker as he walked and he heard the low growl of wild animals in the brush. He heard small creatures scurrying in the underbrush. Shapes appeared and disappeared and he saw familiar faces with unfamiliar names. The man who looked like Martin joined him and they walked together down a narrow defile marked with the strange tracks of unknown beasts. Spiders dangled from glistening silken strands that stretched to the sky. The thread kept wriggling and unwinding in his hand, but when he looked back, he saw only snakes undulating wildly as if someone had cut the cord into several pieces behind him and they had been transformed into serpents. And he knew then that there was no going back to the world he had left.

The way became more complicated and he ventured into other landscapes, each one wilder than the one before, and he kept trying to play out the string in his hand so that he could find his way back, but it kept changing into other things, broken things that he could not define in the normal world, and he knew he was lost and would never find his way back to his starting point.

He saw the riders coming toward him in the distance. There were four of them and they held lances that spouted fire and smoke. The one in the lead wore a dark cloak and there was a black cowl over his face. The others were painted like harlequins and he heard them call like coyotes. And then the riders disappeared like smoke, but he could feel their hot breaths blowing on his face. And the string in his hand coiled up and struck him in the neck and he felt a needle burn into his flesh.

Jack awoke in stark sunlight, sweat clinging to him, the sea breaking foamy on the shore. He slapped a sand flea drawing blood from his neck and looked down at its smashed form in his palm, a pale crimson dot beneath it. He saw that Martin had moved the boat out into deeper water and brought the dinghy ashore. The pain in his leg was subsiding and he knew that was a bad sign. He didn't have the courage to look at it, though he knew he must have developed gangrene, even though Martin had poured liberal doses of whiskey on it during the night.

"Martin," he called, but his voice did not carry far and there was a rasp to it.

The fire burned low, but he could smell the mesquite. He tasted the sea, too, the freshness of it and the dank aroma of the shore, sea plants washed up like dead members of creatures giving off their own scents. Swan-white clouds floated over the Gulf, their shapes like sails on caravels and barques, puffed full by the wind. Overhead, a turkey buzzard circled on invisible currents, only its head moving from side to side as it spiraled down and down.

There were seagulls, too, miniature winged companions to the clouds who soared beneath the sun like offspring of Icarus as if testing the heights they could fly before their wings melted and they plunged into the sea. Killdeer strutted the shoreline on spindly little legs, piping every discovery of shell, mollusk, snail, stitching back and forth, leaving the sand laced with the cross-hatching of their trident feet.

Jack heard a sound, turned to see Martin scrambling down the bank, a pair of freshly gutted jackrabbits in his hand. The fur was still on them, but Jack's mouth watered.

"I didn't hear any shots."

"I set snares early this morning. Found a couple of game trails."

"Busy, ain't you?"

"You're feeling some better, Jack?"

"Yes," Jack lied. He was still trembling inwardly from the dream.

"Hungry?"

"I could eat. You make any coffee?"

"Still early. Won't take long."

"Storm's over."

"Gone on," said Martin. "Boat's sound enough."

"You pump out that bilge, too?"

Martin laughed. He set a kettle already filled with water, dried carrots, chickpeas, onions and seasonings on the fire and began skinning the gutted rabbits. He tossed their hides away and seagulls descended on them like white locusts. Martin cut each rabbit into quarters and threw them in the pot.

Jack watched him as a man will sit on the porch late in life and watch the sunrise, knowing it might be for the last time.

"Smells good," said Jack, wrinkling his nose.

"If you can't eat the rabbit, the broth will do you good."

"I had a bad dream last night. Woke me up."

"Some of it wasn't a dream, Jack."

"I know the difference."

Martin walked over and looked at Jack's leg, but didn't touch it. He could smell it. It stank of whiskey, blood, pus and oil.

"I could take that bandage off, Jack, and pour some gunpowder in that wound. Burn all the poison out."

"I know you could, Martin. I could think of a better use for that gunpowder, though."

"I won't shoot you, Jack. No matter how much it hurts."

"I could do it myself."

"I couldn't let you do that either."

"You'd let a man suffer?"

"I wouldn't want that. But I'll not take a life not my own, nor help anyone cross that bridge."

"You religious or something?"

"No, but I've thought about it—about death and life. I guess I could protect myself and my family, but that's as far as I would go."

"You sound like my pappy. He had some pretty strange, ah, beliefs, I guess you'd call them."

Martin sat down beside Jack, leaned back against the bank. He watched the vapors rising from the stew pot, listened to the lonely cries of the seagulls as they wandered the skies offshore like passing wayfarers from some Grecian isle. Some seamen believed the

gulls were the ghosts of sailors lost at sea and that their
cries were calls to passing ships.

"My pappy talked about a life beyond before he
died," said Martin. "He wondered if there was one."

"My pap said there was. He said that man was really
a spirit inside, that the spirit was trapped in the body
for this lifetime and when we died, the spirit went out
into the world where it had always been."

"I don't think my pap thought that far ahead. He
said it was pretty hard to think of any life beyond this
one. And he thought this one was just one long curse.
A punishment from God."

"I been thinkin' about it pretty hard. Death, that is. I
figure that there's got to be something better than this."

"Might be," said Martin.

"Anyway, if there is nothing, then it won't matter
much. Gone is gone."

"I think you're right."

"But there might be something, eh?"

"I never thought about it much. Why would anyone
want to come back here?"

"I don't mean here. Some other place."

"It would have to be a damned good place."

Jack sighed, looked up at the sky. "And the sea shall
give up its dead," he murmured wistfully.

"That's mighty gruesome," said Martin.

"But poetic." Jack coughed, a dry, raspy scrape in
his throat. "I keep thinking that everything I ever read
or heard might be wrong. Like the Bible and what the
preachers preach."

"So what?" Martin felt uncomfortable listening to
Jack go on about mysteries that would never be
solved. Floating straws out on waters that could not
save him from drowning.

"So there must be something else that we haven't
been told. There must be answers to all the riddles in
life."

"Well, I've never heard any, Jack."

"That's what I mean. Maybe we don't find out until we die. Then, maybe, everything becomes clear."

"All the questions answered."

"Yes. All the questions. Answered."

Jack still stared at the sky and it seemed he could feel his body stretching toward it, something inside him floating out and upward, farther than he could see. And he had felt that way before at night, when he looked up at the stars and imagined that he could float up to them and pass on to other worlds where people lived who knew all the answers.

Over the next few days the skin around the leg wound began to blacken. Martin could see no telltale blue streaks running up Jack's leg.

"Must be inside," he said to Jack. "But I've got to take off that leg."

"Won't make no difference."

"It might. If I don't, you're going to die and it's going to be bad for you, Jack."

"Hell, the cutting will probably kill me." He tried to laugh.

Martin could barely stand to look at Jack. He had lost weight in his legs and stomach and now his ribs were visible under the stretched parchment of his skin. His face was shrinking, too. His eyes were bigger.

"There's a chance we can stop the gangrene from going any further. I could find some maggots or burn off the stump." Martin winced when he said it, but he knew what gangrene was. It was like leprosy. It wolfed down flesh very rapidly.

"How's the whiskey holding out?" asked Jack.

"Plenty left. And rum. More rum than whiskey. Whiskey tastes like coal oil, anyway."

"Let the leg rot, then. I don't fancy walking on a wooden stick, no how."

"Don't let yourself give up so easy, Jack."

"Maybe I want to give it up. There's some things better'n pain."

"Pain goes away."

"So does life."

"Once it's gone, it doesn't come back."

"Some folks say it does."

Martin shook his head. He wished his father had been as rational as Jack. And Jack was at the crazy stage now, he was sure.

"I'll get you some more whiskey."

"How's the boat?"

"It's almost clear clean. Some more swabbing to do. No leaks now."

"You done some caulking?"

"Some. Above water level."

"Good," said Jack and reached for his pipe. They had plenty of tobacco, too. Martin was a man who believed in carrying extra supplies. Running out of some things was plain intolerable when a man had troubles. Martin was good that way. Once they had floated windless for almost two weeks, the sails sagging on the masts. Neither of them got cabin fever. They fished, swam and drank rum and smoked, watched the sunsets and the sunrises. They would have been at each other's throats if they had been short of certain things that calmed a man.

Martin returned with the whiskey and some ship's stores. Lately he had been gone longer and longer each day, leaving Jack alone to brood and smell his rotten leg.

"Where do you go every morning?"

"Hunting. Looking."

"See any Apaches?"

"No. No sign of them. I saw a cow the other day, though."

"A cow?"

"Looked like a cow. Like a patchwork quilt, sort of. Big long horns. It ran wild when it saw me."

"You still think you can settle in this desolate country and raise cattle?"

"I think of it every now and then."

"Do you believe in bad omens?"

"No," said Baron.

"Well, we got us a good 'un here, I think."

"Accidents happen. Yours happened at sea. Not on the land there."

"It happened on account of us coming here, Martin."

"Don't make more of it than it is, my friend."

Jack puffed deeply on his pipe. As if thoughts were in the smoke, as if the smoke could settle his restless mind. He blew the smoke out in a thick cloud and thought of the mornings he had been there when the fog had come in and hidden the boat from sight, cloaked the land, so that he sat, or lay, in a claustrophobic haze that terrified him. As if he had been shut off from the world, as if he was being warned that he was soon to be taken into darkness where he could no longer see the world.

The smoke hung there beyond his pipe and he looked into it as if he could divine his future, as if he could see beyond, into the unknown. But the smoke wafted away on the breeze and the world stood out in relief: the *Mary E* bobbing disconsolately at anchor, the wavelets lapping at the shore, the seagulls calling like lost souls, stitching the blue sky with black-tipped wings and the far clouds floating like white barques on a cerulean sea.

"A man facing death tends to look backward to see where he went wrong," Jack said finally.

"Can't look back and can't look ahead, Jack. My pap taught me that much. He said we have but one single moment in time, at any time, and it's an eternal moment."

"I don't follow you, Martin."

"Well, the way I figure it, in that one moment, we

could be blown to hell or go on to the next. That's why it's eternal, I guess. We could fall dead from heart failure. Everything that happens does so in just one minute, so that's all we have."

"I never could get much of a line on time and what you say makes some sense, but life doesn't last just a single moment."

"Maybe it does," said Martin. He arranged the bottles in the sand so they would stay cool and protected. He dribbled sand on them like a child playing at the beach. It was something to do as long as Jack was talking. "For some, it does. For others, a minute can seem like an eternity."

"You make it sound like we only have one minute of life and that's it."

"Pap said that in all likelihood that's all we do have. Just one minute. That's all we can live at a time. He said we can't do anything about the past. It's done and gone. And the future isn't here yet. So we just have to deal with this one moment. And it's God's moment. Given to us. We can do with it whatever we want."

Jack shook his head, emptied his bottle into the sand.

"Too tangled up for me," he said. "I'll take some of that whiskey."

"You hungry?"

"No. And you've addled my brain so all I want to do is put a damper on it."

Martin laughed. But he knew Jack was thinking about what he had said. He knew it didn't make much sense. It hadn't to him at first, but as he watched his father die, he saw some point to it. It was just not the way people were used to looking at time. So he had never mentioned it to anyone before now. And it did sound kind of silly coming out of his mouth. But it was something his father had talked about as he lay dying, and maybe it might help Jack to come to grips with his own mortality.

Martin pulled the cork on a bottle of whiskey and handed it to Jack. Jack pulled on it generously, his eyelids fluttering like tiny wings. When they opened, his eyes were filled with tears.

"Great suffering Jesuses, Martin. Where did you get that stuff?"

Martin looked at the bottle. It had no label. "Somewhere in New Orleans, I reckon."

"The public bathhouse, likely. God, it tastes like horse piss."

"I didn't know you drank horse piss, Jack."

"Martin, can't you give me something to do? To take my mind off this blamed leg? Haven't you got some sails to mend?"

"Done mended them, Jack."

"When?"

"There were about three days when you were in and out, up and down."

"I don't remember that."

"I thought you were going to leave me. You ran a high fever. I bathed that leg with salt water twice a day and threw wet blankets on you to bring the fever down."

"Jesus."

"You called his name a time or two."

"I didn't know. Thanks for pulling me through."

"You done it, Jack. I just sat here mending sail and throwing buckets of water on you."

Jack laughed. "No wonder I dreamed I was drowning."

Martin kept a sea watch every day, hoping he would see Juanito's sails break over the horizon. Jack held on as his leg began to turn black and the gangrene crept slowly up past the wound. Martin did what he could, soaking it in salt water, packing it in kelp to keep the smell down. Finally he took a knife and hatchet with him when he went hunting and he didn't return until late in the day. His arms and hands were covered with dirt.

"Where you been, Martin?"

"Hunting." Martin took off his shirt and waded into the water of the cay to wash off the soil.

"I seen you carry a hatchet and butcher knife up yonder. You forget 'em?"

"I must have," said Martin, wading back to shore.

"What you doing with them?"

"Cutting wood."

"I don't see no wood."

"I'll have to go back and get it. Tomorrow, maybe."

"We got plenty of wood."

"Never can tell," said Martin.

But every day Martin spent on land while Jack brooded and looked down inside himself to see if he could catch sight of his death lurking in the darkness. At such times he floated above himself and outside himself and shed his flesh like a coat. It was very peaceful down there in the silence, and he felt warm and safe there. He felt beyond the bounds of flesh and free of the shackles of pain.

Jack stayed down there at his center for hours and always hated it when he returned. The sound of the gentle surf took him down, and when he was in the silence he was no longer aware of where he was and he could not hear the soft soughing of the sea, but only the murmur of his heart and the whispers of his own immortality somewhere beyond that place where he lay dying. At first he bobbed up and down like a cork and his thoughts ran wild, but as each day passed, he felt himself level off and began to believe that he was spirit at such times, freely floating somewhere in a calm world that had no boundaries, an in-between universe where there was no pain, no feeling from his body at all.

Sometimes when he came back up into the real

world, Jack felt as if he was still floating above the ground. He soon lost all appetite for food, but he drank water and chewed on whatever Martin gave him, just to keep in the habit.

"I don't see any new wood," he said to Martin one day when Baron came back from hunting.

"I'll bring it down when we need it."

"Any sign of Juanito?"

"No."

"You been looking for him?"

"I keep an eye out."

"From up there?"

"I'm never very far away."

"Where'd you get all that dirt on you?"

"In the brush, I guess."

"You digging for something up there?"

Martin turned away, washed himself in the water of the cay. He didn't answer.

Jack squinted at Martin and began to wonder again what Baron did all day long. He did bring in fresh game from time to time, rabbits, ground squirrels, a turkey or two. And one day he brought in a small pig that didn't seem to have much meat on it.

"Never seen a pig like that," said Jack.

"Me neither," said Martin.

"Maybe it's poison."

"Well, we'll find out tonight when I cook it."

"I don't want any."

"Suit yourself, Jack."

Martin never argued with Jack anymore. The man looked like a derelict, one of those men scarred in battle at New Orleans back when Andy Jackson stormed the city and became a hero, legs and arms just stumps, eyes empty as olive pits, skin stretched over their bones like old yellow parchment. Jack's eyes were watery and yellow where the whites should be. It was painful to look at him. He was just skin and bones, yet he held on, still lived.

Cackle Jack seemed different the past several days, though. Martin could not explain it. As if he was calm and resigned to his fate, as if he had no pain and meant to starve himself to death before the gangrene ate him up. Martin could not bear to look at his leg anymore, either. He wanted to take the hatchet and chop it off, bury it or throw it out to sea. He shuddered every time he thought of that leg, black and shriveling into something that resembled one of those wind-bent trees that dotted the shoreline.

"Tomorrow," said Jack one night.

"Tomorrow?"

"That's when I'll go."

Martin was stirring the stew with the peccary remnants still floating in it. The night was warm and he did not need much fire to heat their supper.

"How do you know?"

"It come to me today when I was down there."

Martin's scalp prickled.

"Down where?"

"Down where I go, where I'm just spirit, with no body. It's deep inside. Probably hid there by whoever made us."

"More dreams, Jack."

"No, this ain't no dream. It's real. I found where I really live, way inside my body. That's what will go when I go, when I give up my breath. That's what can't be sick or hurt or poor or anything mortal. I think God hid it from us, but meant us to find it."

"Find what?"

"Whatever makes the stars shine and the clouds to float, Martin. Whatever makes the wind and the rivers run and the land high with mountains."

"You're just a man. Like me. Like everyone else."

"No. That's what I thought. Now I know better."

"You going to eat some of this stew. You have to admit that pig was pretty good last night."

"It tasted all right. No sense in eating much. When

I go, you'll have to carry me up on dry land and bury me in that hole you been digging."

"What?" Martin turned to look at Jack squarely for the first time in several days. The man's eyes were clear and he seemed to glow with an inner light.

"That grave you been diggin' for me, Martin. It deep enough? Is it finished?"

"It's finished," Martin said finally.

Jack smiled and Martin wondered how he knew he had been digging his grave with an axe, a bucket, a knife and his bare hands.

"I know. I knowed all along," Jack said, grinning wide.

And Martin hadn't even asked the question aloud.

5

JACK MCTAVISH DIED the next morning. He called out to Martin just before dawn.

"Come set with me, Martin," he said.

"I'm still asleep."

"Wake up, then. Might be the last time we have to talk. I want to tell you something. Something important."

"All right." Martin got up, rubbed the sleep from his eyes and pulled on a jacket. It was cold and he stirred the fire, put a pot of water on for tea. A heavy mist hugged the shoreline and he could not see the *Mary E,* but he could hear it creak on its moorings like a rocking chair in an empty parlor.

Martin put fresh wood on the fire, fed it until he had it blazing. The flames painted the mist a pale orange and cleared a path to the stars just above the beach. He looked up at the glittering pinpoints, shivered in the chill. Jack sat up in his blankets, bedding crumpled up for a backrest. His face looked eerily skeletal in the firelight. But he was wide awake and his eyes bright. He seemed unusually alert.

"Coffee'll be ready soon. Or tea. What's up, Jack?"

"I'm going on this morning, Martin. I've been awake for hours. Looking at the stars until the fog came in and then I went down inside of me and took the mist with me. It was very peaceful."

"I'm sure it was," said Martin sarcastically. "I wish you were still down in there."

"That's what I wanted to talk to you about, Marty."

"God, I can't even think. I need something warm inside me first."

"It won't take long. I've been thinking."

"I figured that."

"Hear me out, will you?"

"Sure, Jack. I'm sorry. Grumpy this morning. My bones are stiff and cold."

"I'm warm all over, Marty. Warm and at peace with myself."

"That's good." This time he wasn't sarcastic.

"I know you're going to go on and probably settle on this wild land. I can't stop you. I just want to give you something to carry with you."

"What's that, Jack?"

"Something I found out when I let myself go down inside myself and just listen. Listen to the big silence. All the answers are there. All the meaning I've been looking for all my life. I wish I had gone down there sooner."

"I'm trying to understand you, Jack. Really, I am."

"I know. It doesn't make much sense unless you've been down there. But listen. That's the place you can go anytime. If you've got troubles, if you're hurt, if you're worried. It's safe down there. Safe and quiet."

"How do you go down there?"

"Just think yourself down. Just leave your body and sink down. Easy as anything."

Martin shook his head. He heard the water boiling

in the pot, rattling the lid. He stood up, walked to the fire. He threw tea into a tin cup and filled it with hot water. "You want some tea or coffee, Jack?"

Jack shook his head.

The aroma from the tea leaves wafted to Martin's nostrils. He breathed it in and blew on the surface before he drank. He shook the cup in a circular motion to make the tea leaves swirl, emit their savory, aromatic ink in the water.

"I don't have the dreams anymore, Marty."

"That's good, I guess."

"Yes. I had the feeling that God was poking around in my mind with his finger. Trying to get me to do something. Pushing here and pushing there, touching spots in my skull."

Martin resisted the urge to shut Jack up. He was starting to babble again. It was hard watching a man die, especially a good man like Jack McTavish. He had been strong, robust, full of life and energy a week ago, and now he was broken in mind and body, a shell of the man he once was.

"So now what do you think?"

"I think I was supposed to give up the dreams and go down inside myself. See what was real."

"And did you, Jack?" Martin sat down, blew the steam off his tea and sipped the hot liquid into his mouth, let it cool before swallowing.

"I saw that I was part of everything, that I was the spirit part of leaves and trees and rocks and birds and animals, even the sea. That everything has a spark to it and you just have to blow on it."

"You're pretty weak, Jack. It could be you're imagining a lot of this."

Jack cackled softly. "Listen, Marty, listen to me. If you go onto this land, you might run into trouble down the line. I just want to tell you that you can go to a place where nothing or nobody can harm you."

"And where is that?"

"Inside, in the quiet. You do it after I'm gone, and you'll find all the answers to every question you have. You'll always know what to do. There's no confusion in the deep where the spirit lives. Where that tiny spark is so bright it blinds you."

"I'll keep it in my mind, Jack."

"I saw a river down there once, and land that stretched to the stars and mountains in the distance all snowcapped and eagles flying over them. Beautiful."

Martin didn't say anything. He shook his head sadly and thought of the days at sea when he and Jack had laughed and joked and when they had anchored at night and looked at moonlight spangling the waters, sat and listened to the sea slap against the hull, never needing to speak because they were sharing the open sky and the endless sea with pipe smoke wafting on the breeze and bright and warm in their lungs.

The sun was well up and the mist almost dissipated. Sun sparkled on the Gulf waters, shooting off silver sparks like a sharpening wheel.

"I can go anytime I want, you know."

"Go?"

"Die, Marty. That's what I'm going to do. I've lived my life. It was pretty good. But now I know I don't have to live it anymore."

"That's just foam in the churn, Jack."

"You remember what I told you, Martin Baron."

Martin sighed and took another sip of his tea. "All right, Jack."

"I'm going to leave pretty quick. I won't say good-bye. Just remember when you look at the sky or pick up a clump of dirt or see a rabbit run that old Jack is part of all you see."

Martin shook his head. He couldn't believe Jack was talking like this. He must have gone over the edge into madness. That was the only explanation for such empty, meaningless babble.

"I'll say farewell to you, Martin. I'll be getting along right soon. You go after that land. Raise cattle and make your mark."

"You just hang on, Jack. Juanito will show up any day and he'll have fresh food aboard, maybe some medicine for that leg."

But Jack closed his eyes and leaned back against the sandy wall of the bank. Martin watched him carefully. His chest was moving, slowly, but moving. He looked very peaceful. Jack put his hands in his lap, the palms upward, and seemed to go into a deep sleep. Tired from all that talking probably, Martin thought. He turned away, looked out to sea. He thought he could see a white sail in the distance.

Martin stood up to get a better look, but the sun was bright on the water now. He had to squint to shut out the silver glaze. He saw no sail, but he was sure he had seen one.

"That could be Juanito," he said to Jack. "I thought I saw his sail yonder."

But Jack didn't answer.

Martin turned to look at him. Jack's chest was no longer undulating. Alarmed, Martin threw his cup down and rushed to Jack's side. He knelt down, grasped his shoulders, shook him.

"Jack, Jack, wake up!"

But Jack didn't move.

Martin put his ear close to Jack's mouth. He could detect no breathing. He put his hand on Jack's chest. It was still. He shook Jack again, harder this time. He put a finger against the pulse in Jack's throat. There was none.

"Oh, God, Jack, don't do this. Come back."

When he released his grip on Jack's shoulders, Jack fell sideways and didn't move. Martin knew then that his friend was dead. He sucked in a breath and clenched his fists. Then he closed his eyes and the tears exploded from their ducts and he felt the sting of them. His throat ached and he began sobbing to release the pressure he felt.

He cried for himself and for Jack, and he could not stop himself for several moments. The sobs tore at his throat and chest and he hammered the sandy ground with his fists and still could not stem the flood of tears until he was all cried out and empty and hollow in his heart.

And it seemed as if he could feel Jack's spirit all around him, could sense it in the breeze that blew soft against his face and reduced his tears to dust streaks that striped his tanned cheeks. He choked up as he looked at Jack's face, peaceful now in repose, but the hard lines of his illness etched still in his frozen visage.

Martin began to sob again, but it was only a dry, hacking cough that wrenched his body, scratched his throat raw. He stood up and gulped air and still he could feel Jack's ghostly presence. He crabbed up the slope of the bank and stood on the flat, staring at the land, willing himself under control.

"Jack, why did you have to kill yourself?" he whispered. "I could have saved you. Stubborn bastard."

Suddenly the land did not seem so important. Not without McTavish. He had hoped to persuade Jack to throw in with him and help him build something permanent, something that would not sink at sea or be blown to pieces on some rocky shoal. But now he was alone and there seemed no reason to change, to go on and pursue his dream.

Martin had not realized the depth of his feelings for Jack McTavish until this moment. He had liked him and they had had plenty of good times in New Orleans and some damned fine catches in the Gulf. But he had never faced up to his attachment to Jack. He wasn't like his father at all, but he had been like a father to him. And it was just like losing his pap all over again. Only worse, somehow.

An incredible feeling of loneliness swept over him, and he felt the tug of deep despair. He felt more alone than when his father had died, because at least he had known him as a father. He knew very little about Jack. He did not know if Jack had kin or, if he did, where they might be. There was no one to talk to about Jack. He was just gone, and he had left a big hole where he had once been.

Martin gulped in air, shook his head to free it from the dark thoughts that clouded his thinking. There was nothing left to do but bury Jack and put him out of his mind. He could not bring him back. He would not rise from the dead in three days or ever.

He plodded back down to the small beach. He shuddered when he saw Jack's body again. He picked the corpse up in his arms. The remains were strangely light and he walked up the bank easily. He carried Jack to the open grave at the edge of the mesquite thicket. Dirt lay piled up on three sides. Atop the biggest mound lay the axe and bucket he had used to dig the grave. He leaned over and slowly let Jack's body down, holding on to his shirtfront and legs. He dropped him gently the rest of the way and stood up, breathed deeply.

"It's not much, Jack, but the critters won't get to you."

Tears stung Martin's eyes once again and he shut them tight and began to breathe deeply. A ten-knot breeze blew against his face, dried his tears. He opened his eyes and looked up at the sky.

"I reckon I should say a prayer over you, Jack." He felt awkward talking to himself like that, but the silence was eerie. He did not want to look at Jack again, did not want to see the dirt hitting his face. And it didn't seem right to just bury him without saying words over him.

The sky swam above him, all blue, pocked with white clouds drifting easterly in the light wind, little puffs of cotton batting torn from some far-off storm, he imagined.

"Good Lord," Martin said, bowing his head, "take this man, Jack McTavish, into heaven. I liked him and he died too young. I pray you welcome him. I reckon he would rather have been buried at sea, but I didn't want the fish getting to him. Rest in peace, Jack. And so long to you, my friend. Amen."

Martin's throat constricted as he fought back tears. The finality of the prayer choked him and he wondered if he could summon the courage to shovel dirt over his friend's body.

"Damn it all," he said. Then "Pardon me, Lord, but I got a hard chore to do here."

Martin grabbed up the bucket without looking into the grave and began pushing dirt over Jack's body. He heard the sand and clods strike the corpse and every thud tore at him, wrenched his senses. Blindly he shoveled furiously, going all around the grave. He did not see the Apache on horseback a hundred yards away, sitting on his mount like a statue, watching him.

The Indian had been watching Martin ever since he had carried Jack's body up to the open grave. He was alone. He heard the words Martin said and understood most of them. He and his companions had known that Jack was hurt and that Martin had dug a grave for him.

The Apache carried a lance with an obsidian blade. He wore a breechclout, a bright headband, moccasins decorated with porcupine quills and painted symbols. He carried a quiver over his shoulder and a bow in a sheath attached to the quiver that bristled with hunting arrows made with tin arrowheads and fletched with wild turkey feathers.

The Apache was a Lipan, and he had an unpronounceable name in his own language. But the Mexicans called him Abeja, Bee, because of his sting with arrow, lance and knife. He was one of the band who had seen the *Mary E* blown to shore in the storm, and since he was curious, he had gotten the habit of riding in close to observe the white man every few days. He had wondered whether it would be possible to kill him and board his ship and take what goods he could find. But he and his brothers had had bad experiences with boats before and he was reluctant to attack. Besides, the white man always carried a rifle and a pistol and was probably a good fighter.

Abeja watched as Martin Baron filled the grave and made a little mound atop it with the extra dirt that the dead man had displaced.

Martin patted the mound all around until the earth was firm over the grave. Then he placed a stone where Jack's head was resting. He picked up the bucket and stood by the grave for a long moment.

Then he caught something out of the corner of his eye. He turned and saw Abeja sitting his horse. As he gazed at him, the Apache lifted his lance in a kind of salute and then whirled his brown pony in a tight circle and rode away, not fast, but at a gentle lope. He did not look back.

Sighing deeply, Martin turned his steps back toward the little shore where he and Jack had spent the last two weeks or more. It was then that a glint of white caught his eye and he stopped suddenly and shaded his brow with his right palm.

The sail was no illusion this time. And it was Juanito's little boat, *El Viento*. There was a small swatch of orange at the top of the sail. Juanito had dyed a piece of canvas, sewn it to the topmost triangle as a kind of trademark.

Martin waved, but the sloop was too far out, he knew. He took off his shirt and flapped it wildly. He raced along the bank, waving the shirt. His heart tugged when he saw the boom swing and the prow head in his direction under full billowing sail.

Martin jumped up and down then, and he saw the

hull cut the waves and swing to a course that would bring Juanito directly to the cove. He felt like shouting, but his throat was raw as scored ham and he knew the Argentine could not hear him.

By then, Martin knew Juanito could see the *Mary E* at anchor. He raced down toward the cove and stopped at the inlet to wait for his friend. A great weight seemed to lift from his shoulders as he watched the ship tack toward the cay. An offshore wind gave *El Viento* plenty of energy. The sail billowed out as Juanito expertly manned the tiller.

Nearly an hour later, *El Viento* eased into the cove and Martin ran down to the beach to greet Juanito, the sadness in him beginning to diminish the closer the Argentine drifted toward shore.

"Hi, you Martin!" called Juanito Salazar, his swarthy face broken by a white-toothed grin. He waved, then collapsed his mainsail.

"Hi, Juanito. Throw me a line."

"Sure, Martin. Where is Cackle Jack, eh?"

Salazar threw a monkey fist down at Martin, who dodged it. When the lead weight struck the shore, Baron grabbed up the line and pulled it taut, secured it to a scrub tree. Juanito pitched his bow anchor out and set it. He was still grinning widely when he threw a rope ladder over the side. He anchored some fifty yards away from the *Mary E,* set the stern anchor so that there was little chance of *Viento* drifting into the other craft.

Juanito scrambled down the ladder and waded to shore.

"Eh, Martin, did you not think I would come?" He slapped Baron's back. "Did you see the land? Did you see any cattle? What do you think? It is beautiful, no? How long have you been here? What passes, my friend?"

"Belay all that, Juanito," said Martin, swept back by

Juanito's stream of questions. "I just buried Jack Mc-Tavish. Up there."

"Bury? Cackle Jack?"

"Yes. We had a storm and he got hurt. I wanted to cut off his leg, but he wanted—he wanted to die, I guess."

"Sumbitch. For true?"

"For true, Juanito. Just this morning."

"Damn, that is bad news, I think. He did not like the land?"

"He never saw much of it. He lay against that bank yonder. Out of his head most of the time."

Martin told him the whole story, of the storm, the anchor that damaged Jack's leg, the nightmares, the dreams, the ravings. He told him about seeing the Apaches on their fleet horses, with their fearsome faces and ancient weapons, and how they rode off as if they were a single being and left no trace of their passage. He told him of digging Jack's grave every day and hating himself for doing it. He told him of the long nights and the mist of morning off the sea with the salty tang of death in it and how he had prayed Jack to heaven as if he knew there really was one and how Jack had believed at the last that he would not die forever, but become spirit like the wind that blew clear to the stars and beyond. All of it. They sat in Martin's camp and Baron did not stop talking. Juanito watched as his friend bared his soul, and his face, clean-lined and bronze from the sun, never changed expression.

When Martin was finished, Juanito did not say anything for a long time. Instead, he put his hand on Martin's shoulder and patted him affectionately as he would comfort any grieving person.

"Well, that is good that you told me, Martin. I think Jack, he was a pretty fine man. He died in peace, then?"

"Yes. I guess so. He just said good-bye, and when I looked back at him, he was gone."

"That is a good way to die, my friend."

"His leg, Juanito. It ate him up. I could have taken it off and he'd be here, laughing and joking, like always."

"No. I think Jack wanted to die. One way or another. We make our worlds, my friend. We make our own worlds."

"Well, Jack did not have a very good one toward the last."

"Maybe he did, Martin. He found out who he was, no?"

"I don't know. I don't understand any of it."

"When I was a boy, my father, he read to me. He read the English and he loved the books. He read me once from an old manuscript he copied by Thomas Traherne, who was some kind of an English priest and a poet. I learned the English from this, and others, that my father gave me. I memorized much of what I read and there was one thing this Traherne wrote, I think maybe two hundred years ago, that I have always remembered."

"What's that, Juanito? I never heard of this man."

"He wrote a manuscript with many truths in it. This part I remember might be what Jack found for himself as he lay dying."

"What was it?"

"Traherne wrote: 'You never enjoy the world aright, till the sea itself floweth in your veins, till you are clothed with the stars; and perceive yourself to be sole heir of the whole world, and more than so, because men are in it who are every one sole heirs as well as you.' "

"I don't understand it."

"Perhaps Cackle Jack would have understood it. It may be as the Prashna Upanishad, an ancient Sanscrit text, tells us, that 'the dreaming mind recalls past impressions. It sees again what has been seen; it hears again what has been heard.' "

"I don't understand," Martin said.

"The mind sees all," Juanito replied.

"I didn't know you were so educated, Juanito."

"My father taught me. The books he gave me taught me. And my old grandfather taught me, too. Things they do not teach in the schools."

"Well, no matter. Jack's dead and I miss him."

Juanito put his hand on Martin's shoulder. "Let us go and find land for us to raise cattle. Let us carry Jack's memory with us."

"You still think we can raise cattle here? It does not seem a good place from what I've seen of it."

"I have seen it. I have walked it."

"You've been on the land?"

"I have seen it in my dreams. I have seen cattle in the brasada, the thickets of mesquite. It would not have been a place for Jack. It will be a place for us."

"You think so?"

"Jack was of the sea. I am of the land. You must sometimes give up one life in order to live another."

"Me, you mean?"

"You—and me, Martin. We are not of the sea, you and I. We are of the land. That is where we belong."

Martin breathed deeply and he saw the sense of what Juanito had said. He looked at the boats bobbing gently in the harbor and he closed his eyes and felt the tug of the land. He saw again the Apache riders wheeling their horses and riding off as if to some secret place, and he wanted to know where they had come from and where they had gone that day. Yes, he said to himself, this is where I belong. This land is where I will go with Juanito and we will leave the sea and walk on the land.

"We'll set out tomorrow, Juanito. I want you to show me the land."

"We will show it to each other, my friend," said

Juanito. "Now, let us have some rum and eat the shrimp and oysters I have on board *El Viento*."

"I have wine," said Martin.

"Ah, *perfecto*. We will have wine and talk of our dreams, eh?"

"Yes," said Martin with a sigh, and the saying of it was like a whispered prayer.

6

✝

MARTIN WOKE UP with fur on his tongue. He and Juanito had drunk much wine the night before. They had sung songs together by the firelight and howled at the moon. They had eaten the shrimp and oysters that Juanito had traded his catch for at Port Aransas. He had spoken to men who knew about the land they were going to walk into and he said he would tell Martin all about it the following day.

"Ah, you have come awake," said Juanito as Martin rubbed the dust of sleep from his eyes.

"I am coming awake. My eyes are awake, that's all. And they hurt."

Juanito laughed.

"Fried oysters, Martin, and strong coffee. See, the fire burns the fog away and the sun is just coming up. It is a fine day."

"You still want to go and look the land over? Without Jack?"

"Yes, that is what we will do. *Puesto ya el pie en el estribo.*"

"What the hell does that mean?" asked Martin.

"One foot is already in the stirrup, my friend. We are ashore and we will walk inland this morning."

Juanito sat near the fire cleaning his rifle, an old Kentucky flintlock, German made, with a fine curly maple stock, brass patchbox and buttplate. It was big bore, .64 caliber. He kept it wrapped in oilcloth aboard his boat. He told Martin that he sometimes shot sharks with it at sea, but his father had hunted with it on the pampas and in the cordilleras of Argentina.

"You might need that," said Martin.

"I hope to use it only for game, not Apaches or Comanches."

"Comanches?"

"I have heard they are here in this country sometimes. Very fierce. Very good on horseback."

"We're going to be pretty helpless without horses. We can't outrun 'em on foot."

"I have a map," said Juanito, wiping his rifle dry.

"What good will a map do us?"

"There are some ranches. We might be able to buy horses—or rent them."

Martin's face lit up with his grin. "You think so?"

"That is what I have heard."

Martin stepped down to the shore, bent over and scooped up seawater in his hands. He dashed his face with water several times, then walked back, sat down on his bedroll.

"Why did you have me come to this place, instead of taking shelter at the big long island to the west?" he asked Juanito. "This seems a pretty desolate spot, exposed as it is."

"That is Padre Island and is not a safe place. I thought about putting in above Corpus Christi, or sailing to the mouth of the Rio Bravo, but there are too many ships plying their trade in all those places."

"What are you afraid of, pirates?"

Juanito laughed. "Yes, there are pirates, but there are also seeing eyes. We could have sailed into Aransas, too, but here is better."

"Why?"

"We will find the Nueces River and ride over the lands to the south. Above the Nueces, there are already many ranches. Not so many west of there."

"But some," Martin said.

"Some. And Comanches, too. It is cheap land we want, land where the longhorn Mexican cattle roam free."

"And that's where we'll find it, you think?"

"The mesquite is thick through there and the Comanches have given the Mexican ranchers much worry."

"You are not afraid of the Comanches?"

"The man who tames them will become a king. He can own much land, raise many cattle. That is why I want to ride or walk through this country, Martin."

"Well, let's go and look at the country, then. We ought to put our boats out to sea and then get started on our walk."

"I am ready," said Juanito.

The two men weighed anchor and sailed their boats well away from shore. They rowed back in their dinghies carrying supplies for the journey overland.

After Juanito stepped ashore, he unwrapped a bundle that lay among his goods.

Martin watched him untie the cord around a small wool blanket. Juanito knelt down and lay the bundle on the beach, then unrolled it so that it lay open, revealing its contents.

"What are those?" asked Martin.

"Machetes. The Mexicans use them to cut brush—and for other things."

Juanito handed one of the long-bladed machetes to Martin.

"What other things?"

"Heads," Juanito said.

Martin took the object in his hand. The blade was smaller at the handle, widened out. He touched a finger to the edge. "It's very sharp," he said.

"We'll need these in some of that brush. These machetes will be useful for many things."

Martin swung the blade like a sword. It was surprisingly light. The handle had a hole in it and there was a leather thong through it. He tugged on the thong and it was strong.

"You can carry it on your belt or on your shoulder," Juanito said.

"I've never seen a blade like this."

"There are many such in the shops in New Orleans. I first saw them when I came to this country. At Matamoros, I have seen the Mexicans use these to chop fruit and vegetables, meat, cane, and they fight with them as well."

"Thank you, Juanito. I can see that such a blade might come in handy."

"Oh, yes, very useful, Martin." Juanito grinned and looped his belt through the thong on his own machete. "I am ready now. Let us go."

"We'd better hide our dinghies in the brush," Martin said.

"Show me the way."

The two men filled their packs and slung them and their rifles over their shoulders. They each wore floppy felt hats with wide brims, duck trousers, sturdy, handmade boots bought in New Orleans, shirts of a coarse weave. They tied bandannas around their necks before they set out.

Carrying their dinghies on their backs, they trudged to the brush and entered the thicket of mesquite trees, Martin in the lead, Juanito following him. The brush scratched at them, blocked their way. Finally Martin stopped and, panting, set down his dinghy.

"Far enough, I think."

"A blind man could follow our tracks in here. I will try and brush them out," Juanito said.

"It's really thick, isn't it?"

"This is mesquite. The cattle feed on it. That is why there is so much of it. The seeds go through them and are fertilized. When they leave their dung, the seeds grow."

"How do you know all this, Juanito?"

Juanito grinned. "I have been asking the questions," he said.

"Ah. I have a question."

"Say it, Martin."

"If you wipe out our tracks, how will we find our dinghies again?"

Juanito laughed. "I will find them. Do not worry."

The two returned along the path they came in, with Juanito carefully brushing away their tracks, and when they emerged, the Argentine seemed satisfied.

"Now we will walk up and down and leave many tracks. We will go in and we will go out. It will drive the Apaches crazy if they try to find the true path to the boats."

The two men did this for an hour and left a maze of tracks all along the brasada. Finally they returned to the shore and began packing provisions for their journey overland.

"You know where we are going, Juanito?"

"Yes. And we will see many wild cattle along the way. I have seen animals with horns wider than a wagon, six feet, eight feet."

"That's hard to believe."

"Let us hope they do not chase us while we are on foot."

When they were packed up, the two men took one last look at their boats as they stood atop the bank. Martin felt a tug at his heart as the *Mary E* bobbed at anchor. She was all battened down, her bilge pumped out. She could weather most any storm, he thought.

"You must put her out of your mind," said Juanito.
"Huh?"

"Do not worry about the *Mary E.* That is your past floating there. We are walking into the future."

"I don't want to lose her."

"If you are to see her again, she will be here, waiting for you."

"Aren't you worried about your boat?"

Juanito laughed. "What will be, will be."

With that, the Argentine turned on his heel and Martin had to break into a trot to catch up with him. They crossed the floodplain and circled the brasada on a westerly course. Martin looked back once, but he could no longer see the boats at anchor.

The two men carried bedrolls and light packs, a half a pound of powder each, knives, hatchets and rifles; each had a brace of pistols, loaded and primed. They also packed coffee, salt pork, flour, dried figs and onions. Juanito figured they would find enough game to fill their bellies as they trekked overland.

Both sailors carried compasses, but Juanito brought his out more often each time he studied his map. The map was crude, but he was able to show Martin the Nueces River and the Rio Bravo. The Argentine quickly set a northwesterly course.

"There are several creeks through here and we must find them or we will lose both our bearings and a source for water."

"How did anyone ever map the land in this maze of bushes?" Martin asked.

"The man I got this map from was a surveyor. He worked for an American named O. B. Clarke, who settled here two years ago. He saw one of the land-sale signs in New Orleans and came here."

"Does this man Clarke own the land where he lives?"

Juanito laughed. "Yes, he bought it from a Mexican

who had a Spanish land grant from the king. He has built a house and he raises cattle and food."

"I would like to meet this man," Martin said.

"I have met him once. He came to New Orleans and sold tallow and hides from the longhorn cattle he raises."

"Why didn't you tell me about this man before?"

"I only met him after you left New Orleans. Besides, do you not like surprises?"

"How did you meet him?"

"I met the surveyor, who introduced him to me," Juanito replied. "He stayed with Clarke for a year before he came back and he was bragging about the country, how big it was and the many wild cattle that roamed the brasada."

"Brasada?"

"The mesquite trees you see," Juanito said.

"How can you see the country?"

"Oh, we will soon pass through this barrier."

"You must have talked to this man a lot."

"Oh yes, Martin. We became good friends. You will meet him one day."

"Who is this man?" Martin asked.

"He is called James McCairn. He is from a place called Scotland."

"A Scot?"

"He plays a funny musical instrument that looks like a carpetbag with many horns sticking from it. It sounds like animals screaming."

Martin laughed. "He plays the bagpipes."

"He blows on one of the horns and the bag fills with air."

"I look forward to meeting this man. I have not heard a bagpipe since I was a boy."

Juanito snorted in disgust.

At times the two men had to use their machetes to cut through the thick brush. Martin heard noises of game fleeing at their approach, but never saw anything but snakes and lizards in the shadowy world of the mesquite grove. At times he felt claustrophobic and wondered if they would ever find their way through the impenetrable maze.

Juanito stopped often to check his map and lay his compass out to take his bearings. At such times, both men lit their pipes and rested in the shade.

"How much more of this jungle do we have to go through?" asked Martin at one such stop.

"Jungle? This is not a jungle. You should come to Argentina if you want to see a jungle. Or Brazil. This is an olive grove, an apple orchard, my friend."

"You can't see twenty yards ahead in any direction."

"Ah, but these are little trees and there are no large snakes hanging from their branches. There is no jaguar prowling through them."

"I've stepped on at least three snakes," Martin said.

"Yes, and I have stepped on five and beheaded one with the machete. These are small snakes that run from you. Not those in Argentina. They wait for a man to pass under and then they fall on him and swallow him whole."

Martin felt his stomach churn. "How much longer, Juanito?"

"I do not know. Another day, maybe two. These are very small trees, but there are many of them."

"I hate every damned one of them."

Juanito laughed. "Someday you will come to love them. I will bet on that."

"You'll lose," Martin said, and they put out their pipes and started off again through the interminable maze of mesquite.

They found clearings here and there, but always the mesquite rose up, seemingly out of nowhere, to close them in again. They walked through sun and shadow, stopping once to eat lightly and talk of the land they sought.

"This is much different than the country I first saw here three years ago," Juanito told Martin. "I went to the Matagorda. Landed up at a place called Cox's Point. Do you know it?"

Martin shook his head.

"It is a little ways up the coast from here. I went to a place called Brazoria, then set out on my own. I saw many head of cattle and I hid from wild Indians who rode through the country with their faces painted and I saw some with fresh scalps hanging from their bridles and lances."

"Weren't you afraid, Juanito?"

"I was afraid sometimes, yes. But I knew that some-day, those Indians would ride no more through this country, killing the people and cutting off their hair. It is the same in my country. A few bandidos can scare many people, but when the people rise up and fight, the bandidos go away. It will be the same here."

The two men walked through the afternoon under a sky laced with thin high clouds, a blue sky that seemed endless under the canopy of mesquite. They found a spring near an open place late that first day and set up camp well inside the mesquite forest.

"The trees will break up our smoke," Juanito explained.

"You do not want someone to see our smoke?"

"Those who would see it have red skin and would kill us just for the few goods we have. For the ma-chetes if nothing else."

Martin felt a shiver dance up his spine, and he began to look around everywhere for the sight of a painted Indian.

"I'll cut us some wood for a fire," Martin said. "I want to see what this machete can do."

Juanito chuckled and began setting up the camp. He

tied tarps to the mesquite for shelter, dug a hole for a fire and then circled the camp, keeping to the fringe of the trees. Curly mesquite grass grew in the opening and he covered that, looking for tracks. Here and there were patches of prickly pear, gamma grass and the delicate cholla, with its dangerous thorns that were like fine thin hairs. He saw hoof marks of wild cattle, deer and javelina. The bare spots were laced with the tracks of quail and other birds, and he found the wavy marks of a passing snake.

When he returned, Martin had already started the fire. The pungent aroma of mesquite wood clung to the air under the trees. Juanito stepped back and looked at the smoke. By the time it rose above the trees it was no thicker than a light mist.

"We must stand guard tonight," Juanito said.

"Did you see Indian tracks?"

"No, but this is a place where game passes and I think we should take the care to watch for hunters."

"I'll take the first watch."

Juanito shrugged. "I do not expect we will be disturbed."

Martin felt his skin crawl slightly and he knelt down to go through his pack and lay out foodstuffs, the coffeepot. He filled the pot at the spring, felt the loamy wet clay surrounding the seep, sniffed it as a man used to the smell of soil.

When he returned to camp, Martin banged the pots around, jumped at every sound.

"You seem very nervous, Martin. What passes with you?"

"I don't know. I just can't get Cackle Jack out of my mind, I guess."

"I know how that is. When a friend or a loved one dies, there is a big empty space. You keep expecting him to walk up and greet you."

Martin laughed nervously. "Yeah, I guess that's it.

Something like that. But I can see him in his grave. I know he's gone."

"Gone from this earth, yes."

"You believe he's still alive somewhere. Heaven?"

"I do not believe in heaven as you believe it. That is a place. The Spirit is everywhere."

"Spirit? You mean a ghost?"

Juanito smiled. He sat down and filled his pipe, lit it with a stick from the fire. Martin sat down, too, no longer interested in mashing coffee beans.

"I think it is the Spirit that lives within everything. Maybe Jack, he saw this Spirit before he died."

"He saw something. But he was out of his head."

"Was he, you think? *Loco,* eh?" Juanito drew deeply on his pipe and held the smoke in his lungs for a couple of seconds. He breathed it back out slowly. "Maybe he seemed crazy to you, but he did not think he was crazy, did he?"

"No," Martin said. The weight of Jack's death was still on his shoulders, heavy as a lead weight.

Juanito seemed lost in thought. He did not speak for a long time. When he did speak, his voice was very rich and timbrous, as if it came from some hollow cavern deep inside him.

"I am going to ask you a question in a little while, Martin. But first I want to tell you a story that my father told me when I was a very young man."

"You tell good stories sometimes, Juanito. I've wondered where you heard them, how you seemed to have lived so long when you are not much older than I am."

"Well, I have lived in books and I have lived in my life, so it seems I have lived beyond my years. My father, Don Francisco Salazar, was a scholar and a teacher. He translated many Eastern languages, including Sanskrit, Hindi, Egyptian and Babylonian. He taught me many things and I began reading his translations when I was a small boy."

"How come you never told me this before? I thought your father was a rancher. You said you grew up on the pampas and worked cattle."

"I did, but I worked for my mother's brother who owned a large ranch and did some mining in the cordilleras, as well."

"You've lived a very big life, then."

Juanito laughed and blew vaporous smoke through his mouth and nostrils. "True. Anyway, my father told me this story long ago. He said it was an ancient Hindu legend."

"Aren't those the fellows who make snakes come out of baskets by playing on a flute or something?"

"Oh, the snake charmers, yes, but a very old people, older than we, I think."

"What was the story, then?"

Juanito puffed on his pipe and talked through the smoke. "It seems there was a time when only gods lived on earth and they had made man from their own image and gave him divinity. When the men abused their divinity, Brahma, the god of them all, he became angry and said he was going to take away every man's divinity and hide it where none would ever find it.

"But the little gods wondered where they could hide it so man could never find it. They argued about it at a meeting with Brahma. One god said that they should bury man's divinity deep inside the earth. But Brahma said that this was not a good place, for eventually man would dig deep down in the earth and find it.

"Then another lesser god said they should sink it in the deepest part of the ocean. 'Man will never think of looking down there.' But Brahma disagreed. He said that man would eventually find a way to the bottom of the ocean and find his divinity. Another god said they should hide it on the highest mountain peak on the earth, a place so cold and airless that man would never climb to the summit. But Brahma told them that man would surely climb the highest mountain one day and find his divinity and take it back.

"So the lesser gods gave up and said that there was no place on earth to hide man's divinity. Neither in the sea, on the desert, deep inside the earth or atop the highest mountain. Brahma listened to them and said, 'I know where we can hide man's divinity where he will never find it.' And the lesser gods wanted to know where this was. Brahma told them he would hide it deep down inside man himself. Man would never think of looking for it there.

"And the Hindus say this is where man's divinity yet lies while he searches high and low for it, looking everywhere but inside himself."

"Is that the story?" Martin asked. "I don't understand it. Are you saying that man is a god and doesn't know it?"

Juanito smiled. "That is what the ancient peoples thought."

"What do you think?"

"I thought we were talking about Cackle Jack. You wondered what he saw at the end, and when he told you you did not believe him."

"Oh, Juanito, you're pulling my leg. Come on. It's just a story made up by a bunch of men who make snakes dance by playing the flute."

"I told you that I would tell you this story and then ask you a question."

"That's right, you did. What's the question?"

"It is a question you must ask yourself. And if you know the answer, maybe you will know what happened with Cackle Jack and what he saw at the end of his life."

"Go ahead, Juanito, ask it, then to hell with it. You're full of riddles today and I'm not a patient man."

"When your father died, you told me you were with him. You watched him die as you watched Cackle Jack die. What did your father say before he died?"

Martin glared at Juanito. "I don't remember what he said. He just died, that's all."

"Well, Martin, if you ever remember what he said to you when he was dying and if you ever understand it, then maybe you will know what Cackle Jack saw inside himself before he died."

"Oh, I'll never know that. And neither will you."

"No, perhaps not. But if you ever do remember, then you will know whether the story I told you about Brahma is true."

"Juanito," Martin said, "I don't give a damn what the Hindus thought or did. Jack died. My father died. And that's that."

But when he arose from the ground, the weight of Jack's death was still riding on his shoulders like some terrible beast that would not go away.

7

LATE IN THE afternoon of the second day, the sky
scrawled with torn remnants of clouds, Martin and
Juanito came upon the abandoned adobe. They flushed
a covey of Gambel's quail from a patch of curly
mesquite grass in front of the hut. The sound of
whirring wings startled both men, and they crouched
with rifles at the ready as the flock scattered and
coasted to separate landings like debris flung from an
unearthly explosion.

The silence after the birds had whirred away was
profound. There was a desolate emptiness about the
forlorn adobe building. A strong aroma of sweetbrier
and the musty, cloying odor of dead animals filled the
air. The hut was small, with no visible doors or windows. The wind made a sound as it breathed through
it as if the dead still sighed within its hollow shell.

"Is this place on your map?" Martin asked.

"Yes." Both men were good navigators, and Juanito
had been marking their progress by the sun and com-

pass all day. The sky was clear except for those high streamers of dusky clouds shredded by the wind, flung like widows' scarves to drift on some eternal sea toward heaven.

"Let's take a look."

"There are only ghosts inside," Juanito said.

"Are you afraid of ghosts?"

"No, I mean the house is empty."

"Who lived here?"

"I do not know," Juanito admitted. "But you can almost smell the blood. I have seen such places before, in the cordilleras and on the pampas."

"Someone went to a lot of trouble to build it."

"It is very old," Juanito said as he stepped past a patch of prickly pear. "But there are fresh cattle tracks all around. Coyotes, too."

"I see them," Martin said. He walked to the doorway and peered inside. A hairy brown tarantula crabbed across a bare window ledge, then jumped outside. The dirt floor was a shambles of rotted pieces of cowhide and shriveled clumps of fur from dead animals. Bones lay strewn in the corners, small bones from rabbits and rats and quail.

Martin stepped inside and heard a rattle that froze his blood. He did not see the snake, but its brittle clatter sounded as if it came from inside his own ear. The sound sent shivers up his spine and his flesh felt clammy even in the heat of the afternoon, as if he had been plunged into ice water that quickly evaporated.

Juanito laughed as Martin stepped back outside.

"Ghosts, you say, Juanito."

"And rattlesnakes."

Martin breathed deeply and looked around. "I don't see any corrals or fences. So why would someone live here? What did they do?"

Juanito shrugged. "Perhaps they hunted or just wanted to be alone."

"Something or someone drove them away."

"Or they were killed here and the coyotes and wolves ate them. I see no graves here. Just the place where they made the adobe bricks." Juanito looked up and pointed to the birds circling high in the sky like stringless black kites drifting in lazy spirals. "Or the buzzards."

Martin grimaced. "Do you always think the worst?"

"It is a very lonely place. Perhaps the Comanches did not like whoever lived here."

"What does it say on your map? Does it have a name?"

"It says 'adobe,' that is all," Juanito said. "Look, there is a well, and that is on the map, too."

Martin and Juanito walked over to the well. It had been filled in with dirt and rotted timber. A black widow spider sat on a thin cloud of silk that clung to an arc that lay in shadow.

"Do we have far to go, then?"

"Tomorrow we will reach our destination."

"Let's get away from this place."

"Yes. There is nothing here for us. That adobe is very old. I did not see the forms for making the bricks and the walls are wearing away and crumbling."

Martin saw the huge square spot where the bricks had been formed. Not a scrap of lumber; not even a weed grew there.

"You see a lot, Juanito."

"I see what is there," said the Argentine. He untied his bandanna and wiped grimy sweat from his forehead, dabbed at his eyes. Both men's shirts were soaked with perspiration, the cloth clinging to their oily torsos like sodden plaster.

They had not walked far when they began to see fresh tracks of cattle. Juanito studied them for several moments. He picked up droppings and crumbled them in his hands. He sniffed. They seemed very fresh to Martin.

"The herd passed through here early this morning," Juanito said. "Fifteen or twenty head, maybe."

Two hours later, they came upon the herd.

"Longhorns," Juanito said. "Make no noise. We will watch them for a while."

"I've never seen so many at once, or so close," Martin whispered. "Their horns are large, aren't they? And twisted, some of them." They looked to Martin like strange beasts in some ancient painting, not of this world, but of another. Their hides were varicolored and their horns sleek and graceful, twisted into grotesque shapes. They looked, he thought, like some moving tapestry on a wall that was itself in motion.

"The ancestors of those cattle were brought here five hundred years ago."

"By the Spaniards."

"That is so. There were three kinds. The retinto, colored reddish like those there, the berenda, with a white hide and black markings on its head and neck, and the Ganada Prieto, a great fighting bull from Andalusia. I have seen these grand bulls in Argentina. I see no prieto blood in those longhorns."

"How come you know so much about them cattle, Juanito?"

"Because I ask a lot of questions and I read the books. Before I came here, my father and I talked about these breeds of cattle. He said they could live on anything that grows and do not mind the heat of Texas."

"I wish I knew more about them."

"Maybe you will learn someday, Martin."

The herd drifted slowly across the plain, nibbling the gamma grass and the mesquite. When Martin squinted his eyes, they looked like a moving patchwork quilt. He knew they were very wild, like the buffalo he had heard about, and Juanito had told him they were dangerous. Their long graceful horns looked sharp and lethal.

As the two men were gazing at the feeding longhorns, they both heard a twig snap. It sounded like a
rifle shot in the silence.

Martin did not see the bull at first. He heard its
hoofbeats thundering in his ears and turned to see an
enormous animal with long curly horns charging at
him from out of the brush. In the background, Martin
saw one or two of the grazing cattle look disconsolately in his direction.

The charging bull was a blur in the corner of Martin's eye.

Juanito yelled and started running, which probably
saved Martin's life. The big longhorn saw the running
man and changed course, swinging its huge horns
away from Martin, who stood rooted in surprise at the
size of the bull and the sweep of its horns.

"Shoot him!" Juanito shouted as he dropped his
pack and shot forward in a burst of speed. The longhorn, with mottled liver spots and gray brindle hide,
was amazingly fast, Martin thought as he lifted his
rifle to his shoulder. The beast would surely catch
Juanito in a few seconds if he did not act fast.

Martin cocked the hammer on the flintlock rifle and
led the bull, swinging the muzzle just past the longhorn's chest. He kept swinging the barrel until the barrel passed the bull's head; then he squeezed the
trigger. Powder flashed in the pan and a tiny cloud of
smoke billowed from the iron. The fire shot through
the touchhole and ignited the charge in the breech. The
rifle boomed and bucked against Martin's shoulder.
Smoke and orange flame burst from the muzzle.

Martin saw a plume of dust erupt from the longhorn's hide about four inches behind its left leg. The
bull staggered and lurched to its right, its forelegs
crumpling. The animal went down and raised a cloud
of dust as it skidded several feet on its side. Martin
heard the crack of its right horn as it snapped at the
boss with the weight of its body.

Juanito stopped and lifted his own rifle, cocked the hammer back. He approached it from the left, the barrel pointed at the animal's head.

Martin stood there, his hands shaking, his knees trembling as if they were made of currant jelly. The acrid smell of black powder assailed his nostrils, but his eyes were fixed on the great bull lying in the dirt, blood gushing from its side, one horn sticking skyward like a huge lance.

"You killed him, I think," Juanito panted. "We will wait a minute. Stay where you are and reload, just in case."

Martin's hands were still shaking as he pulled on the wiping stick and set the rifle on its butt. He blew through the barrel and a small amount of smoke emerged from the touchhole by the pan. He looked up and turned his head to see if the herd was still there. The cattle were gone and he hadn't heard them. Dust hung in the air where they had stood moments before.

Juanito stepped gingerly up to the bull and poked it with the barrel of his rifle. The bull did not move.

"He is dead, Martin. A very good shot."

Martin stood there, his shaking worse now, unable to speak.

"I almost didn't shoot him," Martin said.

"A few more steps and he would have hooked me."

Martin felt sick inside. He forced himself to look at the bull. Such a magnificent animal, lying there so still and huge, torn from life in his prime. The longhorn's eye stared up at the sky, wet and glassy, frozen at the moment of death.

"It seems a damned shame," Martin said.

Juanito looked hard at Baron. Then he looked at the dead bull and prodded it again with his rifle barrel.

"It is a shame," Juanito said. "But this bull knew what it was here for."

"What?"

"He died protecting his herd. Look at his hind legs. Look at his chest, the one horn."

"I don't see anything."

"This bull has fought before."

Martin looked closely at the downed longhorn. There were scars on its hind legs. One of them looked pretty deep, scabbed over long ago, like a leather patch on its leg, a thong glued into the hide. He walked around to look at the bull's lone remaining horn and its muzzle, its chest. Its nose was scarred, too, but he had to look close to see the lacerations in the black rubbery snout. There were ragged scars on its chest, too, and on its shoulders, he could see nicks, places where the hair stood crooked, growing the wrong way.

"Yes, it looks as if he's been in a scrape or two. So?"

"So this was the bull's destiny. To fight, to give protection to the herd. It knew it would die one day."

"Bullshit, Juanito."

"Bullshit? You have a lot to learn, my friend."

"About what? Longhorns?"

"About life, Martin. Consider the lilies of the field."

"Huh?"

"They do not labor, they do not run, they do not fly. They do what lilies do. They grow and laugh in the sun."

"So? Lilies grow. Everything grows."

"Everything knows its purpose in life. Like this great long-horned bull. I am glad you shot it, or you'd be looking down at me right now and feeling sorry for yourself."

Martin's hands stopped shaking. "I'd be feeling sorry for you, Juanito."

"No, you would wish you had shot the bull because it was a thing you had to do. It is why you are here with me now."

"You make too much of a small thing, Juanito."

"Yes, that is one of my many faults, Martin. But it is better to make much of a little thing than to disregard everything one sees in this life."

Martin looked at the dead bull again. "I feel like I just robbed somebody," he said to Juanito.

Juanito walked over to Martin, slapped him on the back. "Did you reload your rifle, my friend?"

Martin looked sheepishly down at his rifle and shook his head. "No, I reckon I didn't."

"Take off your pack and rest in the shade and reload. I will cut us out some meat for our supper tonight."

"You going to butcher that bull?"

"Yes. That is what one does when one kills an animal for food."

"I wasn't hunting cattle."

"No, you were not. This one was hunting you, and if I had not started to run, I would be looking down at you right now."

"Juanito, sometimes you don't make any sense."

"Consider the lilies of the field, Martin."

Martin slapped the air with one hand as if to push Juanito away. He shook his head in bewilderment and walked over to a mesquite tree and wriggled out of his pack. He sat down and began to reload. He heard the leather hiss in Juanito's scabbard. A moment later, he looked up and saw the Argentine cutting the bull open from brisket to balls, and he savagely pulled his wiping stick free of the underside of the barrel. The stench of the bull's bowels rose on the light breeze and wafted to his nostrils.

The two men finished butchering the bull and packing prime cuts of beef—part of the brisket, the heart, liver, the soft meat beneath the spine, chops from the legs— to carry with them.

"The coyotes will feed well tonight," Juanito said after they had left the clearing. "And so shall we."

"That much meat would have fed us most of a winter back home."

"Is that not the way, Martin? That will be our plan. To bring such plenty to those who starve in winter."

"It would be a job."

"So it will," Juanito said.

They traveled in more open country, avoiding the cactus that grew in profusion. Juanito read tracks eagerly, for the plain was littered with the spoor of wild game. Blackbirds flushed from the swampy low places, some with red scapulars on their wings, and more than one covey of quail shattered the stillness of their journey. The sound of the quail flushing, Martin thought, sounded very similar to the rattlesnake's warning at the old adobe.

They camped that evening near the edge of a broad plain where live oaks and cactus grew, a strange landscape unlike any Martin had ever seen before. The grass was thick and there were signs that wild cattle and deer had been feeding there recently. His heartbeat quickened when he saw the tracks of wild turkey and the tiny, almost human handprints of squirrels and rabbits.

"There must be a lot of game here," Martin said to Juanito. "Did you see all the tracks across that flat?"

"I saw them. Other tracks, too."

"What do you mean?"

"Unshod horses, for one thing."

"I didn't see any. Are you talking about wild horses?"

"No, these tracks showed that the horses had weight on them. The hooves were trimmed, too."

"What are you saying?"

Juanito shrugged and the faintest curve of a smile bowed his lips slightly. "Maybe Indians come here to hunt."

"Fresh tracks?"

"From this morning. There are droppings, too. You

must look for these things, Martin, when you are walking. You must expect trouble even when the sky is clear and the birds are singing."

"Tracks aren't trouble, are they?"

"Horse tracks could be. Might be Comanches or Apaches."

"Aw, Juanito. You worry too much."

"Oh, I do not worry. I just keep my eyes and ears open, and I walk with care."

Juanito's talk gave an entirely new dimension to the flat. It was no longer a serene plain where wild game tracks crisscrossed in hieroglyphic patterns, but a place where Comanches rode their horses looking for white men to kill and scalp. Looking out there now, beyond the tree fringe, gave Martin a very odd feeling, as if he was looking at an empty stage on which at any moment animals, horses and painted men would emerge and perform some kind of mystic dance, a dance of death. He shivered in the shade of an oak tree and gripped his rifle more tightly as sweat oozed out of the skin of his palms.

They made camp and Juanito began to clear a place for a fire. "I will cut the mesquite wood," the Argentine said. "Why do you not look around the edge of this thicket and see what you see?"

"Are you expecting trouble because of those tracks?" Martin asked.

Juanito shrugged and continued digging a small pit for the fire.

Martin walked across the open plain, looking at all the crisscrossings of tracks. He heard a small sound, like a sigh, when he was halfway across. He stopped to listen. It seemed he could hear someone breathing, but the sound was very loud and it was not natural. He began to doubt his senses when he felt a tug at his sleeve.

He turned around and saw no one. Three seconds later, a sharp gust of wind flattened him to the ground before he knew what had hit him.

Then his shirt began to billow out and the loose cloth on his trousers and shirt began to flap and whip like sheets in a gale. A cloud of dust rose up around him and swirled madly in a gritty spiral.

Particles of dust stung his face, spat into his eyes like tiny needles, blinding him. He felt his loins rise up slightly off the ground and he thought he was going to be lifted up and carried away by the whirlwind.

After a few moments, the wind danced away from him and his hips settled back to earth. He opened his eyes and stared in bewilderment at the funnel-shaped swirl of dust as it twisted across the plain, veering sharply, bending and wending its way on a zigzag course, gathering speed and spewing dust in its wild wake.

When the sound subsided, Martin heard Juanito laughing.

"What the hell was that?" Martin asked.

"That is what they call a dust devil," Juanito replied.

"It looks like a small hurricane."

"That is what it is. You are lucky it was small."

Martin got to his feet and dusted himself off, patting his trousers, shaking out his shirtsleeves. "I hate this country," he said, rubbing the grit from his eyes. "Dust devils and mean cattle and Indians all around. We'd play hob trying to make a ranch here."

Juanito did not say anything, for then the wind came up in earnest and blew away their words. They ate a supper that was full of sand and their teeth ground the sand down to dust and they swallowed dryly as the flames whipped in the fire pit as if mirroring their angry thoughts.

And the wind blew sand in the tracks and wiped out all trails in that part of the country so that when they started out again it was like a new country filled with savage whispers from the blowing wind that they could not understand.

8

THE RIVER SEEMED to stand still for a long time. Then as Juanito and Martin walked closer, the river began to move as if it had been frozen in time until, at their approach, it began to flow.

"That's the Nueces," Juanito said.

"Not much of a river."

"It is at least a river in dry country."

"It looked like a city street for a time. I thought it was made of dried mud," Martin said.

"There is mud in it. We must cross it."

"Why did we not come in below it?"

"We could have and then we would have been lost. The river is a boundary and a landmark. It is the blood of the land and we must fill our canteens and mark the crossing of it as a good omen."

"Maybe it is just a bath," Martin said, but Juanito did not laugh.

The river curled through the mesquite and cactus like a brown snake, and when they came to the bank,

Martin saw that it seemed deeper than he had thought and swifter. The fierce wind that had blown all night and all morning licked whitecaps from its surface and sent spray dashing into nothingness, whipped the shallows into froth. The two men, eyes red from the blowing sand, bent into the wind to keep from falling down.

"You will not bathe in that," Juanito said. "You will not swim it either."

"Is there a crossing?"

Juanito looked at the map. "There is a ford not far from here. But rivers change course and we might have to look for another."

"Maybe this Nueces will keep us from where we want to go."

"No. We can always cross one way or another."

But Martin was not so sure as they followed the Nueces northward for a time. Then the river widened and he saw sandbanks and small islands and narrows where a man could wade across. The wind was not as strong here and the two men had stopped shouting at each other.

"Let's go across," Martin said.

"Take the care," Juanito said. "Follow me."

"Is this the place you crossed before?"

"I do not know. I do not think this is the place."

"I hope you don't get us lost."

Juanito laughed and started down the bank toward the shallows as if he had not a care in the world. Martin followed him through water up to his knees. When they reached the opposite bank, a cloud of mosquitoes rose up out of a slough they had not seen from the other side.

The two men slapped at the insects, drawing blood from the dead ones as they scrambled to get to dry ground. A swarm followed Martin, zinging in his ears, eluding his flattened hands as he smacked his cheeks.

"Damned skeeters," Martin said. "Damned Texas."

"You want to go back?" Juanito asked.

"I ought to. Cackle Jack would have turned back long before now."

Juanito smashed a mosquito on Martin's shoulder. Its needle was buried deep in his flesh. "We must get away from here or be eaten alive, Martin."

Blood streaked Martin's face where he had slain the stinging mosquitoes. "It's just one more thing," he said, his ears ringing with the whine of a dozen or so insects searching for his blood. "One more damned thing. Christ."

They left the mosquitoes behind and found a shade tree with prickly pear cactus ringing its base.

"You didn't get bit so much, Juanito."

"It's the blood. They don't like Spanish much. Or Indian."

"Just white man's."

Juanito smiled. "That's right."

"This is god-awful country. I've got cholla burning my ankles and skeeter bites all over me. Next I'll probably get snake-bit."

"It will take some time before you hear the heartbeat of this land, before you taste and smell the blood spilled into the earth," Juanito said.

"It's my own blood I smell."

"That is not what I mean. You must not fight nature, but accept it, go into it as you would a door in a house."

"You speak pretty good English, Juanito, but I don't understand half of what you say. It was you who got me to come here in the first place. You said we could raise cattle. I don't know anything about cattle and I just killed a longhorn yesterday. It wasn't like killing a deer. It was like killing something that gives milk."

"That was a bull you killed. You would not want to drink the milk it has."

"You know what I mean."

"Killing the longhorn was a good start for you. Now

you have some of the blood of this country on your hands."

"You've changed, Juanito. Since we came here. In New Orleans, you were happy-go-lucky, full of plans about cattle raising. Now you talk about death and blood and I don't know what all. It just don't make any sense."

"When I was a little boy," Juanito said, "my father gave me a calf. He told me to raise it. I had to feed it, clean up its mess, comb its hide, watch out for the wolves and the jaguars that waited to kill and eat it. I loved that baby cow. I treated it like a pet. It followed me everywhere. It wanted to come inside the house and sleep in my bed. My mother would not let the animal inside the house. I hated her for that. I thought she was cruel and without feeling.

"I slept outside in a corral with my calf. In winter, I slept with it in the barn. The calf was mine. I was its father and mother. It grew into a cow and one day my father told me to kill and butcher it. I told him I could not do this thing. He told me that I must. I hated my father then as I had hated my mother.

"But he made me do it—not with a knife, but with an axe. He told me how to do it. I cried and cried. My mother would not feed me until I killed the cow and cut it up. I wanted to run away and take my beautiful child with me."

"What happened then?" Martin asked.

"I ran away from home. I was turned away from every ranch I went to. My father sent riders all around to warn them I might ask for shelter. I had no place to go."

"What did you do then?"

"I went back home. I took the axe and struck my cow between the eyes. I did it with hatred in my heart, and in my heart I was killing my father. I killed the cow and got its blood all over me. My father stood over me while I butchered it. I cried with every cut of the knife and in my heart I was cutting up my father, carving him into a thousand pieces.

"Then my father helped me with the butchering. I cried even more, but my father never said a word. He showed me how to skin the cow and open its belly up. He showed me how to save the entrails, the kidneys, the brains, the heart. I bathed my hands and arms in the blood of my beloved cow and sawed the bones and cut the meat into many pieces."

"God," Martin said.

"When I was finished it was no longer my cow. It was no longer a cow. It was just meat."

"What then?"

"I cooked some of the meat in Mother's kitchen while she watched me, and then she made me sit down at the table and eat some of my cow."

"Was that all then?"

"No. My mother and father brought many people to the house and we all feasted on my dead child."

"It sounds so cruel, Juanito."

"That is what I thought. The meat made me very sick. I wanted to run away from home again."

"Did you?"

"No. My father made me stand there while all the people thanked me for giving them the meat of the cow."

Martin shook his head in bewilderment.

"My father told me that the cow was born to feed us and that I had to know and understand that if I was to survive in the world. 'All creatures have a purpose,' he said. 'God put the fish in the sea, the birds in the air and the cattle in the field to feed us so that we could live and make things in the world.' He said God gave us everything to use and that if we did not use those things we would lose them; we would die for no good reason."

"Did you believe him?"

"When I became a man, I understood. Yes, that is the way of the world. Every creature feeds on another. Life is death and death is life. It is all one thing. We kill to live. We die to give life."

"I don't see how you could kill a pet calf, even if it was a cow."

"My father was teaching me what was important. I was dying. I killed my child so that I could live. My father told me that I owed the cow my thanks, my gratitude, for it had taught me about life and had fed many people, had made them happy. It was a good lesson."

"My father never did anything like that to me," Martin said.

"Perhaps you were not ready to learn."

"Were you?"

"My father thought so. I am very grateful to him. When I think of that cow now, I know how selfish I was. I did not own the cow. The calf was a gift and I was not willing to share it because I loved it. But when I saw the pleasure it gave to many people, I knew that the cow had fulfilled its destiny and I had done well in raising it so that its meat could feed us. It was one of many good lessons my father taught me."

"And now you want to raise beef."

Juanito grinned. "That is so. That one calf shall become many cows. Feed many people."

"You are very strange, Juanito. And you and I are different."

"Are we?"

"Yes, I probably would have killed my father and let the cow live."

"I do not think so. Sometimes we cannot see a thing when it is right in front of our eyes. I only saw the calf. I did not see the beef inside. You would have come to see the same thing."

Martin shook his head and walked away to collect his scattered thoughts.

The wind died down just before sundown and both

men felt the coolness waft in from the Gulf on light whispering zephyrs laced with the tang of salt and wet sand. Juanito built a fire from the gathered mesquite and began to unpack the beef Martin had provided.

"What part of that longhorn do you want to eat, Martin?"

"I'm not very hungry, Juanito," Martin said.

The wagon tracks wound through open spaces in the mesquite, over huisache and creosote and black chaparral and ocotillo in bloom. Juanito and Martin had come upon the ruts early the next morning. Wind had blown sand fine as the grains in an hourglass into the ruts, but they were clearly visible.

Martin stared at them as if peering backward into time, as if looking at the ruins of a civilization long since crumbled to dust.

"Old tracks," Baron said.

"Yes."

Martin was disappointed. It was like the abandoned adobe cabin. An emptiness filled him. A sense of isolation suddenly gripped him with cold skeletal fingers, squeezed his heart until his belly swirled with newly hatched swarms of tiny winged insects.

"How old?" Martin asked. His throat felt dry and tight, as if the vocal cords might snap at any moment.

Juanito shrugged. "A month, two. A year. Older, maybe."

Martin looked at the faint traces of wagon wheels on the cracked bare ground. They might have been made by a wagon that had passed through this desolate place a thousand years ago. A million. As if left by men long gone to ghosts.

Martin's throat constricted as he felt swept up in a tide of almost overwhelming grief and heart-wrenching loss. He felt like a man stranded on an island or on a distant uninhabited planet. Lost. Abandoned by God and man. Lost in a deserted wilderness far from the sea he had known, the boyhood he had left behind in the East, left in his father's grave, bones upon bones.

Windblown and rain-washed wagon tracks, like indecipherable hieroglyphs, mute as fossil bones in stone, yet strangely articulate. Someone passed by, God knows when, he thought, and disappeared into the trackless maw of time, never to be seen again. Who? When? Why?

Martin had no answers to his questions. He wished he had never seen the tracks, for they gave him no comfort, no reassurance that he was not alone in this burning backcountry of earth.

"Let's follow the tracks," Juanito said. "They look familiar to me."

"Familiar? You mean you've seen them before?"

"I saw a lot of wagon tracks when I first came here."

"And where did they lead?"

"To a road," Juanito said.

They walked through the blood-soaked land, a land of cactus and mesquite and chaparral, like refugees from a sacked city somewhere out of time, past the gaunt skulls of longhorn cattle and the shed antlers of deer, skirting the cholla and prickly pear, wary of the warning rattles from the brush as they crossed a dry slough, passed over animal tracks frozen in an open-air kiln: mice, rats, raccoon, deer, coyote, cattle, the pear-shaped spoor of a wolf. Lizards from another age peered at them with centuries-old eyes and birds fled from their dust wallows like leaves before a wind.

The wagon tracks faded in the gamma grass and emerged again like the twin trails of a pair of snakes on open ground. Martin felt as if they were being lured to an even more desolate and empty region, where they would be impaled on giant cactus and devoured by the ever-present buzzards floating overhead, vultures that watched them to see if they stumbled and fell and lay unmoving in the sun.

Baron watched the sun arc toward the western horizon until he was staring into its fiery face and had to squint or go blind, and he wore sweat on his body like a second skin and drank the warm water from his canteen until his belly rebelled and he had to fight to keep from vomiting it back up. Blisters erupted on his feet and broke open, exposing raw flesh that raged from the salt of his sweat and sent shoots of fire into his brain that matched the sun's intensity.

Juanito seemed not to be bothered by the heat or the dryness. He wore a bandanna around his forehead that soaked up the sweat and kept the perspiration from dripping into his eyes. Martin was beyond caring as he blindly followed the tracks and Juanito, wondering where they would wind up when the sun fell beyond the horizon. He was scarcely aware, hours later, when the old wagon tracks converged with newer ones and then faded entirely away on a road marked with wagon ruts less than a week old.

"This is the road," Juanito said as he stopped and consulted his map and compass once again.

"Huh?"

"We have been on the road to O. B. Clarke's rancho for the past half hour. Did you not notice?"

"Christ no, Juanito. That sun's been peeling my eyes off my head. I stepped on a cactus back there and it threw a prickly pear into my shin like a slingshot."

"You better get those spines out of your leg."

"I got 'em all, I think."

"You are tired, eh?"

"Tired? Hell, I'm way past tired, Juanito. I'm half dead from the heat, sick from drinking the hot water in my canteen, bleeding from the holes in my shin, and sore-footed as a man walking on hot coals."

Juanito laughed, but as always, Martin did not take it as a mean thing. That was just the way Juanito was, and he accepted that. Juanito laughed at everything that hurt or troubled an ordinary man. Juanito seemed to be always above pain and worry, like a little kid on a summer outing with not a care in the dadblamed world.

"It ain't funny," Martin said. "This pack weighs a ton and my rifle feels like its full of melted lead balls."

Juanito just grinned.

"That must mean we're getting close to our first destination."

"Our first destination? How many do we have?"

"We will talk to O.B. and then look the land over."

"What land?"

"The land that lies in the direction he points his finger."

"I think Cackle Jack was right. This ain't no place for a sailor or for cattle, either. The ones we seen were wild, and they didn't look none too fat."

"You must be patient and you must have vision."

"Vision?"

"You must look into the future and see what can be."

"I've been looking at the here and now and it don't look none too good."

"The present always becomes the future, Martin. And the future is what you make of it. We will raise fine cattle here and we will be rich and happy men."

"Hell, Juanito, even if we did find a place to make a ranch and ran herds of cattle on it, it would be way out in the middle of nowhere. Nobody would know we were there and we'd have to eat all the beef ourselves."

Juanito grinned and hefted his canteen up to his mouth. He drank sparingly and swirled the water around before he swallowed it. "We will take the cattle to the buyers."

"Where?"

"To New Orleans, first. Then to other places."

"Did you ever see any beef in New Orleans? Fish and mutton and pork, that's all."

"So we will be the first. We will make a lot of money."

"You're crazy," Martin said. "The sun has burned into your skull, too."

Juanito laughed again. The same laugh. Always the same bright laugh. Not a damned care in the world. Thick-skinned as a pampas bull.

"The sun will go down," Juanito said. "Come, let us go where it goes."

Juanito stoppered his canteen and walked along the road. He seemed as fresh as when they had started out that morning. A boy on a lark, Martin thought. Or a man so crazed by the heat he did not suffer.

Just before dusk they came upon the remains of the wagon, the one that had made the first tracks they followed. For there were its burnt wheels, left where they had stopped. Pieces of the wagon—the charred bed, the burnt tailgate, the scorched tongue—lay scattered around a plot of blackened earth that told some of the story.

Juanito found a broken arrow next to a rock. He dug down and came up with the rest of it. A flint arrowhead wrapped to the shaft with yellow sinew, with colored markings bled into the wood. Martin looked beyond and saw two mounds flanking a huge anthill.

"Someone buried them, I guess," Martin said.

Juanito stood up.

"Yes, there were probably crosses put there."

"Long since rotted away."

"Or burnt by the Apaches."

"You think the people were killed by Apaches."

"I do not know. I have heard many bad things about them."

The two men walked over to the graves, inspected the anthill. Large red ants swarmed in and out of the center hole, roamed the ground in search of food.

"I've never seen an anthill that size," Martin said.

"It is new. They are still building it." Ants swarmed

over the graves as if looking for something that once was there. "I think the people were buried in the old hill. Perhaps sweet water or honey was poured over their faces, stuffed in their ears and mouths."

"What?" Martin shuddered with the image of people buried alive in an anthill.

"That is one of the stories of the Apache I have heard," Juanito said.

Martin started scratching his arms. "Let's get out of here," he said. "It feels like I've got ants all over me."

"It is a slow way to die," Juanito mused.

"Shut up, Juanito. Just shut your damned mouth."

Juanito shrugged, and the two men continued their journey along the road. Martin looked back at the twin mounds once and shuddered again. When a flock of crows cawed at their intrusion, it seemed to him that he could hear the screams of the people buried back there by the anthill so long ago.

9

■

THE SUN BLISTERED the blue sky until its clouds
rusted and the horizon turned the color of copper.
Shadows stretched across the land like the tattered
shrouds of dead things blown from faraway graves,
like the soft crepe that draped unearthly caskets.

"Be dark soon, Juanito. You going to stop?"

"We should be close to the rancho of O. B. Clarke."

"What if it's burnt to the ground like that wagon we
saw?"

"You have not met O.B. yet. He is as tough as boot
leather."

So are you, Juanito, Martin thought. Tough inside,
tough outside. Baron's feet were raw and he was sure
they were bleeding into his boots. The back of his neck
was tender where the sun had burnt it and the lining of
his hat was wet with sweat. His legs ached and felt like
wooden pegs. Every step jarred pain into his bones
from the soles of his feet to his hips. They must have

covered fifteen miles since they came upon the road, but it felt more like fifty.

"Think you can find this place in the dark?" Martin asked sarcastically.

"This is the road that leads there. One of the roads."

"One of the roads? How many are there?"

"Two or three, at least, I think."

"It isn't much of a road."

"No, but now there are cattle tracks crossing it and the tracks of horses wearing iron shoes."

"Ah, that means something?"

Suddenly Juanito stopped. "Listen," he said.

Martin hesitated. He hated to stop, because he knew that if he did he would not want to go another step on his bleeding feet. He listened, then stopped when he heard nothing.

"What did you hear?" Baron asked.

"Listen," Juanito said again.

Martin heard it then, heard it against the blazing sky and out of the gathering shadows of afternoon. The lowing of cattle, the mooing calls of longhorns that reminded him of the cows his father had raised, cows that called to each other at dusk and formed herds for protection against critters of the night.

"I hear them, Juanito."

"A large herd, eh?"

"If you say so."

Juanito grinned and started toward the sound at a brisk walk. Groaning inwardly, Martin followed, and the pain in his feet started up again and lay on the cushion of his mind like some festering beast. He wanted to cry out that he could not take another step, but the lowing of the cattle sounded strangely comforting, somehow inviting.

They came upon the brush fence ten minutes later. The road led right to the gate, an old wagon bed roped to the brush firmly on one side and tied to a skinned pole on the other. The fence was over ten feet high, a tangle of mesquite, huisache, cátclaw and half a dozen other thorny plants.

"I never saw anything like it," Martin said.

"What do you think you have been chopping with your machete?"

"But a whole long fence? Nothing could get through that."

"Only the small animals," Juanito said.

"Damned small."

"Seguro."

"Is this the right place, then?"

"We are here," Juanito said, his voice bright with excitement. "This is O.B.'s rancho."

Juanito opened the gate, beckoned for Martin to come through. Dozens of white-winged doves resting in the brush fence took flight with a whistling of wings. Martin stepped through the gate, still marveling at the strange fence that stretched from horizon to horizon. Juanito closed the gate. A roadrunner streaked past them from out of the thicket, head stretched forward on its elongated neck, tail feathers straight back.

Martin saw the cattle then, bunches of them walking in single file, grazing, lying down. Dozens of cattle, and not all of them were longhorns. The falling sun made their backs glisten and their deep lowing sounds filled the air like a welcoming chorus.

"How far is it to the house?" Martin asked.

"About two kilometers, I think. The road goes right to it."

Martin's gaze followed the road to where it disappeared a thousand yards ahead of them. He ignored the pain in his feet as he followed after Juanito, who strode down the road at a brisk pace, almost a trot. His rifle and pack both felt lighter as they headed toward the sunset. The sun flared in one last lingering blaze as if lighting their way. When they crested the small hill,

Martin saw the ranch in the center of a broad savannah, surrounded by hundreds of cattle as far as he could see. Little adobes lay helter-skelter atop higher ground, their sides bronzed by the flanking sun, their fronts dark with gold-rimmed shadows. Trees grew nearby, some providing shade for the adobes, others near watering troughs set on the plain.

There were pole corrals near the adobe huts, and in them horses milled and stamped their hooves at the sight of the two strangers. Martin heard them whicker and whinny, and he thought they were making them welcome.

"Horses," he breathed.

"Look over there," Juanito said, pointing to the north. "Riders coming in."

"I see them."

Four riders were heading for the ranch, and when Martin's gaze swept the plain, he saw another, well to the rear. The men wore large sombreros and the rowels of their spurs glinted in the slanting rays of the sun.

"That last rider is O.B.," Juanito said.

"You recognize him at this distance?"

"The others are Mexicans. O.B. is not wearing a sombrero. He has a hat on I have seen before. In New Orleans."

Martin saw the difference. O.B. was wearing a smaller hat, but it had a brim and was dark, either brown or black. The sombreros were yellow as wheat stalks in late summer.

Juanito waved to O.B. O.B. lifted a hand, then dropped it. But the rider turned his horse and headed in their direction while the four Mexicans continued on toward the cluster of adobes.

"There are more adobes here now," Juanito said. "And a bigger garden. More people."

Martin saw the garden then, some distance from the adobes. Women were working in it. The corn was knee-high; there were beans climbing thin mesquite poles. He recognized tomato plants. There were other things growing in it too and he could smell the rich aroma of compost wafting on the evening breeze.

"What are those little huts, Juanito?"

"Jacales. I think O.B. lived in one when he first came here."

"That a hay field way over yonder?"

"I think so," Juanito said, then turned his attention to O.B., who trotted his horse the last few yards to stop in front of them.

"Is that you, Juanito? By heck and Harry, it is. And who you got with you? This the man you told me about at Pierre's? Bascomb? Barton?"

Juanito laughed. "This is the man I told you about. Martin Baron."

Clarke rode up close and stretched out his hand. He was a short, burly man with a sun-tanned face and bright hazel eyes set in narrow, fleshy slits. He had wide jowls, a square chin that was rimed with black sweat in the folds of excess flesh. His hair was graying at the sides, streaming straight from under his hat to his neckline. His grip was strong and Martin could feel the hard calluses that edged his palm.

"I wish I had of been your age when I first come here," O.B. said.

"How long have you been here?" Martin asked.

"Almost two years," Clarke said wearily. "Wasn't nothing here but twenty-foot-high brush, a damned tangle of huisache, mesquite, catclaw, granjeno, retama, black chaparral, prickly pear, yucca, rattail cactus, vines, grass thick as rope, and resacas, them damned sloughs full of mud and skeeter water. I got more thorn holes in me than a Gulf sponge. I cleared the land and gathered longhorn, brought in some British breeds and planted and replanted grass for the past two springs. Come on to the house and I'll pour you boys a drink and you can tell me how you got here and what you think of this country."

Martin liked Clarke instantly. He seemed open and friendly. As they rode toward the adobes, he looked at the land, trying to imagine how it had been before O.B. had cut through the brush, dried up the resacas. He had seen brush along the way that was impenetrable. He and Juanito had walked around it or chopped through the least of it until their arm muscles ached and lost every ounce of energy.

"How many horses do you have?" Martin asked Clarke after O.B. had put his mount up in the corral with the lean-to, fed him grain and hay. He had not seen the corrals out back, nor had he ever seen so many horses in one place. They were all sizes and colors: paints, roans, Appaloosas, duns, bays, sorrels. A rainbow of horses in huge rope-and-pole corrals hooked up to shade trees.

"I have a hundred, more or less, in my remuda. Most of the boys here have twenty or so. A man can't have too many horses in this country."

Martin whistled.

"Where did you get so many horses?"

O.B. winked at Juanito. "Why, we find all we want over yonder." He pointed to the south. "Over the Rio Bravo, or the Rio Grande, as they're callin' it now. Oh, sometimes the Mexes come back for their stock, but we've managed to hold on to most of what we caught."

Juanito and Martin followed Clarke to the main adobe. It was larger than the ones surrounding it. Its doorway faced the east like the others. Martin saw that it had been started with a single room and others had been added. He could see the seams, the different shades of mud.

A woman opened the door and stepped aside as O.B. walked through it. Juanito nodded to the woman and beckoned for Martin to follow him. Both Martin and Juanito took off their hats as they passed the woman. She did not smile at them.

"This here's Casey, my wife," O.B. said, his face turned away from the woman. "Homely, ain't she? Deaf as a stone. But she reads lips, so watch what you say. She's real handy with a fry pan if you get her riled. She makes a real good home for me and cooks grub like an angel."

"Pleased to meet you, ma'am," Martin said. Casey smiled at him.

"Con mucho gusto a ver usted otra vez," Juanito said, and Casey curtsied and blushed.

"Oh, Casey likes Juanito, she does," Clarke said, "and she can lip-read the Spanish better'n I can understand it spoke."

"Does she talk?" Martin asked.

"She talks right good once she knows a person. She got the fever when she was a kid and it made her deaf. Her words sound funny, but she talks all right."

Martin wondered why O.B. had married such a woman. When she smiled, she was some comely, but because of her deafness, he supposed, she looked like an old hag. She was round with mouse-colored hair long enough to be tied back in a bun. She wore a cotton dress with faded flowers and whatnots painted on it. The dress had a high neck and stretched over a large bosom.

"Just foller me," O.B. said, walking into another room. His spurs jingled faintly as his boots scuffed the hard dirt floor of the adobe.

Clarke continued on into a small room that jutted off the main room at the center of the house. It was cool inside, with white walls and Mexican blankets on the handmade furniture, a cowhide rug. There were guns on the wall, old flintlock rifles and pistols of unknown make—some large caliber, some with enormous locks and chunks of flint that, if cut up into smaller pieces, would service Martin's rifle for years of striking sparks. O.B. opened a rustic cabinet and took out an unmarked bottle filled with a pale amber liquid. Casey appeared a few seconds later carrying a tray with three tin cups on it.

"Squat," O.B. said, pointing to wooden trunks draped with varicolored Mexican blankets. He poured the three cups nearly full and took one for himself. Casey passed the tray to Martin and Juanito. After they had taken their cups, she left the room, pulling a blanket over the doorway to give the men privacy.

"Drink up, boys." O.B. sat in a cowhide-covered chair, slipped his spurs off and lifted his boots onto a small trunk that served as a footstool.

Juanito drank from his cup. Martin smelled his first. "What is it?"

"Ain't polite to ask, Baron, but it's mezcal. Cactus juice. Sheet lightning. Silver fire." O.B. took a swallow from his cup and his eyes lit up as he smiled. "Pure joy, Baron."

Juanito was grinning, watching Martin. Feeling self-conscious, Martin took a swallow. He held the mezcal in his mouth for a moment, then let it slide down his throat. The alcohol burned pleasantly all the way to his stomach. But his eyes didn't sparkle. They watered and his lungs filled with hot smoke and he thought he was going to die on the spot. He choked and then tried to spit out what was no longer there. The mezcal nestled in his belly like lava, burning with that silver fire O.B. had spoken of a moment ago.

"Mighty fine, ain't it?" O.B. said, grinning.

"Strong," gasped Martin.

"You'll get a taste for it, you stay in this country long enough."

"Would it profit a man to raise cattle here?" Martin asked.

Clarke frowned. "Not yet. But a man's got to look ahead."

"You're raising cattle."

"I'm crazy."

"Are you?" Juanito asked. "They told my grandfather that in Argentina a hundred years ago. He became very rich."

"And so will we," O.B. said. "Cattle is the oldest money there is. In the old days, it was the only wealth on earth. Even today, we use the word *chattel* as a hand-me-down word for money."

"Where would I find land that I could buy?" Martin asked.

Clarke took another swig of mezcal. He did not blink nor did his face change expression. He might as well have been drinking water, Martin thought. The fumes from the alcohol he had swallowed still lingered in his nostrils. His stomach twitched with the thought of tasting more of the fiery liquid.

"Most men who came here after Texas got its independence in '36 just took it and worried about getting the Mexican land grants later. Fellows over on the other side of the Nueces. But you want land, go south. There is a man there with lots of legal land and he's fighting for his life."

"Apaches?" Juanito asked.

O.B. nodded.

"Apaches, Comanches. They've raided all of us. If you want land here, you can steal it, buy it or have it give to you, but you got to fight to keep it, that's for damned sure."

"We saw two graves on the way here," Martin said. "A burnt wagon. Apaches?"

Clarke finished his drink, poured another. He offered the bottle to Juanito and Martin. Juanito drank some more of his and tendered his glass. O.B. filled it. Martin shook his head.

"Go ahead and swaller it down, son. We make it by the barrelful here."

"I don't like it," Martin said.

"Suit yourself. But if you've got sore feet from walking here, this stuff will make you forget all about them blisters."

"How did you know?" Martin asked.

"I seen you walking on eggshells. Your boots are probably filled with blood."

"I reckon."

"Then swaller it down and I'll tell you about them two graves you saw."

Martin forced himself to take another drink. He closed his eyes to shut back the tears and drained his glass. The fumes filled his lungs and smothered him, but he kept the drink down and felt its warmth spread through his bones down to his feet. When he opened his eyes again, both Juanito and O.B. were staring at him. Clarke held the bottle poised to pour another drink. Martin stretched out his hand and held the glass under the bottle. O.B. poured it full.

"There you go," he said. "You'll grow hair on your chest a lot faster now."

"It's the worst stuff I ever tasted, Mr. Clarke."

"Call me O.B."

"Awful stuff."

"One day you'll thank me for giving you your first taste of mezcal."

"Not today, sir."

Juanito and O.B. laughed.

"Them graves you saw on the road," O.B. said. "I dug 'em. Nothin' but bones to put in 'em. But I knew the folks. Jorge Pacheco and his woman, Esperanza."

"Was it Apaches killed them?" Martin asked.

O.B. nodded. "Sure as shootin' turtles off a log."

"Did—did the Apaches bury them in an anthill like Juanito said?"

"Nope. They was staked out on either side of the big anthill you saw. Only it wasn't so big then."

"Did the Apaches pour something sweet on them to attract the ants?"

O.B. looked sharply at Juanito. "He tell you that, Baron?"

Martin nodded.

"Well, Juanito got it wrong. They was plumb naked when we found 'em. Apaches took their scalps first. Didn't kill 'em. Just cut a little in front to get the top-knot, slicked the blade in a little circle, yanked the scalp hair loose. I figger the Pachecos screamed some at that. Then those red niggers smeared their own blood all over their faces and private parts. They tied their wrists and ankles with wet rawhide what shrunk in the sun. Them ants took a long time to eat 'em up. I figger it took most of two weeks for them two to die."

Martin's mouth gaped open. "How do you know all this? You weren't there."

"Nope, but their kid was. Luisa. She weren't but twelve years old. Them Apaches made her watch."

"Did they let her go afterwards?" Martin asked.

"Not hardly. They kep' her with 'em. Did some powerful raping of her, in bunches. Beat the fire outen her, made her a goddamned slave. She finally run off and come here."

"She is alive?" Juanito asked incredulously.

"Nope, they come after her. We had two Mexicans guarding her because I figured they might track her here. She was out tending the chickens in the jacal when those Apaches come up. They killed the two Mexicans, shot 'em through with arrows, and cut Luisa up into meat. She took a long time to die, but she died right enough."

"What did you do?" Martin asked.

"Oh, we went after them, but that Apache bunch is wily. They run down into Mexico and we lost 'em in the cordilleras."

"Do you know the Apache who killed that family?" Juanito asked.

"I know his name. What he looks like. He's stole horses and cattle from me. He's as smart as they come."

"What's his name?" Martin wanted to know.

"The Mexicans call him Cuchillo. Means knife."

"Why do they call him that?"

"Because he takes scalps, I reckon. Collects 'em, like souvenirs."

"I hope we don't run across him," Martin said.

"Oh, it's likely you will. He hates Americans more than he hates Mexicans. You watch your back trail when you go south."

"Will you give us an introduction to this Aguilar?" Juanito asked.

"None needed," O.B. said. "I already told him you were coming. He sent two men to ride down with you. So you won't get lost."

"Can we buy horses from you?" Martin asked.

"I'll pick out four good ones for you," O.B. said. "Sell 'em to you real cheap."

"How much?"

"For you, Martin Baron, a dollar apiece. Gold or silver, whichever you like."

"That does not seem like much."

O.B. reared back in his chair and laughed. "I stole them from Cuchillo himself. His best horses. They might prove pretty dear one day."

"I don't get it," Martin said. "Do you want us to fight this Apache?"

"Nope, but it will tell Cuchillo you mean business. He prized them horses and we snuck 'em away from him one day when he wasn't in his camp. He might think you stole them from me."

"I hope they don't get us killed," Martin said.

"They might get Cuchillo killed. Can you fight?"

"I've killed an Indian," Martin said.

"Well, then, you won't have no trouble at all with Cuchillo. But he knows rifle ranges and can sneak up on a man in midday in the middle of a bare flat and cut his throat."

Martin rubbed his neck. He took another swallow of

mezcal. It went down smoother this time and his feet no longer hurt so badly. In fact, his sore muscles seemed to be just fine.

"Let's look at those horses, O.B.," Martin said, downing the rest of his drink.

He felt ten feet tall.

10

THE HORSES CARRIED the Circle B brand. They were in a large jacal so that they could not be seen from a distance. Two Mexican wranglers cut out the four pintos.

"Those are fine horses," Juanito said. "They look strong and healthy."

"Breaks my old heart to give 'em up," O.B. said.

Martin handed the rancher four silver dollars. They disappeared into O.B.'s pocket so quickly, Baron blinked as if he had seen a magician's sleight of hand.

"You'll need saddles and bridles," Clarke said. "No spurs for those pintos. They'll turn any whichway with a touch of the knee. On a dime."

"How much for the saddles?" Martin asked.

"They ain't much. Mexican made. High cantles, oversized horns. You can have the both of 'em for a five-dollar gold piece."

"Done," Martin said and fished a coin from his

pocket. Again the money disappeared into Clarke's pocket without a trace.

"I'll throw in them bridles for free. Leather's cheap out here. And I'll give you two pair of rope halters."

"We will need some rope, too," Juanito said.

"Take what you need out of the tack room next to the main corral out yonder."

"You're mighty generous, O.B.," Martin said.

"It goes both ways, son. I might ride your way someday and I hope you'll treat me kindly."

"I sure will, O.B."

The tack room was dark and O.B. lit a coal-oil lantern when he showed them the saddles.

"Them two," he said, pointing to a corner as he held up the lantern. The saddles sat on a rail atop two sawhorses. "Mexican made, like I said. A thick stem, heavy, but pitched on the front so's the rope won't jam. Enough pinch to hold a good jerk on it even with one dally."

Juanito stepped past the light and knelt down to inspect the saddles. Then he stood up and grabbed one, lifted it off the pole by the single hand slot in the center.

"I've seen 'em with two holes there," O.B. said.

"This tree is covered with rawhide," Juanito said, tilting the saddle under the light.

"Them stirrup leathers is only an inch and a half wide. Don't come with no rosaderos, neither."

"What are those?" Martin asked.

"Fenders, kind of," O.B. explained. "To keep the leathers from slapping against the horse's hide."

"These saddles will do," Juanito said, replacing the one in his hand on the pole.

"Nothing fancy," O.B. said, "just serviceable."

"We're mighty grateful," Martin said.

"You won't be so grateful once you've sat ten miles on one of them saddles, son." O.B. smiled wanly and the lantern light gave his face the look of a large troll.

"Them kind grow teeth well inside of a day under your butt."

Juanito picked out some cotton ropes, hung them, coiled, on the saddle horns.

It was full dark by the time they arrived back at the house. Martin could smell the aroma of food and his stomach rumbled with hunger.

"We ain't got no kids, so there's plenty to eat," O.B. said as they all sat down at the table. Casey set out two baskets full of steaming corn and flour tortillas wrapped in hot towels. There was shredded beef brisket, chili peppers, pinto beans and squash.

They ate in the same room as the kitchen, but it was large enough so that they were well away from the stove at the other end. Ladles and spoons hung from a shelf that held pots and pans within easy reach. The dining area was decorated with painted gourds and dried flowers and chili peppers that added still more color to the drab adobe walls.

"This looks real good, Mrs. Clarke," Martin said.

"My name's Katherine, but everyone calls me Casey for my initials, K.C. And I hope you enjoy the meal."

Martin and Juanito ate like ravenous wolf cubs as they talked to O.B. about ranching.

"The easy part is finding cattle," Clarke told them. "The Spaniards left so many wild cattle here, they outnumber humans. But you got to get 'em out of the brush, and that ain't easy. Finding 'em is easy. Catching 'em ain't so easy."

"How did you catch them?" Martin asked, between mouthfuls of food.

"Got some of 'em tame and used 'em like Judas goats. Cattle are herd animals. They see their kind a-grazin' and they'll come out of the brush. Then you got to catch 'em. You learn to rope like the Mexicans, you'll do all right."

"That's enough of cattle, Owen," Casey said.

Martin looked up sheepishly at Mrs. Clarke. "Sorry, ma'am," he said.

"In his room or out in the fields, Owen talks. At my supper table, I talk," Casey said.

O.B. didn't apologize, but he kept silent, concentrating on the food that filled his plate.

"Thank you, Juanito," Casey said, "for the thread and needles you brung me. And the spices for my pies. I've planted an orchard, and next year we'll have peaches and pears and plums and 'cimmons."

"It was my pleasure," Juanito said. "No apples?"

"Too danged hot out here for apples. Oh, I've been thinking of sending off for some crab apples. They might grow. But we do have pecan trees sprouting, and I might get us some black walnut trees from Missoura."

"You're making yourself a right nice home here, ma'am," Martin said.

"Why, thank you kindly, Martin."

"We had a home like that once. Grew all sorts of things and my ma made pies like you talked about. Growed everything we needed, almost."

"The Lord provides," Casey said.

"He surely does," Martin agreed.

"What brought you here, Martin?" Casey asked. "It's not a country for the weak in spirit or the faint of heart."

"Texas brought me here," Martin replied. "The land. I could see it from my ship and it was green and right promising. I didn't see no houses or people, but I saw wild cattle and horses and I thought it might be a good place to settle."

"That's a good enough reason for anyone," Casey said. "Now that Texas has its independence, more people like you will come and take to the land. Someday we'll have towns and roads all through this wilderness."

"Likely it won't be in our lifetime," O.B. said.

"There's so much open country here, a man can get lost and never find his way out."

When supper was finished, Martin's head was spinning with all that he had heard and learned. In a short time, he had come to like the Clarkes, admire them for their fortitude and perseverance. He was flushed with excitement over owning a portion of Texas land. He was inspired by what Casey and O.B. had done in such a short time.

"Martin," Casey said when he started to get up and follow O.B. and Juanito outside for an after-dinner smoke, "would you help me with the dishes?"

"But I—" he started to say. "Why, sure, Casey. Least I can do for such a fine meal."

"I'd be much obliged," she said.

Martin watched disconsolately as O.B. and Juanito left the dining room without so much as a backward glance. He felt left out and wondered why they hadn't asked him to go with them.

"Don't you worry about them two none," Casey said. "They got things to talk about that don't concern you, Martin."

"I—well, I guess so, ma'am."

"They be knowin' each other a while."

Martin wondered how she knew that O.B. wanted to talk to Juanito alone. Some secret signal between man and wife? Or had they planned this for months? Why, that was crazy, he thought.

"I'll wash, you dry," Casey said brightly. "Then you can go outside and have your smoke."

"Yes'm," he said, and stood there like a post while Casey poured hot water from a kettle on the stove into a pan. He listened to her scrape plates and pots, straining all the while to see if he could overhear O.B. and Juanito. But he had no idea where they had gone and heard nothing beyond the walls of the kitchen.

* * *

O.B. and Juanito walked out by the young orchard, lighting their pipes under a canopy of bright stars. Insects spoke in their crackling talk, and somewhere beyond the broad savannah, coyote yelps floated like bright ribbons of song.

"Well, Juanito," O.B. said, "will you be partners with young Baron? Or will you just teach him the business of cattle raising and go back to Argentina?"

"I will do what Martin asks me to do. I will serve him as best I can or be his partner. Whatever he wishes."

"Why?" O.B. asked bluntly.

"Martin is a man with vision, and he has courage. He has saved his money and he is a very good fisherman, a better one than I."

Clarke touched his hand to a pecan tree, felt its bark slowly, thoughtfully. "Do you trust him, Juanito? You know more about cattle than I do. This lad knows nothing."

"I trust him," replied Juanito. "It is true that I know cattle. But Martin, he knows men. He is a born leader. He picked me and a man called Cackle Jack to help him gain that which he wanted. Jack was a good man who would have gone to hell for Martin. He did not like the land, but Martin persuaded him to come to this place. Unfortunately, Jack died, but Martin is here. He has doubts, *por claro,* but all great men have doubts."

"So he picked you. Did you also pick him?"

O.B. stepped away from the palm tree and blew a spume of smoke skyward.

"My father told me that if you could not do a thing, pick a man who can. Martin is determined to make his fortune raising cattle. I think Martin will make us both rich."

O.B. suppressed a laugh.

"You doubt this, O.B.?"

"You are both very young. But that ain't no crime.

Hell, young Baron reminds me of myself, only he's thirty years ahead of where I was at his age."

"There is another thing, O.B."

"What's that?"

"You can't stop a man with a dream. Martin has a dream. A very big one."

"Then he will do well," O.B. said.

"Like you, O.B."

This time Clarke laughed, a deep hearty laugh that resonated with infectious pleasure. He slapped Juanito soundly on the back.

"Buena suerte, 'migo," he said.

"Mil gracias, patrón."

Martin and Juanito slept in an empty jacal furnished with crude bunks.

"It's better than sleeping on the ground," Martin said.

"Do you like O.B. and his wife?" Juanito asked as he sat on the edge of a cot and unlaced his boots.

"I like them. I didn't like being left to wash dishes, though."

Juanito laughed lightly. "Did not Casey give you some motherly advice?"

Martin drew back in surprise as he was slipping his shirt off his back. "How did you know?"

"I helped wash the supper dishes the first time I was here. O.B. went outside by himself to smoke."

"I'll be damned."

"She told you to find a wife as soon as possible," Juanito said. "She said no man could be whole in this country without a good strong woman beside him."

"She said all that," Martin said, folding his shirt and laying it under his coat.

"And what did you say to her?"

"I told her I thought a wife would be a hindrance to a man until he was steady on his feet. I told her I could not ask a woman to share nothing."

"And she said that this was not important, didn't she?"

Martin nodded as he sat down on the cot and began taking off his boots. "She said a good woman would want to be with a man at the beginning of any venture, not pick up in the middle of his life."

"And what did you say then?"

"I didn't say what I thought."

"Ah, and what was that, my friend?"

"I think she's crazy."

Juanito tapped the side of his head. "Then you will have to find a crazy woman like her, Martin."

"You're both crazy," Martin said, but he was chuckling to himself.

Juanito blew out the lantern and the room filled with pungent fumes that lingered in the dark. The coyotes sang the two young men to sleep. Martin did not dream that night.

Solemn gray dawn. Then the eastern sky turned peach and the sun rose above the mist of morning, a flaming ball shrouded for a few seconds so that its shape was clearly visible as the fire god men have worshiped since time began.

Alfonso Chávez was waiting for them at the corral. Martin saw that both his and Juanito's horses were saddled. Another Mexican stood with the reins of their horses in his hand. O.B. was nowhere in sight.

"Where's O.B.?" Martin asked.

"El patrón se fué," Chávez said. He waved a hand in the air. "He is gone. I am Alfonso Chávez. I am sending by Don Jaime Aguilar. I am taking you to his rancho."

The other Mexican handed the reins to Martin.

"And who are you?" Martin asked.

"I am called Chuey," said the man. "I am speaking the good English too. That is why Don Jaime has sending me to ride you."

Martin looked at Juanito, who was trying hard not to smile.

"Here, take your own horses," Martin said, thrusting the reins at Juanito.

Juanito spoke in rapid Spanish to the two men. They replied just as rapidly. Martin didn't understand a word.

"What did you three talk about?" Martin asked as he checked the single cinch, tied his bedroll in back of the cantle. Their packs were diamond-hitched to panniers on the extra two horses.

"I asked them if two of them were enough to escort us to the Aguilar rancho."

"And what did they say?"

"They said there had been four of them when they left."

"And what happened to the other two men?"

"They were chased by Apaches wearing war paint. The other two ran off and they never saw them again."

"Killed?" Martin asked.

Juanito shrugged. "I do not know. Neither do they."

"Is that all, then?"

"No, I asked them if it would be dangerous going back over the same trail."

"And what did they say to that?" Martin asked.

"They said we would go another way."

"I heard the name Cuchillo."

"That is the one who chased them."

"Did they say why the Apaches went after them?"

Juanito took in a deep breath and pursed his lips. But he didn't say anything.

"Well?"

"It is not a good thing," Juanito said.

"What is not a good thing? Damn it, Juanito. What did they tell you?"

"Don Aguilar pays his men four silver dollars for every Apache scalp they bring him."

"A bounty?"

"Yes."

"Well, no wonder them Indians are mad as hell."

"That is why they take Mexican scalps."

"It's a hell of a thing," Martin said softly. "One hell of a thing."

Juanito said nothing. Instead he mounted his horse, took the rope of his packhorse.

Martin looked at the two Mexicans. "You won't, by God, take any Indian scalps while I'm riding with you," he said to Chávez. "Nor you either," he said to Chuey.

"*¿Qué dice?*" Chávez asked Juanito.

"*Vámanos.*"

The four men rode out as the sun boiled in the sky and white clouds began to flock to the north, so far away they appeared like tiny balls of cotton plucked from their bolls.

They rode south in a meandering fashion, through acres of thick brush, across cactus-strewn llanos and past shallow arroyos and green sloughs teeming with frogs and insects. Jackrabbits jumped from behind bushes and birds fled from mesquite groves like spattered ink against the blue sky.

"I hope they know the way back to Aguilar's," Martin said. "I'm sure as hell lost."

"They are very nervous," Juanito said.

"No shit."

"Chuey especially. He has been praying to all the saints and the virgin mother for the past half hour."

"I hope it works," Martin said sarcastically.

Chávez left every so often to ride their back trail and circle, only to reappear ahead of them. At such times Chuey prayed more loudly and crossed himself continually. Both Mexicans wore large-caliber pistols and carried old, scarred rifles, the butts wound tight with rawhide to hold the wood together.

When Chávez disappeared again, Martin spoke to Juanito.

"When he comes back, you tell him I said to send Chuey out to check our back trail and scout ahead. That praying sonofabitch is making me nervous."

"I will tell him," Juanito said. "But he might not like to take orders from you."

"Tell him I'll shoot him out of the saddle if he leaves us again. I wouldn't trust Chuey to hit a barn from two paces. He's shaking like a dog shitting peach pits as it is."

"That is pretty strong language. Chávez might shoot you."

"Then tell Chuey to shut up."

"I will do this, but in a polite way."

"You tell him his praying is making me nervous."

Juanito rode ahead and spoke to Chuey in Spanish. The two talked for some time before the Argentinian rode back.

"What did he say?" Martin asked.

"He said he would pray silently. He is afraid. He says Chávez is very nervous."

"There must be something those two are not telling us."

"Apparently Cuchillo told them he would come after them on their way back. They believe him a man who keeps his promises."

"They understand Apache?"

"The Apaches speak Spanish."

When they encountered Chávez again, he was resting under a cottonwood tree by a small creek. But he sat in the saddle with his rifle at the ready.

"You tell him what I told you, Juanito," Martin said.

"I will talk to him."

"I wish it could be in English."

"It will be clearer to him in Spanish."

Martin said nothing. He got down off his horse, whom he had named Spot. He rubbed his butt, pinched the skin to get the blood back. O.B. had been right. The saddle had grown teeth and then his butt had gone numb. His legs ached in places they never hurt when he had been walking.

Juanito and Chávez talked for a long while. Chuey kept looking around, swinging his rifle every time he turned a different direction. Martin walked around, trying to take the kinks out of his leg muscles. The ground felt good to him—solid, no surprises. He looked at his saddle, wondered how such an innocent-looking thing could cause such pain. When he was riding, he could feel its tree growing into him, like stakes plunged into his buttocks, splinters and all.

Finally Juanito returned, dismounted and patted his horse's withers.

"Well, did Chávez agree to send Chuey to scout?" Martin asked.

"It is too late for that. The Apaches have found us."

"What?"

"Chávez counted six. Then he saw only five. He thinks one rode off to bring Cuchillo here."

Martin looked around. "Where are they?" he asked.

"Oh, you won't see them."

"Chávez saw them."

"They wanted him to see them," Juanito said. "They are playing with us."

"What do we do now, then?"

"We ride on, find a place to make a stand."

"Does Chávez know where that might be?"

"He does not. He is afraid. Like Chuey."

"Well, why not make a stand right here?"

"Because that's where the Apaches want us to make a stand. They have surrounded us."

"Five Apaches? Surrounded us?"

"We will have to fight our way out, I think."

"You don't seem too worried, Juanito."

"I am worried, my friend. Very worried."

Before Martin could say anything else, he heard a strange sound. It sounded like a large bee, then like someone stropping a razor on wet leather, like a whiffling of wings in the darkness, like a whispering ghost.

And then Chuey sprouted an arrow in his throat. The Mexican reached up and grabbed the shaft with both hands, tried to pull it out. Then he tumbled out of the saddle, blood gushing from his throat in a crimson flood. He made no sound as he fell.

His body hit the ground with a thud and Martin heard the arrow crack as it broke off.

"Take cover," Juanito said.

Just as Martin moved, an arrow whistled over his head; the hackles rose on the back of his neck. He pulled himself up into the saddle and clapped heels to Spot's flanks just as the air filled with the chilling yells of Apaches on the attack.

11

MARTIN'S HORSE SPRANG forward with a lunge and he had to hold on to the saddle horn to keep from being left behind. Spot charged straight at an Apache as if bred for war. The Apache's eyes opened wide and he turned his horse to avoid being rammed and unseated.

Martin pulled his rifle to his shoulder, cocked it as he gripped the horse with his knees. The single loop of the rein held on the saddle horn. Martin fired straight at the Apache from a distance of no more than ten yards. A cloud of white smoke billowed from the barrel of the rifle. But as he rode through the smoke, Martin saw the Apache clutch his side and struggle to stay atop his pony.

Martin let his rifle drop from his shoulder and picked up the rein, wheeled his horse in a tight circle. He saw Juanito, using his horse for cover, fire at another Indian. The Indian threw up his arms and fell backward off his horse. Smoke and the smell of burnt black powder filled the air.

The Apache Martin had shot stared at him with glazed eyes filled with hatred. Then he coughed and blood gushed from his mouth. The Indian tried to nock an arrow to his bow, but he couldn't lift his arms above his waist. A second later, he slid from his pony's back and fell headfirst to the ground.

Chávez rode past at full gallop and Martin put his horse into motion.

"Come on, Juanito. Follow me."

Out of the corner of his eye, Martin saw Juanito mount his horse. Both men were carrying empty rifles, but there was no chance to reload on horseback. Spot ran after Chávez as if demons were chasing him.

Chávez rode in a wide circle, came back on the place where the fight had begun. He slowed his horse and Martin followed suit. Juanito caught up to him a few moments later.

"Why is he coming back here?" Martin asked.

"I do not know. To help Chuey, maybe."

"Chuey's deader'n a doornail."

"I know."

Chávez approached the killing place warily. He had not fired his rifle and now he held it at the ready, with both hands, one clutching the reins.

Martin called out to the Mexican. "Chávez, why did you come back here?"

The Mexican turned and put a finger to his lips, then grasped the rifle again with his left hand.

Chávez slipped from the saddle of his horse and began to stalk something. He crouched over and stepped carefully so that he made no sound. Martin turned to look at Juanito.

Juanito shrugged, but gestured for Martin to dismount. Martin stepped down from the saddle. Juanito came up beside him. Together they followed Chávez as the Mexican crept through the brush toward the place where they were attacked by the Apaches.

Slowly Juanito and Martin caught up with Chávez, who motioned for them to stay behind him. The three of them continued forward, each stepping in unison with the others so that they moved in a tight group.

Martin heard someone ahead of Chávez grunt. Chávez went into a crouch, froze. He stood motionless like a stalking cat, then brought his rifle to his shoulder. Martin looked in the direction Chávez was aiming and saw two Apaches. One was kneeling over Chuey's body while the other stood guard.

The Apache on the ground spoke softly to the other. Then Martin heard a *snick snick* and a scratching sound. The kneeling Apache held up a bloody scalp, Chuey's, triumphantly.

Chávez squeezed the trigger of his rifle at that moment. The standing Apache pitched forward, a small black hole in his chest. The kneeling Apache stood up. Chávez pulled his pistol and shot the scalper in the belly. The Apache dropped the scalp and reached for his knife.

The Indian didn't have a chance. Chávez rushed toward him, brained him with his pistol. The Apache fell on his back. Chávez put a boot on the Indian's throat and held it down until the Indian stopped kicking. Then the Mexican lifted his foot and bent down over him, setting his pistol down and drawing his knife.

"You make one cut," Martin said, "and I'll shoot you dead."

Chávez turned to look at Martin, a savage look in his eyes. He held the knife poised just above the Apache's head.

"I mean it," Martin said, drawing his own pistol. He cocked it and the sound was like a rifle shot in the stillness.

"It is money for me and my family," Chávez said in English. "The bounty."

"No," Martin said.

Juanito put a hand on Martin's arm. Martin jerked it away.

"It is only fair," Juanito said. "The Apache took Chuey's scalp."

"Fair? Do we act like animals because animals act a certain way? I won't see a man butchered like that."

"Martin," Juanito said soothingly, "this is not your business. It is between Chávez and the Apache."

"I mean what I said, Juanito. He touches that knife to that Apache's head and I'll drop him where he sits."

Chávez rose up slowly. He turned to face Martin. He held the knife as if he meant to use it on Baron.

"You damned gringo," Chávez said. "You do not know what the Apaches do to my people. You have not seen the womens and the childrens with their throats cut. You have not seen them burnt alife. You have not seen my people's scalps hanging from lances."

"No, I have not," Martin said. "But I do not have to see you cut up a dead man, either. Step away from that man."

Juanito spoke to Chávez in Spanish. Chávez sheathed his knife, cursing under his breath.

"We will bury Chuey," Martin said in a mollifying tone.

"That might get us all killed," Juanito said.

"We go now," Chávez said. "The ants and the vultures will take care of the dead ones." Then he crossed himself. He snatched Chuey's scalp from the dead Apache's hand and stuffed it in his shirt. He knelt down and closed Chuey's dead eyes and crossed himself again. He stood up then and walked back toward Martin and Juanito, passed them as he headed for his horse.

"I guess we got all five of them," Martin said, still dazed by the killings. "I don't feel good about it, though."

"This is a savage land," Juanito said. "You should have let Chávez take those scalps."

"To hell with Chávez and the damned Apaches, too."

"Maybe you are too quick to judge, my friend."

"What do you mean by that?"

"Did you not hear what Chávez said? He has seen bloodier things than this. He wants a little revenge and you took that away from him. He wanted a bandage for his heart and you tore it out of his hands."

"I stopped him from acting like an Apache."

"No, you made an enemy of him. *Ten cuidado, mi amigo.*"

"What's that mean?"

"Be careful of Chávez from now on."

Martin and Juanito walked back to their horses. Chávez was reloading his rifle.

"We had better do the same," Juanito said. "There is still Cuchillo to deal with."

Chávez finished reloading his pistol. Then he mounted his horse and waited until the two men had reloaded their own rifles.

"Make the hurry," the Mexican said. "Cuchillo, he come soon, I think."

Martin and Juanito mounted their horses. Chávez rode off to the southeast, following a wide arc until he turned southwest again. They rode through a trackless jungle of mesquite, circled the open places where hawks floated in the sky like children's kites and above buzzards rode the thermals in lazy scrawling spirals.

"Is he never going to stop?" Martin asked late in the afternoon. They had been riding, aimlessly it seemed, for hours.

"I think he is trying to outrun Cuchillo."

"Can he?"

"I do not know. Perhaps."

The sun crawled across the sky and seemed to hang

over the western horizon for hours. And still they rode, through desolate, bleak country that often showed only a few yards of itself in the mesquite, then opened up to wide, long grasslands teeming with game and wildfowl.

Chávez no longer checked their back trail, but zigzagged in angles measured by the sun. Martin could detect no trails and saw very few tracks. Those he saw were only of cattle, never of horses, shod or unshod. But they were still heading in a southerly direction.

The day shrank up on them and the sun set in a blaze of golden fire and Chávez never slackened his steady, unrelenting pace through thick mesquite and around savannahs. Martin's butt had gone from hurt to numb and back to hurt again. He began to think the saddle had turned into a large, sharp razor and he was sitting on its finely honed edge and it was cutting his ass to ribbons.

"He's never going to stop, is he?" Martin's voice croaked with dryness. But the sweat on him began to cool as the sun sank over the distant horizon.

"Maybe not for a long time," Juanito said. He seemed resigned to the endless ride. Martin noted that he had not complained once all day.

"I suppose we have to trust him."

"He knows the way. We do not."

"I don't trust him."

Juanito laughed.

"What's so funny?" Martin asked.

"You must trust a man you do not trust. Is this not funny?"

"I don't trust Chávez. I'm not trusting him."

"Yet he leads the way to your destination."

"There you go again, Juanito. That double-talk that doesn't make sense."

"There is none so blind as those who will not see, Martin."

"What's that supposed to mean?"

"If you do not know what it means, then you are truly blind. But, I don't believe that. You are just someone who is unwilling to see."

"I still don't understand a word you're saying."

"Deaf, too," Juanito said with a laugh. "Maybe you had better follow Cackle Jack's path during his last hours, go where he went. Then you might understand everything."

Juanito rode away just as Martin opened his mouth to say something. But then Martin realized it would have done no good—Juanito just didn't make any sense most of the time. He wondered what Juanito meant by telling him to follow Cackle Jack's path. Did Juanito think he, Martin Baron, was an idiot? Jack had been delirious and appeared to have lost his mind at the last. Juanito talked in riddles—as Jack had done before he died.

Martin shook his head and followed after Juanito as the sky darkened and the blue turned to black. The stars began to appear, winking, winking, like tiny lights on a dark prairie.

"Isn't that Mexican ever going to stop?" he said aloud. Spot whickered at the sound of the human voice.

On through the night the three men rode, Juanito and Martin following Chávez blindly, the horses in a straight line. None spoke and Martin wanted to scream into the silence. His butt had turned numb again and he was sure it was mortified, dead as a fire-blackened tree stump.

The sky was ablaze with stars. Martin stared upward until he found the Big Dipper, the polestar. Mentally he calculated their direction. They were heading south. Perhaps Chávez was sighting on the same star. He felt more comfortable about that. They were not lost, just wallowing in irons as they struggled through the doldrums at night.

Later, Martin became sleepy and started nodding off. When he felt himself about to fall out of the saddle, he jerked back upright and opened his eyes. He rubbed them to stay awake. Slapped his cheeks lightly with his right hand. Dimly he made out Juanito's shape in front of him and beyond, the small back of Chávez atop his horse.

Martin continued to fight against sleepiness. He began to see things that were not there. He saw men emerge out of the darkness, only to pass their figures and see that they were just cactus. He saw other horsemen who turned into trees and bushes when he drew close.

He was tired, so tired. Every muscle in his body ached. His bones hurt. His butt began to itch and he could never find the right spot to scratch. Then his scalp itched, and his back, at the hardest spots to reach. He twisted in the saddle, trying to stop the itching, and when he finally found the right place to scratch, another part—his ankle or his elbow—would start itching. It was maddening, but it helped keep him awake.

He fell asleep toward morning, knew he was rocking gently in the saddle. It gave him pure pleasure to close his eyes and drift off into dream. When he would start to fall, he would catch himself and awaken only briefly before dropping off into a deep slumber again.

Then the rocking stopped and he awoke and realized his horse had stopped. Someone was shaking him.

"Martin, Martin, wake up," Juanito whispered.

"Huh? Where are we?" It was still pitch-dark and the stars swirled when he looked up at them, blurred as if they were moving at high speed.

"You fell asleep and your horse just stopped. You have to stay awake."

"Where's Chávez?"

"Right here," Juanito said.

Martin turned slightly and saw Chávez, or what he

took to be Chávez, a dark man on a dark horse silhou-
etted against the light of the stars.

"What's he made of? Iron? Christ, Juanito, we've
been riding for hours."

"It is necessary, I think."

"Necessary? Hell, if Cuchillo came up on us now,
none of us could fight him. We're all dead tired and
half asleep."

"Not Chávez."

"No, not Chávez, that bastard. He's not human.
Hell, isn't he tired?"

"I think he is tired, but he says we must go on. He
does not think the Apache will ride at night. He does
not think they will fight at night."

"Why not?"

"He says they are afraid their spirits will be lost if
they are killed."

Martin snorted. "Well, my spirit's been lost for the
past fifty miles. How far have we come?"

"About fifteen, I think."

"Fifteen miles? What time is it?"

"I do not know. Before midnight."

Martin groaned at the thought of riding in the darkness for another six or eight hours. He rubbed his eyes,
shook off the sleepiness.

"We ought to stop and make some coffee, at least."

"Chávez says we must go on."

"Chávez says," Martin mocked. "What does Chávez
know? If the Apaches aren't riding at night, why do
we have to?"

"He says it is far to the rancho of Don Aguilar. If we
get far enough away from Cuchillo, he will not catch
us."

Martin sighed deeply. "If I don't get some sleep, it
will be a blessing if Cuchillo comes up and kills me."

Juanito did not laugh. Instead, he slapped Spot's
rump and rode away. Chávez had already started toward the south again. Spot jumped ahead and fell into

line, like some obedient beast, following the Mexican's lead.

Martin fought off the weariness over another ten miles of twisting, slow, agonizing riding through oceans of stygian darkness, seas of smothering night, tunnels of mesquite, broad swells of star-dusted savannahs. He began to believe he was in a nightmare, dreaming it all, his senses lost somewhere in the vastness of the sky overhead.

Baron's mind began to wander. Suddenly he felt very lucid, could see very clearly into the darkness. The moon had risen, but it wasn't that. It was something else. Something like delirium. Like what Cackle Jack had gone through when he was dying. Martin felt like giggling, as if he were half drunk.

He thought of Cackle Jack and the things he had said. The things he had seen when he was floundering in the depths of delirium. And then Martin remembered something he had meant to talk to Juanito about. Something Juanito had been doing ever since they had left the Gulf shore.

At first Martin had paid no attention. He had thought Juanito was catching a catnap before they set out each day and before they went to bed at night. But tonight he realized that Juanito was doing what Cackle Jack had done. He was going on some inner journey. It was perfectly clear. Juanito had been oblivious to his surroundings during those times when he sat quietly alone, closed his eyes and did God knows what. But there was a cleanness to Juanito's face at such times, morning and evening, a shining as if a light burned from within. The same look he had seen on Jack's face when he was slowly drifting toward his own death.

"I must ask Juanito about this," he whispered to himself. "But I think I already know. I want to know what he sees in there. Where he goes. What he does. Maybe that's what he meant when he told me to follow Cackle Jack's path. Maybe he wants me to follow his path now. Eh?"

"Shhhh!" Juanito whispered.

"Huh? Oh, was I talking out loud?"

"Be quiet," Juanito warned.

Martin smiled inwardly. I've got you now, Juanito. I'll dig it out of you. You don't fool me.

And the lucidity left him as quickly as it had come and he rocked in the saddle like a somnambulist, eyes open but sleeping, stuporous, half-delirious mutterings scrambling through his brain like snatches of conversation at a gathering of idiots.

The night seemed endless, and soon Martin's backside began to throb. The saddle had turned to iron heated to a cherry glow, burning through his flesh, eating him alive. Just when he thought he could stand it no longer, Chávez halted.

Martin almost rode into Juanito before he realized that they had stopped. Chávez dismounted, walked back to talk to the two mariners.

"We will walk for a time," he said. "The horses need to get some resteds, I think."

"We need some resteds," Martin said sarcastically. He couldn't move. He doubted if he could get out of the saddle. He felt as if he was welded to it.

"The walk will rest us," Juanito said, climbing down from his saddle. "Need some help?"

"I don't know if I can walk," Martin said.

Juanito laughed that laugh of his and Martin wanted to slap his mouth. Instead, he pushed up from the saddle and stood in the stirrups a moment or two until the feeling returned to his battered buttocks. They felt as if they had swollen to an enormous size.

Martin stepped a long way down out of the saddle. Finally his right foot touched the earth. He steadied himself and swung the other leg out of the stirrup. The ground felt alien. His body still rocked to the rhythm of Spot's easy gait. He felt light-headed, almost giddy.

Juanito touched Martin on the shoulder for a moment.

Martin hung his head down, closed his eyes. He leaned against the saddle, crossing his wrists.

"Are you all right, Martin?"

"No, I died about four hours ago. Have they lit the fires yet?"

"Fires?"

"We're in hell, aren't we?"

Juanito laughed softly. "We are going through a trial, yes. We are not in hell. We are safe."

"Safe? Safe from Cuchillo, maybe. But not safe from Chávez." Martin laughed inanely at that. "Chávez the torturer. Chávez the Cruel. King Chávez."

"You will feel better after a while. I think it is getting cooler."

It was getting cooler, and to Martin that meant that it was probably past midnight and he might even see the light of day again.

"Do you know what time it is, Juanito?" Martin asked.

"Chávez thinks the hour is three in the morning."

"When do you and Chávez talk? I haven't heard him say two words all night."

"He does not say much."

Martin lifted his head and turned away from the horse. "I'll sell you this stolen Indian pony real cheap, Juanito."

"Ah, you will come to love him. Has he not carried you through the night safely to this place of rest?"

Before Martin could reply, Chávez said something in Spanish to Juanito.

"What'd he say?" Martin asked.

"He said that we must go now."

"I take it back, then, Juanito."

"What's that?"

"Chávez has said four words all night. The same four words."

"I do not understand."

"We must go now," Martin said.

And Juanito laughed, but this time Martin did not want to strike him. It was a good laugh, well meant, harmless.

"Let us go, then," Martin said. "After all, we wouldn't want Cuchillo to catch us on the ground like quail wallowing in a dust bath, would we?"

Single file, the three men and six horses walked through the dark and forbidding forest of night, like bedouin following a path across trackless sands in an unknown country.

12

FOR ANOTHER DAY and into the next night they rode, three men on tired horses. They changed mounts twice. Martin learned to sleep in the saddle and only fell from his horse once. Spot followed the other two horses. The only time Martin was unseated was when the horse shied at a pool of smelly ooze.

"What was that stuff seeping out of the ground?" he asked Juanito.

"Oil."

"Oil?"

"There is oil under the ground," Juanito said.

Martin went back to sleep on horseback and thought no more about it. But the smell of the crude oil lingered in his nostrils for a long time.

They slept, taking turns on watch for two hours apiece in the heat of the day. The horses fed on the mesquite that hid the men and their mounts from view. After they had rested, they rode again in the cool of the evening. Martin felt refreshed. Chávez had slept the least, and Martin wondered if he even slept on horse-back. Probably not, he decided, since he was the pathfinder, their guide to the Aguilar rancho.

On the third day, they stopped at a small creek that threaded through the mesquite.

Chávez spoke to Juanito in Spanish.

"What did he say?" Martin asked.

"He says that Cuchillo is not following us."

"How does he know that?"

"He knows."

"He must be a mighty smart man."

Juanito and Chávez spoke some more and Martin wished he could speak Spanish. He knew a few words, that was all.

"We are going to rest up. Tomorrow we will be on Aguilar land."

"The rancho?"

"No, just the land. We have many miles before we reach the rancho."

"How many miles?"

"Chávez does not know how to measure distance. He said it would be a two- or three-day ride."

"Good lord. Aguilar must own a lot of land."

"He does," Juanito replied.

Martin looked over at Chávez. He was asleep under a live oak tree, his sombrero pulled over his face. He looked dead, Martin thought.

"So he's not made of iron, after all."

"He has plenty of iron in him, that man," Juanito said. "Let's get some sleep. There is no need to set watches."

"You're sure?"

"Chávez is sure."

"You trust him, then."

"He is a man who has lived in this country for a long time. He is part of it. If he sleeps, we can sleep."

"I wish I had your confidence in Chávez. Maybe

he's just faking it. We'll go to sleep and he'll ride off and leave us to be scalped."

"Such thoughts can only bring trouble to you, Martin. Get some sleep."

"Wake me if I don't wake up, will you, Juanito?"

For once, Juanito did not laugh. He was too tired. He was snoring lightly before Martin even closed his eyes.

Two days later, Martin saw vaqueros working the longhorn herds. They passed little clusters of jacales grimly attached to the land, with flowers growing around each hovel. Women waved to them and little children laughed and chased their horses, yelling in Spanish.

The men, Martin noticed, were all armed with rifles and pistols. They did not call out, but only waved to Chávez, and from the dark holes in their faces, Martin could feel their eyes burning into his.

On the third day, they saw more cattle, and riders far in the distance, driving strays toward the main bunch. Martin felt an excitement he had never known before when he saw a bunch of men branding calves near a small corral made of spindly mesquite limbs. He could smell the hair burning.

"You would think Chávez would stop and talk to some of these men," Martin remarked to Juanito.

"I think he is in a hurry to get rid of us."

"Is that all?"

"No, he is worried, I think. He told me that Cuchillo does not give up on a thing very easily."

"I thought he said Cuchillo was not following us any longer."

"He said that. But it may be that Cuchillo has ridden around us and is waiting up ahead somewhere."

Martin's scalp prickled. "You think that?"

"I don't know. Chávez is more alert today, did you not notice?"

"He seems to be looking around more, yes."

"He is as much instinct as intelligence," Juanito said.

"Boy, there's a bone to chew on. Where do you get all that fancy stuff?"

"From books. From my father. Reading is a way of meeting the great minds of the world, listening to men long since dead."

"Like the Bible?"

"The Bible. The Vedas. The Upanishads. The Dhammapada."

"I never heard of them others."

"They were written thousands of years before the Bible."

"You don't say."

Juanito laughed and they rode on, but Martin started looking beyond the gently rolling land to the farthest reaches of the horizon. He expected to see Apaches rise up out of the earth at any moment, screaming and yelling, shooting arrows at them.

On the fourth day, following their big day of rest, Chávez reined up his horse and turned to them. *"Mira!"* he said to Juanito. "Look."

On the distant horizon, a small black wisp of smoke hung in the sky like a charcoal scarf.

"Is that the rancho?" Juanito asked in Spanish.

"Yes," replied Chávez. And then he checked his rifle and his pistols. "There is trouble, I think."

"What's that smoke?" Martin asked.

"The rancho, Chávez says. It may be that Cuchillo has beaten us to our destination."

Martin checked his rifle, poured fresh powder into the pan, blew away the excess. Juanito did the same.

"How do you feel about shooting an Apache?" Juanito asked.

Martin patted his rifle stock, laid it across his lap. "I don't know how I'd feel."

But he did. He remembered what happened after his

father died. Smoky mist of morning. He followed a cold trail, riding after the Shawnees who murdered his family. Riding an old plow horse with soft feet. Carrying his daddy's rifle and a pistol almost too heavy for him to lift, enough grub for a week, beef jerky, dried apples, flour, salt, a skillet, a knife, a spoon, a fork, some hardtack, a canteen, a blanket, an extra shirt.

Following the trail through thick woods, across creeks, and once a river, and seeing the tracks and remembering the Shawnee who had told the others what to do: a thick-armed, big-bellied man with greasy skin and wrinkled face, eyes like daggers and a smell to him so strong Martin thought he would never get it out of his nostrils. The Indian had dirty feathers and beads tied to his roach and red rouge on his face, with white crosses and black arrows on his cheeks and a forehead streaked with blood from his mother's throat.

Tracking them, tracking them, and hating them all, all four of them—hating their skins, their smells, their eyes, their breechclouts, their bows, their knives, their moccasins. Learning about them. Knowing where they pissed and where they shat and hating them more each day, each week. Smelling their night beds and poking in the ashes of their fires and always getting closer and finding a pig's head at one camp and seeing smoke in the sky from a cabin they had raided and burnt and more dead people staring into the sun—their privates mutilated, their heads fouled with blood and white patches where their hair had been and chicken feathers at one place littering the ground like dirty snow, heads lying on leaves, yellow eyes staring into nothingness. And then he found them all, drinking firewater from earthen jugs stolen from some settler, all laughing and farting and belching, and he had shot the leader first and then cut one with his knife, clubbed another with his rifle and shot the last with his daddy's pistol; he stabbed the other two to death after they grappled with him and knifed him bad, killed them both with a savagery that surprised him until he was covered with blood and out of breath and screaming inside and crying for his mother, bawling over his pa like a baby and hating the Shawnees and hating himself until he found a creek and washed the blood from his clothes and skin and rode off along and back home, where he looked at the sad graves and cried once more before he burnt down the house and barn and never went back even in his mind until now, just now, when Juanito was asking him how he felt about killing an Apache and it dredged up all the memories out of the dark dungeon of his mind and he could almost feel the blood on his clothes and soaking his skin and he could smell that Shawnee so strong in his nostrils that he wanted to puke right there.

"It is hard to kill a living man," Martin said, and his voice was so sepulchral and solemn that Juanito sucked in his breath and his eyes widened in surprise for a moment.

"Yes, that is so," Juanito said. "But if you think too long about it, the Apache will kill you."

"Then I won't think about it at all."

And the voice was different this time, but older, as if an aging man had taken over Martin's vocal cords, as if someone ancient was speaking through him.

"Vamos," Chávez said.

They rode toward the smoke hanging in the sky.

Martin's stomach was tight as a drumhead as they drew closer and the smoke thickened at the base of the column and he smelled the scent of burning wood and that, too, became linked with the memories that had boiled to the surface of his mind. This smell was different from that of wood burning in a cookfire. This smell had the stench of man's hand in it, the smell of not just wood, but of something a man had made and cherished as a possession, something someone had built with his hands and that was now afire, the work and the pride lost in the smoke, lost forever in the black smoke rising to the sky.

As they rode over the slight rise, Chávez halted his horse for a moment. Juanito rode up beside him, followed by Martin.

"Listen," Chávez said.

"I hear them." Juanito glanced at Martin.

"I hear them, too," Martin said. The yips and yells of Apaches, the smattering of rifle fire. *Pop. Pop. Pop.* He thought he could hear the hiss of flames eating at the wood, but he knew that was impossible. He just knew how it sounded, for he had heard the same sound before.

"We must be careful," Chávez said in Spanish. "There are many of them."

"Is it Cuchillo?" Juanito knew that Chávez probably could not tell at that distance.

But Chávez replied: "I think it is Cuchillo. Yes."

"Too far to shoot from here," Martin said. "I count eight Apaches."

"I think there are nine or ten."

"You could be right, Juanito."

Chávez kicked his horse and yelled at them as he rode toward the Apaches. "To the fight!"

"Well, let's go," Martin said, caught up with the excitement of the moment. He and Juanito kicked their horses at the same time, leaving the packhorses trailing their reins as Chávez had done.

There were more Apaches than either Juanito or Martin had counted. They seemed to appear everywhere Martin looked, rising up out of the ground or appearing from behind a cactus or a structure, on foot or on horseback. Something rose up in his throat and he gripped his rifle tightly, afraid he might drop it and have only his pistol for defense.

Then there was that other feeling, the one he had known before when he tracked the Shawnee who had slain his parents. When he had killed the Shawnees, just before he fired his rifle, Martin had felt a strange sensation.

It was like being in an empty room with the floor moving underneath his feet. And then his body had gone hollow. He could feel a soft hot wind blow through his hollow stomach and up to his hollow head. But his stomach muscles had been taut then, as they were now, and his eyes had been able to see every small detail where the Shawnees sat drinking their stolen whiskey: the bloody scalps, the cheap jewelry, a mirror, a skillet, a man's hat, a woman's dress. He saw all that was in that camp as now he could see the Indians hugging the sides of their ponies, then peering over to shoot their arrows. He saw everything in slowed-down motion: the dust, the smoke from rifles inside the house, the orange flowers of flame from the muzzles. Beyond the large, sprawling ranch house he saw Apaches driving off horses and cattle, with some of them carrying on a rear-guard action. They rode their horses in tight circles and he saw the dark lines of arrows arcing toward the house.

From another position, Apaches hidden behind haystacks shot burning arrows at the house and barn. Mexicans fought the fires from outside with blankets and buckets of water, while others fired pistols and rifles at sporadic intervals.

The demonic yips and blood-freezing yells of the Apaches made Martin's skin jump like a shirt flapping on a clothesline.

Chávez veered off from his flying course and rode after an Apache who had just shot an arrow toward the house. The other Indians looked in the Mexican's direction and began to turn their horses to give aid to their brother.

Chávez rode up close and fired his rifle at point-blank range at the fleeing Apache's back. Martin saw the Indian's body stiffen. Then the Apache threw up his arms, leaving his bow hanging in the air for a split second before it fell to the ground. The wounded man tumbled from his horse, landing on one leg, which snapped, throwing him to the ground.

Chávez ran his own mount right over the down man, swung his rifle like a polo mallet. The rifle butt struck the Apache in the head and blood flew like meat from an exploded tomato.

Martin turned away and saw Apaches riding toward Chávez. Juanito swung his horse to cut them off, bringing his rifle up chest-high with one hand. Martin turned his pinto to catch up to the stragglers riding to get into the fray.

Two men ran from the house, stood with rifles to their shoulders, tracking the Apaches riding away.

Chávez drew his pistol and shot an Apache in the chest from a dozen yards away. The Indian's pony ran right out from under his master and the Apache struck the ground, rolled over and over like a broken doll.

One Apache charged straight at Martin. Baron felt the floor drop from under him as the Apache drew back his bow, slid to one side of his pony in an amazing feat of horsemanship. He clung to the side like a spider on a fragile web, his legs locked tightly around the horse's belly and back.

Martin knew he could never hit the Indian if he fired his rifle from the saddle while his horse was running. There was only the smallest target and it, too, was moving. The floor in the empty room rose up under him and he felt the hollowness inside him fill up with solid iron.

The Apache released the arrow. Martin ducked and hugged Spot as he hid behind the horse's neck. He heard the arrow sizzle over his head, whisper past with a feathery, whiffling sound. He sat up straight and saw the Indian do the same. Martin swung his rifle in one smooth motion, leading the man about two feet, and squeezed the trigger. The rifle bucked against his side and smoke and hot powder blew back in his face.

He saw the Indian jerk as the ball struck him just below the neckline. Blood spurted from his throat and he pitched from the pony's back in a sidelong dive.

Martin dropped his rifle, knowing he'd never reload it while atop the horse. He drew his pistol and looked for another target. He saw Juanito grappling with an Apache, horse to horse, and then Chávez rode by and swung his machete, slicing into the Indian's side, nearly cutting the man in half. Juanito was drenched with gore as he broke free of the dying Indian and grabbed up a pistol. Martin saw that he had dropped his rifle to the ground as well.

Men yelled and Apaches yipped as they rode away, leaving a scrim of dust hanging in the air. Martin heard one or two shots, and then it was silent. He reined Spot to a halt and felt the tremors ripple through his veins and flesh as the excitement inside him died down.

Juanito rode up, a wan smile on his face. "Some fight, huh, Martin?"

"I never saw so many Indians in one place. Now they've all gone."

"Did you see Chávez chop that Apache?"

"I saw it. You look like a damned butcher, Juanito. Your face is covered in blood."

Juanito grinned. "We drove them off."

"We'd better help put out those fires."

Juanito turned and saw men forming a bucket brigade from a fortified well in the courtyard of the main house. Men were at the barn, stomping out the least of the fires, smothering the larger ones with wet blankets. To Martin it was a scene from hell, with smoke billowing up into the sky, the blackened faces of men tired beyond feeling, dead bodies lying everywhere he looked.

Chávez dismounted and ran to the first Apache he had killed. As Martin watched, the Mexican deftly cut the scalp lock from the dead man. Then he walked over to the man he had cut with his machete, dispatched him by cutting his throat, then took his scalp. Chávez looked over at Martin Baron, held up the scalps so that the blood dripped from over his head onto the ground. Then Chávez smiled at Martin.

"You sonofabitch," Martin breathed.

"Better not say that out loud," Juanito said. "There's nothing you can do to stop the scalping on Aguilar land."

"I know. It's just the man's arrogance that riles me."

"Hey, gringo!" Chávez yelled. "What do you think of that, eh?"

"Do not answer him," Juanito said.

"No, I won't give him the satisfaction."

Martin and Juanito turned their horses, rode up to the house. The fire there was almost under control. They dismounted. A Mexican, dressed more finely than the others, walked up to them. He wore a brace of Spanish pistols. His hands were blackened from smoke. His hair sported long sideburns and a trim moustache. He wore calfskin boots, and a pair of gloves were tucked into his back pocket.

"You are from the north?" he asked, his tone affable. "The Circle B?"

"O. B. Clarke sent us to see Mr. Jaime Aguilar," Martin said, holding out his hand. "I'm Martin Baron."

"I am Benito Aguilar, Jaime's brother." Benito shook Martin's hand, turned to Juanito. "You must be Juanito Salazar."

"I am."

"Then welcome." The two men shook hands.

"Do you need any help?" Juanito asked.

"We have the fires under control." Benito's English was accented, but Martin could find no fault with it. "I offer you my hospitality and apologize for the conditions you encountered upon your arrival."

"We accept your hospitality. You need not apologize."

"I see that only Chávez came with you. Where are the other men my brother sent to bring you here?"

"They are all dead, I'm sorry to say," Juanito said.

"Apaches?" Benito looked at Martin for confirmation. Martin nodded.

"Chávez said it was Cuchillo," Juanito said.

"That is the one who just raided my brother's rancho. He is a very bad man, that one."

"Yes," said Martin.

Benito looked over in Chávez's direction. He beckoned for the Mexican to come over. "Excuse me for a moment, gentlemen. I must take care of this matter right away."

Puzzled, Juanito and Martin stepped back a foot or two as Chávez walked toward them. When he came up, he bowed his head slightly, regarded Benito with a smirk.

"I will speak to you in English so both my guests may hear, Chávez. I ask that you reply in the same tongue. What is that you have in your hand?"

"Scalps from the two Apaches I killed. We killed some more, but this gringo here would not let me scalp them."

Benito looked at Martin. A flicker of a smile rippled on his face. "And what are you going to do with those scalps, Chávez?"

"I am show them to Don Jaime. He give me money for them."

"Give me the scalps." Benito snatched them from Chávez's hand.

"You will pay me, Don Benito?"

"I won't pay you a centavo. There is no more bounty on Apache or Comanche scalps."

Chávez spoke in rapid Spanish, protesting Benito's edict.

"Close your mouth and get to work, Chávez. Or draw your pay. The scalping is over."

"I will tell Don Jaime—"

"You will not tell my brother anything," Benito said. "If you have anything to say, you will tell me. Now go."

Chávez started to protest, but Benito stood his ground. His eyes flashed and every man there knew that Chávez was a hairsbreadth away from being gunned down where he stood. Chávez bowed his head and walked away without saying a word.

"I am sorry, gentlemen," Benito said, "but that was necessary. My brother's policy has cost us dearly. It cost him most dearly of all."

"You mean paying for scalps?" Martin asked.

"Yes, it was a bad policy. The irony is that this morning I bought out my brother's interest in the ranch and he had agreed to return to Mexico. I had hoped to make a treaty with Cuchillo and the other raiders who have stolen our cattle, killed our vaqueros, raped our women. Now it's too late."

"Too late?" Martin asked.

"When the Apaches came, they caught us by surprise," Benito said. "My brother Jaime was killed in the first volley of arrows."

"Your brother is . . ." Martin searched the man's face for some sign of grief.

"My brother is dead," Benito said.

13

⊹

BENITO AGUILAR STOOD there like an embattled general surveying the battlefield as the dead and wounded were carried away. Martin and Juanito, locked in the silence of their own thoughts, followed his gaze, wondering which of the dead was Jaime Aguilar.

"My brother is in the house," Benito said as if reading their thoughts. "Come, you must be hungry after your journey. Have you tasted the Mexican aguardiente? Perhaps you would like a glass of tepache before you eat."

Without waiting for a reply, Benito walked toward the house, Baron and Salazar following. They heard the sound of shovels ringing from somewhere beyond the house and watched the men at the barn douse the last of the fire on the roof. The air was filled with the sour smell of burnt wet wood; tendrils of smoke still rose from half a dozen hot spots.

A light breeze rose up out of the mesquite groves,

stiffened into a wind that had the taint of blood threaded through its zephyrs like vagrant wisps of crimson twine. It swirled around the dead and carried the scent of death into the upper currents of air, where the buzzards were already circling like dark paper kites on invisible tethers.

Martin was surprised to see that the main house was made of logs and adobe mud, with rifle holes cut in the logs and window shutters. There was powder blow-back embedded in the adobe like sprinkled pepper. The house was cool and low-ceilinged, but high enough so that Martin did not have to lower his head. Benito led them to a dining room that was spacious, windowless. Beyond, through a doorway, Martin could see part of the kitchen. He smelled corn tortillas and beans, the enticing aroma of beef. His stomach coiled with the pangs of hunger.

"Sit down, gentlemen. I will have some tepache brought to you and give orders to the cook."

Benito walked through the kitchen doorway as Juanito and Martin sat at the large oak table, polished and smoothed and varnished to a high sheen. Religious icons—bultos and santos—stood on small shelves bolted to the walls. There was a large china cabinet and a small bar on one side of the room, extra chairs stacked in the corner. The chairs were wood, covered with soft leather and stuffing, high-backed, baronial.

"Very nice," Martin said.

"Elegant."

"Too bad about Benito's brother."

"It is sad."

"It was that damned bounty on scalps, Juanito."

"Perhaps."

Martin snorted. Just then a woman arrived carrying an olla, which she set on a woven mat in the center of the table. Another woman came in bearing a tray and glasses. Benito's voice could be heard speaking Spanish from the kitchen. The two women left and Benito entered the room a few seconds later.

"It will only be a few moments," he said, "before the food will be brought to us."

"You are very gracious, Don Benito," Juanito said. "We are humbled by your hospitality."

"Uh, yes," Martin added. "Nice of you, under the circumstances."

"We will bury my brother tomorrow. Tonight those who wish to pay their respects will come by and say good-bye to Jaime. There will be wine and music and remembrances."

"We're very sorry," Martin said. "Didn't mean to come at a bad time."

"Let us have a drink," Benito said. "Then we will talk while we wait for the food."

Benito sat down at the head of the table, poured tepache from the sweating olla. He filled three glasses, passed two to his visitors. "The olla keeps the tepache cool. You will like the taste of peach in the beer.

"Many years ago, my brother Jaime had a dream. He obtained a Spanish land grant for many thousands of hectares of land. He felt rich and he was rich. But he did not realize that so much land comes with much responsibility. It was very hard for him, though many of us tried to help."

"Too much land?" Martin asked.

"The land came with Apaches and Comanches. Mexican raiders riding over the border to catch horses and steal cattle."

"But you have many men here on the rancho," Juanito said.

"Too many for the amount of land we're able to manage. Not enough for all of it."

Martin liked the taste of the tepache. The pineapple made it sweet. The beer gave it a buzz. He was very hungry after a couple of swallows and he could still smell the food cooking.

"I came here to look for land I might buy," Martin said. Juanito glared at him. "But I realize this is not the time to talk business."

"There will be time to talk of land," Benito said. "There is much of it in Texas."

"Have you been here long?" Martin asked.

"Jaime came here ten years ago. I have been here for three. I visited before, but he never asked me to stay until just before Texas gained its independence."

"What changed his mind?"

"He had been having trouble with the Apaches and Comanches raided him now and then. He began to lose men. Then he started paying a bounty on Indian scalps. That was a very unwise decision. Just after he put that order into effect, something happened that aged Jaime overnight."

"What was that?" Juanito asked.

"One day some Apaches sneaked up and kidnapped one of the vaqueros. They made a lot of noise when they left. They tortured the man so that he screamed. And he kept screaming. This man was the brother of Jaime's wife. Jaime and this man were very good friends."

"They must have wanted him to scream," Martin said.

"*Si*, they wanted Jaime to follow them."

"Why?" Martin asked.

"You will soon see."

"It was a trick?" Juanito asked.

"Yes, in a way," Benito said. "They took this man, whose name was Federico Delgado, to a place where small trees grew. Young trees. Before my brother Jaime got there, they stripped Federico naked and bent two trees down. They tied one of his legs to one tree, his other leg to another. They tied the trees down with a single rope. As Jaime and I rode up with some other men, Cuchillo cut the rope that held down the two trees."

Two women brought the food in and Benito spoke no more while they were serving lunch. After they left, their host passed the plates to them first before taking any for himself.

Martin helped himself to hot flour tortillas, carne asada, beans, salsa casera, gazpacho. One of the women brought a bottle of red wine and glasses. Benito poured glasses for the three of them.

"Are you married?" Martin asked Aguilar.

"My wife is bathing Jaime. Her name is Pilar. Jaime's widow is also preparing her husband for burial."

"I'm sorry," Martin said. "I didn't know."

"That is all right."

"You were talking about Delgado," Juanito reminded Aguilar.

"Yes. When Cuchillo cut the rope, the trees swung back upright very fast, in opposite directions. They ripped Federico's legs, split him up the middle with much force. His screams were horrible. I had to dispatch him with a pistol ball."

"You shot him?" Martin asked.

"It was necessary," Benito said, biting into a fatly rolled tortilla loaded with meat and beans. "No one could stand the screaming. We could not sew the man back up with all the sinew or thread in the world."

Martin shuddered as he thought about it.

"Jaime was never the same after that. He was mad at the Apaches all the time. He was especially mad at Cuchillo for killing Federico so horribly."

"So he put a bounty on Indian scalps," Martin said.

"And he formed hunting parties to go out and kill Apaches. He was a little bit crazy, I think."

"Were the Apaches just attacking this rancho?" Martin asked. "I mean, did Cuchillo just hate your brother?"

"No, it has always been this way. From the time San Antonio was built, the Apaches raided the missions and the farms and ranchos of settlers. There were several tribes to blame: the Lipan, the Mescalero and the Natagés. They brought terror to all the roads leading from San Antonio to the Rio Grande, to Los Adaes and to La Bahía."

"But people came to Texas and settled here," Juanito pointed out.

"Only the most brave," Benito said.

"I thought there were soldiers in San Antonio," Juanito said. "Did they not fight the Apaches, protect the settlers?" He sipped his soup. Martin washed a swallow of food down with a drink of the red wine.

"The soldiers went out sometimes and killed Apaches in their rancherías. But mostly they defended San Antonio. The Apaches are like hornets. When you come near them, they attack and attack, they sting and sting. That is what Jaime had forgotten, I think."

"Then there will be more trouble with Cuchillo," Martin said.

"As long as there are Apaches, there will be trouble."

"As I told you, I want to buy some land here, raise cattle," Martin said.

"Yes, I remember."

"Will you sell me some of your land?"

Benito belched and sat back in his chair, patted his belly. He picked up his glass of wine and drank heartily before answering.

"Do you have money?"

"Some. I would have to pay on it."

"Yes, of course."

"Would that be all right with you?"

"I am sure we can come to terms. But first, you must see the land, live on it. See what it gives you. Think about what you can give it. It would not be wise of me to sell you land that you do not know. Even I do not know all of it."

"But you know what you own."

"Yes. I have a plot map that tells the name of the ranchos. I will make you a copy."

Martin tried to hold back his excitement. Although he had not eaten much, he was too nervous to eat more, and the wine was making him drowsy. The thought of owning his own land ballooned in his mind. He would not even ask Aguilar about the taxes because he did not care if they were low or high. Nor did the cost of the land shrink his dreams. Somehow he would pay for it, pay for it all, if he had to work from sunup to sunset.

The women came back and cleared the table.

"Aguardiente," Aguilar said, *"y vasos limpios, por favor."*

The woman brought a bottle of brandy and fresh glasses.

"Now you must taste the hospitality of the old country, of Spain," Benito said. He poured aguardiente into three glasses and held his up in a toast. "May you have much money and time to spend it."

Martin swallowed a mouthful of the brandy. It bit hard and sharp into his throat, swarmed into his stomach like wildfire. The fumes streamed up into his nostrils and it seemed his brain became enveloped in a warm rosy cloud. Oddly, the brandy seemed to settle his stomach, make the food he had eaten more palatable.

"Good," he said, and Benito smiled at the young American.

"I think you will someday make a fine rancher," Aguilar said. "If you can take the strong drink, you can take what Texas may bring to you."

Martin didn't know exactly what Aguilar meant, but he didn't care. He had the Mexican's blessing and that was enough for him. He swallowed more of the aguardiente and dreamed of owning land and cattle and fine horses that were like his own flesh and blood.

Pilar Aguilar wore a black dress with lace borders. She had a sleepy left eye and Martin felt its piercing gaze as she curtsied and muttered something in Spanish.

"She says she is pleased to meet you," Benito translated.

"I am pleased to meet her," Martin said.

Pilar was a dark-skinned woman of proud bearing. Though small, she appeared tall in the black dress with the mantilla as a crown. She said more words to her husband, then left the room. It was only after she left that Martin realized she was pregnant. Standing still, she had appeared normal, but when she walked, she leaned backward and he realized she was carrying her baby high.

"She says to tell you that Victoria, my brother's wife, is too grief-stricken to meet you right now, but she wishes to speak to you alone after her husband is buried."

"To me?" Martin asked.

"Yes. She has been watching you from beyond the curtain there."

Martin looked around quickly. He understood then. Jaime Aguilar was laid out in a casket for all to see who came by, but they had partitioned off part of the room with a heavy curtain. The immediate family sat behind it so they could see the faces of the mourners without being seen themselves.

The procession of people paying their respects seemed endless, but there was lots of food to eat and strong drink for the men. The room was filled with smoke from pipes and cigars and the little cigarillos some of the women smoked.

Juanito took Martin aside. "Want to take a little walk and breathe some fresh air?"

"Yes, there's too much death in this room."

"It's not the dead, but the mourners who make you sad. Those left behind."

"I think you're right."

"I will tell Benito we are leaving."

Martin felt uncomfortable with so many strangers and the man he had come to see lying in a casket, his eyes closed, his features frozen in death. When Juanito tapped him on the arm, he was ready to leave.

"How long will that go on in there?" Martin asked when they had walked well away from the house.

"Most of the night, probably." Even as they spoke, riders called to the night pickets as they rode in from the other ranchos and the corrals filled up with horses.

"Why do you think the widow wants to talk to me?" Martin asked.

"I do not know. But, it was Jaime we came to see, and now that he is dead, his widow may wish to discuss business with you."

"I thought Benito—"

"Benito was only being polite. I think Victoria Aguilar owns all this land and he will only work for her."

"But—"

"I do not know the terms of the will, of course, but I think you must be very nice and respectful to the widow of Jaime Aguilar."

"Well, sure, Juanito, but I don't know how to deal with no woman."

Juanito laughed. They stopped on a rise beyond earshot of the pickets or anyone outside the house who might overhear them. "Women are very good at business. Especially widows. They know the value of the land, the work that went into it. She will carry out her husband's wishes, Martin. I am sure that they discussed you. And I am also sure that Jaime wanted to get away from this place before it killed him."

Martin and Juanito stood well behind the pack of mourners at the grave site. But they could hear the women weeping and sobbing. Their exclamations of faith and grief whisked past Martin and Juanito on the Texas wind that blew across the plain that day. When Jaime Aguilar was lowered into the ground and dirt thrown onto his wooden coffin, Martin breathed a long sigh of gratitude that it was over. He didn't know which was worse, the death or the mourning afterward that seemed to drag the grief out of even the most hardened mortal until it was almost a palpable thing.

That afternoon, he was summoned to the house at Victoria Aguilar's request. He had been impatient all day to set out and find the man Benito had told him he must see. Martin and Juanito had been given a small jacal for the night. There were sleeping mats on the dirt floor, a couple of kegs covered with cowhide for chairs. The rats kept them awake at night; the scorpions and a sullen tarantula kept them company during the day.

"Wish me luck, Juanito."

"You will have luck."

"Good or bad?"

Juanito laughed. "Whichever you desire," he said cryptically.

"Ah, that is very comforting. I'm as nervous as a cat."

"That is good. It will keep you on your toes."

Neither of them had gotten a good look at Victoria Aguilar at the funeral or at the burial. Her face was veiled in black. Martin thought she looked like a strange bird with the high mantilla, the lace dress. Two men had braced her against falling or swooning, but she had neither stumbled nor fainted and Martin gave her credit for that.

Martin slicked down his hair and straightened his cap as he set off for the house. A servant let him inside and directed him to a dark parlor he had not seen before. The beaded doorway rattled as he went into the room.

Victoria Aguilar sat in a rocking chair next to a win-

dow with the curtain only partly open. The sun
streamed through just enough to backlight her profile.

"*Siéntase,*" she said, her voice strangely gruff and
musical.

"Uh, ma'am, I don't speak Spanish. Begging your
pardon."

"Take a seat," she said.

Martin groped for a chair nearby. It was placed so
that he could see her face clearly when he sat down.
She was a beautiful, haughty woman, with an aquiline
nose, dark flashing eyes, a delicate throat, features that
seemed chiseled out of grainless wood. She was still
wearing the black clothes of mourning, but not the
mantilla. Her black hair was wrapped tightly in a bun
that lay against her neck like a loaf of rye bread. Martin thought she must have very long hair.

"Thank you, ma'am," Martin said.

"You came to see my husband about buying some
land from us." She spoke perfect English, but with a
strong accent. She made the words sound almost lyri-
cal.

"Yes, ma'am, I did. Uh, I'm sorry about . . . about
what happened and all."

"You will not deal with Benito, my worthless
brother-in-law," she said.

"No'm. I mean, if you don't want me to."

"I own all the land now, young man."

"Yes'm."

"My husband wanted to sell his holdings, but I do
not."

"You don't?"

"Not all of it. This is Aguilar land. It has my husband's blood on it. What Benito told you to do is what
you must do. You must ride through the land, you
must live in it and look at everything and see if you
want to settle here. It is a very dangerous land."

"Yes'm, I guess it is."

"If you still want to buy land from me, then we will

talk about it. There is too much for me to manage, but I want to keep the largest portion for my family."

"That would be just fine, ma'am. I wouldn't need much."

"You will need a great deal if you are to . . ."—she groped for the words—"to make a fine ranch and raise a family."

Martin nodded. He was fascinated by Victoria Aguilar, surprised at her strength just after her husband had been killed by Apaches. She seemed to be made of iron, despite her delicate appearance, her small, thin hands, her fragile neck.

"Is that what you want? A family?"

"Why, yes'm, I reckon I do."

"Then you must find a good strong woman to help you. She must be of your race or you will be unhappy and she will be unhappy."

"Yes'm."

"Can you keep the secret?" she asked abruptly, leaning forward and whispering.

"Why, sure, ma'am."

"Then listen to me. And do not tell anyone of this, even your friend the Argentine."

"I sure won't."

"If something happens to me before you return, I will make sure that land is set aside for you to purchase. Do you understand?"

"Well, sure, but I hope nothing happens to you. I know it won't."

"I will draw up my will in a few days. Did you meet Pilar, Benito's wife?"

"Yes'm."

"She is with child."

"I know."

"That child is my husband's. Benito cannot father children. He was in an accident. I want that child to inherit the Aguilar rancho, the Rocking A brand. It is with the child you must deal, not the father."

"But I don't see how—"

"It will all be arranged. Someday my husband's child will grow up and all of this will be his or hers. Unless you are able to pay for all the land at once, you will have to do business with this person. Do you understand me?"

"Yes'm."

"I do not trust Benito. He is a weakling. He plays the grand don, but he is, how do you say, without spine?"

"Spineless, yes'm."

"Spineless. Ambitious, greedy. My husband was strong. He put the bounty on the Apaches. Benito is stupid. I will keep the bounty, despite what Benito has tried to do."

"I don't know about that. Seems it cost you dear, losing your husband and all."

"We will beat the Apache. They will not take us away from our land."

Martin did not know what to say. He was confounded by Victoria Aguilar's fervency. He wondered if she had run the ranch while Jaime was still alive.

"Remember my words. If you want to buy Aguilar land, you must know the truth of what I say. That child in Pilar's belly is my husband's flesh and blood. He or she will inherit all that my husband owned. Not Benito and not Pilar."

"I'll remember, ma'am."

Then the woman rocked back in her chair and smiled at Martin. She spoke to him in a normal tone of voice.

"You must call me Victoria from now on, Señor Baron."

"Sure," he said, but could not bring himself to say her name.

"Go now. Go with God. I hope to see you when you return in a few months."

"I hope so too, m . . . ah, Victoria."

And she smiled again, but it was not a real smile. It was the smile of a woman who had triumphed in battle and stood alone in victory while all around her lay bloody and dead.

14

✝

BENITO AGUILAR CAME to the jacal where Juanito and Martin were staying just after Martin blew out the lamp.

"*Abre la luz,*" he said softly.

"Huh?" Martin gasped.

"He wants you to light the lamp," Juanito said.

Martin struck sparks off a flint, blew on the warm wick. The glow spread and the flame erupted. He eased the chimney back down and hung the lamp on a hook hanging from a ceiling branch of wood.

"I have given you four good horses in exchange for those of the Apache Cuchillo," Benito said. Martin thought he looked very sad or angry. His face was long and he appeared to be weary.

"We thank you," Juanito said.

"I have come to talk and to give you a letter from the widow Victoria."

"A letter?" Martin asked.

"It is for a friend, an American. He will help you, I think."

"Please thank Mrs. Aguilar for me," Martin said.

Benito gave Baron the letter and a sheaf of papers. "Here are the maps of the Aguilar ranchos I promised you and directions for your journey tomorrow."

"Thanks." Martin looked at the letter.

"It is addressed to Samuel Robbins," Benito said. "Do not open it."

Martin saw that the letter was sealed in wax and bore the imprint of the Rocking A ranch. The wax smelled fresh.

"I won't." Martin gave the letter to Juanito. The envelope was deckle-edged and the paper was thick and heavy. SAMUEL ROBBINS was scrawled in large letters across the front.

Benito sat on one of the kegs. He rubbed his hands together as if washing them. For a long time he said nothing. Martin and Juanito exchanged looks. Juanito signaled for Martin to wait. Martin shrugged. Finally Benito looked up. He stared at Martin for a long time.

"She told you, did she not? My brother's wife. Told you all about me."

"I am not at liberty to say what Mrs. Aguilar and I spoke about," Martin said.

"Very well. I will not question you. I would just tell you that all things are not as they seem. I am sure she did not tell you the whole truth."

Martin said nothing.

"I wish you both a good journey," Benito said, and abruptly stood up. "*Buen viaje,* Juanito."

"*Gracias,*" Juanito said.

"Someday, perhaps, you will hear the whole story of my brother and me. And the truth about his wife, the widow Victoria. Good night." Benito left without another word.

"Well, if that ain't the damnedest thing," Martin said. "I wonder what that was all about."

"Perhaps it had to do with your conversation with Victoria Aguilar, eh?"

"I can't talk about that. She made me promise not to."

"Well, my friend, I have been talking, too."

"To Mrs. Aguilar?"

"No. To the vaqueros who work on this ranch. They are afraid of Victoria Aguilar. They fear her as they never did her husband."

"Why?"

"They say she is more cruel than the Apaches."

"I don't believe that. She seemed like a refined lady to me."

Juanito's mouth twisted in the faintest of smiles. "Perhaps it is as Benito said, appearances can be deceiving."

"I can't believe you listen to gossip, especially about a fine woman like Mrs. Aguilar."

"The ears have no discrimination."

"What's that mean?"

"I listen. I do not comment."

"Good, 'cause I won't listen to it. Let's get some shut-eye. We'll be riding off early, on our own."

"I know," said Juanito. "It will be good to leave this place of death."

Martin paused before blowing out the lamp again. "Yeah. There's something about this place that gets under your skin." He lifted the chimney and blew out the lamp.

"Death," Juanito said as the room went dark.

Martin watched the land light up and take shape as the dawn spread across the sky, winking out the stars, paling the black of night to the blue of morning. His blood tingled with the freshness of the land, the clean, brisk air that blew the scent of sage and cactus to his

nostrils. It was like watching a magic land suddenly
rising up out of the darkness as if it had never been
there before.

"I feel like I'm really in Texas now," he said to
Juanito.

"It is like leaving a bad port and seeing only the sea
around you."

"Yes, that's what it's like."

Martin Baron liked the horses Benito had traded
them. They were larger than the Indian ponies and responded quicker to the rein. Before they left, Benito
had given both of them spurs and these had taken
some getting used to. He felt their tug when he
walked, but atop his horse, they felt as if they belonged. And when he gently raked the horse's flanks
with both heels, the horses moved faster.

A month later, Martin was still enchanted by the dry
Texas mornings when he watched the stars fade and
the land come to life.

His butt had toughened up and he was no longer
saddle sore at the end of a day. He and Juanito had
roamed the vast Aguilar rancho, finding all the mark-
ers indicated on the maps Benito had given them.

Martin was amazed at the size of the ranchos and
wondered how one man could ever tend such vast
acreages, even with help. The first rancho they saw
was called La Plata; it was laced with creeks and brush
so thick he wondered if he and Juanito were not the
first to ride through it. But he envisioned clearing it
and being able to see for miles across its breadth.

They found La Paloma and noticed that it was sep-
arated from the other ranchos by unmarked land, thousands of acres of it. Martin wondered who owned the
lands in between. Indeed, the Aguilar holdings looked
like a patchwork quilt on the big map that showed all
the ranchos. The Rocking A main rancho was called
Palos Verdes, probably from all the mesquite trees that
had been stripped of branches and leaves to make

poles for the corrals and fences. Martin had lost count
of the trees he had climbed. He and Juanito were able
to see vast distances only by crawling up in the live
oaks and staring all around them at endless vistas of
mesquite, endless llanos and smaller savannahs.

And always above them was the enormous sky.
Across its broad seas sailed hawks and buzzards and
doves and blackbirds and eagles and bright white
clouds like ancient galleons slowly making their way
across calm blue waters.

Martin felt the changes in him at every night camp
and dawn strike, on every ride into new country, at
every sign that an Aguilar rider had passed that way
before them. He looked for deer in the mornings and
was seldom disappointed. Sometimes they heard
turkeys fly to roost in the oaks, heard them call in the
mornings and disappear without a trace before they
could be sighted. He and Juanito shot and ate rabbit,
deer, dove and ducks; quail they brought down with
slingshots before the birds could take flight.

"I love this country," Martin said when they had
been six weeks in the wilderness of the Aguilar holdings.

"Have you found the place you want to set your
house yet?"

"No."

"Do you know what you are looking for?"

"I don't know. Sometimes it seems like there's so
much of it that you want and so little that you can
have."

Juanito smiled. They had stopped at a seeping
spring where birds drank and flew away at their approach. Time, for them, had disappeared into another
dimension, and they no longer tracked it or marked its
passing. Each day seemed endless; each night brought
a calm to them such as they had known only on clear
starry nights asea. When it rained, they took shelter in

the mesquite and washed the sand fleas from their hair, filled their canteens and scrubbed the grime from their necks.

"You will know the place when you find it," Juanito said. It was not a question, but one of the enigmatic oracles that Martin had come to accept from his Argentine friend.

"Yes, I will know it. It will have a hill and a place for a garden. I will clear it and plant trees where I want them. It will have water and a long view of the grazing fields."

Juanito laughed.

"You have seen it already, Martin."

"Yes, a thousand times in my mind. But I have not seen it yet."

And so they rode and looked and breathed each day in and out of their lungs without hurry or care. Martin became as brown of face as Juanito, and they might have been brothers except for Martin's hair, which was lighter, and his eyes, which were hazel-brown, flecked with gold, while Juanito's were brown.

"I wonder how many more springs there are around here," Martin said suddenly.

Juanito shrugged.

"Let's ride around here, make some big circles, see what we find."

"We might as well."

"I'll meet you back here in a couple of hours."

"You want to ride alone?"

"Yes, I feel something. I don't know what it is. We might be near the kind of place I'm looking for."

"Good. When you find this place, there is something else you must look for."

"What is that?"

"A place nearby where you may wish to build a town."

"A town?"

"Yes. Someday people may want to come here and live and work for you. They cannot all stay on the ranch."

"You are a pretty smart man, Juanito. Sometimes you plumb knock me out of my socks."

"Is that so?"

"A town, you say. Well, I will look for a place to build a town then."

Juanito smiled. *"Bueno,"* he said.

"Adios, amigo." Martin had been learning Spanish, asking Juanito the names of the things they encountered each day. At night he practiced, and Juanito thought Martin might one day be fluent. Martin had not yet put it all together, but he was eager to learn and was absorbing a great deal of information. His vocabulary was extensive and he was now trying to learn the verb forms, especially the irregular ones, so that he could converse intelligently with the Argentine.

"Hasta luego," Juanito replied, and the two men rode off in opposite directions.

Martin rode in a straight line for a mile or two until he encountered a maze of longhorn cattle tracks leading to the southwest. He followed the tracks through the mesquite, knowing he was on the trail of a sizable herd. He reasoned that the cattle would go to water and grass and safe bedding for the night.

He followed the trail slowly, knowing it was fresh. He did not want to startle the herd from its intended destination. The trail meandered and he saw where some of the herd wandered off and then returned sometime later.

An hour or so later, he came to a broad plain, and in the distance he saw a hill on which trees grew. And the land shimmered in the sunlight, bathed in a vaporous haze that danced with shining lakes that appeared and disappeared, mirages that hypnotized him as the land opened up and he saw the cattle in the distance, nearly a hundred grazing, lying in the shade of live and post oaks.

The plain was dotted with potholes, small ponds, a couple of lagoons. Despite the dryness, Martin knew, there was water underneath the soil, and that meant he could water stock and grow gardens and trees.

Martin rode straight for the small hill. The cattle did not spook when they saw him—at least not right away, for his course led him away from them on a slant. He came to the hill and rode around it and atop it and dismounted and sat in the shade of an oak while his horses grazed. Nearby there grew a kind of palm that he had never seen before. There were five or six of them. Their leaves stuck out in all directions so that their tops looked like the tops of dandelions, perfect spheres. He watched the sun dapple his hands with shadows and listened to the susurrant ripple of the grasses as they bent to the light breeze.

He looked around him and envisioned a house, a small one at first, then added onto it until it sprawled from the hill onto the plain. He filled in the empty spaces with barns and stables. On the far reaches of his gaze, he built pastures and grassed them over. He fashioned corrals and stock tanks, drilled wells and built windmills.

He saw horses and cattle dotting the plain, grazing peacefully. He saw an orchard and a garden in bloom. Wagons trundled down crooked roads and men waved from the fields. He built a pond with ducks floating serenely on its still, mirrored surface, and he created geese that strutted regally past the barn in single file, their long necks stretched out, their tails waggling as they waddled to their own pond beyond the pigpen. For good measure he added a place where goats grazed on the greenest grass he had ever seen.

The longhorns stopped grazing suddenly and all seemed to stare in his direction. Martin waved at them, and they wheeled and rumbled away into the distance like a phantom herd that he had only imagined.

"This is the place where I will build my home," he said to the horses. "I will call it La Loma de Sombra. That's Spanish I learned from Juanito. *Loma* means hill and *sombra* means shadow. Shadow Hill. For the trees that grow here. And I will plant more and they will give me shade in the summer, a place for birds to nest and give me song when I awake in the morning. Yes, sir, boys, this will be my home someday."

And after a time of musing and daydreaming, Martin remounted his horse and led the other one away from La Loma de Sombra and rode a wide circle and saw a place where a town might be built, for there were creeks and gamma grass thick as clover. He looked at his compass and at the sun falling away in the sky and knew that he had lost all track of time.

He set a course to return to the place where he and Juanito had parted company and spurred his horse to a brisk gait. He had been gone much longer than he had intended and he hoped Juanito would not worry and still be there waiting for him.

He figured he had ridden almost ten miles to La Loma de Sombra and nearly that far to the town site. But by riding straight back, cutting through the center of the circle, he would cut down the length of his ride back.

But when Martin passed by La Loma de Sombra, he heard his name called.

"*Hola,* Martin."

There, leaning against a tree, his horses tied to another, Juanito Salazar waved a hand in the air.

"Well, I'll be damned," Martin said and turned his horse toward his friend.

"This is a good place," Juanito said when Martin rode up.

"How did you find it?"

"I followed your tracks."

"But I thought you were going to scout in the other direction."

Juanito laughed. "I started out to do that," he said. "But then I realized that there was no need."

"Oh, how did you figure that out?"

"You said you knew what you were looking for. I did not know what you were looking for, so such a search would be useless. No?"

"You're right, Juanito," Martin said, grinning.

"Well, is this the place?"

"Yes. Do you like it?"

"It seems a fine place to build a home."

"I call it La Loma de Sombra."

"That is a good name, my friend. And did you also find a place to build a town?"

"Just over yonder," Martin said, pointing. "It's got water and it's flat and big enough to plat out a township, I think."

"Well, now we must measure and write it all down and you must see how much Señora Aguilar wants for it."

"How much do you think she will want?"

Juanito shrugged. "I do not know. But whatever it is, you must bargain with her. I would think that the more land you buy, the cheaper it will be."

"Really?"

"Perhaps when we talk to this Samuel Robbins, he will be able to help you establish a good price."

"Well, I hope it's not more than two bits an acre."

"That would be too much."

Martin scratched his head. He had saved a considerable amount of money over the years, but he would need more to tend the land, to hire help, to bring in lumber and buy hammers and nails and saws. His stomach swirled with worry.

"Maybe we should just ride back to the Rocking A rancho and find out what Victoria Aguilar wants for this land."

"I doubt if she has ever seen it. But it is part of her holdings."

"Yes, I know."

"I think we should see this Samuel first."

Martin sighed. He stepped down from his horse. The sun was lower on the horizon. This would be a good place to spend the night. Give him a better feel for the land. There was a spring no more than a hundred yards away, feeding the roots of the trees that grew there.

"I'll sleep on it," he said.

"I think that is wise," Juanito said, nodding in agreement.

Whitewing doves crisscrossed the vast llano at dusk, when the western sky was a dark purple bruise laced with ocher and goldenrod. Juanito built a small fire and they filled their rifles with small shot and brought down doves, gutted them out and packed them in moist clay. Juanito placed them under coals and turned them until they could smell the aroma of the cooked meat.

"A fine night," Martin said.

"You sound like a man who is very content."

"I am. This is grand country."

"It is hard country, too."

"Yes, I know. I think that's what I like about it. Its wildness."

"Maybe that is your heart talking."

"I will tame it."

"Your heart?"

"The land, Juanito, the land."

So they ate and talked and basked in the glow of the setting sun and listened to the whistle of wings as the doves flew back to their roosts in the brasada. After they took to their bedrolls, Martin stayed awake a long time, staring up at the stars, dreaming of a roof over his head.

The sound of Juanito's snoring put Martin to sleep

after a while, and he slept dreamless and soundly until dawn.

The two men did not eat breakfast, but they drank coffee and each smoked a pipe. There was the tang of the sea on the morning air and it brought a thrill to Martin's heart. He was anxious to measure the land, stake it out, learn more about it.

"How do you want to do this, Juanito?"

"We can use compass directions and estimate the square mileage. I am used to working in hectares, but I think I can figure it out."

"Good. I will show you the land I want for a ranch and a town."

So they rode the wide plain all day and found numerous springs and water holes. They were amazed at the number of wild cattle they saw at these watering places, and the game that drank at them as well. Juanito made notations in his ship's log, using the back pages of the book he had brought.

At the end of the day they were far south of La Loma de Sombra, having traversed a huge section of land that Martin could not even estimate. He was not used to measuring land by riding a horse, but by walking off rods and footage on acreage, so he quadrupled every estimate and knew that he was probably way off in his figuring.

"Well, Juanito, what did we cover today? A thousand acres? Ten thousand?"

Juanito laughed. He opened his book and did some arithmetic. His scribbles made a rustling sound. They held their horses at a spring that made a small pond in an opening where the brush had been trampled back over eons by cattle and wild game.

"From where you stand on the hill with the trees," Juanito said, "there is a square of about a hundred thousand acres, I think. In every direction."

"How did you figure that?"

"I took the longest measure and multiplied it by the four corners."

"Hmph, that's what I was trying to do. But I was using walking feet."

"I was using kilometers."

"And what about to here?"

"Another hundred thousand acres or more."

"So we bargain for two hundred thousand acres."

"Do you want some advice?"

"Sure," Martin said.

"Buy a hundred and fifty thousand acres, and lease eight hundred fifty thousand acres more. Then you would have a million acres."

Martin whistled. "A million acres? I can't even count that high."

"There is much land here. Empty land. Worthless land until it produces something. The Aguilar family would not even miss a million acres."

"You sound as if you've been figuring the land ever since we left the Aguilar rancho."

"I have," Juanito said, smiling. "I looked at their maps and at all the places we have been. There must be over three million acres that is just Aguilar land. That is too much for one family."

"Maybe a million acres is too much for me."

"It will be at first. But later on, you may be able to take on more. If you control it, you own it. Later on, you can buy the land with money you make so that it will not be difficult to acquire."

Martin took off his cap, scratched his head. The dream was growing bigger. A million acres. He would never live to see it all in his lifetime.

A million acres. He looked at the surrounding mesquite, the small pond. How much mesquite on a million acres? How many such ponds and water holes and springs? Was there any limit to what a man could do with such a large amount of land?

Suddenly Martin could see it all, every square inch

of a million acres. Did he dare to dream so big? His stomach swirled with the thrill of owning so much land.

"Damn," he said, "a million acres." And even as he said it, Martin liked the sound of it.

15

✛

MARTIN DREW IN a deep breath and found his voice. "What makes you think Victoria Aguilar will let me have so much land?"

"There are many reasons," Juanito said. "I think they need money. The Apaches are costing them much. If the señora sold you only fifty thousand acres, they would spend the money right away. She will feel better about selling a hundred or a hundred and fifty thousand acres because that will not cost her much land. She has much. If you lease more, then she will have an income each year. With this money she can make up for losses and improve her stock, her rancho. She will believe that you will never be able to pay for the land you are leasing, so she will always have a yearly income."

"What if I can't buy the rest?"

"Then you have not lost much. But if you want the land, you will find a way to pay for it. That is the way the spirit works, my friend. That is the way the world and the universe works. There is always plenty of everything."

Martin snorted. "There you go again, Juanito. Taking off in a different direction."

Juanito only smiled.

But Martin's blood ran hot with the thought of so much land, so much opportunity.

Samuel Robbins had dug a deep cave in the side of the hill, shored it up with thick beams. The cave was well underground. Inside, hanging from beams and stacked on shelves were cheeses made from goat's milk, in baskets woven of cheesecloth, aging in the dark coolness. He was a stocky, jowly man, florid of face, with muttonchop whiskers, complete with matching bushy eyebrows, that only emphasized the squareness of his massive jaws. He grunted as he trundled around the cave, checking the cheeses, smacking his fat lips in satisfaction.

When he emerged from the cave, he blinked in the lucid brightness of the sun, like some marmot emerging from a winter's den at first thaw. He wore patched clothes and patched boots and carried a pistol in his belt, a ball pouch, with spare flints and leather, in his pants pocket, and powder in a tin tucked in his shirt pocket.

The cave was guarded by trees he had planted for that purpose, and he stood in their shade until his eyes adjusted to the light, then stepped out into the sun toward the house. Goats bleated as he approached, the billies looking at him like satyrs guarding their flocks. Sam's hands were gnarled and cracked from milking, scabbed over with mottled patches of mordant skin; they were powerful hands that could crack walnuts between thumb and forefinger.

"Señor, someone is coming," said a Mexican who stepped out from the long barn where Samuel milked the goats.

"Apaches or Mexicans, Lorenzo?"

"I do not know," Lorenzo Machado said, shading his eyes. "They are strangers."

"You get that double-barrel and hide yourself."

"*Sí, patrón.*"

Lorenzo disappeared inside the barn. Sam heard the rattle of the lock on the old smooth-barreled flinter that was the only weapon Machado could shoot and be fairly certain of hitting something. He was piss poor with a rifle and not much better with a scattergun.

Robbins stepped beyond the barn to view the strangers for himself. He shaded his eyes with a craggy hand and stood in plain sight so the riders could see him. They did not look threatening, but one never knew in this coastal region of the Matagordos. The riders looked tired and they were leading pack-horses.

"Chato, *ven,*" he said, and a black-and-white dog sleeping under the front porch of the house came running to his side. "Chato, *búscalo.*"

The dog's ears perked to sharp cones and he turned his head until he saw the riders. Then he streaked away in a beeline to intercept them, barking in a rapid staccato.

Men appeared out of nowhere—stepping from behind haystacks, emerging from the mesquite, riding out from far unseen pastures on horseback—all carrying rifles and machetes. They stepped from jacales bare-chested, sleepy-eyed from their siestas, but armed and ready to fight.

"Now let's see who we have here," Samuel said to himself, stepping over to his porch, where he stood in the shade, knowing his rifle leaned against one of the posts holding up the porch roof.

Martin saw the dog running toward them barking loudly and reined up. "What the hell?"

Juanito stopped his horse a second later, looking

around. There were sheep and cattle in the pastures and suddenly men rose up out of the earth and surrounded them, all carrying weapons, converging on them like a phantom army.

"I hope these men do not shoot first and ask questions later," Juanito said.

"Damned right."

"Let us wait and see what they do."

"I'll wait until by God somebody starts shooting. You got that letter from Victoria Aguilar handy?"

"I have it," Juanito said.

"It might save our lives."

The barking dog ran around them in circles, first one way, then another, as if holding the two riders in place until the men with rifles could come up and put them under submission.

"Nice dog," Martin said. The dog only barked louder and more often. He fingered the trigger guard on his rifle, but did not lift it from his lap. His palms turned slick with sweat as he waited for one of the men to come near and ask their business.

Then a man stepped out from the porch. He was unarmed. He beckoned to them and called to the dog.

"Chato, *ven!*" Samuel yelled. The dog turned quickly and romped back to the house. The men in the fields held their position. None came near.

"Let's ride on up. Maybe that's Robbins," Martin said.

"I think that is what he wants us to do."

Martin and Juanito rode slowly toward the house. To Martin, it seemed that it took them an hour to reach the porch from a couple of hundred yards away. All the men with rifles made him nervous. But at least the dog had stopped barking. It lay at its master's feet, tongue lolling, sides heaving.

"Are you Mr. Samuel Robbins?" Martin asked when they drew near.

"I am. Who might you be?"

Martin told him who they were. "I have a letter from Mrs. Aguilar addressed to you, sir."

"Light down, then. I'll have a look at the letter." Robbins then turned to Machado and spoke to him in Spanish. "I told Lorenzo to take care of your horses. He will water and feed them after he unsaddles them."

"Thank you, sir," Martin said. Juanito hadn't said a word.

Martin and Juanito stepped down from their saddles and handed the reins and trailing ropes to Lorenzo, who led them away toward the barn. Martin's legs were still quivering from the ride. He rubbed the palms of his hands on his trousers to dry them. His cap was sodden from sweat, and he took it off and wiped his forehead, slicked back his hair.

"Come inside where it's cool," Robbins said. "You have the letter?"

"Juanito?"

Juanito took the letter from inside his shirt. He had wrapped it in oilcloth to keep it dry. He removed it from its wrappings and handed it to Robbins.

"You're not a Mexican," Robbins said.

"I am an Argentine," Juanito said.

"Ah. You have come far."

Juanito said nothing. Martin looked at him, wondering if his friend was suspicious of Robbins. Juanito's face and manner gave no sign.

"*A trabajo,*" Robbins said to one of the men from the field, and Martin heard the Mexicans talking. He watched as they all rode or walked away from the house.

They followed their host inside the house, which was partly frame, partly adobe. It was cool inside. The front room was spartan, but there was handmade furniture, benches and chairs.

"Take a seat," Robbins said. He took the letter over to a window for light and opened it. He read it and folded it back up and stuck it in one of his trouser pockets. Martin and Juanito sat in separate chairs.

Robbins sat on a bench draped with a colorful blanket made of sheep's wool.

"So you want to buy land and raise cattle," Robbins said.

"Yes," Martin replied.

"I've seen many like you come to these parts. Some are good friends, men I've sailed with. You are both sailors."

"Fishermen," Martin said.

Robbins smiled. "Do you have your boat?"

"Yes, we both have boats," Martin said.

"Might be a good way to have an income. I raise mutton and cattle. Not much market for the beef, but some like it."

"We don't want to haul freight," Martin said.

"Ho, and why not?"

"I think we can raise cattle and find markets for the beef. Juanito does, too."

"Juanito doesn't say much, does he? Probably not used to our ways."

"He's a right smart man, Mr. Robbins."

"Call me Sam."

"Sam."

"Well, Juanito, what makes you think you can find people to buy beef when nobody else seems able to?"

Juanito waited a few seconds before answering. He looked Robbins up and down as if measuring his mind and body.

"The Spaniards would not have brought cattle from Andalusia to this country if they did not intend to feed a great many people," Juanito said. "I think this country is ideal for raising very good cattle, maybe the best cattle in the world. If we do that, people will want to buy from us."

"Well spoke," Robbins said. "The Spaniards have

gone and their Andalusian cattle went to seed and mixed with the Mexican blood and now you have all these wild longhorns."

"True. But, we can make our own breeds as we did in Argentina," Juanito said.

"You know anything about cross-breeding?"

"Some. My uncle was a rancher and I worked for him."

"Hmm. Well, boys, we fought Mexico to get this land from them and there are some saying we ought to fight 'em again and give it all back."

"Why is that, Sam?" Martin asked. "Is this not good land?"

"Most of the ranchers here have been raising cattle to feed the Comanches and the Apaches. It's a losing proposition. If I didn't sell mutton and cheese and goats now and then, I'd be cash poor."

"But you live here. You've got land. You raise sheep and goats and cattle."

"I love this land," Robbins said. "I want to live out my days on it if I can hold on. Between the Comanches, the Mexicans and the Apaches, it's damned uncertain how much longer I'll be able to stay."

"You seem well prepared. Those men who work for you will fight, I think," Juanito said.

"Yes. They will fight. They have fought. It's just that we are so close to the border, the Rio Bravo being the line, that the Mexicans and Indians come up here to steal and then run back across. Either we go down and steal from them to even things up, or we go broke. This country is littered with abandoned ranches, ranches built by men like yourselves."

"The Aguilar family seems to be doing all right," Martin said, but without certainty in his voice. He was beginning to wonder if Juanito knew what he was talking about. Maybe they couldn't last here. Maybe nobody could.

"The Aguilars are in trouble. They must sell off

some land to survive. They are tired of fighting Comanches and Lipan and Kickapoo and other tribes
who steal their stock. This letter you brought me asks
me to extend you every hospitality. So it appears she
is willing to sell you land. I was sorry to hear that Victoria's husband was killed. It will be hard for her
now."

"She is afraid her brother-in-law might kill her,"
Martin said. "But Benito treated us very well. I
thought he might run the ranch for her."

Robbins closed his eyes, rubbed his forehead. His
eyebrows undulated like a pair of caterpillars. He
cleared his throat before speaking again.

"Well, that is a very touchy situation. Did she tell
you about Benito?"

"Not much," Martin said. He was bound not to tell
this stranger what Victoria had told him about Benito's wife.

"It is a sad story. Benito and Jaime's father was
something of a tyrant. A grand Spanish don who believed in absolute obedience, loyalty from his sons.
Benito raped a village girl in Chihuahua during the an-
nual fair there. Don Alfonso Aguilar was very upset.
He had Benito gelded."

"Gelded?" Martin asked.

"Yes, castrated like a bull or a ram. That was his
punishment."

Martin swore under his breath. So that explained
why Benito was unable to father children. Then he
must know that his wife's child was not his.

"I can't imagine a father doing that to his son," Martin said. Juanito said nothing.

"Neither can I. But it made for an odd relationship
between the two brothers. I think Jaime felt sorry for
Benito. But Jaime's wife hates him."

"Do you think Benito will murder her?"

Robbins shrugged. "Who knows about these
people? They have customs of their own. Jaime was

just like his father. He treated Benito pretty badly, even though he felt sorry for him. He hated weakness. Like his old man."

"Well, I don't want to get into their family feuds," Martin said. "I just want to buy and lease some land from Victoria."

"You are prepared to make her an offer?"

Martin looked at Juanito, who remained impassive. It was Martin's decision.

"Yes," Martin said.

"All right. You might want to talk to someone before you make your offer, though. Do you know anything about animal husbandry?"

"What's that?" Martin asked. Juanito smiled knowingly.

"Breeding cattle."

"Not much, I guess."

"Well, then you must talk to Larry Darnell. He's doing something with the longhorn stock that you might want to know. Cross-breeding with European breeds."

"Why?"

"He thinks he can produce a better beef animal than the wild stock."

"That is good," Juanito said. "I would like to talk to this man."

"I'll tell you how to get to his ranch," Robbins said.

"How are you doing?" Martin asked. "With your ranching?"

"I, too, have a boat. At certain times of the year I take cheeses and mutton to Galveston, sometimes to New Orleans or other places along the coast, and sell them. It's hard to make a living here right now. And I lost my boat to pirates."

"Pirates?" Martin asked.

"Yes, last time I was out a man named Sam Cullers boarded my boat at gunpoint. He robbed me and stole my boat."

"Can you not get it back?" Juanito asked.

"I wouldn't even try. Cullers is a brigand and he has probably long since sold the boat, spent my money."

Martin shook his head, almost in disbelief. He had learned so much in a short time that he began to wonder if he was doing the right thing in trying to acquire land. It seemed there were few people one could completely trust. But it was no different in New Orleans. He had heard about men like Cullers. But he had never heard of a father castrating his son or a brother fathering a child with his brother's wife.

"So how are you going to take your goods to market?" Juanito asked.

"I was hoping you two might want to make some money. You'll need cash, most likely. You'll want to buy lumber and you'll need staples to get you by. If you hire vaqueros, you'll have wages to pay. Might not be much at first—two bits, four bits a day. Maybe six bits for a top hand."

"We had hoped to start ranching, sell our boats," Martin said.

"I would keep them for a while," Robbins said. "You might need something to fall back on."

But all Martin could think of was that pirate who stole Sam Robbins's boat. And now he was starting to worry.

Robbins put Martin and Juanito up in a small jacal that was used to store shears and sheep dip, liniment and other medications, rope and hardware supplies: axes, hammers, nails, saws and shovels. It was little more than a flimsy shed and stank like nothing Martin had ever smelled before.

"What do you think, Juanito?" Martin was tired. They had eaten supper with Robbins, a bachelor, and he had given them directions to Darnell's ranch, a two-day ride.

"About what?"

"About Robbins's offer to freight his cheese and meat to Galveston and New Orleans."

"It is a good offer."

"But I have saved plenty of money. I don't want to buy land and then go back to sea."

"Sometimes we have to do things we don't like to do."

"Let's wait and see whether or not Victoria will sell me the land I want."

"Two trips a year, Martin. That is not much time away from your ranch."

"Long trips."

"I will do it. You can stay at the ranch."

"I can sell my boat in New Orleans, get a pretty good price."

"Or Galveston. You would not have so far to ride."

Martin brightened. "Yes, I'll try there."

"The way will be opened to you," Juanito said with a smile.

"Is that your great wisdom?"

"Borrowed, I fear. If you want something, there is always a way to get it. You want land, you will have it. You will find a way to keep it."

"Well, I knew that."

Juanito laughed. "Of course."

Sam Robbins brought gifts to his guests the next morning.

"Why, that's mighty nice of you, Mr. Robbins," Martin said.

"Call me Sam."

"Well, Sam, thanks."

"Just something to eat while you're traveling. You really don't want to make any cookfire on your journey. There's some cheese in this sack, some wine and some smoked mutton."

"Indians?"

"After the revolution, the Spaniards took out all

their troops. Indians took some revenge. They still are exacting a pretty high toll for the way they were mistreated."

"You seem to be holding your own."

"The Comanches don't like sheep much. And they hate goats."

Juanito laughed. "So that is why you raise them?"

"No, it's just an experiment. I have a few head of cattle. The problem is that you have to watch them night and day. Apaches and Comanches will drive off cattle right under your nose if you don't have riders out."

"I'll keep that in mind," Martin said.

"By the way, if you do buy from Aguilar, you'll have solid title. The old man was Spanish and he had Spanish land grants."

"That's good to know," Martin said. "How'd the old man die, anyway?"

"I've heard two stories," Sam said. "One is that he died in the cholera epidemic of '33."

"And what's the other?"

"That his son murdered him."

"Benito?"

"No, Jaime."

Martin drew a breath. "Which one do you believe?"

Robbins shrugged. "It could have been the cholera. A lot of people died."

"But you think Jaime killed his own father?"

"It's possible."

"Why?"

"Maybe for what the old man did to Benito."

"But I thought Jaime didn't particularly like Benito."

"It's a family thing. Blood. Spaniards don't think like us. Mexicans neither. They go back a long way with bloodlines pure as a thoroughbred's. They have long memories."

"I'll remember that," Martin said.

"Good luck. You'll like the Darnells. They have a daughter about your age."

"They do?"

"Pretty as a currycombed pony," Sam said.

"What's her name?" Martin asked.

"I forget. She's got a brother named Kenneth. I think her name's Angeline or something like that."

"Well, no matter. We'll find out soon enough."

"You tell 'em Sam said howdo."

"I'll do that, Sam."

Juanito and Martin waved good-bye. All of the Mexicans on Robbins's ranch waved to them as they rode to the southwest, following the course Sam had set for them.

"What do you think, Juanito?" Martin asked when they were once again riding through thick brush country.

"About what?"

"About Sam and the Darnells, this whole country."

"I think it is going to take a strong man to raise cattle anywhere in Texas."

"But you told me that before we even came here."

"I know. It is even more so now."

"Why?"

"Because Texas doesn't want to be owned by anyone."

"What's that supposed to mean, Juanito?"

"There has been much blood spilled here. The Spaniards, then the Mexicans, then the Americans, and now the Indians are exacting revenge."

"Might be Texas is worth fighting for."

"Is it worth dying for?" Juanito asked.

And Martin could not answer him.

But the more he rode the country, the more he loved it.

16

LAWRENCE DARNELL'S SMALL ranch lay wedged in between Sam Robbins's and Captain Richard Grimes's places near Matagorda and Tres Palacios. Darnell, at forty, had not been on the land long and he did not expect much from it, just a living for him and his family, consisting of a wife, a son and a daughter. But the coastal country fascinated him and he kept a few head of cattle for food and breeding experiments.

He had some ideas about cattle that interested no one but himself, but he talked about them constantly to Polly, his wife, and sometimes to his son, Kenneth, or to his daughter, Caroline. Both Robbins and Grimes thought Darnell to be eccentric, but both admitted that if anyone could raise cattle for market, it would be Larry Darnell. Perhaps not in their lifetime, they admitted, but they stood in wonder at his determination to put meat on the rangy longhorns by breeding them with European stock.

Polly Darnell, a woman in her mid-thirties, lean,

red-haired, blue-eyed and freckled over most of her body, pursed her lips in determination as she inhaled a deep breath through her nostrils. She pulled on the calf's head, her small hands cupping it behind its sodden ears as the cow lay sprawled in a large stall, wide-eyed and trembling.

"It's stuck," Polly said to her husband.

"Damn." Larry knelt by the cow's head, calming it with light pats to its neck.

"I'm going to reach in and grab its shoulders."

"Be careful."

"I may have to twist the little feller out."

The stall reeked of urine. The Darnells had been with the cow inside the barn for over an hour, watching its contractions until the calf's head popped out. But there the calf had stuck, and Polly had been trying to coax it through the breech.

Sunlight streamed through the open door of the three-stall barn built of driftwood timbers and oak, patched together with nails and rope and wire. The cow and calf lay on tattered blankets made from cotton sacks because they had no straw. The roof, thatched of mesquite and gamma grass, shed the rain, so the barn was dry except for the puddle of birthing fluids at the cow's backside.

"Boss, boss, boss," Larry crooned to the cow. "Good bossy."

Polly slid her hands gently down the calf's neck and over the slope of its shoulders. The cow quivered and tried to kick her. Polly slid to the side to block the cow's leg movement.

The bluebottle flies wove burred wire threads of sound through the tapestry of animal and human breathing that filled the barn. An occasional breeze wafted the strong aroma of sweetbrier through the structure, carrying with it the saline tang of the sea.

"Come on, baby," Polly said as she tried to tug on

the calf. The cow struggled to get up, bunching its leg
and shoulder muscles until they rippled like waves beneath her hide. "Hold bossy down, Larry."

"Hurry," grunted Larry as he scooted up to the cow
and knelt lightly on its shoulder. Then he spoke to the
cow: "Hold on, girl."

"The calf may be too big," Polly said, pausing for a
breath.

"Are you sure?"

"No. Its head came out all right, but I just have a
feeling."

"Well, try, Polly. Try."

"Um, yes."

Her hands were slick with water and blood and she
felt them slipping back toward her. The cow began to
struggle again and Polly felt a hoof graze her buttocks
as the animal gave a sharp kick. She reached down
deeper inside the cavity and tried to find the forelegs
of the calf. She felt a slender stiff bone and tried to pull
it upward.

"Uh-oh," Polly breathed.

"What's the matter, hon?"

"Her forelegs are all tangled up."

"No," Larry breathed.

"She's too big to come out, Larry. I can't get her un-
stuck."

The cow tried once again to rise, and Larry had to
apply more pressure to her shoulder. She was a Here-
ford, weighing several hundred pounds with calf. He
had bred her to a rangy longhorn bull, hoping that at
last he would have a live birth, with no complications.

"Want me to try?" he asked.

"Not yet, Larry. Let me give her one more yank."

Polly settled into a deeper squat and tried to slide
her hands behind the calf's legs where they joined the
trunk. The calf moved under her hands, but only slid
back further inside its mother. Polly let out a sigh as

she lost her grip. She pulled gently on the calf's head, twisting it one way, then the other, but the calf was stuck fast and wouldn't budge an inch.

Larry knew the calf wasn't going to make it. He felt a leaden weight on his shoulders as he looked at his wife's freckled face, the strands of hair dangling from her forehead like tendrils of dark smoke, the sweat stranding beads in the creases of her soft frown.

Polly looked at her husband, saw the darkening of his face as he pulled away from the cow, lurching to his feet.

"I know how disappointed you are," she said.

"I had thought this would work, Polly. A breeding heifer or a crossbreed bull at last."

"You mustn't give up, Larry."

"No," he breathed, rubbing his eyes with his left hand. "We came so close."

"Couldn't we cut her open? Save the calf?"

"I'd have to kill the mother first. It would be a mess."

"Yes," Polly agreed. She stood up, too, refusing to look down at the calf again.

"Polly, we'll have to get help. Where's Ken?"

"I don't know. I think he's out working with Caroline."

"Alone?"

"No, Demetrio is with them."

"Oh, yes," Larry said, "still digging that well."

"It's taking forever without help," Polly said. They all worked from sunup to dark, unable to pay wages even to the Mexicans. Demetrio was different. He had no family, was content to have a roof over his head. Not that it was much of a roof. He lived in a small jacal at the edge of the brasada, helped tend the cattle, cooked for the family, did the chores. Polly knew Larry felt bad about that. He always said a man should be paid for his work, but they had little money, sometimes not any, and they were grateful for Demetrio's loyalty and help.

"If we can't get the calf out, I'll have to destroy them both."

"I know." Polly sighed and knelt down again. She looked at the calf's wide wet eyes. She rubbed its sodden boss, ran her hand down his face. The calf lay there, no longer trying to emerge from its mother's cavity.

Larry walked around the cow, looked down at his wife, the calf. His mind raced with thoughts. Was there a way to get the calf out? He'd have to tie down the mother or kill her if he tried to pull the calf out with a rope.

That would probably kill the calf, too, he thought. God, he hated to have to kill them both. But the cow was suffering now and worn out from trying to give birth.

"There has to be a way," Larry said.

"How?" Polly looked up at her husband. "She's really stuck in there."

"I could try to cut the calf out," Larry said.

"If you kill the mother first."

"Yes."

"You tried that before."

Yes, he had tried to save a calf before by surgery. The calf lived a few days, then refused to eat. It starved to death, breaking both their hearts, Caroline's and Ken's, too. He still remembered all the blood, how horrible it was to cut the cow open to deliver its calf.

"Polly, go on up to the house," Larry said a few seconds later. He looked toward a roof support where he had leaned his rifle. He was never very far away from it. It was loaded and primed, a fine Kentucky in .58 caliber.

"Are you going to do it?"

"Yes," he said.

"All right. If you're going to give up."

"Damn it, Polly. There's nothing else I can do."

She touched his arm, tried a weak smile. She looked wan, he thought, as if she had just given birth herself.

"I know, Larry. I'll get Demetrio and Ken to help you bury them."

Just then a shadow filled the doorway. Larry and Polly looked around as if they were one person. Two men stood there, blocking the light.

"Mr. Darnell?" asked one of them. Larry could not see their faces.

"I'm Larry Darnell."

"My name is Martin Baron. We've come to see you."

"I can't see you now," Larry said. "Wait up by the house."

Juanito stepped past Martin and walked up to the cow and calf.

"The calf is very big," Juanito said.

"Too big," Larry said.

"I think we can get her out."

"Do you know anything about cattle?" Larry asked. Martin stepped forward.

"He's an Argentine from the pampas. This is Juanito Salazar, Mr. Darnell. We were sent here by Samuel Robbins."

"Sam sent you here? Why?"

"I'm going to buy some Aguilar land and raise cattle," Martin replied.

"The hell you say."

Larry looked at the two men sharply, then. Polly moved closer to her husband, slipped her arm in his. "Can you save the calf?" she asked Juanito.

"I can try."

"How?"

"Let's get the cow moved and I'll help her. Martin, you grab the upper leg. Mr. Darnell, you take the other. We'll pull her out straight and then spread her legs, make the opening wider."

"She'll kick you to death," Larry said.

"Then hold her very tight."

The cow started kicking the moment Martin grabbed her high leg. Juanito stepped in and helped him pull the cow straight. Then he helped Larry pull the other leg up. The calf bleated pitiably, moved one of its legs as if trying to climb out.

"Good," Juanito said. "The calf wants to get out of its mother."

"Don't hurt her," Polly said.

"Now pull the cow until she is on her back," Juanito said. "Hold her legs wide."

"That's what you do with humans," Larry said.

"And it works for the cows, too," Juanito said.

The cow struggled, tried to kick free of both men. Martin almost went down before he tightened his grip and held her fast. Larry grunted as he applied pressure to hold the leg in place. The cow kicked harder, with both legs, when she was lying on her spine.

Juanito straddled the cow's belly and knelt down close, bracing himself by gripping the cow's flanks with his knees. Then he began to massage her belly, pushing toward the breech in slow, powerful movements.

"Up and down," Juanito said in rhythm to his kneading. "Up and down."

"Can I help?" Polly asked.

Juanito looked at the freckle-faced woman. She was thin, but looked strong and sinewy under her homespun dress.

"Yes. Pull on the legs and lift up," Juanito told her. "Gently, gently."

"I'll be gentle," Polly said, kneeling down. One leg of the calf was still partially inside, the other was almost all the way out. She could see part of one shoulder. She worked the tucked-in leg outside and pulled on both legs as Juanito continued to work the cow's belly. The cow kicked with both legs and more of the calf slid out. Both legs emerged from the cavity and the calf began to claw the air.

"Now," Juanito said, and stood up. "Push her back over so's the calf's legs can strike the ground. He will pull himself out if you help him."

Polly heaved a sigh of relief. The men pushed the cow back over on its side. She struggled to get up. Larry started to push her back down.

"No, let her kick and try to get on her feet," Juanito said. "The more she moves, the easier it will be for the calf to get out."

When the cow turned back over on its side, the calf's hooves struck the ground and it began to pull itself out from its birth chamber. Polly tugged on the calf's shoulders, her hands slippery from the birthing fluids.

Juanito continued to knead the cow's belly, pushing from the side. Martin squatted down to help Polly. Larry stood watching the cow in case it lurched to its feet. He was visibly nervous, sweating profusely. Flies swarmed over the calf's head and flew into its eyes. Martin batted them away.

"She's coming," Polly said. "I think she can make it."

"Let her mother up," Juanito said, stepping aside. "She wants to help."

The cow lurched to its feet, took two steps and the calf slid free of its mother, plopping onto the ground. The afterbirth followed it like a rumpled yellow slicker, oozing out of the cow's womb.

The calf struggled to its feet, wobbled on four spindly legs, its curly hide slick with fluid. Larry croaked a soft hurrah. Tears welled up in Polly's eyes as she stared at the tiny creature that had appeared so suddenly before her.

"It—it's beautiful," she said. "And it's a she."

"I'm damned," breathed Larry.

"It is a fine calf," Juanito said. "Very big, no?"

"A heifer to boot," Larry said. "The first crossbreed born here."

They all watched as the mother began to lick her calf.

"That is a very pretty calf," Juanito said.

"Prettiest I ever saw," Larry agreed. "Where did you say you boys came from?"

"Uh, it's a long story, Mr. Darnell."

"You can call me, Larry. Why don't we go up to the house where we can talk. Polly, do you need me?"

Polly's face glowed. She shook her head without taking her eyes off the new calf.

"Nice to meet you, ma'am," Martin said.

"Yes, forgive me. I—I want to just stand here and gloat for a while."

"No matter, ma'am," Martin said.

"Come on up when you're through," Larry said.

"I will." Polly wiped the sweat from her face with the back of her hand. She seemed transported, lost in another world. Martin wondered if her daughter was as pretty as she was.

To Martin's surprise, Larry turned back at the door to the barn. "You know, I think I want to look at that calf a little while longer myself. Do you mind?"

Martin shook his head. Juanito grinned and walked to the edge of a stall and squatted down. Martin stepped over to sit by him. Larry touched his wife on the shoulder and stood there transfixed as the mother licked its calf until its hide was as curly as a windswept ocean. Then the mother cow ate its afterbirth. The calf wobbled over to its mother's udder, gave it a couple of bumps with its boss and found a swollen tit.

Larry Darnell beamed as the calf began to suckle its mother. "Ain't that a pretty sight?" he said to no one.

"Sure is," Martin said.

"That calf will make a fine cow," Juanito said.

"You know cattle?" Darnell asked.

"He's from Argentina," Martin said as Juanito nodded. "Lived on a big ranch down there."

"Well, I'll be damned," Larry said, and Polly did not chide him for his cussing, much to Martin's admiration.

"Looks healthy enough," Martin said.

"She's very healthy," Polly said proudly. Then she looked at Martin as if for the first time. "What brings you to these lonesome parts, Mr. Baron?"

"Why, I came to buy some land and raise cattle myself. Juanito's going to help me."

"It's a hard land, Mr. Baron."

"Mrs. Darnell, you don't have to call me mister."

"Why, then you call me Polly, Martin. Now, where is this land you're going to buy?"

"We've been looking over the Aguilar property," Martin replied. "Victoria Aguilar said she would sell some land to me."

"Don Jaime's wife? That's strange. What did Don Jaime say about that?"

"Jaime is dead," Martin said. "He was killed by Apaches the day we came to his ranch."

Polly nodded as if expecting such news. "So sad," she said. "But he always brooded about being killed by Indians."

"We stayed until after they buried Jaime," Martin explained.

"What about Benito?" Larry asked. "He always wanted to run the ranch. I thought he would step in if his brother ever died."

"He may be running it," Martin said, "but Victoria runs him."

"I would not trust any of the Aguilars if I were you," Larry said.

"What do you mean by that?" Martin asked.

"They're a shrewd bunch, every one of them, and about as ruthless as they come. Them putting a bounty on Indian scalps has put all of us in danger." Darnell shook his head.

"Benito says he's going to stop paying bounties," Martin said.

"Well, Don Jaime's widow won't stand still for that. She hates Indians more than her husband did. And now that Don Jaime has been killed by Apaches, she'll never stop until every redskin between the Rio Grande and the Red is dead."

"She seemed very nice to me," Martin said. "Gracious, even. Considering her husband had just been killed, I thought she went out of her way to be kind to me."

"Well, maybe," Larry said. "I'll tell you a story I know firsthand about Victoria Aguilar. And if you believe it, you can make up your own mind about dealing with her."

"Larry, this isn't our business," Polly said. "And you mustn't tattle."

"I'd like to hear what you have to say," Martin said.

Juanito's eyes glittered like winking coals, but he said nothing.

Larry looked at his wife. Polly shrugged and twisted her mouth in a wry little smile.

"There was a feller come to the Matagordos a while back," Larry said, "had him some horses and mules. His horses all had different brands on 'em, and a bunch of them looked mighty funny."

"What do you mean, funny brands?" Martin asked.

"All of 'em different. No two alike. And some looked skewed."

"Skewed?"

"Do you know what a running iron is?"

Martin shook his head. Juanito smiled knowingly.

"Thieves make an iron brand that changes the way letters and signs are. They can make an A into a B, a bar into a cross and so on. Some of this feller's brands looked like he laid a running iron on 'em."

"Did you ask him about the funny brands?"

"No," Larry said. "He wanted to sell some of the horses and mules to me, but I told him I had no cash. He said he'd trade, but I had nothing to trade. He asked me did I know somebody who might have cash money and I told him the Aguilars probably did."

"Did he ask how to find their ranch?"

"He said he'd pay me a commission if I took him over to the Rocking A."

"And did you?" Martin asked.

"I didn't want to," Larry said. "But he gave me cash on account, so I rode over to the Aguilars with him. He had more horses than he showed me at first, because two other fellers were waiting for him just beyond where I could see from the house here. They had forty or fifty horses, I reckon."

"All wearing different brands?"

Larry nodded.

"Then what?" Martin asked.

"They were a rough bunch, scraggly as tumble-weeds. None of the boys had shaved in weeks and probably hadn't washed in a month or more."

"Were you afraid of them?"

"No. They were pretty congenial for all their filthi-ness. They didn't talk none about where they got the horses and they had grub enough. Them boys was pretty good shots, too. One was no more'n a boy, they called him Hap. Never did know his full name. He was always grinnin' and makin' jokes and kind of a like-able feller. The first man I met was called Hardy and the other'n was named Pat. They never used no last names."

"What happened when you got to the Aguilars?"

"Don Jaime and Benito looked the horses over and asked me questions I couldn't answer."

"Like what?"

"Like who were these boys and where they had come from and where did they get the horses? Don Jaime, he asked Hardy if he had bills of sale and Hardy said he sure did, and he showed 'em to Don Jaime and he took them into the house and pretty soon Victoria come out and Pilar, too, and they all talked in Spanish. Hardy, he knew some Spanish. He asked them if they wanted to buy his horses and mules and Don Jaime said he wanted to check the brands and the bills of sales, but Victoria she never took her eyes off those boys and before I knew it, there was a whole bunch of Aguilar hands come up and standin' around with machetes and pistols and rifles and they got the drop on these gringo boys. Victoria, she gave her hands the high sign and they grabbed the boys and took their pistols away."

"Something wrong with the brands?" Martin asked.

"Well, it was worse than that," Larry said. "Some of the horses had been stole from the Aguilars and others had belonged to people they knew in Mexico and all of the bills of sale were forgeries."

"So then what?"

"Larry," Polly interrupted, "I don't think you ought to say any more about this."

"Well, I got this far. Might as well tell Martin here what he wants to know."

Polly looked back at the little calf, but her face had clouded up and her eyes had dulled down to slitted shadows.

"Go on," Martin said. "Please. I want to hear the rest of it."

"Hardy, he raised a ruckus, said he'd bought the stock fair and square and that those were the bills of sale he'd been given. Victoria told him he was a thief and said that they were all thieves and they would have to hang."

"Hang?"

Larry nodded. "Victoria called for the ropes and

even tied the hangman's knots. They rode those boys over to a live oak. I wanted to get out of there, but Don Jaime made me stay. The whole bunch of hands and their wives and kids came out to watch. Some of the Mexicans strung up those American boys and Victoria handed them the ropes. Hap, he started crying, and I asked Victoria to have mercy on him at least, but she was as cold as a cinder. I had to watch the whole thing. The Mexicans whipped them horses out from under those boys and they choked and kicked and died a-hangin' like a bunch of marionettes. It was a god-awful sight. I got sick and Victoria made me some soup that settled me down. She said I could have any horse I wanted, but I just wanted to get home to Polly and the kids and forget about what I saw."

Martin resisted the urge to swear. He looked at Polly, then at Juanito, his mind swirling with images of the men dangling from ropes.

"Did you think Victoria was wrong to hang them?" Martin asked.

"I don't know," Larry said. "This is a hard country and I've heard they hang cattle rustlers without batting an eye, but I had rode with those boys for a week and I hated to see them die like that, with no chance."

"But they did steal those horses?"

"I guess they did. Hardy kept saying they didn't. But Hap never said anything and Pat didn't open his mouth. I just don't know the right nor wrong of it."

"But you don't trust Victoria Aguilar?" Martin asked.

Larry paused and took a deep breath. "I never saw a colder woman. It sends chills up my back to think of how she looked at those men and how cool she was wrapping those knots. I guess I'm kind of afraid of her. She's got some kind of iron in her that don't seem womanly."

"Sounds to me like the men around her do what she says."

"I think you'd better think twice before you do any business with that woman," Larry said.

Polly stood up and looked straight into Martin's eyes. "I don't trust her," she said. "I think she's cruel and mean. If you ever did anything she didn't like, I think she'd kill you as soon as look at you."

Larry seemed surprised at his wife's outburst. He shook his head and looked away.

"Well, I thank you both for your advice," Martin said. "I'll give it some thought."

Juanito said nothing, but he looked at Martin with a look that could only have been described as admiring and a slow smile played on his face.

Seconds later, they heard voices and then a young woman raced into the barn, her long hair in pigtails, a hat bouncing off her back, pulling on the thong around her delicate throat. She wore a loose blouse and home-spun pants and handmade Mexican boots. She stopped short and looked at Martin with wide staring eyes of the purest blue.

"Caroline," Polly said. "Look at our new calf."

Juanito leaned over close to Martin and whispered in his ear. "This is the one. This is the woman for you. She will take you on the rest of your journey."

Martin stood transfixed, staring at Caroline Darnell, stunned by her radiance, shot through with her simple beauty.

"Yes," Martin breathed, and his voice sounded in his mind like a fervent prayer.

The girl stared directly at Martin. He felt the blaze of her eyes on his. Then like the crack of a whip across the seething plain of his mind, he heard Polly's voice again.

"Caroline, stop staring like that. What has come over you?"

Martin heard Polly's words, but Caroline did not break her stare, nor could he drop his gaze from her. He looked into her eyes and knew that Caroline was the woman he was meant to love, the woman he was destined to marry.

17

THE MAN RODE out of the brasada on a windy day, leading two packhorses. He wore a Remington .44 pistol on his right hip, carried a .54 caliber Kentucky rifle in a cowhide sheath strapped at an angle to the saddle under his right leg. He wore a flat-brimmed Mexican hat of pressed beaver, a loose Mexican shirt made of cotton and dyed brown, black wool pants and leather Mexican boots, stitched flowery scrawls for adornment. A blue bandanna encircled his neck. The man had a shock of red hair springing from his scalp in tight wiry coils, a tanned face, a florid complexion, full lips chapped and cracked from the scorching sun and moisture-leaching wind. He wore a large belt-knife, made for him by no less a man than Jim Bowie, and from his saddle horn dangled a dozen scalps that were unmistakably Apache in origin.

John Fitzroy Killian rode with seeming purpose atop a charcoal-black Missouri trotter that was fifteen hands tall, with three white stockings and a star blaze on its forehead. Killian rode as if he owned every square foot of land he traveled, with shoulders set square and back straight as a leveling rod. But his blue eyes missed nothing, turned on liquid axles for 180 degrees. He seldom looked back, because ranging well behind the horses was a bluetick hound bred in Kentucky with a rubbery nose and as keen an eyesight as Jack Killian's.

Killian hummed a little Irish ditty sotto voce as if he had not a care in the world. His rifle sheath was hard and cocked at such an angle that he could easily jerk it from its scabbard. He kept all six cylinders of his Remington .44 loaded with powder and ball. Each nipple on the cylinder was tightly capped and the copper jackets gleamed bright in the sun.

There was an edge to his humming, a falling off of the notes until they sounded almost like the keening tones of a mourner, and when he roamed into the high register, his throaty voice hummed whole notes that were inflected with the quavery sound of a man in pain.

Killian winced as he reached inside his shirt and drew out a bloody kerchief from beneath his armpit. He stopped humming abruptly as he held out his hand and squeezed blood from the kerchief. He watched in fascination as a stream of crimson blood dripped to the ground. He replaced the kerchief, winced again as it touched the bare wound next to his armpit.

He wondered how much blood he had lost. He felt light-headed, giddy. He blinked his eyes and tried to concentrate on the trail ahead. The earth swam woozily as it wobbled into focus. "Damn," he breathed.

Another dog ranged ahead of Jack, while two more covered his flanks as they had been trained to do. They all responded to whistles varying in pitch. The dogs were Jack's eyes and ears in the brush, but they were also hunters, of wild game and of men. The animals were silent now, but Jack knew that they would strike spoor soon. He could feel it under his skin. When they started belling, he would know that they had struck scent, and from the pitch of their yelps, he would know whether they had run onto the track of man or beast.

Buzzards spun lazily in the cloudless blue sky, and somewhere far off, Jack heard the scree of a hawk. The sound was muffled inside his head, as if he had cotton stuffed in his ears. He thought of the dogs he could not see, wondered if they had lost the scent of the Apache who had wounded him, who rode somewhere up ahead on a spent pony with a .54-caliber lead ball in its rump.

The blackbirds were silent and that bothered him. Bothered him more than the crows that had suddenly lost their voices. But he trusted the dogs: Bull, the mongrel on his left flank; the mastiff, Duke, on his right; and Digger, the big Airedale that took the lead. Jasper, behind him, would pick up any scent that Digger missed.

The Apache had half a day's start on him. They had jumped him at dawn, and the only reason he was still alive was that the Indians had fallen for his trick of setting out a false bedroll by the campfire. When they rode in, he and the dogs had been asleep. There were six of them. Five had fallen to his guns, but the sixth had shot him in the side, grazing a rib, tearing out a chunk of meat under his armpit. He thought now that one rib, perhaps two, might be cracked. The pain stabbed him with every step the trotter took, and the trotter had an easy gait, soft and silky, as if he walked on air.

He gave the Apaches credit. They had tracked him clear across the Rio Grande and he'd never seen them. Nor had the dogs picked up their scent. Sometime he'd have to find out how they had done that. Probably smeared their bodies with creosote or crushed mesquite berries. Or smoked themselves in some scent. He knew some would come after him, for he had taken scalps from a bunch he jumped in Mexico, but he thought he could lose them in the brasada.

Jack cracked a wry grin. He had made a mistake. A big mistake. The Apaches had outsmarted him. It had not been the first time. Ever since his brother had disappeared, Jack had been convinced that Apaches had killed him, stolen his horses. Then he had met a Mexican who told him what had really happened to Hardy. All those years of riding the vengeance trail and he had been after smoke, chased images in cloudy mirrors.

The Mexican had worked for Jaime Aguilar up in Texas and Jack knew that's where his brother had gone to sell horses. Stolen horses and mules, to be sure. But the Aguilars had executed him without so much as a formal trial, and that didn't sit well with Jack Killian. Jack kept plying the Mexican with tequila and had learned a great deal about the Aguilars.

The Mexican's name was Miguel Fuentes and he had left the Rocking A ranch in fear of Victoria Aguilar, whom he had called a *bruja*, a witch.

"She is a tyrant," Fuentes had told Killian in Spanish. "*Sin corazón, sin vergüenza.* Without heart, without shame."

"Tell me more, Miguel," Killian had said, and through the night in Matamoros, he had listened to tales stranger than any he had ever heard. Before the night was over, Miguel had taken his shirt off and shown Jack the scars from many whippings he had endured at the orders of Victoria Aguilar.

"So you ran away," Jack said.

"Yes. When Benito Aguilar drowned my son in a watering trough after torturing him for hours."

"Why?"

"The señora said that my boy had stolen some of her jewelry."

"And did he?"

"No. My son was not a thief."

"Why did you not go to the authorities?" Jack had asked.

"What authorities? The Aguilars are the law of the land. There is no law, but theirs. I took my wife and left the rancho and now I am *borracho* and my son is dead at the hands of that witch. And my wife is weeping and has plucked her head of hair and she is blaming me for the death of our son."

And Miguel had told him about the bounty on the Apaches and the hanging of the American horse thieves and the man they called Hardy.

"Hardesty," Jack had said.

"You knew this man?"

"He was my brother. I thought the Apaches had killed him."

"He was a thief?"

"Yes."

"Then he was given justice," Miguel had said.

"Justice? No, I think not, my friend. He was murdered without a trial."

"Ha! The Aguilars give no trials. They are the judges. They are the law."

"We'll see," Jack had said. He had left Mexico the next morning, but ran into trouble at the river when the Apaches jumped him. He had been to the Rio Grande Valley before, had seen the ranches springing up in Tres Palacios and Matagorda and to the north and east, and he had thought that he might seek land for himself, for he loved the country, the wildness of it, and yes, even its distance from the laws that governed the United States.

He and Hardy had worked as lads with Jim Bowie and his brothers, smuggling contraband slaves into the country, but he had left that life, as had Jim Bowie. Hardesty had ridden with the outlaws, preferring that life, and Jack had to admit to its appeal. But while

Hardy had stolen horses from Mexicans and sold them in the States, Jack had lived off the land, worked for his money, striving for an honesty that his older brother seemed to lack and have no care for in his life.

Killian did not yet know what he was going to do about the murder of his brother, but he wanted to look Victoria Aguilar in the eye and ask her why she had ordered his brother to be hanged, and he wanted to call Benito out as well, and exact revenge for Hardesty's murder.

One of the dogs barked, and he recognized the bark as the Airedale's, Digger. Digger had the best nose of the bunch, better even than the bluetick's, Jasper. Then he heard Bull, the mongrel, let out a yelp. Digger went silent, and Jack knew the Airedale had his nose to the ground. Jasper shot by him a moment later, heading in the direction of Bull's high-pitched yelp.

After a few minutes Jasper picked up the scent, and his sonorous cries rang on the still air of afternoon. Jack winced as he clapped spurs to his horse's flanks and took the trotter into the next gait, a lope.

Now, the dogs were in full cry and Killian's blood raced as the trotter, caught up in the excitement, took up a gallop. The packhorses jerked on the reins, but Jack pulled them along until their speed matched his mount's. Pain shot through his shoulder and side and he felt the warm sticky flow of blood start up again.

"Damn," he said, wondering if one of his ribs would puncture a lung. He was sure the ball had gone clean through, but there was a lot of flesh missing and he had been too much in a hurry to check his wound thoroughly.

Killian listened carefully for any pitch change in Digger's bark, and to the hound, Jasper, who would mark the treeing of his prey. As he pictured it in his mind, the dogs had not yet sighted their quarry, but were in hot pursuit, dead on the Apache's tracks, the spoor strong in their nostrils. Indeed, the dogs were in full cry, chasing after the Airedale. The mastiff could easily outdistance the other canines, but Killian knew that he lacked the fierce heart of Digger, the killing instincts of the mongrel, Bull, and the perfect nose of Jasper. But Duke was an intimidating dog. He astonished the Apaches, kept them at bay. One Apache had told him they thought he was a spirit dog and they feared him. Duke ran like a deer and looked like one, and stood almost as tall as the Indian ponies. It was a strange pack, but they were loyal to Killian and he had trained them with patience to hunt the Apache and to obey his whistled commands.

Jack noticed a change in the Airedale's bark, as it went to a slightly higher pitch. But the bluetick had not yet sighted the fleeing Apache, for his voice was still wavering among the same notes. Then abruptly Jasper's belling went to a high pitch and Jack knew that they had the Apache cornered somewhere on the plain or in the brush.

He slowed his horse, the pain in his side massive now. There was no need to hurry. The dogs would keep the Indian at bay. The trotter slowed to a walk, and Jack put his hand under his armpit and felt the bandanna. It was soaked with fresh blood. He drew it out and squeezed it, watching the sanguine drippings as they fell to the ground.

High thin cirrus clouds striped the blue sky and Jack felt a twinge of apprehension as he put the bandanna back under his arm, laid it gently against the open wound. Something was wrong, but he couldn't put a name to it. Then he realized that the dogs had gone silent one by one, and the apprehension he felt rose up in him like unseen smoke.

"Digger," he called. "Jasper?"

Only silence as his call died away, and it deepened as he listened to the soft sound of his horse's hooves striking the ground.

"Bull!" he yelled, and pulled his rifle free of its

scabbard. No bark, nothing. He whistled three times, waited. He looked for the dogs to come bounding toward him, but nothing stirred in the silence of the afternoon. Jack whistled three times again, but still no dogs appeared.

Now Jack knew something was wrong, terribly wrong. He tried to think which dog had stopped barking first. Jasper? Yes, maybe. Digger? Bull? Why hadn't he noticed that Jasper had stopped yelping? Perhaps his mind had been on his wound instead of on the dogs.

Killian cocked the rifle and jabbed his mount gently with his spurs. The horse, used to his master's commands, picked up the step, but did not break into a trot. Jack tried to remember when he had last seen Jasper, which direction the dog had gone in. He reined the horse to turn so that he could approach where he had last seen Jasper take to the brush and come in at an angle in case the Apache was waiting for him.

Somehow the Indian had silenced the dogs. But how? He'd never had that happen before. Usually the dogs kept the Indians at bay until he came up. The mongrel and the Airedale usually ragged the redskins until Jack could approach close enough for a shot.

But not this time.

It was as if the dogs had been swallowed up into the earth itself. One minute they had been there—barking, chasing their prey—and the next thing he knew, they had vanished into the open maw of the wilderness.

It didn't make sense. Not four dogs. Not four trained hunting and fighting dogs like these. Against one Indian? One lone Apache. It didn't seem possible to John Killian that dry summer afternoon.

Jack kept the horse quiet, and the horse, as if sensing the danger, stepped carefully, following every touch of the rein, every tap of the spur against his flanks. The horse and the rider moved quiet as shadows through the mesquite forest, and the silence rose up around them like a curtain. Even the crows were silent. Not so much as a lizard stirred.

Killian hunched over the trotter's neck, his rifle across the pommel, his finger inside the trigger guard. His senses tautened into an acute state of alert, his ears attuned for the slightest sound. He held the horse to a slow, sporadic walk, stopping him after every step to test the animal's senses as well as his own.

Jack wanted to whistle for the dogs again, but he knew that he was wishing for something that was not to be. Something had happened to the dogs, he knew not what, and they would not be coming to his calls. He felt a pang of sadness constrict his throat, well up as tears in his eyes. He loved those dogs. They had been his friends for a long time. Now it was as if he was riding blind into the unknown. He could not see, he could not hear. There was only the long hard silence of a granite tomb.

Killian searched the brush with his eyes, criss-crossed the terrain so that he didn't miss anything. He knew he was in the general area where the dogs had gone and felt sure that he would either find them or their tracks. Each step the horse took, though, heightened his sense of dread.

Ahead Jack saw movement. He halted the trotter and peered intently through the mesquite thicket. He prodded the horse ahead another foot or two. Then he saw something move once again. He leaned over the horse's side and saw an object swinging from a mesquite branch. Something familiar.

"Easy, boy," he whispered to the horse and held the reins taut as he stepped down from the saddle, silent as a cat, careful not to scrape the rifle on the leather-clad horn. He loosened the pistol in its holster and checked his rifle again. He held his thumb on the hammer, ready to cock it at the slightest sign of danger. The pain under his armpit pulled like a frayed nerve in his brain.

Killian tied the horses to a trio of mesquite trees and crept toward the swinging object on foot. He circled it warily, keeping a part of the strange silhouette in sight at all times. He looked for tracks on the bare ground, any sign of a pebble overturned, a bent grass or twig, anything mussed or amiss. But the earth was as clean and smooth as a cue ball. Almost too clean, he thought.

When Jack had completed a full circle, he approached the mysterious object warily. Curious, he thought it might be a rag or a piece of clothing, something that might have rubbed off a passing rider's saddle.

When Killian stepped to within ten feet of the thing he had seen from horseback, the small hairs on the back of his neck bristled. It was then that he realized that there should have been tracks on the ground. Someone had been to this place. Someone had swept all signs of his presence clear. The mastiff. "Duke," he breathed.

The mastiff hung from a mesquite tree, a braided thong around its neck, its brindle coat drenched in blood where its throat had been cut, sliced through to the spine. Its chest was ripped open, and the heart torn from between its lungs. The blood was almost dried.

Bile rose up in Killian's throat and he had to turn away and gulp in great drafts of air to keep the vomit down.

"Oh, Duke," Jack breathed as the dead dog twisted slowly on its gibbet.

Killian drew his Bowie knife from its scabbard and winced with pain as he cut the braided thong from the tree. The dog fell to the ground. Jack slit the thong in two and snatched it from Duke's neck. He stuffed the thong in his pocket for later examination.

Killian knew he could not stay there. Even now someone might be watching him. And he had three more dogs to find. He set out in another circular pattern, hoping to locate the other dogs and find them alive.

Jack did not have far to go. Forty yards beyond the place where he had found Duke, Jasper and Bull lay in a small clearing, each with an arrow jutting from its neck. Killian shuddered. He wondered where the Airedale was. He looked around, saw no sign of him.

Cautiously Jack approached the dogs. Their throats gaped, too, as if whoever had killed them had wanted to be sure. Again, he could find no tracks. A light breeze ruffled the hair around the neck wounds and Killian felt the bile rise in his throat. He turned and retched, spewing vomit on the ground. He gasped for air and let it all come up until he was hawking dry-throated and felt the cords in his neck tauten and threaten to break. His movements aggravated the pain in his side once more.

"Jesus," he said, and it was a soft curse on his lips.

It took him several moments to recover and he wished he had brought his canteen to rinse his mouth of the vile taste of vomit. He realized suddenly that he was still in the middle of a clearing, an easy bow shot for any lurking Apache.

Gingerly, Jack moved on in the same direction he had come. A sickening thought occurred to him. The Airedale had to have been the first to catch up to the Apache. The Indian had killed him and then gone after the others. But the mastiff had been snared, so whoever had done it had been expecting the dogs. Perhaps Duke had been the first. Where, then, was Digger, the lead dog?

Killian ranged over a wide path on foot, and it paid off a few minutes later when he encountered moccasin tracks. Bold, deep, with no attempt at concealment, the tracks stood out like a handful of sore thumbs.

Trying not to think of the other dogs, Jack followed the tracks warily, but he had the odd sensation that the Apache who made them wanted him to see them. The footprints were in a straight line. Jack crouched low, despite the pain, and used the mesquite for cover, never following the moccasin prints directly, but crossing them every few yards.

In a small clearing, he saw what looked like a bundle of clothing. He circled and approached the pile carefully. What he saw next, when he was no more than five feet away, made his skin crawl. Without knowing for sure what it was, he knew what it was.

Jack ran to the pile of fur and stopped, aghast, his face frozen in a dark scowl.

"You sonofabitch," he said crisply. There was no need to pick up the bundle of fur. He knew it was Digger, the Airedale. The Apache had killed him and skinned him neatly. When he kicked the bundle, four paws scattered in the dirt, ringed at the cuts with blood. The head rolled out, too, and Killian felt his stomach twist and jerk as if to spill its contents. Yet he knew there was nothing left to throw up. He turned away from the remains of Digger, his eyes closed. "I ain't goin' to blubber for you boys none," he said. "You did what you had to do and saved my skin. I'm mighty grateful." Then he clenched a fist and opened his eyes. "I'll get you for this, you bastard," he yelled.

And, by the deadened sound of his voice, Jack knew there was no one there to hear him. No one anywhere near. Suddenly he felt terribly alone, and for the first time in his life, afraid.

18

JACK KILLIAN RETURNED to the place where he had tied his horses. They were gone, packs and all. And, where they had stood, the Apache had smoothed a place in the dirt. Killian bent down to see what the Indian had scratched in the smooth dirt. It was an easily identifiable icon.

The Apache had drawn the outline of a dagger or knife.

The sign held no meaning for Jack.

But he knew he was a man on foot with no food, just the arms and ammunition he packed with him, and no idea of where he was. And he knew he could not stay in this place. There was nothing to stop the Apache from taking the horses to some hiding place, then returning to kill him.

Yet he could have done that at any time. No, this Indian wanted to rub Jack's nose in it, he decided. He had killed Jack's dogs and stolen his horses and now

he would go back to his scabrous tribe and brag about
how he had bested the white man.

Killian knew that he dared not linger at this spot.
The Apache could well bring others of his tribe back
to this place and do him in. It took Jack only a moment
to make up his mind. He could not head south, back
toward Mexico, for surely that was the way the
Apache was going. To make sure, Killian followed the
tracks of the horses far enough so that he was certain
the direction the Apache had taken. When he was satisfied, Jack turned on his heels. He headed north,
where he knew he would eventually run into other
people, ranchers that had settled well away from the
Rio Bravo.

He moved quickly, alternately running, then walking, as the pain in his side rose in intensity, and cover-
ing his tracks at various places. His belly growled with
hunger, but he knew he could not afford the luxury of
hunting until he had put some distance between him
and the Apache who had killed his dogs and stolen his
horses.

Killian kept his bearings as he zigzagged up-coun-
try, traversing vast mesquite forests, skirting broad savannahs, fording creeks, where he drank greedily until
he thought his stomach would burst, over low sand
hills, heading north, always north. The sun, daylight,
was his enemy, and he longed for the safety of darkness. The soles of his feet were sore and his leg
muscles ached, the tendons so tender that to touch
them was to scourge them with fire. Gradually, the
pain in his side subsided.

The weary Jack Killian trudged long into the day
across the trackless and scorching land, his stomach
racked with hunger pangs, his arm leaden with the
weight of the rifle, his bruised ribs burning with a soft
pain. He missed the dogs, yearned for even one horse
to ride. His feet were sore, his boots bristling with the
spines of prickly pear, and more than once he'd had to

stop and scrape the stinging cholla out of his britches with the blade of his knife.

He had made a serious mistake, he knew. One that could have cost him his life. He had known men who had died for lesser transgressions. A broken leg, a careless handling of a firearm, even such a small thing as a sprained ankle could put a man down permanently. As the sun drew long shadows across the basin, Jack thought ruefully of that day and knew that he was lucky to be alive. His wound was a constant reminder of his carelessness and his good fortune.

Killian sensed a change in himself as he moved through that alien land, where even the shadows burned with the fire from the sun. He did not discern the change all at once, but gradually, as if he was leaving part of himself in the ancient earth and as if part of the earth was growing into him. There was something about the brilliance of the light—the shadows themselves seemed to be afire—and something about the sky and the way the mesquite forests framed it and somehow seemed a part of the vast blue ocean overhead. And he felt himself being drawn into those fiery shadows and into the mesquite and up to the sky, as if he was just one part of a gigantic whole and where he walked and looked was all one thing, majestic and simple at the same time, immense and yet somehow oddly homelike and small.

Strangely, Killian felt at peace in this wild, unknown country. It was not at all like Mexico, where he had never felt completely at home. Rather, he felt a sense of belonging—of safety, even. Despite the realization that he was running for his life, the deeper he went into the country, the safer he felt, the more it seemed like a home that had been waiting for his return.

As the shadows began to darken, the sky softened and paled, and the fire clung to the clouds, burnishing their undersides with golden flame. Killian took great stock in the sky. He used it for guidance, both night and day, and he looked to it for weather signs, since he knew the danger of sudden flash floods in such country.

So many years on the plains had taught him other things, too, and he knew where he was going for the night, what he was looking for that would keep him safe. As the clouds began to rust, he knew there would be fair weather on the morrow, and this caused him some concern. He would rather that it rain, so that his tracks would be hidden from any Apache pursuer. Still, he felt confident that he could make the best of it and trudged on, alert to the slightest sound. Every so often, Killian stopped and put his ear to the ground, listening for any rumble or pounding that would warn him of approaching footsteps or hoofbeats. He heard nothing and continued on, his eyes constantly on the move.

Jack turned northeast as the sun began to fall away, leaving a mottled bruise on the western sky, purple and yellow clouds, dark patches like thumb smudges on the horizon. Finally he heard the sound he had been waiting to hear, and seconds later, he trotted out onto a broad plain. There before him lay what he had been searching for all afternoon.

He stopped and stood there for a long moment. He touched his wound and it was dry and bloodless. "Perfect," he said aloud.

The plain was dotted with small mounds and there wasn't a sign of movement. But Killian knew they were there. He smiled. Beyond the plain, a vast mesquite thicket stood like a dark impenetrable wall. There, he thought, he would sleep tonight, giving his wound a chance to scab over, safe from anyone trying to cross that broad expanse.

Jack drew a deep breath of satisfaction. In front of him stood the largest prairie dog town he had ever seen. Miles of mounds in all directions. The sound he had heard had been the high-pitched whistle of a sentry dog, warning of his own advance.

He let out his breath and began to circle the huge underground town, but he could not outdistance it. The sky grew darker, and he hurried his pace until he had completed a circle, treading carefully between mounds of dirt pushed up around escape holes. It was so quiet he might have been walking through a cemetery at midnight.

When he reached the mesquite grove, Killian entered it, found a shelter in a copse of trees and sat down to rest and think. He was close enough to hear the prairie dogs as they emerged from their subterranean dens for one last look at the dying day. And he could see the edge of the town beneath the leafy mesquite branches. All he had to do was sit and wait. He would have guard dogs and a meal if his patience paid off.

Jack carefully checked his rifle, set the stock against his shoulder, bracing himself against the tree, using one knee to steady the rifle in case a prairie dog presented itself for a clean shot. The growling in his stomach had grown worse and it seemed that the sound could be heard from far away.

The sky gradually darkened and Killian knew his chances to bag a prairie dog were fading with the dying rays of the sun. Although he peered intently through the mesquite grove, he saw not a living thing. Nothing moved and he heard no sound. The boisterous crows on the far side of the town had fled and no longer were raucous in the trees. And the clouds were now dark smudges in the sky, slowly turning invisible.

The stillness of eventide was eerie. Even the birds had gone silent and he knew he could not rely on even the crows to sound an alarm once the sun had set. Soon he sat in darkness listening to the sound of his heart beating, the rumble of his empty stomach.

Killian knew he would have no protection that

night, even so close to a prairie dog town. But he also knew that the Apaches could not track him after the sun went down. The darkness closed down on Jack, and with the darkness, the terrible hunger, bringing memories flooding in on him, memories of the last letters he had received from back home, from Ireland.

His mother had written him in 1846, after a long year of famine, telling him of the potato blight, something Jack found hard to understand. His mother, bless her soul, had told him that their potatoes had been stricken with a blight, a kind of mildew that made the potato skins develop white, gray or purplish patches. The way she explained it, the potatoes became covered with a downy mildew that made them inedible.

Maureen Killian had said that thousands had died the previous year and that millions more were starving to death. She also said that people were leaving Ireland in droves, and if they could afford it, they were coming to America, as he and his brother Hardesty had done.

Jack had sent his mother and father money for passage, but it had reached them too late. They died in 1847, and the other relatives blamed their deaths on the accursed English who would not let them own land or have sovereignty. Every time Jack was hungry, he thought of his parents slowly starving to death when he was in a land of plenty, where a man could own land and property and raise crops to feed a family. He thought bitterly of those letters now as claws raked his stomach and his innards roared and rumbled with the emptiness.

And now he was the only one left. And he owned no land, did not have food. He had a wife and son in Fort Worth, but he had not seen them in years. The irony of it made Jack laugh aloud. The sound of his voice startled him in the stillness and he found a soft spot of earth where he could lie down and sleep.

The ground grew cold and dissipated his body heat. Jack dozed fitfully the entire night, his hunger an animal thing that gnawed at his guts, his feet so cold, they turned wooden. Finally he awakened and looked at the stars and estimated the hours until morning. He walked around in circles to restore the circulation to his feet. He tucked his hands under his armpits and tried to keep his teeth from chattering. His wound had not broken open during the night and he knew that his ribs were only bruised, not broken.

Before dawn, he was heading north again, steering his way by the stars until they faded and disappeared in the glow of morning light. He wandered a zigzag course, no longer concerned about his back trail, but hoping to find game—a rabbit, a deer, a turkey or even a squirrel.

It seemed to Killian that the land had risen against him. He saw no prairie dog towns. He saw no wild cattle, nor game of any kind. He found tracks, lots of them, but they were old and stale.

Late in the afternoon, Jack jumped a deer. By then he was so hungry and weary that he was not prepared. The deer startled him, and by the time he brought his rifle to his shoulder, the animal was almost out of range. In frustration, Killian fired, and knew before he had finished squeezing the trigger that he had missed. The deer bounded into the brush and Jack slumped down on the ground to reload his rifle. The pain under his armpit returned, but it was a distant low throb, not a full-blown flare-up.

Killian fumbled with the powder and ball, forgot to spit on the patch. "Get your ox out of the ditch," he said aloud. The agony of his hunger was a roar in his ears, blotting out all sensation. Finally he finished reloading his rifle and then began to worry if he had done it right.

Jack carried his doubts with him the rest of the day and he cursed himself for being such a weakling that he allowed himself to succumb to the weight of such thoughts.

Killian went to sleep on the hard ground that night without assuaging his hunger and dreamed of food the entire night: not just any food, but hot apple pies and johnnycakes and beef stew, smoked ham, chicken and dumplings. When he awoke from his tortuous and ragged sleep the next morning, the sun had not yet risen and his hunger had turned into a murderous anger that boiled inside him. But his wound had started to scab over and he favored it so it would not break open. It did not hurt to breathe, so he knew the ribs were not cracked.

"I've got to find game," he said when his eyes came open and he had rubbed the sand of sleep from his lids. "Food. That's prime."

He hunted all morning, following tracks that took him into bewildering mazes in giant mesquite thickets. He sat near a watering hole for most of the afternoon, watching the birds, the maddening birds, fly in every direction. Desperation mingled with the hunger that clutched his belly like some crazed beast and he drank from the watering hole until he was sick to his stomach and had to fight to keep the liquid down.

He stumbled on a jackrabbit late in the day and swung his rifle as it zigzagged across the plain. He led it smoothly, squeezed the trigger and, through the white smoke, saw a puff of dust rise up where the rabbit had been a split-second before. When the smoke cleared, the silence rose up around him and he could still hear the fading echoes of the report ringing in his ears long after all sound had died.

On the third day, Killian fired the ball from his rifle and reloaded it with shot he kept in his possibles pouch for emergencies. He had shot at another jackrabbit and missed, wincing with the pain of his healing wound. Now he was looking for birds, any small game he could bring down with lead pellets. His stomach had knotted up on him, constricted so tightly from lack of water that he knew he had to have both food and drink or he would shrivel up and die an agonizing death.

At times Jack lost all sense of direction, and it took an inordinate amount of concentration for him to realize that he had lost his bearings. When he took a sighting on the sun, he would lurch northward again and find that he had drifted eastward and probably had lost ground, as well.

He hunted all day, his wound starting to itch. The few birds he saw flying were all out of range. He became determined to go on, although all of his instincts told him to turn around and go back over ground that he had already covered. He had thought Mexico was a wilderness when he was deep down in it, but this place called Texas was maddening. At times the mesquite was so thick that he could not penetrate it and had to walk around—always keeping to an easterly course, but he realized, too, that the thickets were full of game. Occasionally he wondered if it would not be better to crawl inside one of the mesquite forests on his hands and knees and hope to find a game trail, lie down near it, and wait for food to come his way.

But every time Jack thought about going into the brush, he backed away from committing himself. Once inside that thicket, he thought, he might never find his way back out. So Killian stayed to the open places, skirting the thicker brush. He found a small creek that was almost dried up, but managed to dig out enough subsurface water to wet his parched and cracked lips. The fleeting wetness on his lips only increased his hunger, and after a time he realized that he might possibly go mad long before he starved to death.

Late one afternoon, when the sun was beating down on him like Lucifer's own lash, Jack came upon a vast open plain dotted with cactus: cholla, prickly pear, ocotillo, black chaparral. As he watched, the plain filled with water until a lake stood before him, shimmering silver in the sunlight. He stood there transfixed, licking his lips, wondering if this was not a mirage, after all. It looked so real. He thought he saw ducks on the water, and he saw little wavelets bobbing like foam on an inland ocean.

He saw a deer emerge from the far thicket and approach the lake. As Jack watched, the deer entered the water, and he saw it swimming across the water, fighting the current. He thought he might kill it when it emerged from the lagoon on the other side, so he ran as fast as he could to head it off.

He ran right into the water and it evaporated in an instant. The deer bounded away across hard, dry, cracked land. Jack sagged to his knees and sobbed as he raked the dry sand with his hands, hoping they would be wet when he brought them up to his face. He poured the sand over his head and only then knew that it was not water.

Killian began to lose long intervals of time. He did not scratch his wound, although it itched fiercely with the sweat seeping into the scab. Pieces of hours fell from his memory and he could not account for them. He began to distrust his own thinking, his judgment. And he was no longer certain of where he was going, nor even where he had been.

"Didn't I just pass that oak an hour ago?" he asked aloud.

And he answered himself: "Nope, it's a different one." Pause. "Isn't it?"

Jack went on like a semi-blind man, missing whole chunks of country as his mind raged over food, as his throat constricted and his tongue swelled and turned wooden in his mouth. Another day went by. Then another. Half mad from hunger, Jack's mind raged with doubts that inflicted his every move, his every step. He wandered in a delirium, driven close to crazy by the cold nights and the blistering hot days, the endless trek to nowhere.

"Did I just come past here? No. Look at the sky."

The sun seemed at times never to move. And Jack became uncertain which way it had moved when he looked up at the sky again.

"Better quit talkin' to yourself," he warned. But he continued to speak aloud and no longer cared if he was going insane.

"Where are the birds?" he asked, and he saw thousands of them in the sky and he could hear the geese bugling and the raspy burr of ducks high overhead. But he knew they were flying toward the Gulf, having left their winter quarters. He almost cried when he realized how high they were all flying and he saw the Vs waver and break up, re-form, none of the wildfowl within range.

Killian stumbled on through a blurred landscape, often crashing into mesquite trees, scratching his hands and forearms. He felt thin and weak, no longer able to speak above a scratchy whisper. He fell down more than once, and was surprised when he picked himself up again and staggered northeasterly, somehow blindly following the slow arc of the sun across the immense sky.

"God, if there be a God, help me," he rasped when he fell and lay next to a lone oak in the midst of a vast savannah under blessed shade. Jack sat there for a long time, his rifle across his lap, numb to the ache in his stomach, the harsh pain in his throat, the dryness of his mouth.

He dozed there, fell into a fitful, shallow sleep, his mouth open, his swollen tongue, dark and cracked from dehydration, lolling at the corner of his mouth, like some eyeless creature in its den. A breeze ruffled the strands of hair lacing his forehead, but he did not feel it. The sky darkened overhead as clouds scudded in from the northwest. The air temperature dropped and the breeze stiffened. Killian dropped deeper into sleep, and his eyelids quivered as he dreamed of grog shops and tables laden with food, golden-brown meats and tawny glasses of ale, green and red vegetables spilling from gourd cornucopias.

The rain spattered down, and still Jack did not awaken. He was at sea, standing on the deck of a ship, the spray from the whitecapped waves dashing into his face. Seagulls flew all around and he heard their wings whisper as they passed him by and silver fish leaped onto the deck and cooks picked them up and baked them over glowing fires in iron stoves.

The wind quickened and the rain drove down harder, splashing Jack's face, jolting him awake. Water trickled down his face and into his mouth and he lapped at it greedily, letting it soak into his swollen tongue before it could reach his throat.

Killian shoved the rifle to the ground, stood up and stepped out from under the tree. He took off his hat, turned it upside down and laid it on the ground. He cupped his hands and tilted his head back so that the rain would fill his mouth. When his hands were full, he drank from them. He could not get enough of the lifesaving waters, but he gained strength with every drop that trickled down his throat.

"Yes, yes," he murmured, and licked his forearms, then tilted his head backward again and cupped his hands. The wind changed direction and he turned with it, caught the rain on a slant. "More, more," he said, wishing the rain would fall faster, but felt better than he had in days. Now there was hope, he reasoned, and he felt renewed, strength gathering in his bones and limbs.

The rain passed quickly, but the sun did not come out. Killian drank the small amount of water in his hat, wrung out his shirt and trousers and drank the moisture contained in their fibers. He picked up his rifle, cleaned the pan and poured fresh powder into it. The touchhole was protected by a small bird-feather quill and he knew the powder inside was dry.

He thought of going south, in the direction the brief

storm was headed, but thought better of it and continued northward, the spring in his step reflecting the newfound optimism in his heart.

Jack hunted now with a vengeance, and as the shadows of afternoon grew long, he felt sure he would find game before the sun went down. He saw fresh tracks in the damp earth and followed the spoor of three deer until they split up. He tracked the larger set of tracks as they veered off to the east. He watched the sun crawl across the sky with a desperation that he'd never had before, resenting every fraction that it moved toward the western horizon.

He came upon the wagon tracks rutted deep in a road at the same time as he saw the deer. The animal stood upwind in a copse of trees, its head turned away from him, tilted slightly upward as it tested the wind with quivering nostrils. Jack ducked down and held his breath. He removed the quill from the touchhole of his rifle and squeezed the trigger as he cocked the hammer, hoping the lock would not make a noise.

When he looked up the deer was still there, a plump, antlerless animal, frozen there in the trees beyond the road. It dipped its head and drank from a puddle of water left over from the passing storm.

Jack edged closer, measuring the distance in his mind. The deer was at least two hundred yards away and he cursed himself for loading the rifle with bird shot. But he made no sound as he crept closer, hoping to get within range.

"There's a chance," he said soundlessly, only his lips moving.

He hoped the deer would hold until he could get close enough for a shot. He dared not look at it as he continued his stalk. He prayed for it to stay there as he took one step, then another, careful to make no noise.

He looked up finally, and the deer had moved only a few yards from where it had been. He judged the distance to be less than a hundred yards—still out of range. He had to close the distance to under forty yards, he knew, and aim for its head and neck. He went over all of his movements in his mind as he stepped still closer, hunched over like a deformed creature.

Eighty yards, seventy. The deer was browsing in the open, still upwind. Jack glimpsed it every ten yards. Fifty yards, forty. He crept still closer, his heart locked tight in his chest, his breathing so shallow, he felt barely alive.

When he judged that he was about thirty yards away, Jack slowly stood up, bringing the rifle to his shoulder. The deer stiffened as Jack's finger curled around the trigger. Then it jumped just as Jack fired. A puff of smoke and a hiss, no report. The fine powder in the pan ignited, but the coarse grains inside the firing chamber did not explode.

"Powder's wet," Jack breathed as the deer bounded out of sight.

Jack sat down next to the road and bowed his head. He cursed himself silently, then stretched out, all hope for food gone. He lay beside his rifle and wondered if it was time to reload the rifle and blow his brains out. He did not want to die a slow death from starvation. He wanted to end it right there. He did not think he could go another day without food.

It was then that he heard something far off. He listened intently, then sat up, so he could hear better.

He sat there for a long time, wondering what it was he heard. The sounds seemed to be coming closer, but they were muffled and at times faded away. Quietly, quickly, he reloaded his rifle, this time with patch and ball.

Perhaps, he thought, he would not have to kill himself after all. Someone might do it for him.

19

JUANITO SALAZAR WATCHED from horseback as the drovers pulled the wagon out of the mud. He could hear the ropes groan as they stretched taut, and then the wooden spokes of the wheels creaked as the weight of the wagon bore down on them. It had been a trying day, with tired mules and frisky horses, angry men arguing over nothing. Then the cloudburst had turned the primitive road into a mass of mud. For the last hour they had struggled through rain and a quagmire, and finally one wagon had foundered in a muddy sinkhole. It had taken over an hour to pull the wheels out of sandy wash, meaning they had lost most of another day.

"Vámanos," Juanito called and tossed his hand westward as he reined his horse back onto the road. The wagons creaked and the leather whined as the four teams strained at the harness.

The caravan of Springfield wagons had left Galveston over a week ago, having taken goods for sale from the Box B two weeks before and loaded them on ships bound for New Orleans. This was Baron's road, but Juanito had helped build it. Both had tired of hauling their products to Matagorda and sailing to New Orleans, but they still made occasional trips. So Martin had opened up the country in the past ten years, cutting a road to Galveston, buying wagons so they could haul overland, which shortened both the time and the distance they had to cover to get their goods to market.

Juanito looked at the sun. He had sent two scouts ahead. They should have been back by now. Another man rode well behind the caravan, rifle at the ready, to give warning. They had had some trouble over the years with bandits and with small bands of Apache and Comanche. But he didn't expect any trouble this trip. So far they had been able to defend themselves and deliver some punishment to marauders. And word had gotten around that Martin Baron was not a man to let another best him by either cheating or robbery.

The wagons carried lumber and nails, new hammers and saws, adzes, planing knives, froes for making shingles. One wagon was full of staples for the growing number of hired hands: bacon, pork, flour, coffee, rice, beans, seeds for the garden. Martin had been adding onto the main house ever since his wife, Carolyn, had borne him a son, whom he had named Anson Edward Baron.

The Box B had grown in the past eleven years, and Martin had acquired more land as the fortunes of the Aguilar family declined. Juanito figured that Baron now owned more than three hundred thousand acres. The Apaches had continued their depredations against the Aguilar's Rocking A brand, running off cattle, killing stock and men and women. At Juanito's advice, Martin had arranged a meeting between some of the Apache braves and had worked out a system.

"We will give the Apaches one out of every four

cattle we raise if they will leave us alone," Juanito had suggested.

"Why that number?"

"One cow for us, another for illness and one for the Apache."

"That still leaves one cow."

"One cow for God," Juanito had said.

"That's how we used to plant," Martin said. "One seed for us, one for the birds, one for God."

And that is what Baron had done. So far they had been lucky, but a few Apaches were not the whole of the Indian nations who roamed the brush country.

But Victoria Aguilar was still paying a bounty for Apache and Comanche scalps, while Benito decried the policy. Now the bad blood between the two had grown to fearful proportions. Martin had told Juanito that one day Benito would either ride off or murder Victoria or Victoria would kill him. "She would never walk away," Martin said. And Juanito agreed with him. "She's just as much a part of this country as the mesquite trees."

"Or the cactus," Juanito had said.

Victoria Aguilar held a strange fascination for Martin, Juanito knew. And she was fond of Martin, treating him more like a son or a lover. Perhaps she was shrewd enough to know that Baron would husband the land she sold him, and if her luck ever changed for the better he might consider selling some of it back to her. Juanito was sure that she was not beyond a little deceit in her dealings with gringos.

"Mira," called Mánolo, one of the drovers. *"Ya viene,* Tomás."

Tomás, one of the scouts, was approaching cautiously on horseback, riding slowly. But the horse was lathered and Juanito knew he must have been riding hard. Too hard, damn him.

"What's going on?" Juanito asked in Spanish when Tomás drew near.

"There is a strange gringo up ahead by the side of the road. He has a rifle and a mad stare in his eyes."

"A mad stare in his eyes? How do you know that?"

"I was much afraid."

"Did he try to shoot you?"

"He did not try to shoot me. But he was ready to shoot, I think."

"Did he have his rifle to his shoulder?"

"He had his rifle ready to draw to his shoulder, I think."

"Where is this gringo now? Where is Alberto?"

"Alberto, he is watching him. I rode back to tell you this thing."

"Take care of your horse. You rode him too hard. I will ride ahead and see what this gringo is doing here."

"I think I have seen this man before," Tomás said.

"Eh?"

"I think so."

"Where?"

"In Mexico. In Matamoros. And I have seen a drawing of his face."

"Where?"

"In Galveston, I think."

"You think. Do you not know?" Juanito's mouth drew very tight and his eyes narrowed. He tapped a finger on his saddle horn.

"I know. There is a reward for him. Two hundred American dollars. And pesos, many pesos, in Mexico."

"What is his name?"

"I do not know. I think he is a horse thief."

Juanito laughed. "And who is not a stealer of horses in this country, Tomás?"

Tomás shrugged. Juanito turned his horse to leave.

"Keep the wagons coming. Stay out of the mud."

"We will do that. Take care, Juanito."

Juanito fixed Tomás with a withering glare and spat in the dirt. These *cholos,* he thought, did not have the brains of the piss ant. But Juanito, too, had seen the wanted posters in Galveston. Everyone always looked at them. They were posted on a board outside the constable's office. There were always people they knew, but Juanito always checked them so that he would know who came into the country. Many had stopped by since Martin had acquired the lands, began raising cattle. Some were friends they had known or met before, but some were strangers. Some were outlaws.

If there was only one man, there was no reason to worry, Juanito thought. Alberto would shoot if there was trouble. He was glad that Alberto had been the one to stay behind and watch the gringo. Juanito did not like that term, but it was the one the Mexicans used. It was told to him that the first Americans in Texas and Mexico were always singing a song that sounded like "gringo the lilacs." Juanito knew that they had heard it wrong. It was "green grow the lilacs," and he had heard the song himself. In fact, Martin often hummed or sang snatches of it. Some of the Mexicans referred to the Americans as norteamericanos, which seemed more proper to Juanito's ears. But around the Mexicans, he used the term *gringo* just as they did.

Alberto met Juanito as he neared the place where the scouts had encountered the gringo.

"Where is he, Alberto?"

"He is just around the bend. He is just standing there, weaving from side to side. Maybe he is drunk. I do not know."

"Did he try to shoot you?"

"He did not see me."

"Did you not call out to him?"

"I do not know his name. I think there is a reward on his head."

So, thought Juanito, the two men had talked it over. The man was probably wanted alive, not dead.

"Stay here. I will approach the man."

"Take care."

Juanito dismounted. He carried his rifle with him as he rounded the bend in a crouch. When he saw the man, he stopped. The man was no longer standing. He was sitting down. He appeared asleep at first, but as Juanito watched, he saw that the man was only dozing. His eyes were closed, but he held his rifle with both hands, resting it in his lap.

"Hello there," called Juanito. "Do you speak English?"

Jack Killian looked up with bleary eyes. He was too tired and hungry to care anymore.

"Just shoot me, damn you, and get on with it."

"I am not going to shoot you," Juanito said. "And I do not want you to shoot me."

"Who in the devil are you?"

"I am Juanito Salazar. If you need help, we will provide it."

"You got any food?"

"Yes. Are you hungry?"

"I haven't eaten in a week," Killian said.

Juanito whistled and Alberto came running, curiosity blossoming on his face.

"The wagons will be along in a little while," Juanito said, not without compassion. "My friend and I will help you walk. Give Alberto your rifle. It must feel heavy."

Warily Jack looked up at the two men. Mexicans, he thought, although the first one spoke very good English and did not seem to have a Mexican accent, exactly.

"I ain't giving up my gun."

"Very well. Let us help you to your feet. We have food and water. I am leading a caravan of wagons to my friend's ranch."

"Is there a ranch nearby?"

"It is not far," Juanito said. "Come."

He and Alberto helped Killian to his feet.

"What is your name?" Juanito asked.

"John Killian."

"Good. Well, John Killian, you are welcome to what we have, and if you wish, we will take you to the Box B and you can rest up. What happened to your horse?"

"I had three horses. All stolen."

"Do you know who stole them?"

"An Apache I was huntin'."

"You were hunting this Apache?"

"Yes."

"Why?"

"He and his bunch tried to kill me."

"Ah. Do you know who this Apache is?"

Jack shook his head. "He left me a kind of mark on the ground when he took my remuda."

"What did this mark look like?"

"I'll show you." Jack drew the outline he had seen in the dirt. "Looks like a knife to me."

"Ah, it is a knife. That is a very bad Apache. You are lucky he took only your horses."

"Who is he?"

"He is called Cuchillo."

"Knife, in Spanish," Killian said.

The wagons pulled up a short time later. Jack walked toward them like a man walking against the wind. His feet were leaden boots, his legs rubbery, unstable. He felt as if his belly had shrunk against his backbone.

The wagons came to a stop when Juanito held up his hand. All of the men looked at the white man, saw the bright hunger in his eyes, the dirty clothes caked with dirt and mud, the worn-out boots.

Juanito watched Killian, saw that he was in bad shape. But he admired him for going on his own. He had expected the man would need help. He shook his head, barked some orders in Spanish.

"Give this man some bread and jerky, a little water."

Alberto gave Killian the food. Jack wolfed it down, choked, but continued eating.

"Do not take so much," Juanito warned.

"Starved, starved," Killian said.

"There is no reason for a man to go hungry in this country," Juanito said.

"Huh?"

"There is plenty to eat."

"Couldn't get no game. Missed."

"There is the prickly pear, nopales," Juanito said. "The barrel cactus is filled with water. The mesquite is food. There are lizards and toads. A man need not go hungry."

Killian turned sharply and looked at Juanito. "I'm a white man, goddammit. I don't eat lizards and toads."

"To a hungry man, food is food," Juanito said calmly.

Killian eyed Juanito sharply as he chewed on hard-tack and jerky. The lids edged down into a dark squint. "You ain't no Mexican."

"I am Argentine."

"A damned greaser, nonetheless."

Juanito stiffened. But he did not say anything. He stood there, his face impassive, his features frozen in a noncommittal mask.

Killian finished the food, held out his hands for more. Alberto looked at Juanito. Juanito shook his head.

"Ain't you goin' to give me no more?" Killian asked.

"A little at a time. Can you climb up into the wagon? We'll take you to the Box B and you can eat your fill."

"Damn you, man, I ain't had no food in a month of Sundays and damned little water. I'm still hungry."

"You might die if you eat too much right now," Juanito said softly.

"Damned greaser," Killian muttered.

"Mr. Killian, if you call me or any of these men a greaser one more time, I'll blow your gringo head off. Now get in that wagon or we'll leave you where you stand."

"Who in hell do you think you're talkin' to?" Killian blared.

"A man who is in trouble," Juanito said. "A man who starves in a land of plenty. A man who runs from a lone Apache who has stolen his horses. A man who is nothing but a beggar."

Killian stepped back as if Juanito had slapped him across the face. He started to bring his rifle up to his shoulder, but he moved like a man swimming in quicksand. Juanito grabbed the rifle from his hands and sent it flying through the air, twisting like a thrown stick, around and around. Killian reached for his knife, but Juanito's strong hand gripped him at the wrist.

"You bastard," Killian swore.

"I can snap your wrist like a twig," Juanito said quietly. "Do you want to be a cripple, also?"

Juanito applied more pressure until Killian winced with the pain. He relaxed and Juanito let Jack's hand drop away from the knife.

"All right, you win this time," Killian said.

"You should know something about that knife on your belt, Killian. You should not draw it without reason, nor keep it without honor. I could leave you here to die, or my offer still stands. You come to the Box B with us and eat of our food and then decide what you want to do. But I ask you to look at the faces of the men on these wagons. They all know who you are. They know there is a reward for your capture. They are all men who could use some extra money. They have families to feed."

Killian looked at the men sitting on the wagons. They showed no expression on their faces beyond vague smiles that were chilling to behold.

"They have seen your likeness on wanted posters in Galveston. So long as you are my guest, you are safe from harm. If I turn you loose, they'll have you bound in rope before you can reach that rifle of yours or draw your blade."

Killian thought about it. He threw up his hands in surrender.

"Mind if I go get my rifle?" he asked.

"Alberto, bring the rifle," Juanito said in Spanish. To Killian, he said, "Climb up on the wagon. We are less than two days away from the ranch. I hope you have a comfortable trip. We will eat when we make night camp at sundown."

"I—I'm sorry, Salazar. I—I made a mistake."

Juanito smiled thinly. "A man is allowed just so many," he said cryptically. "I will not count this one against you."

"Thanks," said Killian as he climbed up into the wagon.

Alberto carried the rifle to Juanito.

"Keep it until we make camp," he said in Spanish. "Unload it and then give it back to him. I do not think we will have any more trouble from the gringo."

Alberto grinned and scampered away to catch up his horse.

"Move the wagons," Juanito ordered in Spanish as the scouts rode on ahead. He kept his horse to the side of the wagon carrying Killian so that he could keep an eye on the man.

The road took them to a creek lined with small cottonwoods and willows. There the wagons pulled up in a circle. Juanito posted guards and waited for the scout in the rear, Miguel Hueso, to catch up. Two of the cooks began to gather firewood before Juanito dismounted. Killian climbed out of the wagon.

"I'm still hungry," he said.

"First you must slake your thirst," Juanito told him, pointing to the creek. He watched as Killian lay flat and drank from the branch. "Let the water fill your belly," he said. "That way you may be able to keep the food down."

Killian pushed his face into the water, splashed it over his head and back. "Ahhh," he said when he got to his feet. "That feels better."

"Tell me what brings you to this country," Juanito said in a friendly tone.

"That's my business," Killian said.

"Yes, it is, of course."

"What's the name of this creek?" Killian asked.

"We call it Frontera. It borders the Baron ranch on the east."

"Do you know the Aguilar rancho?"

"I do," Juanito replied. "Is that who you came to see?"

"That's my business, too."

"You know them?"

"I don't know them, no. Just curious."

Juanito held his tongue. There was more to this norteamericano than met the eye, he thought. He walked well away from camp to wait for Miguel. Miguel Hueso was a full-blooded Lipan Apache. Juanito had learned much from him, a great deal about Apache ways. Men could learn from each other, he knew. And he wanted to know more about John Killian.

So he watched Killian out of the corner of his eye. The man was beaten, he knew, but it was only temporary. He was carrying something around with him, and it would come out eventually, one way or the other. There was no need to press it. For one thing, the man had a big chip on his shoulder toward Mexicans. But, as Juanito had discovered, that was not uncommon among Americans. Ever since the Alamo had fallen, many Texans carried grudges toward all Mexicans, even though it had happened over twenty years before.

Miguel rode up a few moments later, appearing

mysteriously out of the mesquite, not on the road. Juanito smiled. Miguel was a good man, knew how to stay quiet and out of sight. And he did not miss much. That was why Juanito felt safe with Miguel guarding their rear.

"*Hola*, Miguel. *¿Qué pasó?*"

"*Nada.* I saw nothing."

"Good. We found a man down the road. An American."

"Who is he?"

"His name is John Killian. He has hunger."

"He must be stupid."

"No, just ignorant," Juanito said.

Miguel laughed. "I am tired," he said. "There are too many bones in this saddle."

"Take some rest. There will be food soon."

"Good." Miguel rode into camp and Juanito stood awhile looking at the sky. He was hoping they would make the home ranch by tomorrow—La Loma de Sombra, as Martin called it. That was where they would unload the lumber and supplies. Now that Martin's son was eleven, Martin wanted to build yet another room on the house, and he needed another barn for the milk cows.

The sky had cleared as quickly as it had filled with thunderheads a few hours before. In the west, the horizon was turning crimson. Tomorrow would be a fair day, he thought. They should make good time, although the road wasn't much better past the boundary line. Rough on wagon wheels.

When Juanito got back to camp, the men were talking, pointing to the sky. Killian was sitting down, his back against a wagon wheel, smoking a rolled cigarette that someone must have given him.

Juanito looked in the direction the men were pointing. He walked faster, then started to run.

A huge pall of smoke hung in the western sky, began to spread. It could have been anywhere within forty to fifty miles. But in his heart Juanito knew that in that direction the black cloud could have come from only one place.

La Loma de Sombra. Shadow Hill, the Baron ranch headquarters.

20

JUANITO DID NOT ask any questions, but began barking orders immediately.

"Put out the fire. Hitch up the horses to the wagons. Alberto, you and Miguel saddle fresh mounts."

Killian struggled to his feet. He gave Miguel Hueso a hard look.

"What's goin' on?"

"There is a fire at the Box B," Juanito said. "Find yourself a horse or get in one of the wagons."

"Ain't we gonna eat?"

"We'll eat on the way. There's jerky and hardtack. Hurry. We will not wait for you."

"You goin' to travel this road at night?"

"If we have to burn torches or crawl," Juanito said.

The men scrambled, putting out the fire, shaking out the lines, hitching up the horses. In a few moments there was hardly a sign that they had been there. Killian rode in the lead wagon, sitting atop a load of lumber that rattled and clacked with each bounce. It grew dark suddenly after the sun went down and the trees turned green, then black.

Juanito kept the scouts in close, no more than thirty yards separating them from the caravan, forward or rear. He had run the wagons at night before. He didn't like it, but sometimes it was necessary. Once before, they had an encounter with marauding Comanches and had to endure a day-long running fight. It was only after the sun had gone down that the Indians had stopped harassing them.

This was a different matter. If Martin was in trouble, they would have to drive all night and hope to make the rancho by dawn. Juanito dreaded what he might see. He had watched the smoke crawl across the sky in an ugly dark smear for as long as the light held, and now it seemed he could smell the burning wood.

The dawn broke and the men in the caravan rubbed their eyes as though they had been sleeping. Some of them had. The horses and mules knew the way to the Box B and the road kept them from straying into the brush. Juanito felt as if his saddle had turned to stone, and he shook off the weariness like many an old soldier going into battle without a good night's sleep.

They might yet have to fight, Juanito thought. There was still a pall of smoke in the sky, although it had thinned out considerably. And he thought he could still smell wood smoke. He took note of his surroundings and knew they had not far to go. A couple of rises would bring them within sight of La Loma de Sombra. Already he could make out the shapes of cattle in scattered clumps along the still dim horizon. The cows gave him some comfort. At least these few head had not been run off by marauding Indians.

As he stretched his arms and flexed his legs, he became aware of the emptiness of his belly and the fluttering of butterflies inside. His gut quivered, not in fear, but in anticipation of what he might find over the second rise.

He rode ahead to check on the lead scouts. Killian was asleep in the lead wagon, lying flat on his back atop a tarped-over wooden box full of tools. The man was snoring softly, a ripple of bass notes floating above the crackle of harness, the rattle of D rings and buckles.

Miguel stopped his horse as Juanito rode up to the point. His face was a solemn bronze mask.

"Ten cuidado," Miguel whispered.

"¿Qué pasa?"

"No sé."

Juanito looked around. The cattle had not moved, but seemed to be grazing. Their heads were down. Then one raised its head, but still did not move.

"Something is wrong," Juanito said.

"Something bad is wrong," Miguel replied.

"What?"

"I do not know," Miguel said again.

Juanito looked at the cattle. "They are grazing, but they are not moving."

"Yes. I think . . ."

Before Miguel could finish his sentence, the ground seemed to explode in several places. Juanito's spine crackled with electricity. The hairs on the back of his neck stood on end. The high-pitched screams, the piercing yips of a dozen or more Apaches filled the air, turning Juanito's blood to blue ice.

Miguel shot an Apache who rose up in front of him at point-blank range. Juanito jerked his rifle from its boot, fired at a nearly naked brave charging him from a dozen yards away, his body smeared with red dirt, his face painted like some hideous harlequin mask.

"To arms, to arms," Juanito cried in Spanish to the drovers, and seconds later he heard the crackle of muskets and rifles. Arrows whistled through the air, whiffling past his ear in chilling whispers. And still he heard the high-pitched yelps, the terrible screeches of Apaches running in every direction. Several Indians started after the wagons, and Juanito wheeled his horse just as another Apache appeared out of nowhere, brandishing a deadly spear. He heard it riffle past, missing his horse by scant inches.

Juanito poured powder down the barrel of his flintlock rifle with trembling hands, his horse pounding toward the wagons and five Apaches on the run. He saw his drovers take cover and saw orange flashes from their rifles. Behind him, Miguel wrestled with an Apache trying to pull him from his horse. Alberto knelt down in front of the wagons, his horse shot out from under him. He took aim on an Apache and squeezed the trigger. The Indian's scream cut off and he dove into the ground and crumpled to a dead heap.

Juanito made it to the wagons, wheeled, and jerked his horse to a halt. John Killian stood atop the wagon, his face a mask of concentration. He fired his pistol with deadly accuracy, and an Apache threw up his arms, a look of surprise on his face, a small black hole in his chest. His knees buckled and he sank like a mendicant at prayer, sucking blood through his throat before he choked and fell forward.

Killian looked down at Juanito and grinned as he picked up his rifle and began to pour powder down the barrel. Juanito rammed a ball home with his wiping stick and poured fine powder in the pan of his flintlock, blew it away just as an arrow rammed into his pommel and twanged like a broken banjo string.

A Mexican drover tumbled off a wagon and screamed for what seemed an eternity as Juanito shot an Apache trying to cut the traces of the lead team in the front wagon. Killian tracked a running Apache, led him three feet and squeezed the trigger. The Apache, as if he were tethered on a string, stopped dead in his tracks and shot backward a foot before falling to the ground, a black hole beneath his armpit, blood gushing from the opposite side.

Killian fired another pistol and knocked an Apache

off a mule the Indian was trying to steal. Smoke and screams filled the air as Juanito rode back and forth along the wagons, shooting, reloading, dodging arrows and spears. His drovers fought hard, but he saw one man he couldn't identify go down, his skull crushed by a war club and no Apache in sight.

Juanito soon realized that there were more Apaches attacking them than he had first thought. They swarmed everywhere like a cloud of hornets. Men screamed and went down, Apaches came at them out of the white smoke from their rifles, and there seemed to be no end to them. He saw Killian wrestling with an Indian atop the wagon, both jabbing at each other with knives. He drew his pistol and shot an Indian climbing up the side of the same wagon trying to get at Killian from the rear.

He no longer remembered reloading, but knew he was low on powder. He had not yet fired his pistol and cursed himself that he had two others in his saddlebags, out of reach in the melee. He kept ramming balls down his rifle barrel and seating them atop powder. He adjusted his flint twice and felt it wear down from the chipping of the hammer.

The mules brayed and kicked in their traces. Apaches on horseback rode by and slashed the leather harness and chased the teams off as drovers fired into their backs.

Two Apaches came riding fast up to the wagons, veered and headed straight for Juanito. He had just reloaded, so he took aim at the nearest man and squeezed the trigger when the Indian was right on top of him. Then he grabbed his rifle by the barrel, burning his hands, and swung it, unseating the second Apache. He heard the rifle stock crack and saw the Indian tumble from the saddle. The Apache landed on his feet and rose up to full height and drew his knife. He charged straight at Juanito, screaming at the top of his lungs, his face a grotesque painted mask.

Juanito fumbled for his knife, grabbed his pistol butt instead. He jerked it from its holster, but it was too late to fire it. He lowered his head and met the charge, ramming the Apache in the solar plexus and driving him backward. He felt the sharp rip of the knife in his lower back and flipped the Apache over on his back. Then Juanito waded into him, kicking the Indian in the face. He cocked his pistol and put it to the man's forehead and pulled the trigger.

Brains and blood exploded in a crimson cloud as the ball tore through the Apache's skull and blew out the back of his head like a bowlful of bloody mush. Panting, Juanito staggered away and fell against the wagon just as Killian shoved an Apache off the side, the Indian's throat slashed from ear to ear, spurting blood all over Juanito as he fell.

The firing died down and Juanito no longer heard the yips and yells of the Apaches. White smoke billowed everywhere, hugged the ground like sodden clouds, and the air was filled with the stench of blood and burnt powder, urine and voided excrement. With shaking hands, Juanito reloaded his single-shot pistol with the last of his powder and rammed a ball home through the twist of the rifling. He looked up. Killian grinned back down at him.

"A hell of a fight, eh?"

"It's not over," Juanito said.

"Hell, they're runnin' now, pickin' up their wounded. Know who that was who run the mules off?"

Juanito shook his head.

"That was Cuchillo, sure as snuff in a tin, and I missed him by a wolf cub's curly hair."

"I'm going to see who's still alive, see how many mules we have left. We've got to get these wagons over that next rise."

"I'll give you a hand," said Killian, who seemed to have found an inner strength. He did not look like the man Juanito had picked up on the road the day before. There was a spring in Killian's step when he bounded down from the wagon. Together they walked along the wagons, counting the dead, both Apaches and Mexican drovers.

"I count two of your men dead," Killian said.

"Yes. Four Indians."

"Five. There was one under the back wagon. The Mexes gave a good account of themselves."

Juanito winced, but he said nothing. He was not going to reprimand such a fighter as Killian. He had accounted for at least three Indians himself, perhaps one or two more.

Miguel Hueso walked up, straight-backed, black eyes glittering.

"Baron comes," he said in Spanish. "It was he who drove off the enemy."

"Good, Miguel," Juanito said. "They get any cows? Mules? Horses?"

Miguel held up five fingers on one hand, made the sign for cow, two on the other with the sign for horse.

"Go see if you can pick up their tracks, then come back to the ranch house," Juanito told Miguel, who nodded and trotted away.

"Who is that anyway?" Killian asked. "He don't look like no Mexican to me."

"He's an Apache. Of the Lipan tribe."

"A sure-enough Apache Indian?"

"Yes. He is a good man."

"Well, somebody sure cleaned him up some. But how come you got an Apache workin' for you?"

"He was just a boy when I found him. Badly wounded, half crazy with pain. He had been shot several times, scalped."

"Looks like his hair growed back."

"I sewed him up, taught him Spanish, learned many things from him. And I hope he learned some things from me. Anyway, he stayed on. He said he would take up the white man's way if I would help him."

Killian scratched his head in puzzlement. "A damned Apache. I don't get it."

"He is a man," Juanito said. "Like any other. One of Aguilar's men shot him, scalped him, left him for dead."

"Those damned Aguilars."

"Do you know them?"

"No, I just heard about 'em," Killian said laconically.

But Juanito suspected that Killian knew more about the Aguilar family than he was telling. One more secret the man had inside him.

"Well, let's see if we can't patch things together, get this caravan moving. The Box B lies just over that next rise."

"And Baron, who's he?"

"He is the man who owns all this blood-soaked land," Juanito said wryly.

"I can't wait to meet him," Killian said.

Juanito spoke to Alberto quietly about the dead men, told him to see that they were carried down to the ranch, given to the women to clean up and lay out.

Martin Baron knelt down next to a dead cow. Its feet were hobbled with braided rope. A small boy stood next to him, holding a small-caliber rifle. Martin looked up when he saw Juanito approaching, a stranger at his side. Baron's face was smudged with smoke, his clothes reeked of it. He looked as if he had been a week without sleep. His eyes were red-rimmed and puffy, his hair tangled where it leaked from his battered, begrimed hat.

"They sure foxed you, Juanito," Martin said in English. "Hobbled these cows and hid behind 'em."

"Yes, they did. Pretty smart. I learn more from the Apache all the time."

Martin stood up, looked at the stranger, stuck out his smoke-blackened hand.

"I'm Martin Baron," he said.

"John Killian." He shook Martin's hand with a firm grip.

Martin looked at Juanito, raised his eyebrows.

"We found him on the road," Juanito explained. "He was lost and starving."

"Starving in this country? Hell, there's more to eat out here than in New Orleans, and some of it is better grub."

Juanito and Martin laughed. Killian scowled.

"One year we had it pretty bad," Martin explained. "A diet of jackrabbit, lizard, snake and mesquite cakes. There was cholera in Galveston and all over and the Apaches had run off most our cattle. With the drought and all, we had to eat what we could find. Wasn't meaning to poke fun at you."

Killian's expression softened. "I take no offense," he said.

"Well, we lost a few head of cattle," Martin said to Juanito. "Some horses. Any of your men?"

"Two, I think. Alberto will bring them to the women. Miguel said we lost two horses, five of the cattle."

"They run off six cows down at the house and three good horses. We didn't lose a man."

"What about the house? They burn it?"

Martin laughed. "No, they burnt up a barn and all the hay in it. Kept us busy all day. Guess they knew you were coming with the wagons. We just got through running them off. Caroline's setting the table. We heard your gunfire up here on the flat."

"I am glad they did not burn your house down," Juanito said.

Martin slapped his friend on the back. "Well, you brought enough lumber to get another started, didn't you?"

"We could get a room out of it."

"And you brought the special package?"

"Yes," Juanito replied.

"Killian," Baron said, "come on down to the house with us and we'll have some grub."

"I'm obliged," Killian said.

"How do you like your lizard?"

Killian laughed and Martin and Juanito joined in.

"Pa, are we having lizard?" asked the boy.

"Anson, you can have whatever you want," Martin said, tousling the boy's hair. "Why, I'll bet your mama could even fix you a lizard pie."

Anson Baron frowned. "Aw, you're just funnin' me, Pa."

"Nice boy you got there," said Killian.

"Anson, shake hands with Mr. Killian. I'll bet he's got a tale to tell us over dinner."

Anson shyly stuck out his hand. Killian shook it warmly. "Mighty nice to meet you, Anson," he said, and it sounded genuine.

"Yes, sir," Anson said.

"Let's see about getting those wagons down to the house. Then we'll eat and see about going after those Apaches."

"Miguel is picking up their tracks now," Juanito said.

"Or riding with them," Martin said.

"I trust Miguel."

"I don't," Martin snapped. "But," he added quickly, "I trust you, Juanito."

With Martin taking command, Juanito and his drovers got the wagons hitched that had been cut away by the Indians and the caravan rolled toward La Loma de Sombra. Killian rode in the lead wagon again and was surprised when the wagon topped the rise and started down a shallow hill. There stood the ranch house, some pens, corrals, a half-acre garden; barns— one that was still smoldering—and an endless expanse of flat land, shining green in the sun with waving grasses that made it look like an emerald ocean.

"My God," he breathed and the Mexican drover looked at him and grinned.

"She is pretty, no?"

"I never expected anything like this in such a god-forsaken country."

"Don Martín, he make the grass grow, eh?"

Cattle grazed as far as Killian could see. Here and there he saw adobe huts and children playing, dogs and cats running everywhere. After days of trudging through the thick brush, hiding near prairie dog towns and in mesquite thickets, Killian could hardly trust his eyes. At the main house, he saw men and women gathered together, the men carrying rifles. There were girls and boys, too, and they were all smiling and waving as Martin Baron led the wagons down the hill. A cheer rose up from the various bunches of people as Baron waved back.

Juanito led the wagons to a barn beyond the house. Killian jumped down, began helping the men unload the lumber and goods.

"Come on up to the house with me, Killian," Juanito said. "The men can handle this."

"I'm willin' to work for my keep."

"It is not necessary."

Sheepishly Killian grabbed his rifle, walked away from the others and joined Juanito.

"You speak very good English," he said to Juanito.

"Thank you."

"You sound like an educated man."

"I have been to schools and my father was a scholar."

"You know cattle?"

Juanito nodded.

"Is Baron making a living at it?"

Juanito shook his head. "Not yet."

"I saw me some cattle out there in that grass. Looked fat."

"They are. We are slowly opening up markets for beef."

"Where?"

"New Orleans," Juanito said, then increased his gait as if he no longer wanted to talk to Killian. Killian had to trot to catch up.

"It's a long way from here to New Orleans," Killian said.

"It gets shorter all the time."

"Damn, if that don't beat all. Selling beef to a bunch of pork eaters in New Orleans."

Juanito grinned. "Martin has confidence in himself."

"I can see that," Killian said.

At the house, Martin introduced Killian to his wife, Caroline. Over the years, she had become even more beautiful than she was on the day Martin first saw her. She was just over five feet tall, with black hair and blue eyes, a ruddy complexion from long hours spent in the garden. Her small hands were veined like sculptures, but Killian could sense the strength in her legs and arms. Her son, Anson, was the spitting image of his mother, with his dark curly hair, smoky blue eyes, full lips.

Caroline nodded to Killian, but did not offer her hand or speak. Killian wondered what her voice sounded like. Her chiseled cheekbones and straight nose gave her a patrician look, and even her long hair braided to pigtails gave him the illusion that she was a woman of uncommon bloodlines.

"Nice to meet you, ma'am," Killian said, touching the brim of his hat.

"You'll meet the others later," Martin said. "Wash up out back and we'll get to the feed trough. Juanito, will your men be ready to ride?"

"As soon as you want."

"Eat first, then we'll go after those thieves, get our stock back."

Juanito looked up the rise beyond La Loma de Sombra, but he saw no sign of Miguel Hueso. Then he walked to the back of the house, where Killian and Baron were both washing up at the pump. The two men were talking when he walked up.

"You've worked cattle, then," Martin was saying.

"Some. I've more a feel for horseflesh."

"You looking for work?"

"I might be," Killian said.

"We can talk about it. We could use someone who can ride and shoot until these Indian troubles are over."

"You think they'll ever be over, Baron?"

"Juanito thinks so. I haven't had any trouble for years until yesterday. When the Apaches and Comanches came by, we gave 'em stock."

"Why do you think they jumped on you yesterday?"

Juanito's senses perked up at Killian's question.

Martin looked at his Argentine friend before he replied. "I think the Indians mean to drive all the settlers out of the Rio Bravo Valley. I think they were just testing the waters with me."

"Well, they didn't get much, did they?"

"No, but on those wagons there," Martin said, "there is something that will damned sure put a crimp in their ambitions the next time they come around."

Juanito smiled.

"What's that?" Killian asked.

"It's a secret for now. I don't want word getting out about it."

Killian looked over toward the barn, but he could see nothing to give him an indication of what Baron was talking about. Martin winked at Juanito.

"Even my men don't know," Martin said. "Right now, it's a secret known only to me and Juanito."

"I hope it works," Killian said lamely, feeling put out that Baron wouldn't wouldn't confide in him.

Martin finished washing up and worked the pump for Killian and Juanito. Both men laved their hands in the flowing water.

"If it doesn't," Martin said, "all of this will be Apache land once more."

21

BENITO AGUILAR GRIPPED the glass tightly, squeezing it as if to shatter it in his hand. The glass was full of tequila and he had started drinking during siesta time while Pilar slept in the next room. The glass was strong and did not break. The glass was stronger than he was, and so was the tequila inside it. He unclenched his fist and set the glass on the table, right where a beam of sunlight could shine through it, brighten its pale amber color.

The quart bottle of tequila was over half empty and its fire only deepened the hatred burning inside him, igniting it into a melancholy flame. Benito grabbed the glass and downed the tequila in one mighty swallow, felt it burn all the way down to his innards. Quickly he filled the glass again so that it would be ready when his eyes stopped watering and his stomach stopped boiling.

He listened to Pilar's soft snores in the next room and cursed under his breath. He wiped his eyes and took a deep breath, wondering if the tequila would ever build up his courage, give him the strength to face down his sister-in-law Victoria.

Jaime's widow had taken another husband, Benito's younger brother, Augustino Aguilar. Summoned him from Mexico and married him. And being the barren witch that she was, and Benito being unable to sire a child, had made Augustino bed with Pilar, who was pregnant once again with a child not of his own seed.

"How much can a man take?" Benito said aloud. "She inherited all the land. Jaime left me nothing and she treats me like a servant and a pimp. Is there no justice in the world?" And then Benito answered his own question: *"No hay justicia en todo el mundo."*

He drank again of the tequila, and this time it did not burn so much as it went down his throat. But it warmed his belly and stirred his courage. He did not hate Pilar, he decided. She was an innocent victim in all this. No more than a dam for stallions chosen by Victoria Aguilar.

He, Benito, was not even allowed to show affection for the son Pilar had given light to some nine or ten years before. Victoria kept him in her household, raising him as a prince. The boy, whom she had named Matteo, thought that Victoria was his mother and that his father, Jaime, had died before the boy had been born. Only the latter part of which was true. The deceit ate at Benito's gizzard, had eaten at it all these years.

And he had seen the light die in Pilar's eyes, seen how she looked at the boy, Matteo, her natural-born son, from a distance, unable to give him the love that was in her heart, unable to tell him that she had carried him in her belly for more than nine months of his life.

Matteo was spoiled. Victoria protected him, coached him like a king's son to take over the Aguilar rancho upon her death. She had even arranged a marriage for the boy when he came of age in a few years. The bride had been chosen from among Mexico's gentry, and the deal had been struck before the boy was even a year old.

Benito's son, Antonio, had been treated like dirt by Victoria's household. He had nearly attained manhood himself before he died, yet in the eyes of Victoria, he was no more than a peon. And Antonio, spineless creature that he was, had adopted that view of himself. It broke Benito's heart to see the way his son had looked at him, looked at him as nothing more than the father of a lowborn slave. And it broke Benito's heart that his only child, his son, Antonio, had died of the cholera, caught in Galveston the year before. Died there all alone and friendless, had been buried in a pauper's grave. Only this year had Benito learned of Antonio's death and gone to Galveston to dig him up and bring his bones to the Rocking A where he lay in repose behind the casita, a cross and stones to mark his resting place.

The day after Augustino married Victoria, he had come to his older brother Benito and told him what Victoria wanted.

"Pilar is to move into the grand house," Augustino had said. "My wife wants her to bear my child."

"And you would do this—this thing, Augustino?"

"I would do what Victoria wishes. She is unable to bear children."

"Then she must accept what God has given her. She already has a son. What more does she want?"

"Insurance, I believe."

"Have you gone as cold as that woman so soon, little brother?"

"I will not argue you with you, Benito. I have come for Pilar. She will stay with us until some time after she has conceived."

"Victoria does not even love children. They are things to her, Augustino."

"She loves her family. And I am now her family."

"What of me? What of Pilar, my wife? We are a

family, too. She does not treat us so. She keeps it all to herself. She took from our brother Jaime, took from him his very life with her damned bounty policy."

"Big brother, do not fight with me. I am only conveying Victoria's wishes. She wants me to make Pilar with child and I am going to do this thing for her."

"Over my dead body, you son of a whore."

At that, Augustino had drawn a small pistol from his silk waistband and pointed it at Benito's belly. Benito had heard the cock of the pistol, sharp and loud in the silence of the casita, and he had felt the blood drain from his head.

"You would kill me? Your own brother? Your own flesh and blood?"

"I am sorry, Benito. Victoria has ordered me to take Pilar into our home. She does not care whether you live or die. She says that you are a pest."

"And you believe her? I took care of you when you were a runny-nosed baby. I taught you to ride a horse and hunt the deer and the rabbit."

"I am a man now, Benito, with a man's charges in life. Now give me Pilar and we will be gone from this—this hovel."

"My god, you would murder your own brother to satisfy that evil woman. I cannot believe you would do this thing."

"I will do it, Benito."

And Benito had seen something in Augustino's eyes that told him his brother would do just such a thing. Even murder. What power Victoria had over men. First Jaime, then Augustino. And shamefully, he had to admit, with him as well. He had felt pity for Victoria at first, and had allowed Jaime to place his seed inside Pilar's womb—but to have this younger brother poisoned by such a woman, it was too much to bear.

Yet he had stepped aside, not only to save his own life, but to save his brother's soul, and now Pilar had come home, sick at heart that she was carrying not only another man's child, but Benito's own brother's baby.

He had come this far, Benito reasoned, but he could go no further. He could not allow this sin against God. He could not let Victoria just take what she wanted with no regard for a man's dignity, his holy faith, his conscience.

That morning Pilar had been returned to him. For no reason. She had just appeared at the doorway of the casita, tears in her eyes, a bundle of her clothes in her arms.

"What is wrong?" Benito had asked.

"They do not want the baby."

"Why?"

"I do not know. They brought a doctor to see me. He drew the blood from my arm. He looked at it through a device that I have never seen before. There was much talk, and the señora, she beat her breasts and tore her hair. She struck Augustino and drove him from the room, cursing him."

"Did you not hear what the doctor said, Pilar?"

"No, I did not hear him. I could not understand what they were saying. I heard one word, a word I do not know."

"And, what is that word?" Benito had asked.

"It is something like *cefalis,* I think."

"Syphilis? Was that the word?"

"Yes, I think so. What does it mean?"

He had taken her into the house and she had bathed but would eat no food. She said she was tired and had taken to her bed. And now she slept, in ignorance of what had happened to her. And he had not the heart to tell her that she had been infected, probably by that bastard Augustino.

Something must be done. Benito knew that much. Someone must pay for such a humiliation. He knew what the disease was, what it could do. He had seen the crazy old men drinking in the cantinas, the young women infected and spreading the plague among the men they took to their cots. He had heard the stories of the tiny worm that lived in the milk of the men and burrowed into the wombs of the women. And now such a thing had happened to Pilar and probably to the baby she carried in her womb. It was a thing of the devil, a curse that now had come down upon them all. Because of Victoria Aguilar and her evil heart.

He wondered if Jaime's widow now had the disease. If she had slept with Augustino, she probably had the infection. That was why she had cursed him and struck him and tore at her hair and beat her breasts. Perhaps she would kill Augustino. Perhaps, he thought in his drunken stupor, they would kill each other.

Benito looked at the rifle by the door, at the holstered pistol hanging from a peg just above it. The objects blurred, but he brought them into focus. Someone must pay for this shame, the shame brought down upon Pilar and upon him. Someone must truly pay for this indecency.

"God would want it so," Benito said, and it seemed like a benediction from on high to him. God's own words issuing from his mouth. "God would want the devil driven from the house of Aguilar."

But would he, Benito, be the instrument? At that moment, he did not know.

"This must be given some thought," he murmured. "God willing. Yes, God willing."

He poured more tequila into his glass and looked into the depths of the liquid for some sign, some agitation, perhaps, that would show him a divinity was at work. But the alcohol settled in the glass and he saw no swirl of supernatural forces at work, no shining motes glittering in its depths.

In the silence he heard the chirp of a cricket from somewhere near the hearth. Benito knew that the cricket's voice was a good omen. Some said that crickets were guardians of the household, spirits that watched over the inhabitants. Yes, a good omen.

Benito took a small sip of the tequila and listened to the cricket. Then, as suddenly as the chirping had begun, it stopped and the room filled once again with silence. Had he imagined the cricket? He was not sure.

He looked again at the rifle and pistol near the door, then at the wood he had put together, the adobe chinking. A far cry from the jacal they had once lived in, he and Pilar. It had been a fine little house with its own spirit cricket, and he had truly heard the cricket singing from the hearth. Somewhere among the stones he had carried to this place, chipped to shape and set with mortar, the cricket lived, guardian spirit of the household.

Benito knew what he must do. He crossed himself, muttered a brief prayer to the Virgin Mary, crossed himself again.

Benito downed the glass of tequila, lurched to his feet. The cricket had been sign enough. He grasped the edge of the table to steady himself, drew a deep breath and looked straight ahead until his eyes could focus. He staggered slightly to the doorway, reached up for his gun belt, slipped it off the wooden peg. He strapped it on, drew the flintlock from the holster.

He had put a fresh flint in the day before, and the pan was primed with fine powder. A lead caliber ball nestled snug against the *polvo* in the barrel, snug against the lands and grooves. He put the pistol back in the holster gently so he would not jar the ball loose. He picked up the rifle, checked the pan, tested the action. The rifle, too, was loaded, as it always was, ready to shoot.

As he was about to step out the door, Pilar called to him. "Benito. Where are you going?"

"Hunting," he said.

"You would leave me alone?"

He heard her stirring in the next room. The creak of the bed slats echoed in the silence before he replied.

"I will not be gone long," he said, his voice gruff and gravelly with drink. "I will return in a little while."

"Espérate," she said. "Wait."

He heard her groan as she crawled off the bed. He knew she was bending over to slip on her sandals. A moment later, she waddled into the room, her right hand palming her swollen belly, her faded dress billowed out from the waist to just above her knees. Her sandals whispered across the wooden floor, a luxury Benito had laid in for her half a dozen years before.

"¿Pa' 'onde vas?" she asked.

"I told you. I am going to hunt."

"I do not believe you, Benito." She came close to her husband and he turned his head away. She touched his arm and he sucked in a breath. She reached up and tucked a finger under his chin, turned his head so that he faced her.

"What?" he asked.

"I smell the tequila on your breath." Pilar looked over at the table, saw the bottle and glass.

"So I had some tequila. Is that a crime?"

"No, but you do not hunt when you are drinking. And you do not go out at this hour of the day."

"Sometimes I do," Benito said.

"I do not think so. Why do you lie to me? Have I shamed you so much that you treat me like this?"

Benito cringed at her words. His eyes filled with tears.

"Ah," she said.

"No, you do not shame me. It is that witch Victoria. And my little brother Augustino. They bring shame down upon us all."

"It is my shame," she said meekly and bowed her head. She let her hand fall from her husband's chin and walked over to the table. "Put your rifle away and sit with me. We must talk."

"There is nothing to say. I am going out."

"Do you then wish to bring me more shame, my husband?"

"I do not know what you mean."

"You are going to the big house with those guns."

Benito's shoulders sagged visibly and he hung his head, staring down at the floor. He gripped the rifle more tightly. Where was the courage he had had a few moments before? Where was the resolve he had steeped in his heart with the swallowing of the tequila? He did not know. If only Pilar had not awakened and come into the room. He would have been gone by now and halfway to the big house, less than a thousand meters away from his own.

Where was the cricket in the hearth to give him comfort?

"*Adiós,*" Benito said suddenly, and before Pilar could rise from her chair, he was out the door. She heard the creak of the leather hinges as the door swung shut. She heard his footsteps on the ground outside and listened to them until they faded away.

Then Pilar dipped her head and touched her face with her hands as if to stem the tears that flooded her face.

"Go with God, Benito," she prayed, and then her body shook with racking sobs of sorrow as an immense grief overwhelmed her, shook her to the very foundations of her faith in mankind, the church and the God of the black-robed priests.

She did not dare beseech the madonna for mercy.

Augustino Aguilar had been looking out the window of the big house ever since they had sent Pilar back to her husband. Victoria sat on a couch in the *sala,* her rage still vivid on her face. He stood there, his face partially hidden by the curtains, peering in the direction of Benito's casita.

"How could you have brought such a pestilence into this marriage?" she asked for the hundredth time.

"I do not know."

"Filth. That is what you are. You are not the man your brother Jaime was."

"He was not much. He is nothing now."

Augustino turned and looked at the woman he despised. His slow, mocking smile brought the reaction he wanted. Victoria turned away in disgust.

"You bastard," she murmured. "You filthy syphilitic bastard."

"You have the syphilis, too, Victoria. I wonder which of us will die first. Or more horribly."

"Have you no shame, Augustino?"

"No."

"*Cabrón.*"

Augustino laughed and looked out the window again, pulling the curtain wider.

"Benito has left his house. He is walking this way."

"Alone?"

"No. He is wearing a pistol and he has a rifle in his hands." Augustino's tone was mocking. "I think he is going to shoot someone. He looks like he is going to shoot someone."

Victoria arose from the divan like some startled bird and raced to the window. She snatched the curtain out of Augustino's hand and peered out. She watched Benito for several seconds. "He is *borracho*," she said.

"Yes, I think my brother is very drunk. Or he would not have the *cojones* to come here with a rifle in his hand."

"Well, do something. Get the rifle. Where is my pistol?"

"Do you desire for me to kill my own brother, Victoria?"

"I will kill him, then." Victoria flung the curtain back toward the pane and went to a desk at the far corner of the room. She opened a door and lifted out a finely made Spanish dueling pistol. She rummaged around until she found two powder flasks. She took the smaller of these and poured powder into the pan, blew away the excess.

Augustino walked to the gun cabinet that had belonged to his brother Jaime and selected a German hunting rifle. Calmly he loaded it with coarse-grained powder, seated a patched ball atop the barrel, forced it partway down the barrel with a short ball starter. Then he primed the pan and tested the lock by pulling the hammer back, easing it back down against the frizzen. The flint would strike sparks. He put the hammer at half cock and walked back to the window.

Victoria was already there, gazing outside at Benito, who was still several hundred meters away. She watched as her brother-in-law lurched from side to side, recovered his balance and stepped closer toward the house.

"Muy borracho," she said.

"I will not shoot unless he shoots at me," Augustino said.

"You fool. He will shoot us both while you make up your stupid mind."

Benito drew closer, his gait more steady now, and Victoria watched him as she would watch a spider inching across its web after a fly got caught in the sticky silk at the far edge. Her eyes glittered with an odd light. Her palms leaked sweat and she wiped them on her dress as she shifted the pistol from hand to hand.

A tumbleweed blew across the ground right in front of Benito, but he didn't seem to notice it. His hat brim fluttered slightly in the light breeze that sailed the tumbleweed beyond him and underneath his porch. Victoria squinted her eyes. She saw Pilar standing in the doorway, one hand against the jamb for support, the other shielding her eyes from the sun.

"You stupid fool, Benito," Victoria whispered. "Go back home and sleep off your drunk."

"What will you do, Victoria, if he knocks on the

door? Let him in?" Augustino's voice rippled up and down the scale, with sarcasm in every tonal shift.

"He won't get that far," Victoria said tightly.

"Are you going outside, or will you just shoot through the window and break your fine glass?"

"Do not talk to me that way, Augustino," she said, wheeling to face him. "I would truly take pleasure in shooting you for what you've done to me."

Augustino made a clicking sound with his tongue against his teeth. "Then I would miss seeing you hang."

"Do not tempt me."

Augustino stepped backward, stared at the pistol in Victoria's hand. The barrel was pointed at his belly. Her finger was inside the trigger guard, but she had not cocked it yet.

"Now you are the one who is behaving stupidly," he said.

"Get out of my way, Augustino. I am going outside."

"I will go with you," he said quickly, turning to walk to the door.

Augustino heard the click of the pistol's lock and the hackles rose up on the back of his neck. He turned, saw Victoria raise her arm, point the pistol at him.

"Ai, do not do this, Victoria."

"Puerco," she said and pulled the trigger. Flame flashed from the muzzle of her pistol; a puff of smoke arose from the pan. The ball struck Augustino just below the chin, tearing through his vocal chords and smashing into his spine. He gurgled as blood flooded from the wounds and his eyes rolled back in their sockets. He dropped the rifle to the floor and crashed against the front door, his head shaking out of control.

Then Augustino's body stiffened and blood bubbled from his mouth. He stared up at Victoria as she stood over him, his eyes sightless, glazed over with the final frost of mortality.

"Pig," she said again, and laid the pistol on the floor as she picked up the rifle. She opened the door and stepped outside.

When she walked to the end of the porch, Victoria stared at the spot where she had last seen Benito. He was not there.

She blinked her eyes, wondering if she had imagined it all. She looked back through the open door and saw Augustino's body lying just beyond. No, she hadn't dreamed it. Not all of it.

"Benito?" she called querulously.

"Did you kill Augustino?" Benito's voice startled Victoria and she jerked spasmodically, twisted her head from right to left trying to locate the source of the question.

She did not see Benito. "Yes," she hissed. "He is dead."

"Good. I was going to kill him anyway."

"Where are you?"

Benito raised his head from under the porch. Then he slipped the rifle barrel up and rested it on the lower rail. The muzzle was aimed at Victoria. He cocked the hammer back.

Victoria brought the hunting rifle to her shoulder, knowing she was too late. Her arms seemed to move in slow motion and the barrel waved and bobbed in circles and triangles and rectangles. Her eyes misted over and Benito's face seemed a blur as she curled her finger around the trigger.

"Jesus, Mary and Joseph, please forgive me," Benito said.

Her throat clogged with fear, Victoria pulled the trigger of the rifle, but she knew that her bullet would miss Benito. She could not bring the barrel down to cover his blurred face. Tears welled up in her eyes as she felt the rifle butt buck against her shoulder. The barrel rose up in the air from the recoil.

Benito fired at point-blank range and the boom of

his rifle echoed through the house. Victoria caught the heavy lead ball in her chest, just next to the heart. A crimson flower blossomed on the white lace front of her black dress, and she dropped the rifle as the impact of the bullet propelled her backward, through the front door. She fell atop Augustino's body and watched the darkness descend upon her until there was only the tiniest pinpoint of light.

Then the light winked off as Victoria gave one last sigh through the blood thickening in her mouth.

22

MARTIN SET THE claw of the hammer beneath the edge of the board and pried it upward. The board creaked as the nails pulled free of the wooden box. Then he pried loose the rest of the boards until the top was open. Juanito stepped up beside Martin, and together they pulled the side boards straight down. The object inside was packed with loose sawdust and planed curlings of soft wood. They started removing the packing material until they could see the shining brass barrel of the cannon.

"There she is," Martin said to Jack Killian. "A four-pounder, British made. Juanito got it at a bargain."

Killian whistled as he rubbed his left hand across the gleaming brass barrel. "I've never seen one before. It looks new. Where did you find such a piece?"

"I did not find it," Juanito said. Martin's eyebrows arched and formed a pair of scimitars. "A man I met in Galveston found it for me. A most amazing and capable man."

"Who's that?" Martin asked.

Juanito smiled enigmatically. "I have asked him to come out sometime and meet you. I met him awhile ago in Galveston. His name is Ken Richman, and he is a most resourceful man of many skills and talents."

"A drummer," Killian said to nail it down, put the man in a frame.

"He is a drummer, a horse wrangler, a cowman, a trader, a buyer, a dreamer, a well-read man—educated in the East, I believe—very independent. I think you will like him, Martin."

"I'm sure as hell interested in him," Baron said.

"He sounds interesting," Killian said weakly. Baron had asked him to stay on for a while, work for wages or for a horse, and Jack had decided that he liked Baron and would hire on for a time. He had been curious about a man like Baron, who had bought acres of wilderness and planned to raise cattle on it.

And he wondered about the Argentine, Salazar, and his relationship with Baron. At the table, Juanito had given Martin's wife, Caroline, some seeds wrapped in paper: sweet peas for her trellis, vegetables, flowers. Caroline Baron had beamed and thanked Juanito, and Martin had been pleased, too. Their son, Anson, seemed bright and intelligent, well behaved and quiet. The boy obviously looked up to his father. He seemed more grown-up than his years, for he was only nine or ten, Killian gathered.

"Let's get the cannon unpacked, Juanito."

"What do you aim to do with it?" Killian asked.

"A surprise for your friend Cuchillo."

At lunch, Martin had questioned Jack about his experience with the Apache. But Killian hadn't revealed much about himself. He just told them all the story of how Cuchillo had outfoxed him and stolen his horses.

"You came to trade, then?" Martin had asked.

"To look around, do some trading, yes."

"We have horses here," Juanito had said. "You could buy one if you want to leave."

"Or work it off, saddle to boot," Martin had interjected.

"Why, I'd like to work some for you, Mr. Baron."

"Just call me Martin, Jack."

And the meal had passed in that way, without anyone questioning him, taking him as he was, which was about all he could offer at the moment. He dared not ask about the Aguilar family or show much interest in them. That was something he meant to keep to himself. He was disappointed, though, that the Aguilar family had not come into the conversation except that Baron had told Killian that he had bought all his land from Victoria Aguilar and that her husband Jaime had been killed. Little enough, but he knew more about the Aguilars than he had before.

Killian helped Juanito and Martin unpack the cannon. It was bolted to four-by-four skids and there was no lanyard attached.

"Made for a British man-o'-war," Baron said. "We'll put it to better use."

"It would look formidable on the deck of your ship," Juanito said.

"Yes, it would," Martin agreed.

"You have a ship?" Killian asked.

"We both do," Martin said. "Docked in Galveston now. Every so often we ship goods to New Orleans, pick up goods from the ranchers hereabouts, along the coast. That's how we earn the money we need for this ranching operation."

"How long can you keep that up?" Killian asked.

"Tell you the truth," Martin said, "I've been thinking about selling my boat. Once the cattle business starts to pay off, I can buy more land with the proceeds, do some more building."

Killian was once again impressed, not only with the

industriousness of the two men, but with their careful, well-laid-out plans.

When they got the cannon uncrated, Martin was about to tell Juanito where they were going to set it up when Caroline and Anson came into the barn.

"Juanito, Miguel just came back. He's about half a mile away. You told me to let you know."

"Thanks, Caroline," Juanito said. "Martin, I'll be back."

"This can keep," Martin said. "We have to do some building before we can mount the cannon, anyway. Come on, Jack, I'll show you around the place."

Juanito left as Caroline and Anson walked back to the house. He saw Miguel Hueso riding slowly down the hill. He waved at him and signed for him to wait. Juanito walked out on foot to meet the Apache under the shade of one of the huge oaks that sheltered the house where Martin and his family lived, past the trellis one of the Mexicans had built for Caroline. She was already spading a place to plant the sweet pea seeds he had brought her. Anson was on his hands and knees, playing in the dirt with a small knife.

Beyond the corrals, the vaqueros were digging graves for their dead. Men, women and children stood in solemn clumps around the diggers. Some of the women held up tablecloths and serapes to shade the men with the spades.

Miguel dismounted and waited for Juanito. He paid no attention to the grave diggers, but knelt down in the shade of his horse, the grass green and high around his ankles.

Juanito spoke to Hueso in Spanish, which he had taught the Lipan well.

"What's going on, Miguel?"

Hueso smoothed a patch of dirt in between the grasses and traced lines across it with his finger. "Cuchillo has crossed the creek here," Miguel said, pointing to a line in the dirt, "and rides for the Rio Bravo."

"Straight across?"

"Derecho, sí."

"How many men has he?"

"He has many. They ride fast. Maybe they go to Mexico."

"We will not follow them," Juanito said.

"No? Two days only and we can catch them."

"I know. Let them go this time. They will be back."

"Some Apache circled back and picked up their dead. They rode very fast and I could not catch them. They butchered two cows and carried the best parts of the meat with them. The other cows they had, they drove off and left behind them."

"Cuchillo is very smart. He has no fear."

"Por cierto, Juanito. Cuchillo is very brave."

"Do you miss being with your people, Miguel?"

Hueso did not seem surprised by the question. He touched his short hair, made a sign over his face to show that he wore no paint, touched behind his right ear to tell Juanito he had no paint there either.

"I have become almost white. The Apache walks a short path. They do not plant the seeds to make the land grow." Miguel spoke very slowly and thoughtfully in precise Spanish. "Each year their number grows smaller. They have no country. They are chased by the Mexicans. They are chased by the norteamericanos. They have no home and the wind whispers to them at night like the spirits of their dead. Their women are like the bent trees on the coast, twisted and shriveled and barren of seed."

"They are a tough people," Juanito said. "They are like the coyote. They come and they go, but they do not disappear."

"Their footprints disappear with every wind."

"They will fight to the last man."

"That is true."

"Will you always fight them, Miguel?"

"I will fight them if they fight me. In the old days when there was bad trouble, my people went away and thought about the great circle of life and increased their number. Now they fight and fight and do not think much."

"You have taught me much, Miguel."

"And I have learned much from you, Juanito. You seem wise in the ways of the old ones, more wise than the white men I have seen. More wise than the Mexicans."

"We have the talking books like the ones I showed you. In them, there is much wisdom. Ancient wisdom."

"I know this, Juanito. It is like the wisdom of the old ones. My people have not spoken of these things for a long time."

"Then you must remember them and pass them along to your children."

"What world will my children see?"

"They will see the world you give to them, and then they will see the world they make for themselves."

"As I have done."

"Yes, Miguel. That is so. But come. We will talk more later. There is something I want you to see."

"What is that, Juanito?"

"A surprise for Cuchillo."

"A surprise?"

Juanito smiled and slapped Miguel on the back. The two walked down to the barn together, Hueso leading his horse, a grulla he called Viento Gris. The animal snatched at tufts of grass as they walked, munching it to pulp between his teeth. The bridle he wore had no bit. Miguel guided the horse by the touch of the reins against its neck, touching its flanks with his knees and heels, much as his Apache brethren controlled their mounts.

"I wonder what this surprise is," Miguel said.

"You will be surprised yourself," Juanito said. "I do not think you have ever seen anything like it."

As he spoke, they both heard a loud boom that flattened out in a crack like thunder, and somewhere they heard a whistling like that of a mourning dove in flight.

Beyond the barn, both men saw a cloud of dust spurt up as if the earth had been struck by a meteor. Viento, startled by the noise, backed down on his haunches, tugging the reins taut. Miguel quickly brought the horse under control.

"What was that?" Miguel asked.

"Part of the surprise we have for Cuchillo," Juanito replied.

"This is where we'll mount the cannon," Martin told Juanito. "At just this level. The structure will have to be level and strong and the cannon must not fall off from the recoil."

"I can build such a mount," Juanito said. "I can rig the cannon like a deck gun so that it will return to its position after it is fired."

"Good. You know just what I want."

Martin had fired a ball from the cannon three more times after Juanito and Miguel had come to the barn. He showed Killian and Hueso, Caroline and Anson how the cannon worked, explained to them about elevation and trajectory and then loaded the breech with powder, rammed the ball home and touched a flaming faggot to the touchhole. Anson had jumped up and down and screamed with delight. Caroline had stood her ground, showing no visible signs of surprise beyond the smoky shadows that flickered in her deep blue eyes.

"Shoot it again, Daddy," Anson said. His blue eyes flickered with amber and gold and green. Martin looked at his son and tousled his black hair with his hand.

"We'll not shoot it again, son, until Cuchillo comes back on another raid."

"You are going to shoot him with one of those lead balls, Daddy?"

"No, I'm going to fill the barrel with chopped-up coins and little bits of metal."

"Why?" the boy asked.

"I want a bunch of Apaches to come up to the barn after our horses. When they do, we'll get 'em all, or most of 'em."

"Golly," Anson said.

"Once that cannon is mounted, we'll keep the horses in and around the barn."

"Like wolf bait," Anson said.

"That's right, son."

"Will you kill them or just hurt them, Daddy?"

"Why, I never thought about it. I guess the only way to keep them from stealing our horses and cattle is to kill them."

"You've asked enough questions, Anson," Caroline said. "Let's go back to the house. You can help me plant the sweet peas."

"Aw, can't I stay, Mother? I want to help put up the cannon."

"No, son, your mother's right. You'll just be in the way. Besides, it will take a while to make the cannon mount. I'll let you help me load it when the time comes."

"Oh, goody," Anson said, and gleefully danced alongside his mother as she walked back to the trellis.

"Is that really what you're going to do, Martin?" Killian asked.

"That's my idea. Think it'll work?"

"Well, I don't know. It'll sure scare hell out of Cuchillo and his braves."

"I want to do more than scare him," Martin said. "I want to break him into pieces and scatter his blood and bones all over the outside of this barn."

Killian kept silent. He saw another side to Martin Baron just then, something hard and cold inside him, something determined and powerful, like the awesome power of the four-pounder, so sleek and graceful, its brass gleaming like the sun itself, some terrible secret in the hollow cavern of its dark barrel.

Juanito looked at the two men and thought how different they both were on the outside. But he saw something in Jack Killian that he liked, an independence, a willingness to learn. Juanito also knew that something was burning inside Killian and he had not yet put out the fire. As for Martin, he had become part of the land. He no longer longed for the sea; he even walked different. He had learned to ride and rope, he had learned about cattle and had come to revere them as the chattel they were, the source of wealth and prosperity, the very basis for the world's monetary system.

Baron had learned these things on his own. Juanito knew that he had acted only as a guide, a mentor in the process. Martin was a landsman now, and it was only a question of time before he would sell his sailing ship and let his roots grow deep into the soil of Texas.

Perhaps, Juanito thought, Jack Killian could learn something from Martin Baron, and perhaps Killian would resolve that burning inside of him that was eating away at his life and had almost destroyed him during his encounter with the Apache, Cuchillo. But deep down, Juanito knew that Cuchillo wasn't the only target in Killian's sights. There was something or someone beyond the Apache, and he hoped Killian would learn the value of life, in the most profound sense, before he faced the personal horror he had been pursuing.

Pilar Aguilar screamed into the night, her body swathed in a Gethsemanic sweat, her lips peeled back away from her teeth, her face taut with agony. One of the women stuffed a cloth in her mouth, and still Pilar screamed.

"*Ay, Dios mío,*" whispered Caridad Rojas, the midwife. "Here comes the baby, I think. There is its little head."

"It is big," Flor Santos said. A corpulent woman, she held Pilar's right leg. The woman pinning down Pilar's arms, the one who had stifled her scream, was called Lucinda Ríos. Another woman, Dorita Gutiérrez, held Pilar's left leg at the ankle.

"I see it," Dorita said.

"*Empuje,* Pilar," Caridad urged. "Push."

Caridad reached for the tiny shoulders, her hands dry with flour, which had soaked up the sweat. Hot water stood in a pan on a table next to Pilar's bed. The room was illuminated with candlelight and tilted tin mirrors that reflected onto the bed. The women, their faces dark with shadow, all wore sleeveless dresses and leather sandals.

"She has been long in labor," Dorita said. "She is growing tired."

"You must push, Pilar, just a little more," Caridad said.

Pilar bore down and beads of sweat oozed from her forehead. Lucinda dabbed the sweat away with a dry cloth, one of a small stack she had placed on the far edge of Pilar's bed. The baby's shoulders inched into view and Caridad grabbed them tenderly and slipped her fingers under the babe's armpits. She pulled gently, praying to the Virgin Mary all the while.

Downstairs, Benito paced the floor of the main salon. He was not used to so much room, even though he and Pilar had moved to the big house the month before, a few days after Victoria and Augustino were buried.

"Is she dying?" Matteo asked. The young son of Victoria and Jaime sat in a large chair, one that made him look smaller than he was. It had been Jaime's chair, and he still did not know that Victoria was not his real mother, that Pilar was. Pilar had wanted to tell him, but Benito wanted to wait until the boy was older.

"But he hates me," Pilar had said. "And I am his mother."

"We will tell the boy someday," Benito had said. "When the time is right for him to know."

Benito knew that Matteo hated both him and Pilar, but he could live with that. He remembered when the boy came in from the pastures the evening after Victoria and Augustino had been killed.

"What happened?" Matteo had asked.

"There was a fight, an argument," Benito had told the boy.

"Did they kill each other?"

"Yes," Benito had lied.

"I don't believe you, Uncle Benito. You killed them. They told me that you would try to do that one day."

"No, that is not true, Matteo. Your mother was my sister-in-law. Your stepfather was my own brother."

"You killed them, Uncle Benito. I know you did. Just as my mother said you would."

So that was between him and Matteo now, along with the guilt he felt at killing Victoria. But they had treated Pilar like a dog and had thrown her away. Now Pilar had the syphilis and the baby would probably have it, too.

"No, she is not dying, Matteo. She is giving birth to Augustino's child."

"I hope she dies. Then you will be punished for murdering my mother. Everyone says you did it."

"Did anyone see this happen?"

"No, but they all say you did it."

"Who says this thing?"

"Everybody," Matteo said. "All of the men."

"What else did they tell you?" Benito asked, his suspicions aroused. Matteo was a smart boy, wise for his years. He might have heard rumors about the circumstances of his birth.

"Nothing more. That is enough."

Benito breathed a soft sigh of relief. Someday he must tell the boy the truth, all of it, but not now. He was worried about Pilar, about her baby.

"You should not wish Pilar to die, Matteo. That is a bad thing."

"Not as bad as what you did."

"You believe those men when I am of your blood? That is not fair."

"I believe it because I know it to be true. Mother said that you wanted the ranch, and now you and your bitch wife have moved into their home."

Benito stopped pacing and turned on the boy. "Mind your tongue, boy. You are talking about my wife."

"My mother said she was a bitch. She threw her out, did she not?"

"Yes, but you do not know why she did that."

"Then you tell me why."

"You must ask yourself why Pilar was living here in the first place."

"Because Mother felt sorry for her, that is why."

"Well, you mind your tongue."

"I hate you and I hate Pilar. You do not belong here. The ranch is mine, and so is this house."

"You are very big for your pants, Matteo. I helped build this ranch. My brother and I built this home and I helped pay for all that is in it. You have given nothing."

"I am Jaime's son. Victoria was my mother. The men have told me that the ranch is mine."

"Are any of these men lawyers? For whom do they speak?"

"They know the law," Matteo said sullenly. He sat in the big leather chair like a royal personage, his arms on the rest, his feet barely touching the floor. A young king. An angry young king.

"They know nothing," Benito said. "Nothing but the shit of cows and the stink of their own shit."

"Someday I will kill you, Uncle Benito. And I hope Pilar dies."

Benito fought off the urge to strike the boy. It would do no good. It would only deepen Matteo's hatred for him and his wife.

"Do not say what you do not mean, Matteo. Do not make promises you cannot keep."

"I can keep that one."

"Enough!" Benito shouted as he heard his wife scream again. The scream, high-pitched and piercing, froze his blood. "Do not say another word, Matteo."

Matteo glared fiercely at his uncle, his face pulsing with the raw hatred that flowed in his veins, tautened his muscles. His fists were balled up, the knuckles sharp against the tight skin.

Then there was a silence and Benito strained to hear. A few moments later, he heard a sharp slap, then a baby's cry. The cry was faint and did not sound right.

"Benito, come, come," a voice called. Benito looked up and saw Caridad standing at the railing. "You have a son," she said.

Benito raced up the stairs and into the bedroom. Caridad entered a few steps before him. He saw the women standing next to Pilar's bed. One of them held the child. Pilar's face glistened with sweat. She looked pale and wan, weak.

"A son," Benito croaked.

He halted and took a tentative step forward. The baby was wrapped in linens and he could not see his face.

Pilar turned her head and looked at her husband. "The boy is blind," she said.

Benito walked over to Dorita, took the baby from her. He pulled back the little blanket from his face. The baby was all shriveled and thin, and was crying. His eyes were open and they were as white as milk.

It was true, Benito thought. The boy was sightless, blind as stone.

23

✝

ONE OF THE Baron vaqueros, Carlos Manteca, rode up to La Loma de Sombra early in the morning, his horse lathered, his own body drenched in sweat, despite the coolness. Juanito, who was leading a horse from the barn to put it up in a corral, saw the rider approaching and called to Martin, who was shoeing a horse out back of the big barn.

"Rider coming in," Juanito yelled.

Martin stepped out to look. "Who is it?"

"Carlos, I think. He has been riding hard."

The horse the vaquero rode was near to foundering. Its nostrils were distended as it drew in more air to its tortured lungs.

"*Hola,* Carlos. *¿Qué pasó?*"

Carlos slowed the horse. Its forelegs were quivering from exertion. Foam dripped from its mouth like cream, ropes of lathered sweat clung to its hide, braided with its legs.

"Apaches. *Muchos.* It is Cuchillo, I think. He is running off the cattle at Bandera Creek. We need help."

"Get down, take care of your horse. We will come and help you."

"I am very tired, Juanito."

"Your horse is about to die. Hurry. I will bring help."

"Do you want me to go back with you?"

"No. You take care of your horse and get some rest."

Juanito put the freshly shod horse up in a rope corral, ran behind the barn. Jack Killian was holding a horse while Martin Baron held one hoof up. He was scraping the inside of the hoof with a curved knife. Anson Baron was holding the tongs with a fresh shoe in its grip.

"Martin, we must get some men and ride over to Bandera Creek. Carlos tells me that Cuchillo is running off the herd there. He has many men."

"Jack, you and Juanito start saddling some horses. Anson, run and get your mother."

"Yes, sir," Anson said, and dropped the tongs on the ground next to a small barrel of water used to cool the hot shoes. A fire burned next to an anvil with a bellows leaning against it.

Martin ran the unshod horse into the barn. He put it up in a stall, then walked to the house. Juanito and Jack were lugging saddles and bridles from the tack room.

"Are you going with us, Jack?" Juanito asked.

"I wouldn't miss it."

"Good. When we finish, bring pistols and a rifle or two, plenty of powder and ball. You'll need it."

"I'll have to borrow most of it."

"We have plenty of arms," Juanito said. He kept the ranch's armory in his house, set some distance from Martin's house in a copse of oak trees so that it was shaded and cool.

Quickly the two men saddled five horses. Then, they led them out back and put them in an empty corral. The two men ran off to Juanito's, where Killian was staying. There they loaded pistols and checked their rifles. They carried their weapons out to the corral. Martin was waiting for them, along with Caroline and Anson.

"Caroline, you know what to do," Martin said.

"I—I think so." Martin had instructed her how to fire the cannon and reload it, if necessary. Still, she had not actually set a charge and exploded the weapon.

"You stay by that cannon with a lighted stick, and if any Apaches come toward the barn, you light the fuse and get out of the way. Leave the doors open so you can see them and they can see the horses inside. Get Carlos to help you."

"Can I come with you, Daddy?" Anson asked.

"No, you'd better stay here with your mother."

"But I want to go. I can shoot."

Martin looked at his son. He was almost twelve now, tall and lean. The boy was a good shot and he could ride as well as any man. It would be dangerous where they were going, but it might be just as dangerous staying behind.

"Caroline," Martin said, "you might have to shoot an Apache or two after you fire the cannon. I don't feel good about leaving either you or Anson here."

"It's my job to protect our home and stock," Caroline said. "Anson should stay with me. Carlos and I can handle things here. I don't want to worry about both my men."

"You're sure?"

"Yes. Don't worry about me." She was not afraid of the cannon like he thought most women would be.

"You'll likely get only one shot with the cannon. Make it count."

"I will. I am not afraid, Martin. Now go." She smiled at her husband, hugged Anson. "You do what your daddy tells you to."

"Oh, I will, Mother. I'll run and get my rifle."

Martin and Caroline watched Anson run back to the house. Martin had bought him a .36 caliber flintlock two years before, and a flintlock pistol in .40 caliber. The boy handled both quite well.

Carlos came out of the barn. "I have walked the horse down," he said. "He will live, I think. Do you want me to ride back with you?"

"No," Juanito said. "You stay here and help the señora. Do what she tells you."

"I will do that. Do you think the Apaches will come here?"

"We do not know," Juanito said. "They might do that. Get three rifles from my house and load them well. Keep one rifle for yourself. Protect the señora with your life."

"I will," Carlos said.

"Swear it to me, Carlos."

"I swear, Juanito."

Satisfied, Juanito sheathed two rifles on his saddle and mounted.

Martin and Killian mounted their horses a few moments later. Killian led the spare saddle horses behind his own.

"This could be a trick, Juanito," Martin said.

"I have thought of that. We should find some vaqueros in the fields and send them back here. We will take two with us."

"You would have made a fine general, Juanito."

"Sometimes a man must be what he is not."

"What do you mean by that?"

"If there is no general, and a general is called for, then a man must step up and become the general."

Martin laughed. "You make a man think, Juanito."

"Ah, that is good, then."

As they rode away from La Loma de Sombre, Martin reflected on how far they had come and how far they had to go. A year ago, in 1853, he and Juanito had been riding to Galveston and were nearing the Nueces River when they encountered two men riding through the mesquite flats on the Santa Gertrudis ranch.

One was a young cavalry lieutenant stationed at Brownsville, and the other a man Martin and Juanito knew, Captain Richard King, who, with a friend, Mifflin Kenedy, had recently bought a cargo ship, the *Colonel Cross,* and were operating a successful cargo business up the Rio Grande from Brownsville. Martin had spoken with King about his ranch properties, and King had expressed a desire to conduct a similar operation. He had had a problem with his partner, Kenedy, however.

But since King and Kenedy bought the *Colonel Cross,* they had expanded their business and were running a series of boats up the river and had since taken in two partners, James O'Donnell and Chester Stillman.

"So," Martin said to King when they met that day, "you've decided to look over this country."

"I recently heard about seventy-five thousand acres on the Santa Gertrudis rancho and this young captain was kind enough to accompany me on a survey trip. Martin, shake hands with Lieutenant Robert E. Lee."

The men had shaken hands. Martin remembered he had been quite impressed with Lee. "Aren't you the man who helped lead the charge with Old Zack's men into Mexico, Lieutenant?" Martin had asked.

"Sir, you do me honor in remembering such an insignificant event, but I was indeed with Old Zack when we entered Mexico."

"So what do you think of this country, Mr. Lee?"

Just then a dust devil had twisted across the barren sand dunes and danced into the mesquite forest.

"Well, sir," Lee had said, "this isn't Virginia, but it's a country with a future. Below the line, cattle can be bought for practically nothing, the grass is good . . . in spots . . . and Mexican labor cheap."

"I'm afraid Bob Lee is a bit more optimistic than I or Mifflin," King had said. "He has failed to realize the bare facts of the current situation. The market—there isn't any. And you can't sell cows without a market."

"True enough," Lee had said, "but all that will work itself out, and in time this will become one of the greatest cattle countries in the world."

"Mr. Lee, you are a man with a vision. That is exactly what my friend Juanito here told me back in '38. And that is why I have bought acreage to the west of here."

"Perhaps you and Richard will be neighbors someday," Lee had said.

"I think we just might be," Martin had said. And to Richard King, he had said, "Dick, you had better listen to this young man. He knows country when he sees it, Virginia or not."

"I'm beginning to feel outnumbered," King had said.

"Sir," Lee had then said to Martin, "have you built a herd yet?"

"We have spent years building mesquite fences, developing water holes and planting grass," Martin had told him. "And, we have a sizable herd that we've acquired in the brasada. My friend Juanito is going to have his uncle ship us some herd bulls from Argentina as soon as we have licked another problem we have in this country."

"The Apache," Lee had said perceptively. "We might be able to help you with that. But it will take time."

"Yes. We have managed pretty well with our defenses, but other ranchers have not been so lucky."

"The problem," Lee had said, "is that the Indian does not understand conventional warfare and he does not fight by the rule book. If he did, we would long ago have engaged him in battle and conquered him."

"I think you may be right," Martin had said, and then he had wished Dick King luck and bade farewell to Lieutenant Robert E. Lee.

Juanito had commented afterward. "That Lee is a smart man. He will one day make his mark in this world."

"Well, I hope it's out here and not in Virginia," Martin had said.

"It will be wherever he is, Martin."

Caroline went into the house she and Martin and Juanito had built. They had started with a single room, then built on another in their first year in the house. During their third year in the house, Martin added a bedroom for the two of them. It was not as large as Caroline would have liked, but Martin thought it was big enough. She knew that he was used to living on a boat in tight quarters, so she asked him to make the room half again as big as he had planned. To her delight, he made it large enough for them to have closets to hang their clothes in and to keep their shoes and boots out of sight. She entered the large bedroom at the end of the house, which now had four rooms, giving Anson his own bedroom, and changed into the rough clothing she wore when she was working in the garden or helping with the calving. She put on a pair of trousers and a loose shirt, boots she had bought in Galveston. She knew that Martin did not like her to wear such clothing and she had seen the Mexicans look at her oddly, but there were certain things she did not feel comfortable doing in a dress.

She had left Anson at the barn with his rifle. He was pestering Carlos with a thousand questions about the Apaches. She smiled when she thought of how eager he was to impress his father.

Well, she thought, probably nothing will come of it, but they would wait in the barn in the event that any Apaches showed themselves and tried to steal their horses. So far they had been lucky, thanks to Martin and Juanito. She felt safe with such men. Not because they were brave and strong, but because they were smart, and even in the face of Apache depredations, Martin had tried to work through the problems. In fact he had been partially successful until recently.

The first three years had been hard. For the first three months they slept in a crude tent Martin constructed of mesquite and tarpaulin. He and Juanito had dug two outhouses that looked like miniature jacales while they laid out the plans for both men's houses. She had accompanied Martin on his sailing trips to New Orleans, which brought them money and allowed Martin to buy lumber. The freighting from the coast had been difficult, she remembered, with no trails and the chance of being attacked by Indians.

Gradually they had managed to build the beginnings of a small ranch. Martin worked hard, and so did Juanito. They were able to pay Mexican workers to come and live on the ranch, which they called the Box B, and some brought their families, so that she was not so lonely. She had not seen her parents in a year, but Martin always made it a point to stop by and see them during their trips to the Gulf Coast and on their return. He bought Larry and Polly Darnell presents in New Orleans, and she loved him dearly for that.

Her father was still in good health, but Caroline worried about her mother. She had never been a particularly strong woman, merely an uncomplaining one; the life on the frontier had been difficult for her. The last time Caroline saw her, her mother had been complaining of her legs, and when she showed them to her daughter, Caroline saw the thick blue veins pressing against the skin. Polly's ankles hurt all the time and her wrists and knuckles were often swollen. The skin on her hands was cracked from the dry winds and milking the cows.

Her father could not afford full-time help and he

was showing the strain himself. He hired out to Captain Grimes at Tres Palacios on the Matagorda now and again and earned some cash for supplies and clothing. She looked forward to the day when she could ask Martin to bring her father and mother to the Box B and let them live close by. But she knew now was not the time. There were days when she wondered if they were ever going to live in peace and raise a family, cattle and other livestock for their livelihood. For now, though, they had plenty, with milk cows and chickens and goats, from whose milk she made cheese. She had a fine garden that gave them fresh vegetables virtually year-round. They had no pigs yet, but she and Martin had often discussed buying some shoats and smoking hams, making bacon from the grown hogs.

Someday, she thought, she would have an orchard with figs, persimmons, plums, apples, perhaps even pecans and black walnuts. Whenever she thought of the future, she felt overwhelmed. They had come so far, but had so far to go. They had fought Indians, drought, rains and winds, disease and garden pests. Sometimes she felt that nature was against them, that they were not meant to live on such a harsh land, though Martin assured her that wherever they went, they would have similar problems. But Martin was a dreamer. He believed that someday there would be a market for cattle and that he and Juanito would be rich men. She was not so sure.

When Caroline had finished dressing, she stepped out of the house, wondering where Anson was. She headed for the barn, hoping he was there and not out somewhere by himself.

"Anson," she called when she came near the back of the barn.

"I'm in here, Mother."

When she walked into the barn, Anson was standing next to the cannon, an odd look on his face.

"You haven't touched anything, have you?" she asked.

"I was just looking. I want to shoot it if the Indians come."

"No, it's too dangerous. You stay away from that thing, you hear?"

"It's a cannon, Mother, and I know I can shoot it."

"Never mind. I hope you don't have to shoot your rifle."

"But I want to kill an Indian," Anson said.

"Anson, don't talk that way. You don't know what it's like to take another human's life. It's a terrible thing."

"But Daddy—"

"Daddy had to do it. He didn't want to."

"But—"

"Let's have no more talk about killing. Besides, I don't think we'll see any Indians while your daddy's away."

"Aw, shucks."

Caroline shooed Anson away from the cannon, set about inspecting it. The barn doors at the front were closed and she would have Carlos open them after she finished her inspection. She wanted to be sure she had a fire going in the pot Martin had set beside the four-pounder. There was a stack of kindling wood, sticks that she could use to light the fuse or touch to the powder. Martin had told her not to use a fuse if she didn't have time. At least she didn't have to aim the cannon. Juanito had built a platform that put the barrel at about the height of a man on a pony.

Martin had checked the cannon every few days, fired it once or twice, cleaned it, made sure the powder was dry, the muzzle loaded and tamped snug.

"Anson, you can build a fire in the pot. Don't make it very big."

"I won't," Anson said, eager to help.

Caroline went looking for Carlos, calling his name.

Her voice echoed through the barn. Martin and
Juanito had built it before Anson was born. It had
started out as an adobe structure, forty feet by fifty
feet, but they had enlarged it over the years, adding
height to the adobe walls, then built a sloping roof,
building struts and closing it in with one-by-eight
boards, shingled it with cedar they had hauled in from
a lumberyard in San Antonio. It was now an expen-
sive barn, with lofts to store hay, watering and feeding troughs, sawdust on the dirt floor. Martin had
built a small sawmill, using mules to power the circular saw. They had used froes to make the shingles, a
time-consuming process.

But Caroline knew that Martin was a man who
knew how to use time, and she believed he had learned
that from Juanito, who seemed to be fully self-
sufficient, needing no one, but always helpful with
counsel and solid advice. Juanito knew cattle as even
her father did not, and what Juanito knew, he passed
along to Martin. To her delight, Martin had been passing along his knowledge of cattle and livestock to his
son, Anson.

"Carlos, *ven pa' 'qui*," Caroline called as she
walked past the stalls, looking into the empty ones. At
the last open stall, she saw Carlos sit up and stretch.
He yawned widely.

"*Levántase,*" she said. "*Abre los puertos en
frente.*"

"Sí, señora," he said, rising to his feet. "I fell
asleep."

"You will sleep through your own death," she said
in Spanish that she had learned from Juanito.

"It is some of one thing, some of another," Carlos
said in a jocular tone.

"Yes, one sleep lasts a little longer than the other,"
Caroline retorted.

"You are very quick with the tongue, señora," he
said.

"Much quicker than you are, Carlos. Hurry yourself."

Carlos brushed the straw from his clothing and walked to the front of the barn in what would be for him a hurry. Caroline smiled at his leisurely pace. She returned to the cannon to see how Anson was managing with the fire.

"How are you doing?" she asked.

"I can't get the danged sparks to catch."

"Anson, watch your tongue."

"*Dang* ain't swearin'."

"It's close enough for a boy your age."

Anson struck the chip of flint against the steel bar in his hand. Sparks flew off into the fine tinder beneath the kindling, but winked out like tiny orange lamps.

"Is your tinder dry?" his mother asked.

"Dry as a bone."

"Shave off some smaller curls and put your steel right next to it."

"I done that."

"I did that," Caroline corrected him. She and Martin did their best to give Anson schooling. Martin read the Bible to him every night after supper, and she had taught him the alphabet and ciphers. Anson could read, add, subtract and multiply. He was still having trouble with division, but Caroline thought he was just lazy about arithmetic.

"You did?"

"You know what I mean. Start blowing on the sparks as soon as they fly into the tinder," she told him.

Anson struck the steel with the flint chip and bent over and blew the sparks out.

"Don't blow so hard," Caroline said. "Gently, gently."

"Aw, shucks, Mother. I can't get that dadburned wood to light."

Caroline turned her head slightly and smiled. "Try it again," she said. "Blow softly but steadily."

Anson drew a deep breath, huffing the air into his lungs like a bull getting ready to snort, and began rubbing the flint hard, back and forth, across the steel bar. A flurry of sparks flew into the tinder, and Anson leaned down and blew gently until one of the sparks glowed brightly, grew larger, then another brightened and the spirals of thin tinder burst into miniature flame.

"Keep it going," Caroline said. "That was good."

Anson drew another breath and blew the flames larger, then fanned them harder and harder with his left hand until the flames from the tinder leaped up and licked the kindling. Finally the kindling caught and Anson let out the rest of the air in his lungs and sat back on his legs.

"Whew," he said. "That was hard work."

"And you did it well, Anson. I'm very proud of you."

Anson smiled proudly and continued to fan the flames with his left hand. "I'll have a real good fire for you, Mother." He set down the flint and steel and scooted back away from the flames.

"Keep it going so that we have hot coals and good flames," his mother said.

Carlos opened the barn doors and light spilled into the barn, stopping just short of the cannon, as Martin and Juanito had planned it.

Caroline looked out toward the open field and sighed. Now they would tie horses at the sides of the entrance so that they could be seen, but not be in the line of fire from the cannon. Carlos put chocks under the barn doors to keep them open and then walked back into the barn.

"Let's get the horses ready," she told him. "Anson, you tend that fire real good for me, will you?"

"Yes'm, I surely will," Anson said. "You don't have to worry none about it."

Caroline drew a breath, but decided not to correct the boy's English. The moment would be spoiled, and she knew she might need Anson more than she would wish before Martin returned.

"Be sure you have your rifle close to you," she said as she joined Carlos to walk with him to bridle the horses they would use as decoys.

Cuchillo spoke to the three braves he would leave behind at Bandera Creek. A dozen more waited a few yards away, hidden in the mesquite. Two others unwrapped bundles of arrows, while two more fired at the Mexicans barricaded behind sand dunes and driftwood on the opposite side of the creek.

"You will circle and fire your arrows from both flanks and from the front. You three will be as twelve braves and as many as five more."

"Do you think the white man will come here?"

"He will come," Cuchillo said. "He will leave his horses at the rancho and we will take them."

"When he comes, do we fight him?"

Cuchillo raised one arm and pointed to the sky. "You will fight until the sun goes to sleep. You will join the shadows and ride away to meet us between this place and the rancho of the white man. We will have many horses with us."

"We will do this," said one of the men, who was called Lobito.

"Be many until the sun falls away in the sky," Cuchillo said. Then he mounted his horse. The men on the ground rose up and joined him while the three slunk off to fire their arrows at the barricaded Mexicans.

And the Mexicans never heard a sound nor knew that while they numbered a dozen, they were surrounded by only three Apache braves, who moved back and forth in the thickets like shadows and shot their arrows into the barricades with unerring accuracy.

Cuchillo and his men disappeared in the mesquite like smoke and headed for the Baron rancho, their unshod ponies making little sound on the hard dry ground. From a few yards away, the small band of Apaches might have sounded like a light breeze riffling through the mesquite thicket.

24

BENITO AGUILAR LISTENED to the vaquero Arturo Santiago. He was standing in a corral, his shirt plastered to his chest and back, where he had been working a rangy two-year-old sorrel gelding that he had broken to halter that very morning.

"There is much shooting there, Benito. And we heard the yelling of the Apaches."

"Up Bandera Creek, you say?" He was aware of the fear quivering inside him, a tightening of invisible strings around his throat, a trembling in his heart. After all these years, the mention of Apaches still had that terrible power over his emotions. With the fear came a sense of dread, a foreboding that the Apaches would somehow gain back the free lands they had lost, that they would wipe the settlers off the face of the earth and once again roam the valley as hunters, becoming stronger and stronger until they spread all over Texas like a plague.

"All the morning. The other men have much fear."

"What do you think?" Benito asked, that old sense of dread lying just beneath his caution. The fear still gripped him, constricting his throat, swarming like hornets in his belly.

"I think the Apaches are attacking the herd of the gringo, Baron."

"Baron does have cattle along Bandera Creek. So do we. How many Apaches are there?"

"I do not know. We cannot hear the arrows. Only the rifles. And sometimes we hear the Apaches yelling. The shooting is far away. At the grass where the cattle of Baron graze. But I have the worry. The Apaches perhaps might come and take our cattle."

"I will go with you and see what is happening. Have you much ammunition?"

"We have three rifles and much powder and ball. I do not think the Apaches have the rifles. They would not yell so much if they did. The rifles we have heard are all the same."

"How many rifles do you think the Baron vaqueros have?"

"Maybe a dozen."

"That is good. Maybe we can help Martin Baron drive the Apaches off." His words poured from his mouth like dry cornmeal that crumbled on the air. But he knew that if Baron went down to the north and east of the Aguilar rancho, that his own land holdings would be at the mercy of the Indians. Baron was a buffer to attacks from the northeast, and the more settlers there were in the valley, the less likely it would be that Cuchillo and his band could overcome any of them. But he did not like the sound of this report from Arturo. The Apaches had not attacked Martin Baron in some time, and he offered them cattle now and then to keep them at bay.

"It is a long ride there and the sun is already high in the sky. At best, two hours of riding."

"We will go there, see what's going on."

"Good. I will get a fresh horse and show you the place where the sounds of the rifles are being heard."

Benito's forehead wrinkled in thought. The Apaches had not bothered them for a while and he was surprised that they would attack the Baron rancho. Martin had given them beef and did not pay a bounty on Apache scalps. In fact, he had thought Baron just might be the man to stop the Apache depredations. Instead of paying a bounty for scalps, he gave them stock. And even though the cattle were worth nothing at the present, they might someday be valuable. It was a wish that all of the ranchers in the valley had harbored for a long time.

"What is happening with Matteo?" Benito asked suddenly. "Does he want to fight the Apaches?" In fact, Benito was a little surprised that Matteo had not come himself. It was really his responsibility to make such a decision, to come for help, not Arturo's.

Arturo looked away and it was as if a shadow had passed across his face. He fidgeted with the reins, turning them over and over in his fingers. Matteo was not yet of age, but Arturo was even younger, little more than a boy.

"Matteo, he is gone."

"Gone?"

"When he heard the shooting, he got on his horse and rode away. That was yesterday. Have you not seen him?"

"No. I will ask Pilar if he has come home." For a brief moment, Benito wondered if Matteo had indeed ridden back for help and perhaps had been caught by the Apaches or delayed somehow.

Matteo had moved from the big house the day after the blind baby was born. Pilar called the child Lázaro because she believed God would one day touch him and make him whole. But in a year's time, Lázaro was as blind as the day he was born and he did not babble as other babies do. He did not cry much, either. He just ate and slept and waved his arms in the air as if trying to reach out and find something floating above him just beyond his grasp.

"I will get a fresh horse, Benito. Do you want me to saddle your horse?"

"Yes. I will get my rifle and bring another along. I will ask Pilar if she has seen Matteo," he said again.

Arturo rode toward the barn and corral where Benito kept spare horses and his own, a sorrel gelding he called Fuego. He was tired from the two-hour ride. He and the other men had been building a fence across Bandera Creek and the work was hard.

Matteo had not said that he was leaving the camp or why he was going. He had just saddled his horse and ridden off. None of the men had said anything because they thought of him as their boss. They all knew that there was bad blood between Matteo and his uncle Benito, but they did not know the reason, although they had many suspicions. He had worked alongside them and had never behaved like their boss. But he was intelligent and strong, and the men looked up to him. Now Arturo felt sorry for Benito, who had tried to befriend the boy, but had been treated cruelly by the son of Victoria and Jaime Aguilar.

Benito went into the big hacienda and called out for Pilar. He looked in the bedroom and she was not there, nor was Lázaro in his crib. He went to the kitchen and saw that she had eaten. There was a plate with the dried remnants of beans and scraps of tortillas. He looked out through the window and saw Pilar carrying Lázaro in her arms. She looked like some withered madonna with child, a castoff from the fleshpots of some ancient ruined city. The baby was waving his hands, staring sightless at the sky. Lázaro was still nursing, and Benito wondered when the boy would give up his mother's dugs and begin to eat food. The boy had small sharp teeth and he hurt Pilar when he suckled at her breasts.

He turned from the window and went into the main
salon, where he took two rifles from the gun cabinet, a
powder flask and a ball pouch. He stuffed strips of
oiled cloth in his pockets and slung a pair of powder
horns over his shoulder, along with the flask and
pouch.

He heard the back door to the kitchen open and returned there.

"Pilar, have you seen Matteo?" he asked bluntly.

"I heard some noises in the night, my husband. I
have just returned from his casita, and he is not there.
But he has taken his blankets and clothes."

"Matteo came here last night and then left?"

"I think that is what happened," Pilar said.

"Perhaps he rode back to Bandera Creek."

"No, I think he rode south, to Mexico."

"But why?"

Pilar sat down wearily in a chair and shifted the
baby to her other arm. The boy had stopped suckling
and was asleep. His milky-white eyes were blessedly
closed, Benito thought. Lázaro sometimes looked at
him with those sightless eyes and a peculiar feeling
came over Benito. The eyes seemed to be accusing
him, seemed to stare right through him, even though
he knew with a certainty that the boy could not see a
thing. Sometimes he thought the boy was a living
curse, a horrible legacy somehow left them by Victoria and Augustino. The boy's eyes, though without
sight, seemed to look at him from the depths of hell,
some dank dark cavern where all blind creatures lived
beneath the earth. At such times, Benito shuddered
and fought down the hate that rose up in him, a hate
against the boy and against his accursed father, Augustino. But he knew the child was not evil, only conceived out of evil intentions, and his Catholic
upbringing helped him quell the disgust he felt. Until
the next time Lázaro stared at him with those blind
white eyes.

"Matteo hates us. You should not have told him that I am his mother. He does not believe you."

"It is the truth," Benito said without rancor.

"He believes his own truth. The truth he has heard from the vaqueros, the truth that Victoria breathed into his mind. I think he goes to Mexico to find out if he is the heir to this rancho. I think he will come back someday and make us leave this place."

"What would you have me do, kill him?"

"No, my husband. There has been too much of that in this family. I think you will have to go before a magistrate and swear that the rancho belongs to us and that Matteo is truly my own son."

"I am ashamed to tell anyone the circumstances of Matteo's birth."

"It must be done," Pilar said. "Victoria has seen to it that you did not inherit this rancho from your brother." Pilar paused and looked at her husband. "What are you doing with those guns?"

"There is trouble on Bandera Creek. Perhaps that is why Matteo left. Perhaps he is a coward."

"Matteo is not a coward. He is strong. And he is wise for his years."

"I will be back tomorrow. I will have some of the men look after you."

"We owe them much money."

"They will wait. Take care."

"You take care yourself, Benito."

"Adiós, mi querida."

"Go with God, my husband."

Benito turned before he walked out the door and looked at Pilar and the sleeping baby.

"Matteo will be back," he said.

"I know." She paused and looked down at Lázaro. "And when he returns, then will our troubles begin."

Lobito dropped to his knees after firing an arrow at the barricaded Mexicans. He did not move from that spot, but signed to the other two braves that he wished them to come near, that he wanted to make talk.

"Why do you call us here, Lobito?" asked Dos Perros, a wiry brave with close-set sad eyes and a pug nose.

"Have you not listened to the rifles? Have you not counted the smoke puffs?"

"I have listened. I have heard the boom of the rifles. I have seen the little smoke clouds. I have felt the sting of sand from the bullets scratching at my leggings."

"Many booms from the rifles?"

"Not many. The vaqueros do not shoot so much. They are hot and tired."

Lobito did not say anything for several seconds. He looked at the other brave, Vaca Blanca, whose brow knitted in thought. He blinked several times and swallowed what might have been dust in his throat.

"Perhaps the vaqueros do not have much powder," Vaca Blanca said. "Or perhaps they do not have many of the lead balls yet in their pouches."

"That is what I think. The vaqueros do not shoot so much, and I think they do not have much ammunition."

"Lobito, you have a hairball in your mind. It gives you much worry. Why?" asked Dos Perros.

"We can kill them and take their rifles. Cuchillo would like for us to take their scalps."

"I do not know if Cuchillo wants us to fight the vaqueros in the open."

"I want to fight them," Lobito said. "I can smell their blood in my nose holes. I can smell their sweat, their Mexican stink."

"What if they are only playing the coyote?" asked Vaca Blanca. "What if they are waiting for us to stand up just so they can shoot us dead?"

"They have not looked out from behind the dead trees," Lobito said. "They have not stood up and taunted us to come to them."

"They are cowards," Dos Perros said.

"Yes," said Lobito. "They are cowards and they do not have powder and ball to shoot anymore. Listen to how quiet they are. Do you hear them shooting?"

"We are not shooting," said Vaca Blanca. "So they do not shoot."

"Let us go and fight them," Lobito said. He was a stocky youth of twenty summers with sharp features: a pointed nose, shale cheekbones, small, thin lips and a javelin chin. His dark eyes glittered, but he was in complete control. He made the sign of shooting the bow and cutting the throat.

The two other braves looked at each other and nodded.

"We will do this thing," Dos Perros said. "We have been hiding like old women and sneaking around like the hungry Mexican dogs."

"Let us fight them and kill them," Vaca Blanca said, no longer reticent. "I want to see their ugly faces."

Lobito smiled. "Here is what we will do," he said. "We will flank them on the right, fire three arrows and then run to the left and come up behind them on that flank. We will nock three arrows as we run. When we see them, we will give the warrior's cry and draw our knives. We will be on them before they have a chance to run."

"That is a good plan," Dos Perros said.

"*Estoy listo,*" Vaca Blanca said, the sibilants hissing past his teeth. "I am ready."

"*Vámanos,*" Lobito said.

The three Apaches crouched low and crawled around to the right of the barricade. Then they eased down to the ground on their bellies, taking a long time—several minutes—to outflank the Mexican vaqueros. They became snakes, wriggling forward silently, using the grass and small bushes for cover.

When they were close to the Mexicans, Lobito raised his head. He saw the men behind the barricades.

They leaned their backs against the logs and stared at the empty land around them. The men were smoking, passing a rolled cigarette back and forth among their number. Lobito smelled the pungent aroma of the marijuana leaves burning in the cigarillos.

Lobito rose up to a kneeling position and fired an arrow into the side of the nearest man. He heard the arrow whiffle through the air and strike the Mexican in the ribs. The velvet flint arrowhead pierced a space between the man's ribs and drove into the lung, collapsing it and filling the cavity with blood. The Mexican sank to his side, mortally wounded.

Lobito dropped flat and rolled to his left. Dos Perros shot an arrow in the side of the second man and tumbled to his left. Vaca Blanca loosed an arrow and shot a Mexican in the neck just as he was reaching for his rifle. Blood squirted from the neck wound and the man jumped to his feet and staggered crazily away from the barricade like a jerky puppet.

Lobito raced ahead to the other flank, nocking an arrow on the run. The other two braves followed right behind him. The three braves rounded the far edge of the barricade and fired arrows into bewildered Mexicans, groggy from the marijuana. Then, yelling at high pitch, they descended on the remaining men with their knives at close range, slashing their throats and gutting them before the vaqueros could put up a fight. The Mexicans screamed and uttered oaths before they died, some wrestling with the Apaches in a macabre dance of death before they fell to the ground, slashed and bleeding. The small battle was over in a few moments. Some of the Mexicans were still breathing. The Apaches dispatched them quickly, slashing their throats until their bellies and legs were crimson with blood.

The Apaches, breathing hard, wiped their knives on their leggings. Lobito reached down and grabbed a dead Mexican by the hair, jerked his head up. With surgical precision he cut the scalp lock off the dead man. The other two braves took scalps from the men they had killed, stuffed the bloody locks inside their belts.

"The rifles," Lobito said when they had scalped all of the dead vaqueros. "Powder and ball if you find any."

"What about their horses?" Dos Perros asked.

"Take them."

The Apaches gathered up all the weapons, taking knives and ammunition pouches off the dead. Vaca Blanca gathered up the horses. They tied the rifles they could not carry themselves onto one of the saddled horses that had belonged to the Box B ranch. They loaded the rifles they had stolen and would carry with them.

"Where do we go now?" asked Dos Perros.

"We will ride to the Baron rancho and see Cuchillo. He will be pleased that we have enemy scalps and that we have taken rifles, powder and the lead balls. Let us go quickly."

The Apaches rode away from the scene of carnage without a backward look. The sun stood high in the sky, and the bluebottle flies swarmed over the faces of the dead men and began to drink first from the eyes. Red ants swarmed over the blood pools in a feverish frenzy, following the crimson spoor to the flesh, where they began to tear at the open wounds and carry chunks of meat back to the nearby anthill, which seemed to be a moving thing, though it was still as ancient stone and just as silent.

Martin Baron stared at the dead men, their scalped heads reflecting an eerie light from the sun, their sightless eyes staring up at him accusingly. His stomach swirled with an angry bile and he gulped hard to keep from vomiting. Tears filled his eyes.

Juanito saw the corners of Martin's mouth tighten

and draw back as a muscle twitched in Baron's cheek. He, too, looked at the dead Mexicans, many of them his friends, all of them recruited by him. Two of the men had families back at the rancho, and two were sons of men he would have to tell what had happened to them.

"We should have brought a scout," Martin said. "That Apache, Miguel."

"I can track the Apache," Juanito said softly. "They took all the horses."

"The rifles and knives, too, it seems. God, it all seems so heartless."

"I wonder if they took the cattle or just run 'em off," Killian said. He had been staring at the dead men without comment. The Mexican vaqueros they had brought with them had dismounted and were looking at the dead faces, turning over bodies. Some of them were weeping; others were stony-faced, praying under their breaths.

Martin stared at them as if they were creatures in a dream. They moved among the dead, hunched over like mendicants or grave robbers, and he wondered what they were thinking as they saw the dead hulks of their friends and companions. For the dead men no longer looked human, but like broken statues in a churchyard, like scarecrows made of rags and straw, like dismembered mannequins strewn along the back alley of a dry goods store.

"The Mexicans and Apaches are old enemies," Juanito said.

"Enemies with no respect."

"That is true, Martin. Do you want to bury them or bring a wagon to take them back to their families? Or do you want to track the assassins?"

"Butchers, you mean."

"I have seen worse. So have you."

Martin doubled up in the saddle and began to sob. He knew all of the men, too, and it seemed so senseless. They were peaceful men, men who were helping him to build a ranch on land that he owned, that he had bought with his hard-earned money. He cried for himself as much as for them. He had been responsible for them. He owed them money. He had offered them a chance to improve their lives, and now they were dead, murdered and savagely butchered.

"Yes, we should bury them. I couldn't take them back to the ranch like this. No wife or father should see such horror. Let them keep their memories."

"Perhaps that is best, but the families might want to bury their own dead."

"Dammit, Juanito. Do I have to make the decision on this?"

"Yes," Juanito said. "You do."

"Is there a shovel around here?"

"Yes. Over there by the creek. I will get it."

Martin held up a hand to stay Juanito from dismounting. "Maybe we should ask the vaqueros what they think we should do."

"They will want to take the dead back to the ranch," Killian said. "Mexicans make a lot of fuss over their dead."

"How do you know?" Martin asked.

"I been down in Mexico. I been to a funeral or two myself."

Juanito studied Killian's face. The man was still a puzzle. He was a wanted man, a horse thief, and had probably lived in Mexico, using it as a refuge, as so many American outlaws did. But Juanito still didn't know the man, know what had brought him to Texas, so far north of the comparative safety of the border.

"Listen," Martin said. "I hear hoofbeats."

Juanito straightened up. "Yes, I hear them. Someone riding this way from the direction of the Aguilar ranch."

Killian showed interest as he cupped a hand to his

right ear. The Mexicans heard the oncoming horses, too, and stood up.

"Get your rifles," Juanito ordered. The vaqueros went to the horses and pulled rifles from their scabbards.

"Cock them," Juanito said, and listened to the clicks of the flintlocks as the vaqueros drew the hammers back.

"How many?" Martin asked.

"Half a dozen, perhaps one or two more."

Martin held his rifle at the ready, but he did not cock it. Nor did Killian cock his rifle.

"Apaches wouldn't make that much noise," Killian said.

"Then it must be Benito Aguilar's men, coming to help," Martin said.

A few minutes later, Benito and several men rode into view. Martin lifted his hand in welcome. Benito and Arturo rode in the lead.

"*Hola,*" Aguilar called out. "*¿Qué pasa?*" Then he looked at the dead men. The Baron vaqueros pointed their rifle muzzles at the ground and eased their hammers back down to half cock. "My God, it is true. The Apaches have raided you, Martin."

"Benito, we just got here. Did you hear the fight?"

"My men were building a mesquite fence down the creek from here. Arturo came and told me. Where did the Apaches go?"

"I don't know," Martin said, "but they may be attacking my ranch right now."

"Then we must go and stop them."

"You are a good friend, Benito. I would welcome your help. Did they attack your men?"

Benito shook his head. Then he looked at Jack Killian, a man he did not know. Killian stared at him with such intensity that he felt uncomfortable.

"Who is Benito?" Killian asked Juanito.

"Why, he is Benito Aguilar, who owns the Rocking A ranch. Why do you ask?"

There was a long pause before Jack answered.

"I'm going to kill him," Killian whispered, so softly only Juanito heard his words.

25

✦

CUCHILLO KNEW SOMETHING was wrong. He saw all the horses around the Baron barn, and the open doors. But it was what he didn't see that worried him. He saw no vaqueros. He saw no signs of life at the house or around the corrals, none at any of the little casitas scattered within hailing distance of the main house.

He lay flat on his belly, hidden by brush that he had cut and carried with him as he crawled from where his men waited. He sniffed the breeze like a wolf testing the wind, and he looked carefully at each horse tied outside the entrance to the barn.

He heard no sounds. Not even the horses whinnied, as if they knew they were part of the deception, the trap.

Cuchillo waited there a long time, to make sure that he was not mistaken. He peered into the dark of the barn, trying to detect movement. He gazed at the house, checking every window, looking for a curtain to move, listening for any sound.

But no person came out of the barn or out of the house, and he knew that was unusual. The horses stood hipshot outside of the barn. They had neither feed nor water. That made Cuchillo even more suspicious. He knew how the white men tended their stock. He knew they would never leave horses unwatched, just as the Apaches would not.

The man he called Baron had wanted to make peace. He had offered the Apache cattle, but never horses. But the white men were like ants. If they made a hill in one place, it grew to several hills, and then they built roads between all the hills until there was no place left to hunt, no place to make camp without the smell of the white man in the nostrils. The white man built wealth very quickly. He bred horses and cattle and then would not let them roam free. It did not make any sense. He did not trade with the Apache, but only among his own kind. Cuchillo did not like the white men any more than he liked the Mexicans. They were all the enemy.

Now he was suspicious. He did not trust the man called Martin, *el barón*. All those gifts of cattle, the attempts at friendship, the false words of peace were like dust on the wind, like sweet berries on the tongue. As he lay there watching for any sign of movement, a plan was forming in Cuchillo's mind, and he fed the plan with a building hatred for the white man. He felt as if he had lost some honor in dealing with Baron, as if he had given away the Apache right to ancient lands by allowing the white man to settle there. He had burnt down Martin's barn before. And the white man had built it back. They were like leeches on the skin. They stuck and they sucked out all the blood of the land. They built fences that blocked off all the old game trails. They built houses where once had been a horse trail.

Cuchillo slid back away from the knoll from where he had been watching the Baron rancho. He would talk to his fellow braves and tell them of his plan. They would talk.

When he was beyond the crest of the knoll, Cuchillo turned around. His braves sat their ponies waiting for him. They were ready to fight, he knew. But was there anyone to fight? Had the white men gone away, never to return? No, they would not leave their horses tied up in plain sight. Baron wanted him to attack. But why?

Cuchillo stood up and walked to the waiting braves. He spoke very low and used his hands to sign so that he would not have to talk so much. "It is quiet at the rancho. There are many horses with no one watching them. I have not seen the white man, nor the Mexican vaqueros. I think it is a trap of some kind that I do not know."

"Let us take the horses," the brave called Toro said.

"Let us steal what is in the white man's house," another brave called Tecolote offered.

Cuchillo listened silently to the others as they made suggestions. He did not speak until they were all finished.

"This is what we will do," Cuchillo said. "We will make a small fire and light the cloth we wrap around our arrows. When we get to the hillock we will shoot the flaming arrows into the barn. Then we will walk with our horses in front of us down to the horse house. We have two rifles. The two with rifles will stay on the hill. If anyone runs out from the barn when it is burning, you will shoot them. If we get to the horses, we will take them and ride away. We will not go into the white man's house. He may be inside with many rifles waiting to shoot us."

"That is a good plan," Toro said. "We will take their horses and ride away to join our brothers."

"I do not like it, Father," a young man called Culebra said. He was a boy of only twelve summers, but the older warriors respected him. "This is not a good plan."

"Why do you say this, my son?" Cuchillo asked.

"If we burn the horse house, it will scare the horses. They will be hard to manage and will try to run into the barn. We will be fighting to keep the horses from running away."

"Yes," Cuchillo said. "What you say is true, my son. But let us make the fire and prepare to burn the horse house down if we fail to capture those we see outside. We have plenty of arrows. You, Alcatrez, and you, Caballo, load the two rifles and stay down on the little hill and watch the horse house and the sleeping house. If you see any people come out, you call to us. Make ready the fire arrows. We will walk behind our horses. If we get chased away, shoot the fire arrows into the horse house."

"That is a good plan, my father," Culebra said.

"We are ready," Tecolote said, tapping his chest with his fist.

Then he and Toro began to build a small fire while the others ripped their shirts and cut strips from their trousers and leggings. Toro started chipping his flint at steel and soon the small twigs caught fire. Tecolote fanned the smoke so that it did not rise in the air, but wisped away into invisibility.

Carlos waited in the shadows of the barn, uneasy for some reason he could not explain. Caroline sat next to the cannon, fanning herself with a kerchief. It was hot and she had been perspiring for hours, it seemed. Young Anson was playing with one of the cannon-balls, tossing it from one hand to another like a juggler. The lead smacked his palms until the sound became incessant, annoying.

"I wish you would stop that, Anson," his mother said.

"Well, there's nothing else to do."

"You could help me look outside."

"There's nothing out there," Anson said. "I'll bet we won't see any Indians today."

"I hope you're right," Caroline said. Anson stopped juggling the lead cannonball. But he hunched over and spread his arms wide and now began to roll the ball back and forth, playing catch with himself.

Caroline sighed and continued to try and fan away the heat from her face.

Carlos walked up to the open doors, staying to the shadows, and started to stick his head out.

"Don't do that, Carlos," Caroline ordered. Carlos quickly ducked his head back.

"I thought I heard something," he said.

"What did you think you heard?"

"I do not know. Something. Maybe a horse."

"Maybe one of our horses," she said.

"Maybe."

"Come back inside where you can look out the opposite side." Carlos had paced back and forth between the rear of the barn, which was closed, and the front.

Carlos moved back away from the open doors. He looked at the low hill beyond the flat around the house and barn.

"I think I see smoke," he said.

"Where?" Caroline asked.

Anson stopped rolling the ball back and forth, looked out into the sunlight beyond the open door. He tried to see smoke, but could not tell in the glare of the sun. There seemed to be a slight discoloration on the horizon. A smudge. But he didn't know if it was smoke or just a trick of the light.

"I don't see anything," Caroline said.

But Carlos's observation was enough to put all of them on edge. Anson picked up his rifle, checked the pan, the lock, as he had done a dozen times before. He put the stock to his shoulder and sighted it out the door at an imaginary enemy.

Carlos drew deeper into the shadows of the barn, his own rifle at the ready. Caroline looked at the fire in the pot. It was still burning well. She put another stick of kindling in it, just to be sure the fire would be there if she needed it.

Anson was the first to see the horse on the side of the hill. At first he thought it was one of theirs that had gotten loose. But after several seconds, he was not so sure.

The boy drew a breath and said, "There's a horse out there."

His words startled his mother, who had been peering into the small fire.

"I see it," Carlos said.

"Is it one of ours?" asked Caroline.

"I do not know," Carlos replied.

"I see it now," Caroline said. The more she looked at the horse, the more strange it seemed. Then she saw another horse slip over the small hill, then another and another.

"Apaches," said Carlos, and his voice was full of dread.

Anson froze in terror.

"Are you sure?" Caroline asked.

"Look at the legs of the horses."

Caroline looked hard at one horse, then another. It was then that she saw what Carlos was talking about. The horses moved back and forth in a zigzag fashion down the hill, so that only their sides showed, but she started counting their legs and saw that sometimes each horse had five legs.

"Oh, my God," she said. "They're behind their horses. And they're getting closer."

"Yes," Carlos said. "That is an old Apache trick."

"Then they know we're here."

"Yes, they know."

"Shoot them, Mother," Anson said.

"You be quiet, Anson."

She watched as the horses crisscrossed the plain, the Apaches coming closer and closer.

Soon, she knew, the Apaches would be upon them, and she'd have to fire the cannon. The walking horses were not close together, and each time she looked, there were more and more of them. Then some movement caught her eye and she looked up to the top of the side hill.

"Carlos," she said, "look up at the top of the slope yonder. Do you see anything?"

"I see two Apaches," he said. "They have the rifles."

"That's what I thought."

"Are they going to shoot us, Mother?" Anson asked.

"No," she said, taking a deep breath. And in that moment she made her decision. She looked back outside the barn and knew what she had to do. Martin might be angry with her, but she knew in her heart that she was doing the right thing. "Nobody's going to shoot us, Anson. Now listen. I want you to do exactly what I tell you to do."

"What's that, Mother?"

"I want you to go to the back to the barn and look out. If you don't see any Indians, you run straight back to Juanito's house and go inside and wait for me there. Take your rifle with you and be ready to defend yourself. But don't make any noise and don't look back. Just run as fast as you can. Do you understand?"

"Yes, Mother."

"Now, go quickly. If you see any Indians outside, you come back. But, I don't think there are any out back."

"Yes'm," Anson said. He stood up and trotted to the back of the barn. He looked back once to see if the Indians were any closer. But he could not tell. He lifted the two-by-four out of the angle-iron holders and opened one of the barn doors. He looked outside, right and left, and saw nothing. He stepped from the barn and then started running fast toward Juanito's casita. Caroline saw her son disappear, then called to Carlos.

"Come," she said. "We are leaving."

"Are you not going to shoot the cannon?"

"No. Just be quiet and do what I say."

Carlos walked up to her, a puzzled expression on her face. "What will you do?" he asked.

"I am going to let the Apaches take the horses. Then maybe they will go away. Anson is in Juanito's casita. Go there, out the back, and stay there until I come."

"What are you going to do?"

"I am going to wait here. If any Apaches come into the barn, I'm going to set off the cannon and then run like hell."

"That is dangerous."

"Don't argue with me, Carlos. Go. You protect Anson if anything happens to me."

Reluctantly Carlos left, walking quickly to the back of the barn. He looked back at Caroline and she shooed him away. He walked outside and started running toward Juanito's little house, never looking back.

Caroline stood by the cannon, her hands shaking, her legs quivering. Thoughts flew through her mind like scuttling leaves before an autumn wind, crackled with the brittle electricity of a sudden excitement.

The Apaches moved so achingly slow, each time getting closer and closer until Caroline could feel her own pulse pounding in her ear. Anger boiled her senses, made her want to touch flame to the powder in the cannon's touchhole, but reason fought with her ire and she knew she could not bear to look at the carnage that simple act would cause. In her mind she could see the screaming horses, bleeding and kicking on the ground, could hear the Apaches moaning with terrible wounds.

She stood there, her heart thrashing in her chest, and watched as the Apaches began to untie the horses. One of them walked up to the barn, stood in the opening with his legs widespread, a bow in his hand, the arrow nocked. To her horror, he stepped inside.

"I am called Cuchillo," he said.

"I know who you are."

"We are taking your horses."

"I know."

"Where is your man?"

"He will be here soon. If you come one step closer, I will fire this cannon. You and your men will all be dead."

"I have seen such thundersticks before. I am not afraid."

Caroline reached down and drew a flaming faggot from the fire. She held it just above the touchhole of the cannon.

"Go quickly," Caroline said. "Take the horses. Go now, or I will fire the cannon."

"You are a brave woman," Cuchillo said. He paused, looking at her. Caroline was sure he could hear her knees clapping together. But he turned on his heel and walked outside. In a few moments, she heard the pounding of hoofbeats and then she saw the Apaches chasing all their horses up the hill. In another few moments they disappeared.

She drew in a breath and let it out in a deep sigh. The hand holding the burning wood began to tremble. She dropped it back in the firepot and stepped away from the cannon, suddenly drained of all energy.

She walked to the opening and closed the barn doors. Then she returned to the pot and began to fill it with dirt until the last tendril of smoke disappeared.

"Damn you, Cuchillo," she said. "The next time I won't be so kindhearted, you thieving bastard."

26

✝

JUANITO'S EYES NARROWED to black slits as Killian's threatening words sank in. "If you are going to kill Benito Aguilar," Juanito said softly, "then you will have to shoot me first."

"Get out of the way, Salazar," Killian said.

Juanito drew his pistol, pointed it straight at Jack's chest. He did this so smoothly that Killian's eyes blinked with the speed of the draw. Killian's own rifle was not pointed at anyone, but still lay across his pommel, his hand on its stock.

"If you decide to shoot me, Jack," Juanito said, "it will be the last decision you ever make."

"Damn you, Salazar. This is none of your business."

"What's going on?" Martin asked. "Juanito?"

"Nothing," Juanito said.

"Get out of my way, Juanito," Killian said. He started to swing his rifle to bear on the Argentine.

Martin, sensing something was wrong, turned from Benito and rode over to Juanito and Jack Killian. He looked at Juanito's drawn pistol and the expression on Killian's face.

"What's the matter here?" Baron asked. "Killian, you got something in your craw?"

"That man yonder, Aguilar. He murdered my brother. I aim to send him to hell."

"Are you crazy?" Martin asked. "Where in hell did you get that idea?"

"I heard he hanged my brother and some other men."

"Well, get your hand off the rifle and count slow to ten, Jack. We'll talk to Benito about this. Juanito, if he gets fidgety about that rifle, you blow his Irish ass out of the saddle."

Juanito looked at Killian and smiled.

Killian huffed in a breath and glared at Baron.

"Benito, come over here a minute," Martin said.

Aguilar rode over to Baron, looked at the pistol in Juanito's hand. It was pointed at a man he did not know. His eyebrows arched, but he said nothing.

"Have you ever seen this man before, Benito?" Baron asked.

"No, I do not know him."

"His name is John Killian. We call him Jack. Name ring a bell?"

"I have not heard this name before, Martin."

"He says you killed his brother."

"What is his brother's name?"

Martin looked at Killian.

"We called him Hardy," Jack said.

"Ah, that name I do know," Benito said.

"You murdered him," Jack said.

"He was hanged, but I did not do that," Benito said. "I felt sorry for the man and tried to stop the hanging. It was very tragic. But he was a horse thief, and in Texas, they hang horse thieves."

"Your name is Aguilar, ain't it?" Killian asked.

"Yes."

"Then, they say you are the one who hanged my brother."

"I am one of many who are called Aguilar."

"If you run the Aguilar ranch, then you're just as guilty as any of 'em."

"Now, wait a minute," Martin said. "This isn't getting us anywhere. Killian, you back off. Benito, I'm sorry you have to hear this guff. There's not a man here who lays blame on you for hanging those horse thieves."

"I lay blame on him," Killian said.

"Well, you aren't the law," Martin said.

"I'm law enough, comes to my brother's murder."

"You carry a grudge a long time, Killian," Martin said.

"An eye for an eye, I say. As long as I can remember my brother Hardesty, I'll damned sure remember who killed him. And if I can, I'll take that eye for Hardy's sake."

Martin started to say something, but Juanito held up his hands to make them all keep quiet.

"Gentlemen," Juanito said. "There are dead men here. Killed by a common enemy, the Apache. This is not the time to fight among ourselves. Martin, I think as long as Killian is riding for our brand, we are responsible for him, do you agree?"

"I agree."

"Then would you not say we would be right in restraining Jack Killian from shooting anyone here?"

"I would say that."

"Killian, if you want to ride for our brand, then you must put away your thoughts of shooting Benito Aguilar. If you do not, then I, acting as foreman of the Box B ranch, will order you to give up your firearms and ride away right now."

"That's right," Martin said. "And that's more than you came with."

"I ain't givin' up my rifle," Killian said.

"Then you'll carry it with you all broke up," Martin said. "And no powder or ball to take with you."

"You're seven kinds of bastard, Baron."

"Killian, I don't give a bobtailed fuck what you think of me," Martin said. "Juanito's right. We've got dead men to bury, and if you don't want to let up on Benito, then you can haul your ass out of here."

"You takin' a Mexican's word against mine?"

Martin bristled visibly. Juanito's face showed no emotion. "What's that supposed to mean?" Martin asked.

"I mean you're taking a greaser's word against a white man's. And that ain't right."

"Killian, you've got a lot to learn. I really don't care if Benito had a hand in your brother's death. Benito is my friend, and I've known him a hell of a lot longer than I've known you. Out here, you take a man at his word unless you find out different. I know Benito to be an honest man. All I know about you is that you're a horse thief with a price on your head and too much sand in your damned craw. So you back off right now, or ride on. That's your choice, man. Your only choice."

"I'll ride on, Baron. But that don't mean Benito there is going to get away with murder. He better be lookin' over his greaser shoulder from now on."

"I ought to shoot you right now for that kind of talk," Martin said, "but my offer still stands. Let it go or ride out."

Killian shot a savage look at Benito, then wheeled his horse. "I'm keeping my rifle, Baron, and you can go straight to hell."

Juanito raised his rifle to his shoulder and started to aim it at Killian.

"Let him go, Juanito. Let him keep his damned gun."

"I did not kill your brother, Killian," Benito said.

"You're a goddamned liar," Killian said. Then he clapped spurs to his horse and rode away.

"I'm sorry about that, Benito."

"There is nothing to be sorry about, my friend. I am glad you did not kill him. I would have had his death on my conscience."

"I do not think we have seen the last of that one," Juanito said. "He is like the bad penny of the proverbs."

"Well, he may come back," Martin said. "But he won't be welcome."

"He is of bad seed," Benito said. "I did not want his brother to hang, but that Hardy was a bad man, I think. And his companions were bad, too."

Martin looked at the dead men lying in the sun. He could hear the buzzing of the flies, see the insects swarm over the faces of the murdered men. He thought of Cackle Jack and wondered if any of them had had time to think about dying before they were killed. Probably not, he decided. Their struggles had been brief, and the Apaches had left them no time to pray or seek the spirit within.

"Let's take these men back to their people and clear out of here," Martin said to Juanito.

"Can we be of assistance?" Benito asked.

"No," Martin said. "What's done here is done. The Apaches are long gone. I hope they don't raid your rancho. As I hope they don't raid mine."

"Do you think they did this to get you away from your rancho?" Benito asked.

"The thought crossed my mind."

"Then you must return quickly. I will gladly ride with you."

"No, we will handle it, Benito. Thanks."

"*Adiós,*" Benito said, touching a hand to his hat brim. "*Hasta luego.*"

"So long, Benito."

Juanito gave orders to the men to load the dead vaqueros on the backs of their horses. He and Martin helped tie the corpses down. Many of the horses spooked as the men went about the grisly task of loading bodies onto the backs of their mounts. One horse shied as soon as it felt the weight of a dead man and would not allow the rider to carry the corpse. Juanito loaded the victim onto his own horse.

"It's very sad, Juanito," Martin said as they were riding back to the Box B. "All those men—killed for nothing but a few rifles and a pistol or two, some powder and ball. I was wrong to try and befriend Cuchillo."

"No, Martin, you were not wrong. But Cuchillo does not want peace. Miguel knew that the Apaches would one day want you and the other ranchers off the land. It was only a matter of time."

"Sometimes I wonder if we'll ever make it in this country. The army does not seem to want to fight the Apaches in this part of Texas. So the Indians raid and kill and rob until the settlers give up and go away."

"But you will not go away, Martin."

"I don't know. I have a wife and son to think about."

"And that is why you will stay. But that is not the only reason."

"Oh, and what other reason would there be?"

"You have the heart of the land in you. And the heart of the land has you. I have seen the way you look at it. I look at it the same. It is a fresh new land, a good land. And if you and I do not make a stand, put ourselves in the path of the Apaches, then the land goes back to being the way it was, empty and without the breath of life. The Apaches do not care what happens with the land. They do not want to own it. They do not want to make things grow on it. They just want to plunder and spoil it, and then move on to another place while the land heals itself of their wounds."

"You really believe that, Juanito?"

"I do. And so do you. The Apache has no home, so he wants all of the land for himself. He does not want houses or people in his path. He only wants to take the game from it and never leaves any sign of his passing. You are not like that. And neither am I."

"No, I want to leave the land better 'n I found it."

"And that is what you will do, Martin."

Martin drew in a breath and looked around at the wild country as they rode. Something swelled up in his chest, something that was like the air itself, and he felt strong and full of happiness. There was a smell to the land that made him giddy, made him want to lie down on it and embrace it, hold it close to his heart and listen to its pulse. The thought of losing it choked him up.

"God, I don't know, Juanito," Martin said. "I don't know if I can do it. It's so hard. So damned hard."

"The land?"

"Holding on to it."

"But so are you, Martin. You are hard and you will find a way."

"*We* will find a way, Juanito. I couldn't do it without you."

Juanito smiled. He clucked to his horse and picked up the pace. "Then that is what we will do, Martin, you and I. We will hold on to the land and grow the cattle and the grass and make it into a grand country."

"Oh, it's already that, Juanito. It's a grand country, the grandest I've ever known."

And Martin put spurs to his horse's flanks and broke into the lead. Suddenly he wanted to be back home and hold Caroline in his arms and embrace his son, Anson—hold them both so tight they would gasp for breath and laugh when he let them loose.

Home, he thought. What a beautiful word. The most beautiful word in the English language.

27

IN THE STRANGE alchemy of human nature and the inherent proclivity of people to corrupt each other's names, Miguel Hueso had fallen victim to the anglicization of his name. By that time Miguel had married a half-Yaqui, half-Mexican woman named Flor de Sol, whom some Texans called Sunflower and whom Miguel, possibly as a result of his own experience of losing both his unpronounceable Apache name and his equally awkward Mexican name, called Sunny. And Sunny called her Texan husband Mickey, like everyone else. Some said that Martin Baron had renamed Miguel Hueso, first calling him Mickey Blue, but it was really Ken Richman, the man of many parts, who had done the deed.

Ken had changed a lot of things since he had come to the Box B, but his crowning achievement was in laying out a township of 640 acres, calling it, appropriately and shrewdly, Baronsville. It was the likeable Ken Richman who had filed the necessary papers and attracted merchants and craftsmen to the budding town. His charm and savvy had brought new people into the territory, and he had rolled up his shirtsleeves and sweated alongside them to put up the mercantile store, the bank, the café, the livery stable, the butcher shop, a saloon.

Anson Baron looked in wonder at the growing town of Baronsville. What was once dense mesquite forest that had sheltered wild game and flocks of birds was now a flat plain denuded of brush and grass. Frame structures arose from circumscribed plots scattered here and there along mapped-out streets and avenues. The town hall, with its regal spire spearing the sky, stood tallest of all the buildings in the center of the township, with a town square newly planted with grass and elm trees, box elders and pecan sprawled at its feet like a crude carpet or a scraggly welcome mat.

On the outskirts of the embryonic city, frame houses and adobe dwellings lined the best streets for those who had come first to be a part of founding the new town. Little roofed wells of adobe brick complemented each small castle.

Tumbleweeds, the dried brown skeletons of uprooted bushes, flocked to gates and fences and modest little porches or clustered in drab and shabby rows against the larger buildings and false fronts of the town.

"It's looking real nice, Ken," Anson said.

"She's coming along. Be a newspaper comin' in next week."

"A newspaper?"

Ken laughed. "A man with a printing press. He'll publish all the news of the town and sell the papers in Galveston, Corpus Christi and San Antonio. Your pa might even take some up to N'Orleans next cattle drive he makes."

"Like a book, huh? With printing and everything."

"Sorta. Big sheet of paper. With pictures—drawings

and such. Most towns start with a print press first off. Then people come and build a town around it."

"But you started this town."

"I've seen a number of them go up, seen a lot of them die, too."

"How come you don't live in town?" Anson asked.

"I don't like towns much, except they're a good place to do business. Not to live in."

"So that's why you built your house down yonder?" Anson pointed to a stretch of land to the south of Baronsville. It was a hilly place with sand dunes and little arroyos and dry creek beds crisscrossing it.

"Yep. I saw a little ridge above a grassy kind of flat that I could look down at and imagine kids playing on someday."

"Why do you call it Wolf Ridge?"

"Ah, well, when I first saw it, there was an old lobo on top of it, looking like he owned it. So I thought if he liked that kind of place, so would I."

"I don't understand," Anson said.

"Well, that old wolf seemed like he was calling to me, like he wanted me to see that place. When I rode up, he just stood there for the longest time, and then he just loped away and left me there staring at the sky and filling up with all the emptiness and grandeur of that little ridge. So I called it Wolf Ridge."

"It's a nice name."

"It's a nice place. Quiet, peaceful. Only me and the wolves and coyotes." Ken laughed and Anson laughed easily with him.

Ken was a florid-faced man with bright blue-green eyes and a quick smile, a hearty handshake for strangers. He seemed possessed of a boundless energy, and Anson's dad had said he was smart as a whip. Ken had told Anson that he had been born in New York State and had ridden to Louisiana on a horse. When he had heard about Texas, he just had to see it for himself. He had met Juanito Salazar in New Orleans, and when Juanito had told him about the Baron ranch, Ken had organized a wagon train of settlers and brought them all out to meet Martin Baron.

Ken had opened up the market in New Orleans for beef, which had amazed even Juanito, and certainly Anson's father, who was still shaking his head at his good fortune in meeting Ken Richman.

Anson had dogged Ken's boot heels for the past three years or so, learning much from him. Anson had never been to Galveston or New Orleans, but his father had promised him he could go on the next drive.

"I'm going to New Orleans, Ken," Anson said.

"Why, that's fine, Anson. You'll like it. Lots of pretty Cajun women there."

"What's a cagin' woman?"

"Acadian. French, sorta. Pretty eyes, pretty legs. Good cooks."

"I reckon I won't be doin' any of that."

"Why not? You're eighteen and a grown man. Your pa won't mind."

"He might," Anson said. "And if he doesn't, then my mother would."

"I guess she would. Well, look around. You won't be tied to your ma's apron strings much longer."

"I ain't tied to them now," Anson said, bristling.

"Am not. You ought to watch your English, boy. You hang around them Texicans too much and you'll forget your ma's schoolin'."

"What's wrong with Texans? I'm a Texan."

"Why, not a thing, Anson, not a thing. It's just that since I've come out here I've noticed that they kind of have a language of their own, and the way they talk is like no other speech I've heard."

"Oh?"

"Haven't you noticed? The Texicans I've met have developed a lazy drawl that ol' Juanito described to me as 'twisting all their words into graceful little pretzels.' "

"What's pretzels?"

Ken laughed again. "Oh, you'll find out when you go to New Orleans. Just go to a German tavern or eatery."

"Well, I don't want to talk about New Orleans no more," Anson pouted. "I just wanted to tell you I was goin'."

Ken didn't bother to correct Anson. He knew the boy would find his own way. He had watched him grow from a thin, awkward youth at twelve to a strapping figure of a man at eighteen, hard as a whip handle and wiser than most country lads he had encountered. He knew that was from Martin's reading of the Bible to him every night, his mother's schooling and Juanito's strange and ancient philosophy. Anson would be his own man one day.

"Here comes your shadow," Ken said, looking off to the south.

Anson looked in the direction Ken was pointing and saw a familiar figure on a claybank mare.

"Yep, that's Mickey, all right. Guess I got to go."

"Have fun in New Orleans. When are you leaving?"

"Tomorrow, I think."

"Take it easy."

"Oh, I will," Anson said. He mounted his horse, a pony he called Matador because he liked to chase bulls. "Thanks for showing me around today."

"My pleasure."

Ken waved at Anson as he rode off to meet Mickey Bone. He genuinely liked the boy, wondered how he would turn out with so many men influencing him: Mickey, Martin, Juanito, and perhaps him. And the country had also had a hand in shaping Anson Baron, he knew. It had even shaped him. While he had begun to build a town, he was already looking beyond. New Orleans was only the start of the market for beef. If Baron was going to make it as a cattle rancher, he had to branch out, find markets elsewhere, in the East, perhaps. Martin's vision had touched a chord in Richman's heart, however. Martin's dream had become Ken's dream.

Mickey Bone waited for Anson to ride up, then turned his horse back toward the Box B.

"How come you rode out here for me, Mickey? I was fixin' to come on home directly."

"Your father say come and get."

"Why?"

"Apache come."

Sometimes Mickey exasperated Anson with the way he acted dumb and talked funny, like he didn't know how to talk English real good. He had heard him speak with Juanito many times and use perfectly good English. But around other people, even himself, he talked like a dumb Indian.

"How do you know?"

"Me track."

"Mickey, you can talk better than that."

"Indian talk," Mickey said, and gave Anson the slightest of grins. "Save time."

"You don't worry about time that much."

"Nope," Mickey said and grinned wilder this time.

"Tell me about the Apaches. Is it Cuchillo? Is he going to raid us again?"

"It is Cuchillo, and he is going to attack the ranch again. I went on a scout this morning. They hit Benito Aguilar three days ago. I found sign that the Apache had been watching the house. I recognized the hoofprints of some of Cuchillo's band."

"Did you see any?"

"No. But I know that they are there. They did not want me to see them."

"How many?"

"Many."

"I wonder if Daddy is going to try and use the cannon."

"I think so," Mickey said. "He has moved it again. And, he and Juanito have been working on it."

Ever since Cuchillo had come and stolen the horses that day five years ago, Anson's father had moved the cannon to various places around the house, hiding it with cut mesquite and under sheds. His mother had told his father that Cuchillo had seen the cannon in the barn, and she said that was why he had not come back to steal horses again.

"Where is Daddy moving it to?"

"I do not know. Him and Juanito do not say. They work on it out of sight," Mickey said.

"Out of sight?" Anson asked.

"They do not let anyone see what they are doing."

"Why?"

"You daddy does not trust anyone but Juanito. He thinks that Cuchillo will not come close to the barn because the Apache have fear of the cannon."

"That what my daddy thinks, huh? What do you think, Mickey?"

"I think your daddy is plenty smart. Cuchillo and his son, Culebra, have gone loco. They have drawn blood and they want more blood. That is the way of the Mescalero Apache."

"But you're an Apache. You're not that way, Mickey."

"Yes I am. I am not of the tribe of Cuchillo, but I am of the blood."

"You would not turn against my daddy because you have Apache blood."

"No, your daddy has been a good friend to me. And Juanito, too. I would fight the Mescalero Apache if they attack your daddy. Their days grow short on this land. It is a sad thing. Very sad. But that is the way of the world, Anson. It has always been the way. Even my own people, the Lipan Apaches, know that someday their time will come. The ancient ones said that we were not the first people and we would not be the last."

"What did they mean by that?" Anson asked.

"I do not know. But I believe it."

Anson lifted his soft-brimmed hat and scratched his head, puzzled at what Mickey had told him.

"Will they just die? Or be killed?"

"Who is to say?" Mickey said. "The Apaches do not give up the old ways and they do not learn new ways. They think this time is forever. But it is not. The time of the Apaches is almost over, I think."

"But not for you. You've learned new ways."

"For me too, Anson. Your father sent me after you, but I wanted to talk to you anyway."

"What about?"

"I am going to leave after the fight with Cuchillo is over. It is time I looked for my own people."

"You are leaving the Box B?" Anson's tone was laden with disbelief.

"I am going away. Back to my own people."

"Why?"

"I have been too long away from my own people. I want to get back so that my son, when he is born, will know the ways of my people, the Lipan Apache."

"How will you live?"

"I will live the way my people have always lived. From what the land gives to me, away from the white world."

"Where do your people live?" Anson asked.

"I do not know where they go. Their paths are covered with dust, their trails are like smoke. I will try to find them. They are scattered to the four winds. But I am hoping to find them and make a home for my wife Sunny and my son to be born. I will name my son after Juanito. I will name him John Bone. I will teach him our ways and the white man's ways. And I will let him choose which path he will take."

"It's almost like you can see into the future, Mickey."

"No can do that," Bone replied.

"Do you know where to look for your people?"

"I know some places to look. I know places where they might be. Maybe the holy places. I will find them."

Anson sighed. He did not know what to say. He felt very sad that Mickey was going away.

"Anson?"

"Yes."

"Do not tell your daddy that I am going away."

"Why not?"

"I will tell to him myself."

"When?"

"After we have driven the Apaches away."

"All right, Mickey. Whatever you say."

There was a road to the Baron home, a crude one from Baronsville, but the two men took a shortcut across the fields, where cattle now grazed on fresh grass planted two years before. Martin had hauled in lumber for fencing some of the pastures, but the range between the house and the town was open. Anson had helped nail the fence together and his hands were hard and calloused. He hated fencing.

The year before, Martin and Juanito had taken Anson, Mickey and some vaqueros down to the brush country to the south, what they called El Rincón. Juanito had said that there were many long-horned cattle in the brasada. They took domesticated cattle with them, built pole corrals and lured the wild longhorns out of the brush and chased them into the corrals.

Anson had liked that work, liked the feel of his pony under him, the way the animal responded to his rein and spurs. He liked the power that surged through him when the horse chased the cattle into the corrals. It had been difficult driving all the longhorns and tame cattle back to the fenced pasture near the house. But the longhorns had settled down and the herd was beginning to build.

Martin and Juanito kept certain longhorns and the

Argentine stock together for breeding purposes. They were constantly driving cattle back and forth between fenced pastures, separating the good calves from the culls, mating different bulls with different cows. It made no sense to Anson, but Juanito had tried to explain what they were after—a breed of strong, domestic cattle with long-horned frames and domestic bulk.

"We're raising beef," Juanito told Anson. "We want meat on those big longhorn bones."

And his father and Juanito had created a new breed, which they called rojizo, which Juanito said meant reddish, after the color of their hides. They were bigger than the Argentine cattle but had short horns. They grew fatter than the longhorn and were hardy, able to withstand the Texas heat and the winter chill.

It seemed to Anson that he had much to think about. So many things seemed to be happening at once, important things. Changes. Mickey Bone was going away. His father was preparing for a cattle drive to New Orleans and the Apaches were going to raid them again. It was the eve of his first trip to New Orleans, something he had been looking forward to. But now even that might be spoiled. What if his father was killed? What if the Apaches stole all their horses and cattle?

Questions. Many questions, and underneath all of them was something his mother had told him just two days before. It had come as a shock, but his father had confirmed it.

"I'm going to have a child," his mother had said.

"What?" Anson had asked.

"I have a baby inside me. It will be born in a few months."

"A baby?"

"Yes." His mother had laughed, but Anson had found the news oddly disturbing. He had never thought about his parents that way—mating and having children. That was why he had ridden to

Baronsville to see Ken. He had wanted to get away, to think. To wonder.

When he thought about it now, the arrival of a new baby brother or sister was the biggest wonder of all, the biggest change, bigger than Mickey's leaving, the Apaches coming to raid them, or the trip to New Orleans.

And it was the biggest puzzle of all, finally. How would his own life change when the new baby came?

"Mickey," Anson rasped suddenly. "I don't want you to go away."

Mickey Bone looked at young Anson in surprise.

"I have thought long about this. I will go soon."

Anson felt as if he had been struck by unknown forces. A deep sense of loss engulfed him, despite the fact that nothing had changed. Mickey was right beside him. There was no baby yet. New Orleans was just over the horizon. But he still felt as if the earth was moving beneath his feet, as if parts of his life were being jerked away and nothing would ever be the same again.

"Damn," Anson said softly, and closed his eyes to keep from showing the tears that welled up behind his lids. He did not want Mickey to see him like that. He felt naked, exposed, as if his manhood had been stripped away and he was a boy once again. Only a boy, not the man he wanted to be, a man going to New Orleans with his father, a man coming into a man's world for the first time. A man.

Caroline sighed deeply. The tracks of tears streaked her face, etching her rosy cheeks with dark stripes that looked like the shadows of strands of her hair.

"I hate to see you cry like this," Martin said. "It just tears at me."

"I'm sorry, Marty. I—I can't help it."

He sat next to her on the bed, took her into his arms. As he held her tightly, she began sobbing again softly, as if she was almost all cried out. He rubbed the arch of her back with strong hands, caressed her neck. She felt like a child in his arms, and he felt that tug inside him that told him how much he loved her, how much he cared for her.

"I—I don't want you to go this time, Marty."

"Caroline, Caroline, sweet Caroline. You said that the last time. You know I have to go."

"But it's different this time. I feel real bad about you going to New Orleans."

"Is it because Anson is going with us?" he asked, his voice very soft, almost a whisper.

"No, it's something else."

"The baby?"

"Maybe. I just have this awful feeling about your going away."

"Sugar, it's got to be done. I'm breaking my back trying to make a go of this ranch."

"I know. I—can't you just get somebody else to take your place? Juanito can do it, can't he?"

"I promised Anson. Besides, I think this one might do it. Juanito wants me there."

She broke away from him, dabbed at the tears on her face. She looked him in the eye and her face softened with the love she felt for him. She put her hands on her slightly swollen belly. He touched her hands there and tried to smile away her fears.

"Please stay, Marty. Just this one time."

Martin sighed and steeled himself. He grasped her shoulders in his hands, put pressure there that he hoped might be reassuring.

"Caroline, sugar, there's nothing to be afraid of. The baby's going to be fine. You're not due for several months, and your mother can come up and stay with you when it's time."

"I don't need my mother. I need you."

"I'll be with you if you think of me. And I'll think of you all the time I'm gone."

"It's not the same," she said, pouting.

"You have to go to that center inside yourself I told you about. That's where you'll be safe. No harm can come to you."

"I don't know how to do it."

"Just be still and quiet and don't think of anything and let yourself sink down."

"Oh, that's just something Juanito told you."

"Yes, but he's smart. I do it. I do it all the time when I'm troubled. Cackle Jack did it before he died."

"I didn't know him. I don't care about him. I just care about you."

"Juanito says we're all spiritual beings and we can always be together even if we're apart if we go to that calm place inside of us where the Great Spirit dwells."

"I've never heard anything like that. It's not in the Bible."

"It's in older books than the Bible, sugar."

Caroline shook free of Martin's grip. "I'm scared," she said. "Doesn't that mean anything to you?"

"Yes, but there's nothing to be scared of. I'm not going until after we take care of Cuchillo and his bandits."

"I won't feel safe until he's dead, Marty. I should have killed him that day he came into the barn."

"Yes," he said slowly, "maybe you should have. But he's my responsibility. He won't get away this time. Juanito and I are ready for him."

"You've said that before."

Martin stood up. "Yes. And I meant it. But this time I won't leave until he's lying on the ground stone dead."

"Promise?"

"I promise, Caroline."

She shook her head and tried to smile. She reached out and grasped his hand. She squeezed it briefly. "I feel better, then."

"Is that what you really were worried about, sugar?"

"Yes," she said. "I guess so."

"Well, then, don't worry about it. We won't start the drive until Cuchillo is dead. I promise."

"I love you, Marty."

"I love you, too, Caroline."

He walked from the bedroom and she watched as his frame filled the doorway. And then he was gone. She slumped down and threw herself across the bed. It wasn't Cuchillo she was worried about. It was something else. Something about the baby inside her didn't feel right. She didn't know what it was. Just a feeling, but more than that. It was more than knowing Martin might be killed in a fight with the Apaches and that he was leaving for New Orleans. It was something else, something she could not explain.

It was, she decided, a hideous nameless dread, and that was the worst fear of all—something unseen, hidden, and without a name.

28

JUANITO LOOKED AT the crude map of the Baron ranch properties he had drawn the night before. He made Xs on the map at various places, scratched his head, and drew lines from X to X and then upside-down question marks at other places. He squinted at the map and listened to the wind building outside, pushing slabs of air in every direction. He had to hold the map down with every gust that tore at it.

"Cuchillo is smart, very smart," he said, his throat gravelly from lack of sleep.

"We know that, damn it, Juanito. What in the hell's the bastard up to?" Martin asked.

"I do not know. But look at the Xs and the lines. This is where he has been. This is where he was seen."

Martin looked at the map. He recognized all the landmarks and houses Juanito had drawn. At the Argentine's suggestion, Martin had ordered houses built at strategic locations along the borders of the ranchlands, each site occupied by at least two families, the more remote ones more densely populated.

In this way, the main ranch house was protected, and runners could be sent from each outlying site in case the camps were attacked or the Apaches were on the move. For the past three days, riders had come in from several of the outlying camps, reporting Apaches.

"But they haven't attacked," Martin said.

"No. Cuchillo is playing with us," Juanito said, rubbing one sleepy eye. "Mickey Bone says they are circling, retreating, coming back to threaten us. Always from a different direction."

"What's the bastard up to, Juanito?"

"I wish that I knew, Martin."

Martin groaned. He and Juanito had put the cannon on heavy skids, planed like the runners of a sled. They had dragged the cannon around to various places for the past three days, setting it up where they thought Cuchillo was likely to strike. They had always concealed it in brush or behind trees, houses or barns. Martin had reasoned that if the cannon were mobile, they would have a better chance of causing damage to Cuchillo's band.

But the Apaches had not come close enough for a shot.

"It doesn't make sense. He hit Aguilar."

"Yes, and took two small girls from a family who works for Benito."

"That galls me, too," Martin said. "What in hell does he want from us?"

"He could have taken children from any of the camps," Juanito said.

"Yes, he could have."

One of Benito's men had ridden in three days before to report the kidnapping. Benito wanted to know if Cuchillo had stolen from the Baron rancho. The man

waited around for a day, then rode back. He had said
Benito was worried that Cuchillo might come back, so
he could not stay to help Martin fight off the Apaches.

"Caroline's scared out of her wits," Martin said.
The two men stood next to the cannon behind
Juanito's house. A mule was hooked up to pull the
cannon into firing position. The map was spread atop
the cannon, rattling whenever freshets of breeze
snicked at its edges.

"*Seguro*. Anson keeps asking when we are going to
New Orleans."

"Maybe never," Martin said bitterly. He looked out
at the cleared land on all sides of La Loma de Sombra.
The cattle grazed peacefully, the sky was achingly
blue and little white puffs of clouds floated overhead,
casting shadows on the ground as they passed.

"We could go after Cuchillo," Juanito said.

"*If* we knew where he was."

"Mickey will be back soon. Maybe he has seen
him."

"Did he see him yesterday? The day before?" The
bitterness in Martin's voice did not escape Juanito. For
some time now, Martin had been suspicious of Mickey
Bone, and Juanito knew that Martin did not completely trust the Apache. Often Martin gave Bone
meaningless tasks to do or assigned him to watch the
ranch house while Baron was gone and Caroline and
Anson were alone in the house. "That damned wind is
going to blow away every track for a hundred miles if
it keeps up."

"Do not be angry, Martin. You know that will not
help. You cannot harness the wind, and it will grow
stronger instead of lighter as this day goes on." Juanito
looked up at the darkening sky and knew that they
were in for a storm right on the heels of that building
West Texas wind that tore at their shirts and hats,
stung their eyes with grit.

"No. It's just that Cuchillo has made us prisoners and we haven't fired a shot."

"And neither has he."

"Juanito, do you always have to be so damned right?" Martin had to hold his hat on to keep it from blowing away as a gust of wind whipped at him, flattening his shirt against his chest, twisting his pants in a dancer's pirouette while he stood stock-still.

"I am not always right, Martin. But I think Cuchillo watched us make the gather and knew we were going to drive cattle to New Orleans. I am puzzled that he did not let us go and then attack the ranch to steal what he could. Instead, he keeps us here. It does not make sense."

"Well, we can't make the drive as long as he's around."

"No," Juanito said, studying the map again, nailing it to the cannon barrel with both flattened hands. He circled an X that marked the last place Mickey had seen Cuchillo. He drew a line from there to the ranch headquarters, estimated the distance. The map told him much, but not enough. He looked for a pattern to Cuchillo's movements, could find no such design in the tracings. "He makes circles that come close and then go far away. It is a strange warpath this man follows."

"What do you mean?"

"How does he eat? When does he sleep? Where does he go when he goes far away? He is not wandering. He has a purpose. Is he singing war chants? What does he tell his braves?"

"Are you trying to find out how an Apache thinks?" Martin asked, one hand holding fast to his hat brim.

"An Apache thinks like any other man. This one has a reason for what he does. That is what is so strange about this journey of Cuchillo's. He goes nowhere. And he goes everywhere."

"That makes a hell of a lot of sense," Martin said sarcastically. He turned back to the map, stared at it as if it were written in classical Greek. He knew what the map meant, but Juanito's lines and Xs seemed like gibberish to him. Now he noticed that there were numbers next to the Xs. "What do those numbers mean?"

"The days he has been seen or tracked. The order of the sightings."

"Does that tell you anything?"

"I am hoping that it will tell me where the next number should be put."

"Well, what do you think? The last time he was spotted, he was way off at Frontera Creek."

"Yes, and that is a puzzle, no? And how long does he stay there and where does he go next?"

"Here would seem most likely."

"I agree, Martin. But from which direction? And what if he does not want to be seen? He is deliberate." Juanito closed his eyes as dust stung his face. The map clattered under his hands like the fluttering leaves of a book.

"What do you mean?"

"I mean he goes where he can be seen. But he does not steal, nor does he fight."

"Maybe he's trying to drive us all loco."

Juanito laughed, but there was no mirth in his voice. "There is more to it than that. I think he wants to see what we do. I think he counts the men at each of the vaquero camps, and sees if they go away."

"So maybe he's not coming here next."

"Maybe not. Maybe he will go to the Aguilar rancho again."

Martin thought of the two little Mexican girls that had been taken from the Aguilar rancho. But he could not think of what the Apaches would do to them. He had heard stories. They were ugly stories and he did not like to think of such things. He knew that Caroline was worried, that she was even more fearful now that she had heard about the kidnapping. The girls were small: one was eight years old, the other ten. They would become Apache slaves or worse. They might go mad or be killed when the bucks tired of them.

Juanito interrupted Martin's thoughts. "Here comes Mickey now."

Martin looked up and saw the anglicized Apache riding toward them from the east.

"So Cuchillo must still be around Frontera Creek," Martin said.

"Perhaps."

Anson ran out of the house to intercept Mickey. Martin watched his son, realized how much he had grown, how tall he had gotten over the past few years. Anson was taller than he was now, still filling out those stringy muscles of his.

"Did you know Anson has his horse saddled?" Juanito asked.

"No, I didn't. Why?"

"He wants to go out with Mickey the next time you send him to track."

"He does?" A scowl froze on Martin's face for a moment, then quickly evaporated. No, Juanito thought, he does not like Bone, not deep down inside.

"Yes. Anson is disappointed that we did not make the drive to New Orleans. He is restless."

"Well, there's plenty of goddamned work to do. He doesn't have to go riding off with no red . . ." Martin said, a sharp edge to his words.

"He is not one to dig postholes all his life."

Martin looked at Juanito sharply. "What the hell does that mean? He think he's too good to get his hands dirty?"

"No. He is a good worker, a hard worker. He likes the adventure. Like you, Martin."

"Well, there's plenty of adventure putting up a good fence."

"Look at him real close, Martin. The boy is a natural leader. He listens. He learns. He reminds me of you."

"He'll have plenty of time to learn without riding off with a gringo Apache."

Juanito winced. "Is that what you think Mickey is? A gringo Apache?"

"Well, he used to be an Apache, remember?"

"He still is," Juanito said quietly, and as Martin looked at his friend there seemed to be smoke in his dark eyes. In the distance, Martin heard a hawk scream.

"I haven't seen no war paint on him lately."

Juanito let it drop as Mickey rode toward them, Anson sitting on the back of the saddleless horse. When Mickey was scouting, he rode bareback.

Martin scowled as the two men rode up and Mickey halted his horse. Anson slid off the horse, a grin on his face.

"He spotted Cuchillo," he said. "Mickey says he's not far off."

"Let Mickey tell us," Martin said.

"Well, okay, Daddy."

Mickey dismounted, let the reins trail. The wind picked them up and turned them into snaking whips. He walked up to Martin and Juanito, looked at the map atop the cannon, leaning against the wind.

"Where is he?" Martin asked.

"I can show you on the map or tell you," Mickey said.

"Just tell me," Martin said.

"He is coming this way from Frontera. He has thirty braves. He left the women and children someplace. He has rifles and pistols. I saw smoke. I think he made a raid on the Frontera camp."

"But you don't know."

"I think he did. I recognized the horse of Rafael Mendoza and a rifle that belonged to Jorge Pedroza."

Martin looked at Juanito. "They were working the Frontera range?"

Juanito nodded.

"Damn," Martin said.

"I saw smoke from the camp," Mickey said. "One of the braves had fresh scalps hanging from his lance."

"So Cuchillo has finally struck," Juanito said. "He has tasted our blood."

"He'll taste his own goddamned blood before I'm through with him," Martin said.

"Daddy, if Mickey's going out again, can I go with him?"

"No," Martin snapped.

"But, Daddy—"

"That ends it, Anson. Mickey's not going back out, anyway. Juanito, send a rider to the closest adobes, get some men up here. Leave one behind at each place to watch the cattle and guard the womenfolk and children."

Anson sulked as the wind snatched his hat away and sailed it a dozen yards. He chased after it, his face stinging from sand blown hard against his skin. "Damned wind," he cursed, but no one heard him. His words blew back into his mouth and he spit out the dust that grated against his teeth.

Juanito watched Anson and felt sorry for him. Not only had his father rebuked him, but now the wind had humiliated him. He shielded his eyes from the blowing dust and sand and looked up at the sky. It was almost black now and he knew that Cuchillo would not come this day. He gathered up the map, folded it and stuffed it inside his shirt.

Martin seemed to be worrying over something as he looked long and hard at Juanito. Finally he spoke. "Juanito, how come you don't want to buy land for yourself? I've asked you again and again."

"For many reasons. This is not my time to hold property. I will wait."

"Wait for what?"

"Until you have your dream."

"What about your dream?"

"It is part of your dream. This is a troubled land, and I do not want to give up a friendship by going into competition with you."

"We could be partners," Martin said lamely.

"No, I do not think so," Juanito said. "Partners often end up enemies."

"Not you and me."

Juanito's eyes seemed to cloud over for a moment and Martin could not read his thoughts. But he suddenly felt uncomfortable with this Argentine, whom he had known for a long time, but did not know at all. The silence grew between the two men like a smoke screen.

"Martin," Juanito said, breaking the uncomfortable spell between the two men, "I do not think you will have to worry about Cuchillo right now. The wind will blow him to cover like the quail in the thickets. He will hole up somewhere until the storm blows over."

"What storm?" Martin asked.

"Truly, there will be a big storm."

"How can you be so damned sure?"

"This wind did not come out of nowhere. There is something pushing it. Look at the sky. Those are Gulf clouds and that is a north wind. See how the wind circles? Two winds and heavy, wet clouds. It is going to make rain, much rain, and Cuchillo will have to guard against the flash floods, as will our own vaqueros."

Martin looked up at the sky as if he had never seen it before. He had to hold his hat down to keep it from blowing away. He sniffed the air. "I don't smell any rain."

"It will come," Juanito said.

"Are you always right, by God?"

"By God, I always am," Juanito replied cryptically. "You can read weather as well as I, Martin. Do you now wish to go against nature in your anger? There are some things you cannot control, even though you are a man of determination. Do not send for the vaque-ros."

"Just sit here and wait?"

"Cuchillo will not come here. Not this day."

"Damn," Martin said.

"You may curse your fortune," Juanito said. "But you must also accept it."

Mickey Bone stood there watching the two men. Anson came back and stopped next to Bone, wondering what was going on. He slitted his eyes against the wind and held on to his hat with both hands, his clothes wrinkling on his frame as if they were electrified.

"Well, maybe we ought to send some men over to Frontera and see if anyone's still alive," Martin said.

"Not now, Martin. We'll have our hands full here when that storm hits."

"Hell, it could blow right on by us and never drop a nickel's worth of rain."

"Not this one," Juanito said.

Martin snorted in disgust. He felt frustrated, unable to move. If it was not the Apaches, it was the weather. He had cattle he wanted to get to market and Caroline was begging him to sell the boat and hire drovers. She wanted to keep him prisoner, too. Just like Cuchillo. Just like the damned weather.

"All right, Juanito. Let's get this cannon inside the barn and unhook it. We'll sit it out and see if this storm really does materialize."

Juanito said nothing. He walked over to the horse and grabbed up the lead rope. He spoke to it in Spanish.

"Daddy, what are you going to do?" Anson asked.

"Not a damned thing," Martin replied. "Mickey, put up your horse and get ready to swim. I'm going to build an ark. Juanito thinks we're going to have the second great flood."

Mickey nodded, but he had no idea what Baron was talking about. He led his horse toward the barn, Anson following him like a shadow blowing in the wind.

The storm hit that part of Texas later that night, just as Juanito had said it would. Martin was still in a foul mood and the shutters rattling, the tattoo of the rain on the roof, the cascades of water dripping from the eaves served only to stir his anger into a worse storm inside the house than outside.

"Martin, what's the matter?" Caroline asked as she cleaned up the supper dishes. The two stood there in the dining area of the kitchen like combatants on a field of battle.

"Not a damned thing."

"Why didn't Juanito come up for supper tonight?"

"How the hell should I know? I don't keep track of Juanito. He can cook. He doesn't have to eat supper with us every damned night."

Anson had left the house, slamming the front door, as soon as he was through eating. The silence in the house swelled up around Caroline and Martin, so thick it was almost palpable. The hard wind and driving rain did nothing to lessen the soundlessness in the room, in the space between the two people.

"Anson barely said a word during supper. Did you two quarrel?"

"No," Martin snapped.

"Something's wrong, Martin. I want to know what's going on."

"You want to know what's going on, Caroline?" Martin fixed his wife with a withering stare. "You want to know what's wrong? Well, I'll tell you what's wrong. Everything's wrong."

"Everything?"

"You know damned well what I mean. We were supposed to drive cattle to New Orleans three days ago. Cuchillo burned out the vaqueros at Frontera. All the rain in the world is coming down on top of us, and you want to know what's wrong."

"Is there something wrong with me? With our marriage?"

Martin turned away from her, started to walk out of the room. "No, damn it."

"Martin, come back here. Sit down."

"I'm not going to sit down. I'll be in the front room."

"Then so will I," she said, slipping her apron off and tossing it on the table. She stalked after Martin, determined to force her husband to vent his frustrations, to clear the heavy air that filled the house.

Martin sat down in his big chair, a stuffed frame covered with cowhide, his back against a pillow Caroline had made from goose down and cotton fabric. Caroline sat on the small divan at right angles to Martin's chair.

They sat silently for a few moments, listening to the rain spatter against the windows, feeling the tug of wind against the house. Brilliant flashes of lightning, followed by cracks and rumbles of thunder, splashed the room with light.

"I'm sorry you're unhappy, Martin," Caroline said finally.

"I'm not unhappy."

"Frustrated, then."

"Maybe that's the word."

"Is there anything I can do?"

"What? We're trapped here. Cuchillo is on the warpath. We need money to pay the men. We're just getting nowhere."

"We're getting somewhere. The breeding is going well. You have a market for beef in New Orleans."

"Which I can't get to."

"You'll get there." Caroline paused, composed herself. "Marty, have you thought about selling your boat?"

"I've thought about it. Why?"

"It seems to me you could raise some cash and pay the vaqueros, buy some things we need."

"I'm thinking I ought to get back into the shipping business."

"You could do that, but I would prefer you stay here, work the ranch."

Martin sighed deeply. These were questions droning incessantly in his mind. Dilemmas he dearly wanted to solve. Money was becoming more and more of a problem for him, and for Juanito, too. The Apaches were keeping him at bay and ruining every opportunity to get his cattle to market. The marine shipping business was becoming more and more competitive. He and Juanito would now be competing with fleets of shipping vessels and might not be able to earn a fair wage anymore.

"I'll think about it," Martin said, softening.

"That's all I ask," Caroline said. Then she arose and went to her husband, sat on the armrest of the chair and hugged him tightly. "I love you, Marty. I want you to be happy."

Martin choked up and could not speak for several moments. That was what he wanted for her, too, and he knew she was not happy. He had been thinking only of himself, his own feelings, not hers.

"Damn it, Caroline, I love you, too. And I treated Anson pretty badly today."

"I'm sure he understands, darling."

But Martin knew there was a rift developing between him and his son. Anson wanted to be treated like a man, and Martin just could not let his son go and be what he wanted to be.

"I hope he will someday," Martin said, and breathed in the perfume of his wife, basking in the warmth of her caress.

"I love you, Marty," Caroline said again, and he took her in his arms and pulled her down on his lap.

He kissed her and felt a surge of resolve rise up in him, displacing the despair he had felt when the storm first hit. But he did not feel worthy to tell Caroline that he loved her, too. Not then, but perhaps later, when they were lying in darkness and sheltered in their own private world.

Caroline nestled in her husband's arms, but she could not feel the warmth of his body against hers. It was as if there were a barrier she could not get beyond. In her heart she felt the same cold and wind and rain that was outside, and she knew it was not Marty's fault but her own, a feeling she had so deep inside, she could not get it out, could not express it in words except to say that its name was Dread and it was smothering her and making dark and terrifying clouds in her mind. She wanted to scream, but her throat was dry and something hard and nameless gripped it, too, and no words would come out, no sound but the horror of her own heart beating loud against her eardrums.

Anson ran through the driving rain to Juanito's. By the time he reached the door, he was soaking wet. He pounded on the door, barely hearing his fist strike it above the roar of the wind and the hammering of the rain on the roof.

"Come in," called Juanito, and Anson pushed the door open, rattling the latchkey.

Anson blinked in the orange light of the coal oil lamp hovering above a table in the center of the front room. Juanito smiled at him. Mickey Bone sat at the table across from Juanito and he did not smile.

"Juanito—I—I . . ."

"Come. Sit down," Juanito said, waving a hand toward a third straight-backed chair. Anson walked over and sat down, dripping water on the bare floor. His feet squished and he felt the wetness on his bottom.

"What's happening, Anson?" Juanito asked.

"Daddy's still mad."

"He'll get over it."

Anson looked at Mickey Bone.

"What are you doing here, Mickey?"

"He is leaving us," Juanito said.

"You told him," Anson said accusingly.

"I am not going to wait until Cuchillo comes," Mickey said. "I am going away tonight. I just came to say good-bye to Juanito."

"Tonight? But it's raining and . . ."

Juanito reached over and patted the back of Anson's hand. "It is all right, Anson. He has made up his mind."

"But you said . . ."

"I have changed the mind," Mickey said. "It is time to go."

Anson sat there dumbstruck. He felt a part of his life tearing away before he was ready for it. His father was angry at him and now Mickey Bone was leaving in the middle of a storm. He shook his head and Mickey arose from the table.

"I will go now, Juanito. I will see you someday. Good-bye, Anson."

Juanito said nothing. He just smiled and waved a hand at Mickey.

"G-good-bye, Mickey," Anson said, close to tears.

Mickey strode across the room, opened the door and stepped outside. The sounds of the storm swept into the room and then the door closed and all Anson could hear was the rattle of the rain on the roof.

"He can't go now," Anson said.

"He has gone already."

"But why?"

"He sees this storm as an omen."

"What's a omen?"

"A sign. A prediction. He wants to go, and therefore he must go."

"He could have told Daddy."

"No, Anson, not now. It is better this way."

"Doesn't he like Daddy?"

"No, he likes him. But your daddy represents another way of life that Mickey wants to leave behind. He wants to return to his own people before he forgets the old ways."

"I just don't understand it," Anson said. "I guess I never will."

"Yes, Anson. Someday you will understand. Life is a journey, and there are always changes along the way. It is how you handle those changes that makes you a man."

"I am a man, but Daddy doesn't treat me like one."

"He will. You have to show him you are a man."

"How?"

"Ah, that is something you have to learn to do yourself. And you will."

"Juanito, Daddy says you always talk in riddles. I asked my mother what he meant by that. What riddles are."

"And what did she say?"

"She says riddles are things you have to figure out yourself. They are like puzzles, pieces of things you have to put together to make any sense of them."

"Then your mother is a wise woman."

Anson said nothing for a long time. Juanito let him sit in the silence and gather his thoughts, sort through the questions he felt must be teeming in the young man's mind.

Finally Anson spoke. "I don't want to go back home tonight."

"You can stay here."

"I mean I want to go with Mickey."

"Ah," Juanito said. "This may be your first test as a man, then."

"What do you mean?"

"Running away is easy. We have all done it. But to stay and figure out the puzzle that is your father—that is a big puzzle. If you stay, you might wake up one morning and your father will no longer see a boy before him."

"What will he see?"

"He will see a man," Juanito said.

Available by mail from

TOR FORGE

1812 • David Nevin
The War of 1812 would either make America a global power sweeping to the pacific or break it into small pieces bound to mighty England. Only the courage of James Madison, Andrew Jackson, and their wives could determine the nation's fate.

PRIDE OF LIONS • Morgan Llywelyn
Pride of Lions, the sequel to the immensely popular *Lion of Ireland,* is a stunningly realistic novel of the dreams and bloodshed, passion and treachery, of eleventh-century Ireland and its lusty people.

WALTZING IN RAGTIME • Eileen Charbonneau
The daughter of a lumber baron is struggling to make it as a journalist in turn-of-the-century San Francisco when she meets ranger Matthew Hart, whose passion for nature challenges her deepest held beliefs.

BUFFALO SOLDIERS • Tom Willard
Former slaves had proven they could fight valiantly for their freedom, but in the West they were to fight for the freedom and security of the white settlers who often despised them.

THIN MOON AND COLD MIST • Kathleen O'Neal Gear
Robin Heatherton, a spy for the Confederacy, flees with her son to the Colorado Territory, hoping to escape from Union Army Major Corley, obsessed with her ever since her espionage work led to the death of her brother.

SEMINOLE SONG • Vella Munn
"As the U.S. Army surrounds their reservation in the Florida Everglades, a Seminole warrior chief clings to the slave girl who once saved his life after fleeing from her master, a wife-murderer who is out for blood." —*Hot Picks*

THE OVERLAND TRAIL • Wendi Lee
Based on the authentic diaries of the women who crossed the country in the late 1840s. America, a widowed pioneer, and Dancing Feather, a young Paiute, set out to recover America's kidnapped infant daughter—and to forge a bridge between their two worlds.

Westerns available from